FAMINE

—for Ann Smith, in memoriam

FAMINE

ISBN: 978-1-943661-14-5

Sij Books
booksbysij@gmail.com

Printed in the USA

Flying in from the south, that straight copter shot from Alem Ketema, zooming over flat-topped ambas and creeping canyons hiding mudded rivers thronged with crocs and scurried with gray monkeys, the village of Godo clung to the ridgeline like white on rice. Footpaths wound among compounds enclosed by desert greens, sticks, and thorns to stab any martyr worth his salt. Thatched huts and little square houses with corrugated tin roofing baked and groaned in the Godo sun. Like most places in the Ethiopian Highlands, everywhere in Godo was up or down, strung along ancient paths brimming with rocks, both sharp (good to throw at dogs) and smooth (good for toilet paper).

Ration day, Friday, and the clinic compound buzzed like a happy grasshopper, up from the ground with life, singing for warmth and joy. Long lines of men and women waited to have their yellow cards checked to load up with grain, milk powder, soybean oil, famine biscuits, and maybe a can of bright orange cheese from Australia. The woman measuring out giant scoops of milk powder into empty grain bags looked painted. A puff of wind carried a tornadic cloud of the powder into the air. The line for the clinic stretched from its door to the fence and up the steep, rocky hill. Thin men lingered outside the walls of the compound, waiting to load donkeys and mules.

Emma Smith felt the air shudder long before she could hear it. Three months of famine relief at the mission clinic in Godo, following a year of grueling work in Gundo

Meskel, and she'd seen it all. Bones knit together with blistered skin, staggering corpses placing scraps of fingers to holes like mouths in heavy heads. Starvation potbellies a memory, back when there was still grass to eat. When people stop spitting, cry without tears (an awful high-pitched whine calling upon death), and knock-knock their dried clapper tongues against teeth the size of garage doors, there's no time for salvation (salivation). It's go time. IV fluids might save a life, maybe some Nido powder mixed with water, maybe down a feeding tube if you've got one. Just don't lay them down in the dirt, because they'll choke on it, breathe it in, sticking to bloodless tongues. God, the flies are having a picnic.

Emma stepped to the doorway of the roughshod clinic made of poles hauled in from miles down-canyon and topped with corrugated steel. Only the thick clouds of morning could hide the clinic from Terry, pilot of the Bell 412 helicopter from Canada. *Whump whump whump whump* with a hair-dryer noise riding beneath. Emma watched the sleek blue-and-white machine swing round its cargo net and lower forty, hundred-pound bags of wheat, good old wheat from the US of A. Rumor was, a new nurse was coming to Godo, and he was a he, and he was from Alabama, like Emma. Only the Irish could give the Southern Baptists a run for their money for following in the footsteps of Jesus.

Hungry? Here's some famine biscuits. Naked? Slip into this long-sleeve t-shirt with a duck on it and then slide these baggy jeans over what used to be your hips. Once you're fat and warm, then snag a Bible, printed in your language, Amharic—but you say *Amarinia*, so *Amarinia* it is. King James version, of course. Xavier meskin! Praise to God!

Terry dropped the grain, twirled up, and spun over to the helipad made of small stones. The copter rested with Pratt and Whitney engines droning, drowning the hubbub of ration day. Terry opened the door and hopped out, his golden hair flying wild. Terry was a hunk, although with a unibrow, but all the nurses knew Terry's wife, Lisa, was a gorgeous piece of work. Lisa's long, dark hair hung Gypsy-like in a thick braid across her left shoulder. She liked to twist it when she talked.

Wearing aqua scrubs and a red bandanna, Emma stepped out to receive the mailbag from Terry along with a batch of sugarcane cookies from Lisa. Emma'd had a tough time of it thus far, fifteen months of nip and tuck, malaria from driving through the low places, the kolla, those rolling plains between rivers, and diarrhea from Hell, fulminating amoebiasis, the rotten-egg variety that had you shitting a teaspoonful every five minutes. Not that Emma would say *shit,* being a Southern Baptist, baptized twice—once when she was eight and then again after she woke up on the floor of a strange apartment during nursing school. Emma looked healthy, though, regardless of her trials. Dirty-blonde hair with natural highlights, the kind women paid to imitate. Clear skin from top to bottom. And Terry, the pilot, routinely noticed her healthy chest, which seemed just right in so many ways. And that wonderful (no better way to put it) lopsided smile, like half of her was thinking about laughing, but the other— just as cool as a cucumber.

"Hey, Babe," said Terry. He handed over the mailbag,

cookies, and a box of tetracycline eye ointment, plain tubes printed with black ink.

"You dog," said Emma. "Where's my permethrin and niclosamide? You know the only thing eating around here are the mites and tapeworms."

"Whoa," said Terry. "Taste those cookies."

"Whose got time for cookies?"

Up went Terry's hands. "Well, princess, maybe Jill at Gundo—"

"Yeah, she could use a cookie and a new fiancée."

"Blew his brains out?"

"Said he missed her, was jealous, is all I can tell. Sounded a little nutty to begin with."

"How's she doing?" Terry followed Emma into the clinic. "Really, though. How's Jill? She doing okay?" He ran his hand through his thick golden hair.

"She's still in Gundo Meskel. You know that. Running vaccine clinics, last I heard. Cries a lot at night, but she's good to go. She didn't need that loser sucking the life out of her with his long letters anyway."

"Sad, though."

"For sure." Emma turned, forgot about Terry, and drew up 10 ccs of sterile saline, injected it into a vial of penicillin procaine, and approached a thin priest holding a staff and wearing a large brass Orthodox cross around his neck.

"Two more runs today," said Terry, bounding out the door. He didn't care for needles. He ran back in. "Any mail to go?"

"I'm busy," said Emma.

Terry retreated to the helicopter for the return trip and another load. After Godo, he had cargo nets of grain and soybean oil for Meranya and Rabel as well.

Back in the clinic, a tiny look of fear mixed with pleasure crossed the old priest's face. He pulled his draping aside and exposed his arm-sized thigh.

"Yellum," said Emma. She motioned for him to stand.

A young woman with a small child on her lap, not caring to see the old man's bottom, frowned, laughed, and slipped outside to the front of a line of fifty-eight that snaked beyond the compound and up the hill. The bells sewn to her leather carrier jingled. Outside, the daily laborers hefted and carried the grain to the warehouse under team leader Isaac's watchful eye.

"Afewerki! I need you!" Emma gave the priest a lopsided smile. Her heart fluttered. Mitral valve prolapse acting up. She'd forgotten to ask Terry about the new nurse, the guy from Alabama. That should be fun. She needed someone to talk to. Writing letters to her pastor, so that he could read them from the pulpit, was one thing, but a live human being was another. Since the Mission had pulled her from Gundo Meskel, where she'd done a bang-up job with Jill getting the place under control, Dr. Guthrie had asked her to start a new feeding station and clinic in Godo. She'd said, "Sure! Dynamite. Let me at it." But that was three months ago, and three months without a companion to share tribulations with had been hard, brutal even.

The hills in and around Godo hadn't stopped the steady stream of walking skeletons from the north. Wollo was the worst hit, with hundreds of thousands dead and yet to die. Afewerki, Emma's interpreter and erstwhile nursing assistant with the urgent, precise voice and neat mustache, put it this way:

To our miseries coming from Wollo, naked bones, silent, falling dead and rotting in the paths, in the marketplace. The only things is selling there is to be dirty piles of cloves like black pins, spicy berbere mix-ed with dirt, and turmeric full of sand. My father is kept us safe at night with the rifle, killing three who is not turning from the gate. The problem is to drag them away. My sister and little brothers becomes like starving chickens. Mother is mixing the spices with grass and leaves from the fig tree. There is sometimes the fire still, and when there is no thing to eat, the myrrh is to bubble in the little dish, making smoke into the tukul, which has to become a dry stink. We are in the floor with our teeth white and dry. The smoke is vanilla and is making our cracking mouths to drip. The flies is sleeping in the smoke and is a time of dreaming.

Before the Baptists swooped in, there was food, lots of food, and medicine, *but* it wasn't in Godo yet. The food was far away, lying on the edge of things, spoiling, piling up at the Red Sea ports of Eritrea, Massawa and Assab, little contested keyholes of compassion in colossal doors of despair. The Eritreans were not immune to the catastrophe, but neither were they disheartened. Their underground cities, hospitals woven into caves, their will to be free of Ethiopian rule, an unrelenting conviction to make permanent that line in the sand fingered with blood by the Italians in 1890, that colonial border depriving Ethiopia of the Red Sea. But the ports, by the might of cluster bombs, Russian T-62 tanks, MiG jets, and the ubiquitous AK-47, *pop pop pop,* the precious ports remained in the hands of the Ethiopians, but the roads out—a no-man's land. Massive airlifts finally lowered the piles in the north and the mountains of food as well as in Mombasa and Djibouti, providing the Baptists with the supplies they needed to heal and fatten.

Thank you, Michael Jackson. Thank you, Don Geldof. Thank you, sacks of grain, from Canada and the US of A. Thank you, Italy, for tomato paste. Thank you, Austria, for Steyr flatbed trucks. Thank you, Australia, for blue cans of orange cheese. Thank you, Ireland, for clear plastic bags of powdered stew mix (a bit on the salty side). Thank you, Norway, for bundles of dried cod (makes okay firewood). Thank you, Mennonites, for the warm blankets.

But, even before the Baptists had flooded the countryside with grain and penicillin, until they could shake the rafters for more nurses in Alabama and burn the barns in Georgia, the Baptists did sanction, although reluctantly, a team of Icelanders, partially funded their adventures, and supplied them with rest and recreation on monthly forays back to Addis Ababa. That was 1984, the early horror. The Icelanders—Doctor Gudmunder Thorsson and nurses Svana Olafsdottir and Eydis Jonsdottir—had worked well together. They had met for the first time the day before leaving Reykjavik, flying with three other healthcare professionals, who would find their famine glory farther north, beyond ancient Axum, where Dr. Bjarni Viggosson would step on a land mine manufactured by Accudyne in the town of Janesville, Wisconsin. How the hell it got there, no one could explain. Viggosson lived for three minutes, according to his companions, forming his mouth into the letter O. They buried his mangled legs there in the scrub and carted the rest to Iceland. His son, a photographer, traveled to the spot where his father's legs were buried and took large-format photos with his vintage Hasselblad. He superimposed the image of his father's headstone, a slab of polished granite sitting quietly in the town cemetery of Vik, over the rocky red earth of Axum, creating an eerie ghostlike image that made many people passing through the airport in Vestmannaeyjar, where the collage was on display for eighteen months, think of death and tumbleweeds.

So, it's 1986, July, the fires of famine and legions of armyworms have been burning, marching, for over three years. The Icelanders have left, and Emma is in charge. It seems the worst is over, but the people remain weak, vulnerable, on the edge of implosion. As they had for a thousand years, in response to the specter of famine, they had dispersed cattle, slaughtered goats and sheep, ate their seeds, sold everything, eventually being grateful for a mouthful of black nightshade leaves, *Solanum nigrum,* boiled free of its poison. Famine work was hard and dirty. The work never ending, but just one more ad in *The Alabama Baptist,* a last call to arms: "Nurses needed for relief work in Ethiopia: Follow God's call!" One more batch of nurses should do it.

Afewerki pushed through the crooked door into the medical compound. Behind him trailed a family without the precious yellow card needed for rations.

"Barra!" Afewerki called for Barra, motioned the family ahead, and slipped into the clinic.

Barra, singing, appeared from the warehouse. He was the darkest of them all with the brightest smile of them all, and the best singer as well. "Mendeno?" *What's wrong?* Barra led the anxious father, mother, and three children toward the registration table, just a few biscuit tins with a piece of particleboard balanced on top.

Back inside the clinic... "Afewerki, tell this kind old man that he needs to show me his bottom if he wants this injection." Emma pointed to the man's backside and held up the capped syringe. "He's got a sore big enough to swim in on the bottom of his foot."

Afewerki explained to the old priest what was needed of him. A fly sat in the corner of the priest's left eye, turning clockwise, turning clockwise.

"He wants the injection in his leg as it is closer to his foot," said Afewerki.

"Well, that makes sense, but..." said Emma. "Just bend him over. We got people waiting."

The priest stood and shuffled the layers of cloth curtained across his shoulders. He held his cross up to the ceiling and squatted on the floor.

"No, no," said Emma. "Oh Lord, Afewerki. You know anything about this new nurse?"

Afewerki helped the priest to stand and took his oxtail fly swatter.

Emma moved right in with her alcohol pad. "Get me two more pads, please. He's filthy."

Afewerki opened two and held them out for her. She swabbed the upper outer corner of the old man's starved gluteus maximus, popped the needle cap off with her teeth, and slid in the needle. "Gonna hurt," and she pushed the thick, white solution into the muscle. "Look, he's smiling. Dang. Tough old man."

"Xavier meskin," said the priest.

"He is thanking God," said Afewerki. "This murphy makes him very happy. He will become angry if you give to him pills only."

Emma smiled at the old priest. "Why do they call it a murphy again?"

Afewerki looked puzzled. "It is the injection, the best medicines."

"But why?"

"Because it is the injection, the best medicines."

"Hmm." Emma capped the needle and jammed it into the dirty needle container. "Count him out ten days of penicillin, five hundred milligrams four times a day. And see if he can't keep that bandage clean. Tell him to wash his foot and put the ointment on it twice a day. At least he's got sandals."

The old priest gathered his pills and flyswatter, nodded, and limped outside into the bright world.

"The nurse from Alabama has a strange name," said Afewerki.

"Let's get the next one in here. What's his name?" asked Emma.

"It is Rice." Afewerki looked puzzled.

Emma laughed. "Rice? What kind of name is that?"

Reece Myers was becoming one with his window seat, exhausted. He could see the black of night surging against the wing. Someone was speaking to him.

"Are you going to teach them to pray?" asked the woman with a deep watery accent, standing with her head bent beneath the overhead luggage compartment.

"No, not really," said Reece. He thought she must be Dutch in her precise blue suit. Thick, umber eyebrows. Matching long hair, a shade lighter, that touched her lapels. Violet eyes.

The flight from JFK to Amsterdam was not a short one, eight hours and ten minutes. Amsterdam to Rome and then on to Nairobi and Addis Ababa. The muscles in his lower back made a punching fist. His kidneys hung heavy about his waist like hand grenades. Dehydrated, he took every offer of water given by the tidy crew. Kristin, his fiancée, had wanted to bring him to the airport alone, and he had let her. He thought of his grandparents standing in the driveway so early that morning, less than twelve hours ago. They seemed now like an old photograph pulled from a dusty shoe box.

"What then will you do?" asked the Dutch woman.

"I'm not sure," said Reece.

And, he wasn't. His voice felt hollow as if it might not reach her. The whole mission-work thing was so vague. The woman seemed satisfied and turned away, gazing the length of the airplane and beyond.

Reece cleared his throat as the plane continued its still

arc, the earth rushing beneath them. He slept in fits, ate bites of Kristin's peanut-butter fudge, savoring each one— and she did make very fine peanut-butter fudge. He kept with him a thick, compact flip-book of photos to share with all of Ethiopia. Photos: Kristin, laughing on a couch in her parents' den; at the zoo eating ice cream bars; her pet squirrel, with one leg lost to a cat, lying in its blue plastic swimming pool covered with chicken wire; friends, family, a slice of life. The photo album, toothbrush and toothpaste, passport, wallet, tiny address book, and the small leatherette New Testament he always carried with him. The peanut-butter fudge he drew from a plastic sandwich bag with a green twist tie from a bread bag.

The plane landed with a thud, and Reece was too tired to regret not having a day or two in Amsterdam. The letters of the flight announcement boards flipped like playing cards. He felt his back breaking as he worked his way to international departures. Here was Europe. Here comes Africa. He wanted to anticipate something, but couldn't think of what it should be.

Once on board the nearly empty KLM 747, Reece reminded himself of another missionary, Hattie. They hadn't connected at JFK in New York. And with a glance now from his seat, he knew that the deeply tanned, white-haired lady in the striped, long-sleeve shirt must be Hattie. Dragging three bulging canvas bags with a straw hat smashed between her elbow and hip, she struggled toward him, eyes searching. He asked if she was with the Foreign Mission Service.

She peeled off a clang of laughter, let go of her bags, and clenched her hands to her hips. Reece stood, stumbled, and stuck out his hand, trying to share her glee.

A tall, dark steward inquired if Hattie needed help finding her seat. "We have very few on this flight," he said, being Dutch, with short, blond hair swept back with care, bronze eyes with pinpoint pupils.

Hattie piled her bags into two seats of the middle row. She sat at the end, across from Reece, who had an entire window row to himself.

"Oh my goodness, what have we got ourselves into, Rice?" Hattie squawked versus speaking. Her Mississippi accent roared above the quiet of the silent plane.

Reece stumbled for a reply. "It's Reece."

"That's okay, I forgive you!" she said, and Reece realized, *This is Hattie. This is how she is.*

"You're from Mississippi?" He wanted to show interest, but felt washed out, low on conversation. A trickle of faces slipped onto the plane, seeming to pick seats as far away from others as possible.

"I'm sorry, but I will need to help you store these bags," said the stewardess. Her dark-blue neckerchief and white button-up made her seem ultra-reliable. "Do you like them underneath the seats here?" She leaned down, shielding her breasts with one hand, and tried to push one bag beneath the seat in front, but it wouldn't fit. "Let's have them up here in the bins, okay?"

Reece stood and indicated that he would help Hattie, and the stewardess moved quickly toward the front to intercept an old woman with a life-size cardboard figure of O.J. Simpson, who had been inducted into the Football Hall of Fame the previous year. Reece missed what Hattie said, following the stewardess as she explained Simpson would need to be stored up front. The old woman was complaining. Reece thought back to first grade, living on a U.S. Army base near Nelligan, Germany. At the PX, on Halloween day, there had been one costume box left on the shelf. O.J. Simpson, number 32. The bright colors of the Bills coming through as robin's egg blue and girl's dress pink.

"What does your family think?" Reece said.

Hattie sobered for a moment and laughed. "My daughters are grown. Their children are off to college. My friends at church, well, that's neither here nor there. I'm just doing God's will."

She sat and fiddled with the air nozzle above her head. Reece noticed her full face, her tan arms. He guessed she was on the edge of sixty. She was like so many women he knew back home, the kind who outlived their older husbands, who gardened in the coolest parts of the day, who made sun tea in gallon jugs, and who would surreptitiously cut the crusts from the tuna salad sandwiches that the younger women brought to church suppers. And always with a fashionable straw hat within arm's reach.

Reece pushed off his shoes, feet beginning to swell. The interior lights flashed, air conditioning suddenly *hooshing* through narrow tubes.

"So, you're a nurse, too." Hattie folded her hands in her lap.

He still didn't know exactly why he had become a nurse. He did, though, have this uncanny, almost nagging urge to help others.

"Two years in CCU. How about you?" asked Reece.

Hattie pulled a pick comb from her purse to fluff her

fuzzy, white hair. "Twenty-four years on the same med-surg unit at a hospital in Jackson. Head nurse for ten years until I got sick of that and went part-time days."

"Are you retired?" Reece felt the plane jerk.

"I retired about four years ago, but kept up my license. Bert, my husband, died two years back, so it's time to get out there and finally see what the world is up to."

The steward was holding up a demonstration belt buckle. Buckle, tighten the strap. The engines kicked in, like a Coleman lantern inside a tent, and the vacuous, nearly empty 747 slid backward in sluggish waves of motion, a coiled spring expanding and contracting. For the first time, Reece looked behind and scanned the few faces he could see, more women than men, bright faces, tired faces.

Airborne, he slept and nibbled his fudge like a mouse. He imagined what might be slipping away beneath him as the plane sliced through the night, racing against the sun.

On the descent into Rome, his ears refused to clear. As the plane dropped much too quickly, the sinus over his right eye crushed inward. The pain brought tears, and he stifled what could have become a scream. The stabbing sensation threw him into a mild panic. He leaned forward and pressed his fist hard to his forehead, swallowed, pinched his nostrils, and blew. Nothing. As the plane neared the ground, a piercing pig squeal of air escaped, equalizing the pressure inside his skull with that of Earth.

The stillness of the plane, heavy on the ground, bred silence. A woman dressed in a beige skirt with a matching top trimmed in white came aboard and cleaned the narrow aisles with a cordless vacuum. Another slipped in and out of the bathrooms with a small bucket of supplies. The plane needed attention before venturing off to Africa. Hattie paced with her hand to her back. Reece felt leaden, and his eyes only wanted to close. He pondered saying something to Hattie each time she passed, but nothing would come. He stood and entered the bathroom. The hum of the plane escalated. A fresh smell like lavender. He washed his face, feeling thick with the toil of mechanized travel. A few more people boarded, golden-skinned travelers with high cheekbones, Ethiopians, speakers of Amharic.

The ten-hour flight to Nairobi seemed like twenty. It was as if Reece had known Hattie for a lifetime. He volunteered to her that his fiancée Kristin had made the little, brown squares of peanut-butter fudge and offered her one. Whatever sense Kristin had assumed in his life, though, was slipping away with each bite. *I am eating her out of existence.*

"I have some pictures." Reece pulled the flip-book from his stuff sack and opened it to the close-up of Kristin. Framed in a puff of brown curls, a face lit with a bright smile loomed in the foreground. "This is Kristin." He handed the photo book across the aisle to her.

"She's the fiancée." Hattie held the book with two hands, turning it this way and that, like the steering wheel of a bumper car. "She's so pretty." Hattie fixed a smile and flipped randomly through a few of the other photos.

Before putting the book away, Reece gazed at the photo of himself and Kristin on the plaid couch in her parents' den, a small room with a console TV that joined the kitchen-dining area. In the photo, she was looking at him with a giddy smile. She had been hitting him with a pillow when her sister snapped the picture.

Mid-flight, a man in a white shirt and slacks walked up. He was with the Foreign Mission Service. Reece had seen the man talking with Hattie earlier, and she had mentioned nothing about him. Ted was his name. He and a young woman, sitting one section ahead of them, would be interviewing and filming mission workers for a short documentary.

"Reece, would you mind if I brought my tape recorder over and asked you a few questions?" Ted ran his fingers over the top of his jet-black hair. He looked drained and returned with a small handheld recorder. Reece moved to the window seat, glancing into the darkness. The world seemed to extend only sideways.

"Tell me something about yourself, why you're going, what you'll be doing." Ted held the recorder in his left hand like a cookie, a tiny red light blinking.

Reece wondered where he should begin. Should he mention the doctrinal point regarding the Virgin Mary about which his interviewer had openly questioned him? The Foreign Mission Service, based in Roanoke, Virginia, had flown an interviewer to Birmingham to cull through the dozens of applicants from the area. The famine was big news, striking the desperate as well as the inspired with wonder. History was calling. The dull routine exchanged for adventure. Life and death. But first, one had to answer questions, submit a criminal background check, undergo a complete physical, obtain letters of recommendation, write a statement of faith that addressed specific beliefs held in common by the governing mind of the Southern Baptist collective, a succinct document known as the *Baptist Faith and Message.*

"I'm an Army brat," Reece said. People always knew what Army brat meant. "Oh," they would say.

"Oh," said Ted, "and did you travel a lot?"

The Baptist Faith and Message laid itself out as Articles, each addressing key points that Reece had begun to question. From the scriptures to God to family, the Articles neatly arranged the key ideas of what it meant to celebrate God as a Southern Baptist. He knew he had to reflect those beliefs in his essay, and he did, but he had added a bit about whether some of the finer points mattered. Did it matter if Mary was a virgin or not?

"Yes, a lot of moving. Army base to Army base," said Reece. "I wouldn't call it travel so much as just moving from place to place. It gets in your bones, that constant movement."

"Do you think your past travels will help you on this trip?" asked Ted.

"I'm not sure. I would hope so. I'm not sure what will happen." Reece paused, sensing that Ted had no energy to continue. He waited for Ted to get up and leave, say something polite, and then perhaps step into the bathroom.

From ahead, the snack cart and the steward appeared, blocking Ted from escaping. The steward turned his back and placed a napkin on Hattie's meal tray. He poured her a plastic cup of orange juice on ice and turned toward them. Reece saw his name tag, Olivier. He had an accent, a swirling accent. Drinking his tomato juice, Reece remained in the seat by the window. Ted asked a few more questions and rejoined the young lady up front.

Landing at Jomo Kenyatta in Nairobi, Reece struggled to realize where he was. The last few hours suspended in the dark, seemingly motionless, had left him blank. He stood against a wall with his hands behind his back, waiting for something to make sense.

The long, narrow, sprawling corridors echoed with heat and humidity. Heavy air trickled through transom windows too high to see through. It was after ten p.m., and only a few passengers and a handful of camo-dressed soldiers with Heckler & Koch MP5 submachineguns milled about. The tall, skinny Kenyan soldiers wore berets cocked to the side and walked without seeming to note their surroundings. Reece wasn't sure if they could see him, as if he had become invisible.

The flight for Addis Ababa left at eight-thirty the next morning. The film crew disappeared, leaving Reece and Hattie wondering what to do. Hattie suggested making it into the city for a hotel, but Reece thought it too much trouble and suggested sitting it out. Hattie couldn't bear the thought of not having a bed and left to find a room. Reece wandered up and down the dimly lit corridors. There was nothing to eat or drink. He found what he thought was a restroom, a small, unlit cube with the stump of a toilet, clogged with feces and urine. The room stank of the same, and there was no sink. He emptied his bladder and moved on.

He found a section of chairs welded to one another and settled in. Across the way, two men dressed in brown uniforms slept on the tile floor beneath benches. After the light hubbub of the incoming flight had settled, there seemed to be no activity, as if the airport, too, had decided to sleep.

The air ceased to move. The orange cushion stuck to his pants, and he felt his clothes growing moist. He stared, watching the same two soldiers as they passed by every twenty minutes or so. They had yet to make eye contact. He pulled out a notebook and wrote his first letter to Kristin. He wrote slowly and methodically, using the exercise to serve as a measure against the passing of time. He mentioned the fudge and ate the last piece.

He dozed off and on, never sleeping, rising to walk in slow circles with his bag in easy distance. The rest of his luggage, he assumed, was waiting somewhere to be loaded for the next flight. In addition to a large suitcase and his flight bag, he had brought two blue pasteboard trunks with faux-brass fittings. One contained a wealth of food, including sugar-free drink mixes, a box of peanut brittle, a bag of Snickers bars, and boxes of pasta. The other contained niceties such as a radio, hiking boots, gifts for occasions that called for gifts (in his practical manner, he had packed socks, fingernail clippers, tubes of Chapstick, and small flashlights), a sleeping bag, and sundry other goods one might take on an adventure.

As the sun rose and light began to spill through the open overhead windows lining the hallways, noise re-emerged, and he felt the heat rising, like a bath filling with warm water. Birds, mechanical sounds, a plane landing. And people began to stir. Hungry, Reece searched out what he thought was a restaurant that he had stumbled across during the night. The sign had indicated an opening time of six a.m. He had no idea of the time—he thought it was six-thirty—and after walking down a dark passage, found the sign again beside the elevator. Up and the door opened. Reece surveyed the room, lit only by light from small windows. A dozen waitresses and cooks lay heaped on the floor, dead asleep. He took this in, and the elevator closed. He descended to the main level and decided to check on the departure gate.

He followed the skinny corridors back to a dark, high-ceilinged room in the middle of which was an enormous cage. Inside the cage sat suitcases and trunks. He walked around it as if viewing a dinosaur at a museum. During the night, out of a mist he had felt, a young man in a blue uniform had approached and asked his name. The young man had handed him a long piece of narrow paper, a Telex that indicated something awry with his luggage. After a minute or two of conversation, Reece understood that some of his luggage had been sent back to Rome. The man had smiled and run off without further explanation. Reece peered into the dark piles of luggage but recognized none as his own.

A shrunken man of fifty in a dark-green polyester suit, something a County Agent might wear to a high-school reunion, approached him with confidence, calling out his name.

"Mr. Myers?" the little man said. His eyes sparkled, his accent fully British.

"Yes?"

The man held a paper that Reece did not recognize.

"You have not paid for the luggage to pass through." He looked at Reece matter-of-factly.

"Yes, it's paid for the final destination." Reece had little stubs in his passport wallet to prove it, and he showed them to the man.

"No, no," said the man. "You must pay. You have not paid."

Reece noticed his name tag for the first time. It read "Official." He argued with him, slightly amazed, surprised.

"I have paid," said Reece. A mild panic lifted from his stomach into his chest. *How does he know my name?* Reece pulled a small address book from his bag and showed it to the man, flipping the pages. Reece ran his hand across his oily forehead. "We must first call this person." He pointed to a name. "And then this person." He didn't know what else to do.

The man raised his hand as if to hush Reece and asked him to stay. He went through a heavy wooden door and returned within fifteen minutes.

"Yes, everything is good. Your baggage is fine." The man stood there, unsmiling. Later, Reece realized that the "Official" had expected a tip.

When Reece spotted Hattie, his spirits lifted, and he suggested they go to the restaurant, but she had already eaten. He left her at the gate, which resembled the starting line for a footrace, and hurried. The elevator door opened, and a magic powder lingered inside the space. Tables were nearly full, staff bustled to and fro, and he sat without pause. He had a complimentary breakfast pass from KLM and showed it to the young woman who brought him the laminated menu. She wore a brown outfit with baggy pants and a tight top. Her round face shone, but without smiling. Something not right in her eyes. She took the breakfast pass and asked what he would like.

Reece drank his juice, orange, he thought, and ate his toast with margarine, but did not eat the cold boiled egg, which he hadn't ordered. He paid in US dollars, probably twice what he owed, and did not argue over the disappearance of his free breakfast pass.

Small vendors selling newspapers, candy, and cigarettes opened up along the corridors as the airport came fully alive. Beer and liquor seemed to be the most plentiful items for sale. Reece had never seen his father or mother drink alcohol of any sort. He felt a certain pride that he had resisted for twenty-three years. But he had never felt tempted, really, so strong was his belief that alcohol stood for weakness.

A steady flow of dark-skinned men wearing short-sleeve shirts with neckties and women with tight, coiled braids filled the gates and halls. Instead of ignoring him as the soldiers had done, everyone now seemed to look his way, to look him directly in the eye, especially the few children. Back at his gate, he and Hattie sat next to each other, an hour to wait.

But the plane did not come as scheduled, and there was no announcement at eight-thirty. The outside world, the tarmac, remained hidden, and no one stood behind the small counter inside the gate. Of the few chairs in the tiny departure lounge, all were filled, and people continued squeezing in.

Hattie sat surrounded by her three large carry-on bags, rearranging items, pulling out a bag of rose petals at one point. She held it for Reece to smell, and he did, nodding his head.

"Rose petals," he said, and then, "I wonder if the film crew is flying with us?"

"They're coming later. Ted said they had a few days in Nairobi before they were coming over." Hattie pulled a tissue from her pocket and blew her nose.

"Oh," said Reece. Sweat was gathering in his eyebrows.

A man in a dark-green suit walked among them and unlocked a door. Sunlight that creeps down a hallway showed itself. A woman in a formal green skirt, a less-harsh green, white shirt, and a matching green jacket came through the door. Her straight black hair tapered back tightly. She wore bright red lipstick and had golden skin.

"Do you think she's with the Ethiopian airline?" Reece said. He alternated slumping in his chair with sitting up and leaning forward, elbows on his knees. His back ached.

Hattie ignored him. "Do you think it's safe to go to the bathroom?" she said.

"It was pretty nasty, the one I saw. I'd wait to get on the plane."

"I mean, do you think I'll have enough time?"

She laid her straw hat on her chair. She looked like a white birthday candle on a chocolate cake, standing there in the room bursting with black travelers.

"I don't know. I wish I had an idea."

Hattie took off, Reece watching her things. He thought about the videotapes wrapped in foil in one of his trunks. A friend of the mission director had mailed him the tapes, telling him to disguise them, or they would be confiscated otherwise. The tapes contained old movies, including *Angel in My Pocket, Ben-Hur, and Looking for Mr. Goodbar.* Twenty or so in all. He hadn't been thrilled and packed them as best he could. He was not a movie guy. He felt uncomfortable when people started talking about movies. His parents had never watched movies. They had taken him to see a western when he was in fifth grade and had walked out after a whiskered cowboy said *Damn. Damn, it's a nice day* is what Reece remembered. On more than one occasion, his mother had changed the channel when a Kotex commercial came on. Never said a word.

Hattie asked about the flight, and the man in the green suit said that, yes, the plane had arrived and that it would leave soon. Around eleven, with men and women lying on the floor, the man began shouting, and groups of people rose and pushed. They became agitated like a group of ants, blocked, searching for a way around a deep puddle. Reece reached for his ticket and found it hanging from his back pocket. He hoisted his stuff sack, which others pressed back into him. The passport holder around his neck seemed heavier than ever, and he struggled to pull it from his shirt.

Once through the bottleneck and answering questions, which he did not quite understand, he nodded and handed forward his passport and ticket in reply. The shouting man in the green suit, who also wore an "Official" name tag, put his hand on Reece's back and pushed him toward the open door. Reece resisted the nudge, and a flush rose to his cheeks. Once down a flight of metal steps, he and Hattie followed the long line of passengers toward a jetliner at least half a football field away. The splotched sky seemed unusually high over the surrounding flat landscape. The sun felt good on his face, the heat he had felt inside the terminal now escalating. The fuel smells of idling airplanes mingled with an odor of burning tires.

Climbing steep metal stairs to the white EAL airliner, with its bright swishes of green, yellow, and red on the tail, Reece felt his heart speed. He focused on looking calm as he boarded.

The packed jet took off with a lurch as the pilot accelerated full throttle before completing the turn onto the departure runway. Hattie sat somewhere forward. Reece looked out his tiny window in the rear. A half dozen golden stewardesses glided up and down the aisles wearing demure smiles. He strained at their English, an easy, rapid rolling of new sounds. He wondered at the multiple pauses and the sudden breathy inhalations. Breakfast was served, and he also wondered at that. The idea of famine and these fat sausages with a lump of what seemed to be powdered eggs, all dumped into a foam tray stretched over with plastic wrap, did not quite mesh.

The pilot, a thin man with a sharp, hairless jaw, spoke very clear English, almost with an American flair. His announcements, following those in Amharic, brought a small joy to Reece. The pilot noted for passengers to look out as the plane was passing over Mt. Kenya, the second-highest mountain in Africa. Reece did not catch how many meters high the mountain was and must have been on the wrong side of the plane, because he did not see it.

A thin woman of twenty gathered her long, dark-green dress and ascended the single step into the dim clinic. Forty-seventh patient of the day. Rows of dusty braids swept back to her simple collar. A large front tooth protruded from her mouth, sliding over her lower lip. Gums tattooed blue made her front teeth shine like white stars, but in the back, rotten molars hid from the light.

"Look how dull her nail beds are," said Emma.

Afewerki made his *Tsk, tsk, tsk.*

"Mendeno, mama?" asked Emma. She sat beside the woman on the narrow wooden bench. The woman smelled of milk and wood smoke, the aroma of motherhood in Godo. She spoke in soft tones, playing with a swath of dirty-white cloth that wrapped her waist.

Afewerki interpreted. "Her child has died by one month, and the sores have returned to her legs."

Emma nodded and frowned, the kind of frown directed at the lack of fairness in the world. She lifted the woman's chin and pulled down the lower eyelid to check for anemia. "Jesus, white as a sheet."

"She will show to you the sores," said Afewerki.

A flock of doves hit the metal roof, scratching for traction. Afewerki reached for the homemade broom and gave the underside a swift bang. The doves clawed for dear life, exploding into gray balls of confused feathers on their way to somewhere else.

The anemic woman pulled up her dress without shame, exposing all. Emma stood to block curious eyes peering through the open door.

"Miliary TB," said Emma. "Get me some gauze and peroxide. Let's clean the pus out and then put on some antibiotic ointment."

In the folds of her groin, vicious open wounds glistened through the healing of scar tissue formed and reformed—swollen lymph glands and ruptured nodes. A vague smell of sour infection and decay. Outside, donkeys braying. The ration lines moving. Sacks of grain hoisting to shoulders. In the distance, the *pop pop* of the area's only grain mill, nonstop, day and night, grinding, grinding.

"Get me the can," said Emma.

Afewerki slid an old biscuit tin, the size of four loaves of bread, between the woman's legs to catch the foaming peroxide.

"What's your name?" asked Emma.

"Her name is Abebe."

"Abebe, *flower*," said Emma. She snapped on a pair of latex gloves.

"Yes, flower," said Afewerki.

The woman smiled, and Emma poured, pushing the woman's dress away from the rush of hissing bubbles.

The woman whispered, then coughed into her hand.

"She wants the murphy. To dry the sores."

"Lord. It's gonna be rifampin, the pills. This is long-term, tell her. She'll need to take this medicine for eighteen months. The odds are against her, but she has to try. Is she married?"

"Her husband has left her. He is gone to Gojjam."

Emma applied plenty of antibiotic ointment to the area. Afewerki poured a month's supply of rifampin from a large can into a yellow button envelope.

The woman whispered.

"She wants murphy," said Afewerki.

Without missing a beat, Emma drew up 5 ccs of inject-able saline.

The next-to-last patient of the day was ushered into the clinic by his father, who wore ragged short pants with leg openings the size of storm pipes and a dingy, white dress shirt that hugged his thin chest. He wore a large, limber canvas hat, patched to death. The dust of the paths clung to his lower legs. His son, about five—only God knew his proper age—clung to his leg as well. The child wore tradi-tional shorts, held up with a stiff piece of hemp rope, and a heavy sweater emblazoned *Pariss, French*. Famine clothes. Famine fashion, as Emma called it.

"This man is saying his son has become deaf. He can-not to hear," said Afewerki. He put his hand to his back and winced.

The dull throb of the Bell 412, doing 120 miles per hour, probably within sight of the Wenchit River, became bare-ly audible. Outside, the crowds had diminished, the day's rationing of food over. The silence that follows a heavy meal hung within the fenced compound. The guards chattered like birds, weighing the pros and cons of peas-ant life, gradually settling on the topic of homemade tejj, the honey mead that made life sweet during hard times.

"Can't hear? Just all of a sudden?" asked Emma. She took the otoscope from the shelf and popped on a new plastic tip.

Afewerki queried the father. "Yes, he says, like a door closing."

Emma squatted and smiled at the little boy, who turned and clutched his father's shirt. "Does he have a mother?"

"No. She is died," said Afewerki without asking the man. He knew everyone.

Emma clapped her hands behind the boy's head. He didn't flinch, but turned at the feel of air on his neck. The father laughed.

"I'll need to look in his ears. Just tell him to lean his head over a bit. It won't hurt." She sat on the bench, taking advantage of the square of light coming through the ceiling. "Come here, mamoosh. Bataam taruno," she said, praising his bravery, and then took a look. "Oh my God. Other ear. Turn him around for me." She whistled.

"Infections?" asked Afewerki.

"Flies and pus. Like a ditch choked with trash." She pulled on a pair of latex gloves. "Get me the emesis tray." She took down a bottle of hydrogen peroxide and opened up a ten-cc syringe. "And some hemostats, the ones with the long pinchers on it."

"This one?" asked Afewerki.

"That'll do, I think. Tell him that the liquid will feel cold. That he might hear bubbles popping. Okay?"

The copter's lawnmower-in-the-sky signature showed that Terry had passed the Wenchit, that he was approaching the Jara River.

Afewerki explained the peroxide to the father, who told his son to stand still like the goat facing the lion. Afewerki laughed. The boy's eyes grew wide, and a small whimper escaped. Afewerki went to the door and gazed beyond the small mountain due south. Someone was banging on the compound's metal gate. A guard walked that way to see who it could be. A feeling of dread entered Afewerki's stomach.

"Afewerki, hold this under his ear." She pushed the peroxide into the left ear in spurts. An eruption of foam and yellow detritus spilled from the canal, spread down the child's cheek, and dripped into the pan.

The boy's breathing quickened, and his hands gripped his father's shorts. The copter grew louder and louder. There was shouting in the rocky, dirt yard outside.

Emma looked up from her work and glanced at Afewerki, then went back to the ear. Down into the canal, she lowered the long-nosed hemostats and pinched.

Afewerki could see the copter now, circling to the left around the small mountain, which lay just below the ridge of Godo. He heard the voice of the village administrator, who was drunk and shouting his name.

Emma held up an intact black fly for the father and little boy to see. "There's more where that came from," and she went back to work flushing debris from the boy's ear, catching it with a piece of gauze. "Afewerki!"

"Aiyee!" said Afewerki.

Two guards appeared at the door. Behind them lingered the Hyena, the village administrator, ex-military, appointed by the Derg to rule over the godforsaken town of Godo. His power came via AK-47s, minions who numbered two, a box of hand grenades, a thirst for booze, an appetite for the narcotic leaf qat, and a lust for the local women. Above his desk in the dirt-floored office beside the town jail was nailed the pelt of the unholy and unclean hyena, a horror to all who laid eyes upon it. The Hyena's two front teeth glimmered in outlines of gold.

The Hyena barged into the clinic, slurring his Amharic, holding a Makarov semi-automatic pistol, brown grip and black barrel, a special model that held twelve rounds. It began to rain, the fat drops finger-tapping on the metal roof. The long meher rains that usually fell from June to September had only just started showing signs of returning. All around Godo, hands lifted, but few had been able to plant the vital seeds of teff, sorghum, and peas. Only some rows of scraggly, tooth-jarring corn barely fit for cattle received the dusty splatters.

On the plane, looking down at the brown, twisted canyons, Reece flinched as a stewardess passed. She had smiled at him. She was slim with flower-vase hips. Her features were European, with golden skin, but it was her smile that bored through him.

Below, the canyons greened, and the ground crowded itself with fanning swirls of buildings lining roadways. The surrounding land looked mauve and red with splotches of dark. The 747 circled once and, on a very short runway, screamed to a near halt before lurching to the right. Tufts of tall grass grew in large cracks in the pavement. Rusting hulks of destroyed military vehicles lined the edges of a vast paved runway. A Russian T-72 tank sat forlorn, blown askew, turret on the ground. They had landed at Lideta, the military airport, and would ride through the city on buses bursting with passengers and luggage to Bole, the civilian airport, where a bomb had exploded recently and damaged the control tower.

With heavily armed soldiers in dark-green uniforms and black boots standing about, seeming jaded, Hattie and Reece boarded the same modern bus, filled with padded bench seats like a subway car. Reece squeezed between two thin men, aware for the first time in his life of how big he could seem. At 6 feet and 160 pounds, he had always imagined himself as thin, but now felt unusually large. The weariness of the past twenty-four hours crept higher up his spine and lower into his brain. He stared oblique-ly through a tinted window as the bus inched down wide dirt lanes and narrow paved streets filled with potholes large enough to fall into. A fine dust hung in the air outside, which seemed to be the only thing holding up block after block of ramshackle structures made of tin roofing, twisted poles, plywood, pallets, cardboard, and sheets of plastic. The bus felt like a fat caterpillar inching its way through a maze of razor blades, heaving, rocking with the weight of its belly. The silence of the passengers inside the stuffy, air-conditioned bus numbed him. A boy in the street struggled with three donkeys, flailing at them with a heavy stick.

The bright colors among the dismal browns, the children waving at the bus dressed in rags, patting their mouths like empty bellies, old men stooped to the ground, a woman carrying a bundle of eucalyptus branches, boxy blue-and-white Lada and Fiat taxis, the rust, the dirt, these things entered Reece's tired mind, piling into mountains of unsorted data.

After what seemed an eternity, the buses turned from a wide paved road and wound their way onto the field of what he recognized as a bona fide airport. From the buses, the passengers pushed their way inside, queuing for a long wait to pass through customs. The low ceilings, tan paint, and cement blocks reeked of function. Since 1974, following the overthrow of the publicly genteel Haile Selassie, the last Emperor descended from Solomon and Bathsheba, a military government, headed by the hardcore Mengistu Haile Mariam, had subsumed the ancient country to serve a new master beneath the ideology and gaze of Marx, Lenin, and Engels. Soldiers armed with short-barreled AK-47s inhabited every corner, standing in a kind of half-attention, watching, not pacing like the soldiers in Nairobi.

The images piled higher in his mind, dualities of every ilk and imagination, black and white, rich and poor, smoldering in his head. Inside the large, open room split by plain square columns, the smells of history, sweat, unknown spices, and what felt to Reece like fear, a weary sort of fear that stuck to the bottom of one's shoes. A mild hubbub of conversation bubbled now as the hundreds filtered from amorphous groups into more orderly lines that led to booths followed by long metal tables where golden women in white shirts dissected luggage, noting certain items on a list, taking electronics, laying them aside, asking the owners of items such as tape players to demonstrate whatever magic lay within. To the side, luggage poured in continuously on clanking conveyor belts run by diesel generators, piling in great heaps.

There were few words in Reece's mind, and Hattie seemed preoccupied with her thoughts and worries. After an hour or so, Reece received his first purple stamp, a carefully laid insignia facing the hieroglyphic visa inside his passport. He pointed out his luggage to the woman, a mother he imagined, who spoke English. The mysterious young man in Nairobi with the Telex had been right. One of his trunks was missing, the one with the videotapes and gifts and other things he could no longer remember packing. To open the other trunk, Reece first peeled away a plaster of duct tape, but then couldn't find the stamped metal key that opened the hasp. With his permission, the young woman inserted the end of a broken pair of needle-nose pliers and permanently opened the lock. She smiled as an apology. As the trunk lid opened, the contents seemed foreign to him. What does one bring to a famine? He wanted to open the peanut brittle, tear open the box, pull out the soft foil pouch, and share it with her. She asked him about a few things, the red radio, a compass sealed in its blister pack, but did not open or take anything.

With his luggage in a pile, he stood there wondering what to do next. A gauzy older man who had the stern, kind look of the former emperor indicated that he should follow the others through an arched passageway. The old man called to one of the soldiers, who soon returned with another old man with a graying beard and yellowed eyes, who picked up Reece's trunk and a suitcase. The man wore sandals made from old tires and smelled of cloves, smoke, and sweat.

The old man deposited Reece's trunk and suitcase in the middle of a large gym-like room among a myriad other piles, then stood waiting for his tip as patient as Moses. Reece fumbled in his pocket and came up with a five-dollar bill, which the man took with a grunt. Reece saw Hattie standing near her pile, talking with a stout white man in a short-sleeved, cotton shirt.

Dr. Guthrie waved at Reece, and Reece waved back. Voices in the vaulted room echoed and mingled into ripples of watery noise. Reece scooted his pile toward them but gave that up and walked over to meet the Baptist Mission's veterinarian. At first glance, here was a man who worked hard and who lived by hard rules. His stocky body, buzz haircut, tight, short-sleeved shirt, and permanent sun squint impressed Reece, imprinted Dr. Guthrie onto his brain.

"Howdy," said Dr. Guthrie with a no-nonsense Southern accent. And then he said hello in Amharic, "Tenesteling!" He stuck his short, strong arm out to Reece, giving him a vigorous handshake. Sweat ran from the top of his head. He stood back with his hands on his hips, sizing up the recruits with a look of gusto.

"Nice and warm," said Reece, resorting to the weather.

"It runs about eighty degrees during the day right now. Not too bad. Gets real cool at night. How was your flight?"

Before Reece could answer, a man in khaki pants with a thick head of curly brown hair walked up, followed by two young Ethiopian men wearing odd combinations of clothing. The one who was very dark with a round, oily face wore a red, cabled sweater with a green Christmas-tree pattern. His pinstripe pants belonged to a nice suit. The other fellow, a toasty color with sharp features, wore a pair of very faded jeans with a woman's sleeveless blue top that featured a small appliqué of a teddy bear blowing a horn.

"Hattie, Reece, this is Ben Ashberry, our director," said Dr. Guthrie.

Ben, wearing aviator-style glasses with large lenses, seemed to need a moment to size them up before speaking. He threw his hands to his hips and rolled his eyes as if in disbelief that here were two more volunteers ready for the whipping post. He blew out a heavy, comic sigh and offered his tan hand first to Reece and then to Hattie. Sweat soaked the armpits of his shirt.

"Welcome, welcome," said Ben.

"Thank you, thank you," said Reece, caught up in the repetition.

Ben turned to the two young men and spoke in rapid,

clear Amharic. They hustled Hattie and Reece's luggage out to a waiting van, one of three owned by the Mission. Ben spoke with them for a few minutes and had to run.

Just as Reece's anxiety began to abate, Dr. Guthrie mentioned that a soda was waiting upstairs inside the airport bar. Reece's very full bladder trembled. They stopped by a single restroom, guarded by an old man, a shimogele, there to keep out the riffraff and to guard the toilet paper, according to Dr. Guthrie. He stood at attention as if a great meeting proceeded behind the unmarked varnished wooden door. Inside was a small, fragile toilet, clean, and a sink without knobs. Reece imagined a mirror and looked at himself. What did he know that could help anyone? What business of his was it, this famine? He took a deep breath and shuddered, then stretched his mouth with a huge smile. Dr. Guthrie handed the shimogele a single bill, a birr.

"Xavier meskin," the doorman murmured as they headed up a flight of narrow stairs.

Reece's footsteps echoed. His feet felt bruised, the bones sore. The stairs opened into a high-ceilinged curved room. He remained vaguely aware of Dr. Guthrie and Hattie. The room seemed to spin, or rather turn, as he walked to the small table where sat a scratched bottle of orange Fanta.

Around the table, a lively conversation ensued, breaking the Styrofoam silence. A thin man in slacks and a dark-blue cotton shirt sat two large, green bottles of Ambo on the table. The carbonated water fizzed chains of bubbles. Reece ordered a Pepsi and learned to mix half Ambo and half Pepsi in his glass. There was no ice, and the tepid drinks hissed in the warm brown room.

As the minutes passed, colors brightened. He thought about Kristin. Without warning, he felt that he had lost something precious.

"This is bizarre," said Reece.

"You don't know the half of it," said Dr. Guthrie.

Hattie tossed Reece a serious but knowing look.

Dr. Guthrie's smile faded into a blank expression. "Expect some hard knocks, young man. Got us a nurse up in Godo, where you're headed. Nearly died on us. Malaria the first time, and then some kind of fever that made that seem like a picnic. Could've been dengue with all the pain she was having. I had to knock her out with some IV morphine on the helicopter ride back to Addis. She was one hurtin' little girl."

"Wow," said Hattie.

Hattie then told a story about having a fever as a child. Her story reached beyond the moment and fell flat. Listening to Hattie's languid Mississippi drawl, Dr. Guthrie's clipped Alabama speech, Reece envisioned an Ethiopia entirely in the hands of these Southern Baptists crowded around a small café table drinking warm sodas. Why were they the only ones in the airport enjoying fizzy drinks in the middle of the day? Where did the waiter go? Reece imagined that he unloaded cargo for a few minutes, hurried back up the stairs, grabbed sodas, ran back down the stairs, and so on, which he did.

"You guys ready to head back?" asked Dr. Guthrie.

Reece looked at Hattie. "Sure."

The Mission's Toyota van looked like a blowfish on toy

wheels but rocked along steady, taking huge ruts in the pavement. Rusted blue taxis and Toyota HiAce diesel vans raced along the main road leading from the airport. Sidewalks crowded with old men in dusty concoctions of draped cotton shawls along with women in long patchwork dresses stooped with heavy loads of charcoal, teenagers with short neat hair, who could have been from an American fifties' snapshot, children bursting in and out of traffic slapping the windows, some patting their mouths with their fingers.

The conversation moved between gaps of silence. Reece was exhausted, and Hattie as well. Dr. Guthrie seemed rested but frayed. Reece noticed the four-lane road widen into a vast twenty lanes of traffic. The van approached and passed beneath a gigantic arch with hammer in fist. "Workers of the World Unite!" Off to the left, a giant billboard with the faces of Marx, Lenin, and Engels stared down on the Abiot, or Revolution Square, as explained by Dr. Guthrie. On the wide sidewalk crowded with begging women, a man wobbled beneath a load of five brightly colored mattresses.

The lanes narrowed quickly, six, then four, and, turning from the main road, the van crawled from one pothole crater to the next. Dr. Guthrie put the steering through its maximum capabilities, straining to keep the van upright. The city seemed to be made of corrugated metal sheeting, used as doors, walls, roofs, tables for bananas and oranges, and sleds to drag down the streets. A turbid, brown creek ran alongside the road. Rounding a corner and crossing a narrow bridge of dirt, a smell penetrated the van so foul that Reece thought he might vomit.

"That's the winery right there," said Dr. Guthrie. A small ditch filled with a muddy liquid ran from the property, crossed the road, and splashed toward the creek.

Hattie held her nose and laughed at Reece. The smell reminded him of the liquid that lingered in a wet garbage can, magnified a thousand times. The van splashed through the runoff and continued along at a snail's pace until reaching a straight section of dirt road. The van limped along, plowing through the V of people crowding the way. Dr. Guthrie pointed out his house, set back on the right, and then rolled his window down and spoke in his forced but rapid Amharic to a man leading a maroon humped cow down the road.

Reece's mind raced as they turned into the gated mission compound. A man with a rifle and a blanket over his shoulders greeted them with a wide smile. The van pulled past a white building with a brown front porch, followed by a small American-style ranch house with a pile of what looked to be junk beside it, and then pulled around in front of two tidy white buildings, the guesthouses.

The sun was bright, the air clear. The quiet of the compound seemed edged with a hum. The larger guesthouse on the right had two small bedrooms, a living room, a small kitchen, and a single bathroom with a shower. A rickety bookshelf in the open living room held a dozen or so tattered novels. The smaller house to the left was home to the mission's journeyman missionary, a Stephanie. Reece missed her last name.

"You guys tired?" Without waiting for an answer, Dr. Guthrie told Reece and Hattie to make themselves at home, that there would be dinner later at Ben's house, and that they should relax. He left in a hurry, late for a cattle vaccination clinic that he held in his front yard on Saturdays. Feeling more and more like a stranger in a strange place, Reece put his heavy baggage in his room and lay on the bottom of his bunk for a few minutes, thinking it was all a dream.

In the tiny bathroom, Reece wondered to whom the worn, yellow toothbrush belonged. Without a sense of the time, he peered into the living room.

Hattie emerged wearing white bicycle pants and a white top with a strawberry pattern. She looked like a Popsicle and seemed lost.

"Lord, Rice, I know we'll have some stories to tell," said Hattie. She peeked out through the white curtains. "Well, I know that plane ride over was an adventure in itself." She made a *Hoo!* and cackled.

Reece imagined her gardening in a big floppy hat, drinking sweet tea between gladiolas.

"Dr. Guthrie said something about you going to a place called Gundo," said Reece.

"He did? Gundo?" asked Hattie. She cackled again.

Gundo Meskel was one of five feeding stations, plus the upcountry base at Alem Ketema, all operated by the Baptist Mission. The various relief groups had carved up the country into territories. The Baptists worked a region known as Merhabete, north of Addis Ababa. Emma had been one of the original nurses on the team at Gundo Meskel, but had since taken over at Godo. At Gundo, they had lived in tents until local workers fleshed out one compound complete with living quarters, eating hut, cooking shed, and outhouse, and then another compound with a clinic and a warehouse for the grain and other foodstuffs shipped in from around the world.

Reece had promised Kristin he would call her when he arrived. He looked around, and there was no phone. He looked in the kitchen and then the bedroom. "Is there a phone in your room?"

"Didn't see one." Hattie wandered around in circles, hands on her hips, commenting on the tidy floors, how clean the kitchen was. "Did you notice that the sheets on those beds have been ironed?"

Reece puzzled that bit of news. So many things seemed a bit off. It was small, but almost unbelievable that amid a famine, someone ironed sheets for missionaries. What did it mean? Where was this famine? His stomach rumbled, and a vague sense of hunger along with a palpable lightheadedness trickled down like dust. He walked toward the kitchen, where Hattie propped open the white refrigerator. Its light was out.

"The water in the bottles should be safe to drink," said Hattie. "Don't drink the tap water. Learned that in Mexico one time. There are a couple of Fantas in there."

Reece stuck his head in the kitchen. The dark cabinets were homemade but solid. A small four-burner stove, propane, rounded out the narrow room. After Hattie opened a Fanta, he slipped in and pulled out a large glass bottle of cold water. It had a rubber stopper in the top.

"Looks like an IV bottle," said Hattie. "Pretty."

"Strange." Reece examined the bottle. The glass narrowed at the top, forming a short, thick neck. The mouth of the bottle was smooth. It was pretty or something like that.

"Your fiancée...What's her name again?"

"Kristin."

It's the look of a child going down the slide for the first time. That look of being let go and the sudden drop. Reece looked like that when he said Kristin's name. He felt like he had been jerked back to Alabama on the end of a long, stiff rope. He looked away and then looked at Hattie, who insisted that he show her Kristin's picture again. Reece, not knowing what else to do, walked to his bunk with a sense of dread and pulled the photo album from his bag. He needed to call Kristin. Hattie stood with her hands behind her back.

Reece opened the book to a photo of his grandparents. Hattie said nothing, letting Reece hold the book in front of her like a dead bird.

"Is that her?" asked Hattie.

It was her, the close-up of Kristin, her thin face punctuated by large, wide, brown eyes, framed with wild curls.

"Yes." Reece felt he should have said, "Yes, that's Kristin." And then maybe something about her. Kristin seemed very real in the photo, but her presence felt chalky in the room. He reminded himself that he loved her.

"Well, she's real nice." She looked tired and said she needed to lie down.

His eyes followed Hattie's new blue Nikes to her bedroom door. He held the Fanta bottle up to the fluorescent light. "Looks used," he said. And it was.

Outside, Reece walked along the U-shaped lane that penetrated the Mission compound. The sky seemed very close, a few quadrangles of cloud hanging almost vertical, like pressed cotton fiber. The sun burned his neck. He turned and stared at the guesthouse, walked to the side, and peered downhill. A thin, mangy dog with swollen teats lumbered from beneath the house through a gap in the brick pilings.

"Hey, come here." The dog hung its head and kept an even distance from his outstretched hand, sniffing with her dry, scratched nose. Reece sat in the rough grass. She let him reach out and scratch beneath her chin. It seemed to Reece that he had dropped from the sky into a vast, crowded city, yet this dog would be the limit of his experience. He walked inside and rummaged through the refrigerator, finding a piece of white cheese. At first, he couldn't find the dog, but then he saw her eyes in the black and tossed the cheese. She inhaled it, remaining in the crawl space.

Behind the guesthouse, the rocky ground fell away toward a yellow-brown creek. The color reminded him of diarrhea. A half-dozen stunted trees, most with thorns, dotted the slope. He could see the top half of a man bathing by the creek. Farther away, he could see a small loop of the creek, shimmering like a hook. According to Dr. Guthrie, the long dry season was winding down with the belg, the short rains, and the meher, the long rains, would fall from mid-June to mid-September. In addition to the civil wars in the south and north, the famine had been fueled by drought, excessive taxes, failed crops, and invasions of armyworms and locusts that had devoured what was left.

Reece sat on the hard ground, picked up a rock, and heard a vehicle stop in front of the guesthouse. He worried about dinner with Ben and his family and the social energy it would consume. He needed a day or two of solitude and closed his eyes. He jerked, nearly asleep, and went inside to take a nap. When he awoke, two hours later, Hattie was knocking on his door. He stood and wobbled as his vision went completely blank.

"You okay?" asked Hattie.

"Yeah."

She had combed out her hair into a broom shape.

"Ben's wife Teresa came by a few minutes ago and said that she would be sending some food down for us tonight, that we would meet with them in the morning, to get some rest since we would be getting our permits, whatever that means, tomorrow sometime. Did you know she just had a baby?"

"Who?"

"Teresa. Only a month old and tiny as can be. Had him here in the hospital. I think maybe we passed it coming in."

Reece heard Hattie but did not process what she was saying. Little seemed real. The dog under the house was real, though. He imagined Hattie on her knees weeding a bed of purple pansies. He sat in the armchair that matched the couch. From there, he examined the wooden slat shades in the large front window. They were level, each slat like a narrow, empty bookshelf.

Outside, trucks, jeeps, and vans pulled in and out of the compound. People came and went from the large white building near the entrance. Reece imagined Ethiopia as a game board, that things were happening, that things would soon happen to him as well, but that he would have little or no control over them. "I'm going to walk around," he said.

Hoping not to meet anyone new just yet, Reece watched a dirty, white Toyota van stop in front of the tiny, detached guesthouse beside the main guesthouse. A man and woman in their late sixties emerged and slammed the doors. Reece took a few steps their way. The man took his time, his gray hair too long and thin to stay put in the breeze. He wore silver-framed glasses and a look of refined patience. The woman, his wife, wore a nondescript pantsuit and had a puffy, wrinkled face beneath a thin film of rouge. She waved and pulled two canvas bags filled with groceries from behind the driver's seat.

"I heard you were here. Is it Rice?" asked Sam Woods. He and his wife Shirley were retired missionaries from Cameroon, but had found they couldn't sit still back home in Tennessee.

Reece shook Sam's hand and said Hi to Shirley. "It's Reece. Like the peanut butter cup."

Sam looked at Shirley and chuckled. "We're glad to have you," he said.

"Let us know if we can do anything," said Shirley.

"Will do, just looking around." Reece felt that Sam and Shirley knew something he didn't. They took their time getting into their tiny house, but the conversation was over for now. Sam and Shirley, childless, cared a great deal for Emma and had essentially adopted her since her arrival, staying by her side at the hospital when she became ill and spending time with her when she came into Addis for rest and recreation. Emma was golden.

Emma motioned for the father to remain seated, to stay calm. "Ishi, ishi," she told the young boy, ears filled with wax and pus, and then exploded at the Hyena. "What the heck are you doing, man! Unless you're sick, and I suspect you're only drunk, get the heck out of here! I'm working. I didn't come eight thousand miles to have to deal with the likes of you." Emma felt for sleeves to roll up, but she didn't have any.

The rain unleashed in a fury, and the Hyena's two teenage henchmen carrying AK-47s pushed inside, crowding the small clinic lined with rickety shelves. Their eyes inventoried the precious bottles and cans.

Waving his pistol like a glove, the Hyena glowered and grinned at Emma. She stood eye to eye with him. He barked at his compatriots, who pressed against Afewerki.

"I am under arrest," said Afewerki.

"Arrest, for what?" Emma glanced back at the little boy, ears clogged with flies. The rain beat the roof, drowning their voices.

In the torrent outside, Terry struggled in the Bell 412 to see what he was doing. He wasn't sure if he was even over the village anymore. Terry searched through the curved rectangle of Plexiglas to the side of his left foot, looking for yellow.

"He is to say I am stealing from this compound, some oils and things."

"What? He knows good and well that he's the one sending his buddies in here at night, stealing everything they can get their hands on. If Dr. Guthrie would let us, I'd tell the guards to shoot them next time they come crawling over the fence dead of night. I've never heard such baloney!"

The Hyena's thugs had Afewerki by the arms. It wasn't the first time they'd arrested him on false charges. They seemed eager to leave and murmured to the Hyena, who laughed and took a seat beside the father on the bench. He was content to wait out the storm and relax.

The copter's noise zigzagged in slow motion above the roar of the rain. The compound went from dust and rocks to thick mud and rocks within minutes, frothy rivulets streaming downhill, pooling against the fence.

"You make me so mad." Emma turned her back on the confusion, squatted, and engaged the little boy, whose face shone with sheer terror. "It's okay. Let's get that gunk out of your ears. Afewerki, get over here."

Afewerki's erstwhile guards let him go. He spoke to the father and the little boy.

"Have him bend his head over like before," said Emma. She tilted her head to show him. "Taruno, mamoosh," she said.

No one said a word as she worked in the dimness. Terry had not landed. No sounds of the copter were to be heard as the rain slackened and a sudden burst of sunshine lit the room. Smells of wet and earth mixed with the Hyena's fruity breath, and cool, fresh air drifted through the open door.

With the hemostats, Emma pulled out an inch-long plug of wax, flies, and pus. The little boy's face contorted in alarm, and he whispered to his father in a pained voice.

"Oh, the sounds is come back," said Afewerki. "He is complaining of the bubbles in his ear."

"Great," said Emma, lost in the task and approaching the other ear.

The Hyena sat enraptured, perhaps imagining his childhood, flies trapped in his own ears. Searching for moisture, the tenacious black flies thrust full-throttle into mouths, eyes, noses, and ears. As if in homage to what he was witnessing, the Hyena grabbed a fly from midair, shook it in his hand like dice, threw the disoriented fly onto the dirt floor, and stepped on it with his black Russian combat boot, a real perk in the rocky Highlands where tire sandals were the norm for those who could afford them.

The little boy moved his eyes from the shiny, black rifles to the pistol that now lay limp on the Hyena's lap. The Hyena blurted out something that had a positive ring to it. He grabbed Afewerki's sleeve and nodded toward Emma.

"He says your work is good," said Afewerki.

Emma flushed the left ear with peroxide and watched it erupt. "He's drunk."

"He says you are a gift from God, that God will bless you."

"Tell him that I'll pray for him." She inched the hemostats in and hauled out a bloody mess that looked like manure oozing with melted vanilla ice cream.

The little boy cried out, and the father scolded him for doing so.

"Got a real infection in this one," said Emma. "I'm gonna flush it one more time, and that should take care of it. Can you hear now, little mamoosh?"

He whispered while drawing his breath in, a peculiar

habit of the people that gave local speech a breathy, mysterious quality.

"He says the noises are very loud to his ears."

"Great. Let's send him along with some paracetamol, and he's good to go. Just give him nine pills, and no more than three a day. If his ear still hurts in a couple of days, tell him to come back."

Everyone made way for the father and son to step out into the dripping, muddy world.

"Wait," said Emma. "Caramella?"

The little boy's eyes grew wide like silver coins.

She handed him a peppermint and then one to the father as well.

The little boy smiled. "Amenseganolo," said the father.

The Hyena held out his hand for a peppermint as well Emma laughed.

The slight grayscale of the air around Reece dropped a notch. The air temperature fell just a fraction. He wandered past the ranch house on his left, wondering at the enormous piles of junk around the house. Guthrie had said the mission's business manager and his wife lived there. He couldn't remember his name. They had kids. The front window had no curtain, and the inside looked dim and spare. Grass grew in clumps in the short, cracked sidewalk leading to the narrow cement porch.

At the end of a rutted, dirt driveway sat a steel barrel, and Reece walked closer. Printed in black letters, he read, "Blackstrap molasses. Product of Florida, USA." Fifty gallons of molasses, a hard brown ooze around the seal. He looked across to the administrator Ben Ashberry's house. It was ranch-style as well, but built of large, flat stones. It looked neater and bigger. Both houses sat in the deep shade of tall Eucalyptus trees. Reece breathed deep, but could only smell a vague odor of dirt and sweat that hung in the air.

Several vehicles sat in front of the building near the gate. A wide wooden porch wrapped the front and right side. Reece walked to the door and peered inside, where a few desk chairs sat against the walls and a chalkboard displayed Amharic script. A churning, mechanical sound emanated from within. If there were people inside, he couldn't see them or hear them. He turned away and approached the gate and the small wooden guard shack. The guard there examined him, whisking flies with an ox tail on a stick. He flashed Reece a big smile, stood, and spoke.

Reece felt mute and weak like loose string. He smiled and said, "Thank you. English? Learning." He smiled, nodding at the puzzled guard, determined to push on to the dirt road and beyond. The two halves of the barred gate stood closed, except for a slight gap, wide enough to walk through. When the guard realized Reece's intention to go out, he jumped up and opened both halves of the gate. The wideness of the opening unsettled Reece.

A wash of people moved down the road. No one seemed to be in a hurry, except for the kids who ran up and shouted, "Ferenj!" Men held hands and walked with men. Women walked with women. He noticed a couple of skinny men dressed in dark military fatigues, both on crutches, both missing a leg. They were Cuban soldiers, veterans of battles to the north with Eritrea, and they ignored him as they hobbled by. Reece turned back into the compound, mesmerized, saturated with new things.

The grinning guard burbled in Amharic, a rollercoaster of sounds filled with halting consonants. Reece imagined throwing a Q into the air and swinging at it with a machete. There was a music to it as if the guard's speech could suddenly become a top-forty hit. He turned back, afraid of what he did not know. The shadows from the trees lengthened in front of him as he walked. He went and searched for the dog, but she was gone, and he took another walk around the compound. It did not seem as if the country was being pummeled into the ground by a military dictator. It did not seem that a famine was raging around him. He glimpsed a man with a beard inside the rancher, caught the toe of his shoe on a rock, and stumbled.

As evening fell, Reece and Hattie wound up having dinner with the Ashberrys, after all. Reece needed to call Kristin. It's all he could think of.

"This is Claude," said Ben with his hands on the six-year-old's shoulders. Ben reminded Reece of a sunflower, the way his curly hair radiated. Claude looked just like Ben, except Ben had straight hair. Claude's glasses followed his brow precisely, giving him a mechanical look.

The inside of the house was warm, with breezes flowing through open windows. A dozen flies rattled in the front room, zipping from wall to wall.

"Wah, wah, wah...wah, wah...wah, wah wah, wah," said Claude. He jumped up and down stiff-legged, making pinching motions with his hands like a blind crab. He laughed, shrugged off Ben, and swung at Reece's crotch.

"Whoa, whoa!" Ben said, grabbing Claude from behind in a body hug.

Reece stepped back, nearly falling over a rocking chair. The room smelled of aromatic spices, something like curry. The front room, as Ben's wife Teresa called it, and the adjoining dining room were crammed with furniture, food, the four Ashberrys, and Hattie and Reece.

"Hi, Claude, I'm Reece." Reece stooped down, hands on knees, trying to produce a meaningful look, a smile maybe. He felt awkward with children and avoided them when possible. Claude stared at him.

When Teresa entered the room from the kitchen, clutching her two-week infant to her chest, her breast partially exposed, and little Kimo sucking long and slow, Reece forced himself not to look away. He felt a weight of bricks was being piled on his shoulders, that his head was gradually being forced forward and down, that he had to fight at all costs or risk melting into nothing. Teresa had wispy brown hair that she twisted into what looked like a tube of yarn, very rustic, but plaintive and suggestive. She appeared slightly older than Ben and wore what Reece thought of as a long hippy skirt.

Claude hid his face in his father's loose pants when he saw his mother. She cradled little Kimo, his African name, in one arm, and gestured with the other, as if balancing the weight of Kimo with the weight of the evening. Hattie caught Reece's gaze and gave him a look of sympathy.

"Okay, guys, this is the real deal," said Teresa. "I made the apple pie and macaroni, but we have a super lady who cooks Habasha—that means Ethiopian—food for us ferenjis."

Kimo nuzzled his mother. Reece struggled not to think of Teresa's breast, which she kept exposed, and enjoyed the food, but did not quite understand what he was eating. The wots, or little stews, were tasty, especially the potatoes and the chicken. The dorowot caused the top of his head to break into a weeping sweat, something he had never experienced before. He asked for more water, the bubbling Ambo, and that made Ben happy, Reece thought. He wanted even more, needed a Fanta or something cold and sweet to counter the spicy hotness. The flat round bread, the enjera, served with the wots, puzzled Reece. The gray color and the rich texture of the honeycombed bread, along with its pungent twang—he felt at a loss to describe it that night in a letter to Kristin—made him ponder each bite, desperate to accommodate the unfamiliar taste.

Dinner lasted for an hour, the conversation always lagging. Teresa dominated, exhorting the benefits of Ethiopian culture, praising Ethiopian women for breastfeeding, and doling out insight into peasant life. Did they know that teff, the grain from which enjera was made, the staple of life in Ethiopia, contained the highest concentration of iron of any edible grain? Did they know that it was best not to wash teff too thoroughly so that even more iron from the soil penetrated the peasant diet? Reece nodded his appreciation, but Hattie responded with exclamations, making Reece feel that he appeared unenthusiastic. He couldn't stop thinking about Teresa's large maroon nipple covered with a milky film, slipping from Kimo's mouth, slowly regaining its shape, and pointing directly at him.

"Ben, take them out to the dump to see the hyenas," said Teresa. Claude sat alone at a small wooden table, his head dropping and snapping.

Crammed into the cab of a red Nissan pickup, Reece sat with his legs straddling the stick shift, squeezed between Hattie and Ben. Ben drove with his lights off, only briefly flashing them when he lost all sense of the road. The currency regarding auto lights in the city was that they blinded oncoming pedestrians and drivers. It was rude to drive with them on, in fact.

The truck struggled through small groups of people, slowing as they scattered like buckshot. Whenever the truck slowed, a pair or two of children in rags appeared from nowhere, tapping their mouths with their fingers, begging for money. The Koshe dump, in daylight, offered up its scraps of metal and paper to the poorest of the poor and to residents of the nearby leprosarium, the ALERT Hospital, as Ben called it. At night, hyenas roamed about culling morsels of bone and scraps of food, perhaps lucking onto a chicken head tossed out by one of the wealthier residents of the city.

The truck struggled uphill and through a wide, open gate. The headlight beams revealed a bright tunnel of gray, damp ground. Ben pulled up on top of the leveled mountain of trash, the edges of which dropped away into nothing. He circled until the headlights caught half a dozen sets of blazing yellow eyes, perhaps a hundred feet away. He inched the truck closer.

"They feed at night," he said. "If you were to walk over there, they would run, but then come back, circle you, kill you, and eat you." A dirty, spotted shoulder, yellowish in color, materialized and faded.

Hattie had been reluctant to come along. But Teresa had insisted that this would be a significant event, that it was a rite of passage to see the dump at night, to feel the creeping of hyenas at the edges of the city's waste. "Are these doors locked?" she said.

"Mine is," said Ben, laughing. "Oh, crap!"

"What!" Hattie jerked her head, filling Reece's face with her brittle, white hair.

About thirty feet away, Reece saw a man dressed in a dirty white shamma, a drapery of cotton cloth, and short pants. His eyes peered between the folds of the shawl, which wrapped around his head and fell across his shoulders. He held a shotgun with a very long barrel, pointed directly at the cab. He circled, intending to block their exit down the steep road.

"Damn," said Ben as he ground the gears and backed away. A rickety guard shack, which reminded Reece of an outhouse, flashed in the headlight beams.

The truck jerked backward in fits, headed directly for the edge of the mountainous heap. Anything seemed possible at the moment. The gate appeared to the right, twenty feet away. Ben threw the truck into first and floored it. A flash and a tremendous boom followed. Hattie screamed and Ben said, "Fuck." Reece was pretty sure he said it and couldn't help laughing, as the truck raced and slid downward. Ben cut his lights, and the whole world disappeared. "Sorry about that, guys," he said.

Ben drove very fast with the lights on and off until he reached a narrow, paved road. Hattie had rolled up her window, but now rolled it back down. A smell of rotting garbage flowed into the cab. On top of the landfill, Reece had smelled only smoke. Shanties lined the road, and an occasional lump covered in rags lay on the uneven sidewalk. The air was very cool, much cooler than during the day.

"Ben, you got to be kidding me," said Hattie. Her hair was a mess. She looked like she had been sawn in half and put back together again.

"Claude usually comes with me," Ben said. "Teresa used to come...Holy cow. That's the first time..."

"That was interesting," said Reece. A silence ensued for several turns. "Where is a phone that I can use to call the States?" he said.

A cow with high, elegant hips appeared on the road, and Ben slammed on the brakes.

Emma said *Damn you* in her head, but what came out was, "Do you think I'm here to hand out peppermints to drunks waving pistols in my face and arresting our workers! We've got work to do, man!" She peeked out the door and saw a lone, pitiful woman soaked to the bone hunched next to the rain barrel, which had overflowed. The last patient of the day, hoping for a miracle. Emma made a sound like an angry, groaning donkey.

"Emma. It is okay. Let me go now to the jail. I will ask what is wrong. All is with the hands of God." Afewerki stepped outside, shadowed by his two captors, dropouts lured by the Hyena's power, alcohol, and endless supply of the narcotic qat leaf.

"Well, by God..." said Emma. She didn't quite know what to do and watched the Hyena grab the doorway and step into the mud. She went to the door and called to the frail woman squatting on a stone the size of a small book. "Mendeno, mama?" she said. "Let me help you." Emma's Nike sank into the muck, and she leaned over to give the woman a hand. Bells jingled from the leather baby carrier hiding beneath her wads of dirty cloth.

The crumpled woman with the child on her back had come from beyond the nearby village of Aferbiny, about five miles on foot. Her husband was ill with malaria. She must hurry back to cook, to boil some soybean oil and peppers, and borrow two or three flat rounds of sorghum enjera from her neighbor's basket. Her young son, bundled on her back, was ill. The devil was eating his face.

These things Afewerki had learned in passing and shouted back to Emma as he was led away. Emma helped this shell of a woman to stand, dripping with rain and maybe sweat, her skirts and bare feet caked with mud. That smell of wood smoke and milk, intense smoke, strong milk, like that of an animal.

"I'm sorry, so sorry about the rain," said Emma. She growled to herself, thinking of the Hyena.

The woman stepped inside, as if cowering beneath the weight of a heavy curse. Under the layers of wet cloth covering her head, shoulders, and back was a neat green dress of coarse cloth with a tailored collar, damp and musty. A goiter the size of a softball gently enlarged her lower neck. All in all, she looked rather pleasant, her golden skin soft and glowing, around the eyes an intelligence, but her bucked upper teeth and goiter called out for sympathy.

"Come, nah," and Emma helped the woman into the clinic. "Sit," and Emma made the motion of sitting. She wondered what "the devil eating his face" could mean. Something awful, no doubt. Horrendous, and she prepared to find out.

The woman laid her wraps in a pile on the floor, and Emma picked them up and placed them on the other bench. The child inside the leather carrier did not move but made a low, agonized whine that sent chills across Emma's arms and back. *I'm dying, I'm dying,* the moans seemed to say. *Help me, I'm dying.*

Isaac, the very slow English speaker with the patchy beard and light skin, poked his head inside. A wide smile creased his face. "You are safe. Yes? The evil one is away? Oh, yes, and Afewerki is to jail." He continued to smile, as if this were the safest emotion to exhibit in trying times.

"I know," said Emma. "Can we get him out? Are we working on it?" She touched the woman's cheek.

"We are praying to God for Afewerki. He will be re-lease-ed, God willing," said Isaac.

Emma shook her head at the idea of prayer as the primary intervention with a sadistic drunk. "Let's see this baby. Isaac, help me. Ask her to uncover the baby."

Isaac did, and Emma looked away.

Reece tossed and turned. A persistent altitude headache nagged him behind the eyes. Addis Ababa sat at roughly eight thousand feet, compared to under a thousand back in Alabama. It had been late when they returned from the landfill adventure, and Ben had asked Reece to come over the next morning to make his phone call. Reece awoke with a mild cough and a headache and realized his intestines had stopped working. There seemed to be no plan or schedule for him or his insides. He felt that sense of limbo, of being rocked slowly in a boat, not sure where he was going or if he was moving at all. The sky felt closer than back home, and it was, and weighed heavy as a lid coming down on a pot.

After eating a tiny banana, he walked outside. The mission was alive, and certainly its business was being carried out, but Reece had no idea what it was they did or how. He looked again for the dog under the house. He could see the Ashberrys' front porch and Claude opening and closing the screen door. Twice, Teresa brought him inside, and back again he came to start over the ritual. He was singing.

The door to the tiny guesthouse to the right opened, and a young woman Reece's age stepped out in a robe as if to fetch the morning paper.

"Hi, you must be Rice," she said, reaching back to twist her damp hair into a rope. She wore thick glasses and had lots of freckles. "I'm Cynthia."

"Hey." Reece stepped back. He didn't bother to correct

her. "What do you do here?"

"I'm in the Journeyman program," she said.

"How long have you been here?" he said. She was plain but slightly exotic in her bathrobe on their first encounter.

"Almost two years. I'm supposed to go home next month, but I want to stay," she said. "Well...good to meet you."

She disappeared inside her tiny house and left Reece wondering about the full meaning of journeyman. He remembered the phone call he needed to make and walked to the Ashberrys. He heard Claude yelling inside and wished for a pay phone.

Teresa came to the door with a strained look on her face. She was trying very hard to remain calm, but acted as if she might like to tie Claude to a chair. She held little Kimo in a cloth contraption around her neck.

"Hi, come in. Did Ben tell you to come by for some informal orientation?"

"Uh, no, just to use the phone."

"Oh, that too," she said. "Do you want to call first? If it's not too long, then we can discuss some things about Ethiopian culture, manners, and so on."

Reece did not want to be timed or waited on. "Sure, maybe ten or fifteen minutes if that's okay."

He followed her to her bedroom. The phone sat on a dresser crowded with clothes, a box of diapers with Arabic script, and stacks of letters. The dim space gave them little room to maneuver. She explained how to call the operator and what to say. Most of them spoke good English, she said. The heavy phone receiver felt ancient. He dialed zero and paid careful attention to the double tones, not ringing sounds, but more like buzzes. A woman's voice spoke, but not in English. A bolt of anxiety rushed through him. He always felt that he let people down when he couldn't speak their language. And what had he done about it?

"English?" he said.

"Yes. You would like to call?"

After an eternity—he had almost forgotten Kristin's number—a phone rang somewhere far away. It rang twice, and Kristin answered.

"Hello?" Kristin's voice rose quickly.

"Hello?" Reece felt his throat tighten. He worried Claude would burst into the room. "Kristin? It's me..."

"Reece..." and she stammered.

He felt helpless. "Kristin, I miss you," he said. "It's been so weird, and this is the first chance I've had to dial out."

"Reece...Are you okay?"

"Yes, yes, I'm fine. Tired, miss you so much, but I'm okay." He sat on the bed and tried to relax, to have a conversation. Every thirty seconds, there was a beep on the line.

"I wrote you a letter yesterday," she said. Before Reece could tell her he had written her two letters, she said, "But I tore it up." Now she sounded defiant.

"What?" asked Reece, derailed. This was the sort of thing he did not want to hear. "I would have called sooner, but...It's hard to explain. There's no phone in the guest-house here. I'm in someone's house now, the Ashberrys..."

"Have you met any pretty nurses?" Her voice rose to a squeak.

Reece made a face and shook his head, closing his eyes. "No, no." Reece wished he hadn't called. "We're engaged, right?"

"Yes."

"Okay then, don't worry. I'll call as often as I can, and I've already written two letters. I haven't figured out how to mail anything yet. It's like being in a dream."

"Like a nightmare..."

"Oh, stop...come on, this is all good. I'm here for a good reason, you know that."

"Reece..." and she cried in earnest.

Reece hung his head and butted his hand to his forehead as if shielding himself from a brilliant light. The phone pinched his ear, and he moved the receiver to the other side.

"How's Harvey?" he said to change the subject. Harvey was Kristin's pet squirrel. She had found it when she was a teenager after a cat mauled it. Harvey was blind and missing a back leg and most of his tail. He loved raw peanuts and apples.

"He's okay." Her voice remained a little shaky. "I love you."

"I love you, too." Reece took a deep breath. Those words came so hard to him. "Will you call Dora and Horace?"

"I've talked to them so many times since you left. I think I'm driving Dora crazy, but I'll call her tomorrow. What time is it there?"

Reece searched the room for a clock. "It's...It's nine-twenty-six...a.m. How about there?"

"It's five-thirty. Dad's watching the news and Mom's cooking lasagna." Reece felt turned upside down. He tried to imagine lasagna. He felt like he was on a TV show, that he was on one set and Kristin on another. Claude peeked into the room with his hand over his mouth. He pointed at

Reece and bobbed his head up and down.

"When are you coming home…and don't say it could be two years."

"I don't know. There's so much I don't know."

They talked for a few more minutes and said goodbye. He felt terrible and relieved. The heavy handset rattled into its cradle.

Back in the living room, Teresa rocked in her chair, waiting for him. Kimo, in her lap, stared around the room. "I sent Claude over to the Watsons," she said. "Have you met them yet?"

"Mmm, no. They live across the way there, I think," he said. He pointed.

She nodded. "Thomas is our business manager. His wife is Betsy, and they have two boys." Kimo struggled inside his wrap, swaddled tight.

"Has a beard?" Reece touched an imaginary beard on his face.

"Yes, glasses, and messy hair." She laughed to herself. "Here, sit down." She pointed toward a green armchair.

Reece noticed her eyes, large brown eyes. Her face was serious as it had been the night before, but her eyes dominated now. "So, is this an orientation of sorts, you say? I wasn't clear what you meant. Will there be language classes?" A hundred questions bubbled.

"Usually we have a group, but since it's just you, we can make it informal." She unwrapped Kimo, who had begun to bluster and squint. "You'll have an interpreter, and you'll pick up on the language. Don't worry. But the people there will laugh at you regardless of how well you speak."

And where is "there," he thought. *And why would they*

laugh? Teresa exposed her breast for Kimo. Reece looked away, then looked over her head. She continued to talk, but he did not hear her. Her eyes seemed like whirlpools now. He could see her large breast and the nipple until Kimo latched on. Reece talked and could hear his voice waver. He cleared his throat. He found her attractive, and a flood of emotions poured from a bucket onto his head and ran down his body, straight to his crotch.

"You will eat as a group, usually. There is a cook, too. You'll be able to cook, though. Emma has a stove, but the guys are all single and young, and men just don't cook here. It's the culture. Did you like the enjera last night?"

Reece regained his focus but had lost a large part of the conversation. He chided himself. He couldn't remember what enjera was and said that he had enjoyed it very much.

"You'll have it at every meal. We love it. Claude can eat his weight in enjera and dinich, spicy potatoes."

He wanted to ask where Hattie was. She seemed to have disappeared. "Where will I be stationed?" he said. Everything was so vague.

"Well..." and she sounded unsure. "A place called Godo. It'll be overwhelming at first, but you'll get used to it."

She lifted her shirt, exposing both breasts. Reece took a deep breath and looked away. He knew it shouldn't faze him, but it did. Working in CCU, he had seen plenty of naked people, had given them baths, scrubbed their genitals. But they were usually older or severely injured, dehumanized in a way that negated arousal. His mind wandered, and he wondered if she might be flirting with him. He curled his toes tightly in his shoes, and his left calf cramped as a result.

"Ahh," he said. He made a face and flexed his left foot until the cramp released.

"You okay?" Kimo was on the other side now, completely lost in breastfeeding bliss.

"Just a cramp. Need some water maybe, the elevation, the flying." He fidgeted in his chair.

If there was one area Reece excelled in, it was in matters of hydration. Working the CCU and living with his grandparents—Dora was sixty-one and Horace was seventy-one—had taught him the dull but profound importance of drinking water, keeping the tissues hydrated. Especially with his grandfather, who worked in the garden all day, Reece had a habit of bringing out glasses of ice water. At night, while they watched the Braves play, he would reach over, take his grandmother's wrist, and lightly pinch the skin on the back of her hand. More often than not, the pinch of skin would tent, indicating that she was in serious need of a big glass of water. "See, see," he would say with a grin.

"If you're thirsty, you can get a glass..." A stooped lady in a long dress entered the back door. She had been hanging laundry. "Berta?" Teresa said over her shoulder.

"Abet?" the old lady said. She had a broad smile and white teeth. Her dark, brown forehead glistened with sweat. She smelled of smoke. She looked at Reece and then at Teresa.

"Wuha," and Teresa pointed at Reece.

The lady took a sudden breath inward and hurried to the kitchen.

"That's Berta, who works for us. She cleans and washes clothes. She has eight children and no husband. Really hard worker."

Kimo's mouth came off her livid nipple.

Reece stood when Berta brought him the orange plastic cup of water. She babbled at him, seeming to tell him to sit back down, which he did.

With the doors and front windows open, the heat of the day rose slow but steady. A tongue of sunlight that had been creeping across the floor touched Reece's shoes. He drew his feet underneath the chair. To Reece, the sun in Ethiopia felt hotter and looked brighter than it ever had before. He was hungry.

"I need to change Kimo," said Teresa. She pulled Kimo off her breast, and he grunted and punched his little fists in the air. A wet spot spread on her shirt.

Reece stood, ready to go.

"I think Livvy's coming by to drive you and Hattie down to the market. You can buy some fruit and vegetables. She may go to the supermarket, too." She walked away, clutching Kimo, looking tired. Reece let himself out. He was starving and thought about digging into the food trunk he had brought from Alabama, but decided not to.

The screen door squeaked shut behind him. He felt his world had been reduced to the U-shaped mission compound. It didn't even have an address. There was no mail delivery in Addis, just the boxes at the post office. He wondered who Livvy was and walked back to the guesthouse, which was air-conditioned, unlike the other buildings. Hattie was there, making homemade mayonnaise in a blender.

"I've always wanted to do this. Back home, I always

talked about it and never did it." She pulled the top off the blender. She stuck in a case knife and then licked it. It looked like mayonnaise, maybe yellower than it should be. "Shirley gave me some eggs. Found this vinegar here."

"Making mayonnaise," said Reece. "Looks good."

"I'm gonna make myself a cheese and mayonnaise sandwich." She looked thrilled. "That hot food last night was good, but didn't settle right."

"My dad used to eat mayonnaise sandwiches," he said.

"Did he put bananas on it?" she said, as if she suspected he did.

"He said he liked mayonnaise and banana sandwiches, although I never saw him eat one."

"My husband liked them like that, but I never did."

She offered him bread and cheese, and mayonnaise if he wanted it. He took a thick slice of what appeared to be cheddar, and that was breakfast, along with a glass of water from the fridge. He was starving.

A white van rolled up in front. Through the windows, the woman inside appeared to be shifting things around. Reece hoped it was Livvy. And it was. Her tight curly brown hair looked home-cut. Her sturdy face seemed soft. She wore a pair of light-blue polyester pants, a short-sleeve top, and a pair of white tennis shoes with big red stars on them. She came to the door with two large canvas bags, and Reece hurried to let her in. After wiping her feet, she more or less waltzed in with a friendly, confident smile.

"Hi, I'm Livvy Guthrie, and you must be the new guys." She laughed and planted her hands on her hips.

"You know we're the new guys, and we need all the help we can get!" Hattie grabbed a bag from Livvy's hand.

"Right, Ricky?"

"So it's Hattie, and it's Ricky?" She set the other bag down.

"Reece," said Reece.

"That's right, Reece!"

"That's an unusual name," said Livvy.

"Well, it's not common, I guess."

"I had some things at the house that you guys probably wanted yesterday." She laughed and unloaded bread, crackers, cans of cheese, and some plastic bags of what looked like flour with dried peas, an Irish stew mix. "Y'all up to go to the market?" She replanted her hands on her hips. She was a busy woman, even though her three boys were in boarding school in Kenya.

"I'd love to," said Hattie.

Reece nodded. "Sure. I don't have any money, though."

"Let's stop by the office, and Tesfaw can get you going with fifty birr each. That's plenty to buy a month's worth of groceries. They take dollars at Victory, a supermarket we'll stop by after the fresh market, but checking out takes forever. You'll need some coins for the beggars."

They walked to the white building with the brown porch. The front room was deserted, but beyond that, the building opened into a large space with three desks. A chemical smell of ink filled the air. The mechanical rumble Reece had heard the day before was a sheet-fed offset printer printing the New Testament in Amharic. He peered through the open door. A man in blue overalls watched over the clanking machine as it spat out large sheets of paper printed eight pages to a side. Inside the room was a cutting and binding area as well. The press created a hum in the floor, the air, the walls. One keystone of missionary lore, Reece knew, was the printing and distribution of Bibles in exotic languages. The reality of this hulking black press spooling out page after page of the New Testament made it all seem very plain.

The man at the largest desk, a very short man with a pronounced limp, extended his hand to Reece and then to Hattie. "Welcome, welcome to Ethiopia," he said, smiling, stretching his mouth wide. He wore an ill-fitting but matched suit of aqua polyester with a loose necktie. His eyes sparkled. He pronounced Ethiopia as Eh-ti-o-pia.

"Reece, Hattie," said Livvy, "this is Tesfaw. He's the mission liaison. He's been with us for over ten years."

The gurgling sound of Tesfaw's speech mesmerized Reece. The breathy pauses seemed otherworldly. Little sounds of airy surprise, filling in for volume or a facial expression meant to convey joy, astonishment, or sorrow. The two ladies at the other desks beamed at them, showing brilliant, white teeth. Tesfaw carefully counted out fifty birr to each of them, including coins. The official exchange rate for years had been two Ethiopian birr for one US dollar. Tesfaw stamped a few forms with purple ink and placed the stack of bills back into a large safe behind his desk.

"I almost forgot. Tesfaw, we need to let you see their passports and visas." She said a few words slowly in Amharic, emphasizing each one.

"Ow," he said long and breathily, meaning yes.

"But let's do that when we get back. Then, maybe tomorrow, Tesfaw can go with you to get your work permits. It'll be an all-day affair, so be prepared. But without Tesfaw, it'd take six months."

Tesfaw nodded, affirming what Livvy was saying. The printer stopped, sending the room into intense silence. Reece noted a slight ringing in his ears. As they moved from the room, the floorboards groaned. A dozen flies clung to the outside of the screen door, waiting to zip in. The tenacious flies went straight for moisture.

Once inside the van, Reece felt removed from this strange experience. The lines of people streaming up and down the rutted dirt road, everyone carrying something—wood, bags of charcoal, bananas, mounds of shirts, bags of grain, sheets of corrugated tin. He saw several more men on crutches, all missing a leg.

"Those are Cuban soldiers who have been wounded fighting in Eritrea," Livvy said. She pointed to the right at an open gate made of corrugated tin. A small sign in English read, PHOTOGRAPHING STRICTLY PROHIBITED. Reece strained to see inside the compound, but could only distinguish a field and a building or two.

"Cuba?" The combination of Cuba and Ethiopia baffled Reece.

"They're a communist country, too," said Livvy.

That idea of Ethiopia being communist puzzled Reece. He had a minimal understanding of what communism meant, other than the stopgap rhetoric he had casually learned from the media. He understood communism as a lack of freedom. People in communist countries worked and gave everything to the government. He knew there was more to it than that. He gazed out the window at the people moving endlessly and couldn't imagine that they would move any differently if suddenly communism were swept away by democracy.

The van's suspension groaned with every lurch, every rock and pothole. Even with the windows up, the stench of the winery runoff pierced the van like a gunshot to the head.

The van gradually found graying pavement. At a large traffic circle, buses, taxis, and cargo trucks swirled—Steyr, Mercedes, Ford, many with signs or stickers denoting one of the dozens of relief agencies that had flooded the country. Small groups of ragged children ran from car to car begging. Tiny, ramshackle vendors interjected themselves among larger, ramshackle buildings.

"That's the post office!" Livvy said over the air conditioning as they passed a tall, brick building. Soldiers with machine guns lounged on the steps. Large military trucks dieseled through the city, the open backs filled with men clutching rifles. The puffy white clouds in the hard, blue sky seemed afraid to move.

"Get ready to be assaulted!" said Livvy as she pulled the van into a slot along a dirty, crowded curb. An entourage waited for the van doors to open. The musty smell of clothes heavy with sweat and a smell of rubber burning inundated Reece. "I wouldn't buy anything yet," said Livvy. "Let's go through the market first."

A man with a crude, curved sword inside a roughly sewn, red leather sheath pushed the object at Reece. Reece smiled and said, "Yellum," meaning no. He wished for a more polite rebuttal. The man persisted, followed closely by a woman with colorful, tightly woven straw baskets.

Livvy plowed ahead, and Reece fell in behind Hattie, who was laughing in amazement. A small girl in a long, army-green dress of heavy cotton grabbed her hand, looking up at her with big, brown eyes. She wore a thin, black string around her neck, marking herself as Muslim. They walked past a store with mounds of seeds in baskets and tin cans, some spread on sackcloth. Out front, a woman older than time itself, with no teeth, sat beside a grain sack covered with long, pointed red peppers, the fiery berbere, which would make Reece sweat at every meal and keep his stomach in constant turmoil.

Rounding a corner through a passage into a crowded courtyard shaded in spots with drapes of thin cotton cloth, merchants minded their fruits and vegetables, chatting in low tones. Before Reece could take it in, his gaze latched onto a tall man who teetered back and forth from a skinny brown leg with a sandal made of recycled tires to what did not look like a leg. The left leg nearly reached the girth of his waist. The skin seemed to be on the verge of bursting. Large lumps that looked like water balloons trapped beneath the skin gave his leg the look of a duffel bag stuffed with bowling balls. A small pool of shiny serous fluid leaked from an open sore on the bottom of his un-leg. The man, watching Reece, lifted his foot as much as he could to make sure that Reece could see the weeping wound. Reece took it in, processed the image, and filed it as how things were.

"How do I ask the price?" Reece asked Livvy who had already bargained for a large bag of oranges.

"Just say, 'Sentino?'"

Reece looked around at the vendors. The green beans surprised him. Almost everything surprised him—the limes, the lemons, the heavy weapon-like segments of raw, purple sugarcane, the tiny thumb-sized bananas. He hadn't developed a clear sense of what to expect, but his list of what he had not expected grew longer with each passing minute.

He approached an older woman selling the small bananas. He did not really like bananas, but he felt obligated to buy them, like popcorn at the theater.

"Sentino?" he said, pointing to the bananas lying on a sheet of cloudy plastic.

Pulled back in a kind of ponytail, the woman's hair had begun to gray. A faint tattoo ran across her neck. She looked up at Reece, shielding her eyes from the bright sun. She looked at him as if he were a photograph.

"And kilo, sost birr," she said.

Puzzled, he pulled out a five-birr bill. The woman said something to her neighbor, who was selling lemons. The woman passed an ancient scale with a tin scoop on top. With a surprising weight of bananas in the roomy straw bag Livvy had given him, Reece studied his next purchase.

He bought oranges and potatoes and onions. Each time, a kilo. He only needed a half-kilo at most, but did not know how to say so. Weighted down with his produce, he felt like a rich man accumulating more than he could ever use. Livvy was ready to go and stood near the alleyway entrance. The man with the circus-sized leg remained just as he had been, swaying from one foot to the other. His eyes begged, but the rest of his face remained expressionless, the dirty, orange plastic cup held just at waist level. Little brown birds flitted back and forth, catching a crumb or stray seed here and there.

Reece approached the man with the giant leg. Having

to carry the straw bag, fearing the handle would break, Reece shifted the load onto his hip and placed the folded money into the cup, which the man held with two hands as if it could warm his body. The man did not look at Reece, but peered toward the sky and murmured, "Xavier meskin."

Emma groaned. The woman, the mother, did not bother to look back at her son, three years old and so thin and drawn that he seemed an infant. A teardrop head with no hair. Not even the quntcho, that handful of hair on top for the angels to grab at cliff's edge. The thinnest of eyebrows knotted from the pain, the awful pain of exposed dry bone, the entire lower left jaw filled with rotting teeth, the flesh cleanly demarcated as if cut with a razor, no bleeding, the scapular chin ivory and picked clean of flesh, melding into the intact right side of the child's eaten face.

"Jesus Christ." Emma touched the woman's cheek and then her shoulder. She could think of nothing else to do.

The child cowered, exposed, moaning for relief, a living, dead thing.

"How..." Emma sought Isaac's eyes for understanding, but he looked shocked, unable to discern what this could be.

Isaac asked the mother how this had come to pass. She explained in a hushed, pleading voice that she did not know. That it began fifteen days ago, just fifteen days ago, and now look. *Can you help me? Can you help my son? He is not eating. He is not drinking. Each day, the bone becomes more, the flesh less.*

Emma's mind raced. She wanted to know if the woman could go to Black Lion Hospital in Addis Ababa. The Mission would pay. No problem. The child will die otherwise, she said to the mother.

No, said the mother. My husband is ill with malaria.

There is no one to cook, no one to care for the children. *Aiyee,* my son will die if you cannot help me. Her voice rose to that of a woman begging for mercy, mercy for her, her son, her family.

Emma knew the child would die, and soon. She did not know what could cause the rotting of flesh from the child's face. Was there a snake bite? Perhaps a spider bite? Did the infection start in the teeth? Where did the bone first show?

Yellum, yellum. No, no. The flesh is falling away, and the bone is like death, dry, and full of death.

"Isaac?" asked Emma.

"Yes?"

"Do you have any money with you?"

"I have some birr."

"Go and buy some bananas and eggs, please. Bring them here. I'll give you money later."

"Yes, Emma, yes," and Isaac hurried out the door that framed a gorgeous lavender sky, a shaft of fanned light bursting from a cloud to the west.

And then there was a banging at the gate.

In the downpour, Terry had dropped the grain where he could. The guards let the first man-hauler into the clinic-warehouse compound. He struggled with a hundred-pound sack of grain on his back, having carried the bag for half a mile. Word had traveled quickly, and within minutes, volunteers had dispatched to lumber the grain to its intended destination inside the clinic and warehouse compound.

Emma rose from her seat beside the woman, the dying child covered once more, its weak moans unable to pierce the cloth folds. The sight of the muddy man in shorts and a shirt made from grain bags, balancing the bulging bag on his shoulder, lifted her spirits. "Bataam taruno," she called out. Very good. "Bataam taruno."

The guards directed the man into the warehouse that was beginning to fill again with grain for the next ration cycle on Saturday. Others were arriving with grain at the gate, calling to be let in.

Emma wanted to take the woman and child to the shelter, but the mother was anxious to get back to her family. The child needed IV fluids. The child needed a feeding tube. It was starved in so many ways. But there seemed little hope that the child would live unless evacuated to Addis Ababa and then perhaps out of the country. The woman stood, stooped over with her son strapped to her back.

"No, no, bucka. Stay. Sit. Food." Emma at least wanted to give the woman some foodstuffs that the child might be able to eat in his last days, eggs and smashed bananas. If he couldn't eat it, others would. She took a packet of famine biscuits from a tin and handed it to the woman, who secreted it into the fold of cloth around her waist. The biscuits were similar to Graham crackers, but thicker, drier, and less sweet. And for the husband with malaria, Emma gave her a packet of chloroquine and another of paracetamol for fever. Outside, into the rain barrel, water dripped like a beating heart, slowing, slower.

Victory, as everyone called it, was not far away. It was the only supermarket in the city. Only foreigners and diplomats bothered to shop there, perhaps to maintain some artificial tie to another reality. Reece pushed what he thought must be a military-grade shopping cart from Russia. The few shelves sat far apart. There were no fresh vegetables.

He approached a long line of freezers with iced-over glass doors. He opened one door and looked inside to see a dozen or so frozen chickens. He couldn't tell, but the chickens looked gray beneath a heavy layer of frost. Against his better judgment, he placed one in the buggy. One aisle contained nothing on one side, and boxes of cereal with Arabic script filled the other side. He moved on and selected four cans of tomato paste, a bottle of Merti Hot Ethiopian ketchup, and a box of chamomile tea.

When ready to check out, Reece felt silly pushing his nearly empty buggy toward the register. But there was nothing at Victory supermarket that he needed.

A tall lady wearing a green smock told him in clipped English to go to the back of the store. She gestured as if she had pointed this out to him many times before. He took a breath, looking around for Livvy. She had been chatting with the store manager.

"Okay," Livvy started, almost as if she worked there. "Items from a store department have to be checked by someone from that department. Did you get any meat?"

"A chicken."

Livvy made a face. "Okay, so for the chicken, the line is in the back over there." She pointed. They'll check it off on a form, give you a copy, and then you bring that back up here to the lady at the checkout aisle."

"Oh."

"And you have to do that for items from each department. Then you'll get totaled up, and then you go pay over at that window with the painting beside it." It was a likeness of the dictator, Haile Mariam Mengistu.

"Oh." Reece felt that he had wandered into a puzzle with no edge pieces to guide him. He worried about his oranges and bananas spoiling in the heat of the parked van.

"And you have to pay in dollars. They don't take birr here."

"Really? Why?"

"Because only foreigners shop here, and the government knows it can get dollars here." Livvy seemed to know what she was talking about.

"Why do you come here?" Reece was a little irked at the experience.

"You just never know what they might have," she said in an understanding, motherly tone. "Sometimes they have Corn Flakes. A few months ago, I found some boxes of pudding that Norbert likes. And like that chamomile tea in your basket, I've never seen that here before."

Reece had never had chamomile tea, had always vaguely wanted to try it, but primarily had tossed the soft blue box in the buggy to make it seem like he needed to be there buying things. Hattie was looking at everything twice. She had asked a young man in a white apron if the little cans she pointed to were like Vienna sausage.

"Sausage, yellum," the boy had said. "Just read," and he pointed to the label. His short afro was flat on top and immaculate on the sides. A sharp but strong jaw punctuated his squarish face. He had the look that Reece would peg as classic Amhara, the traditional ruling class of the Ethiopian Highlands—the golden-brown skin, the angled face, the brilliant smile, tall, skinny.

Reece waited behind a dark, dark man in a lovely blue suit. When it came Reece's turn, a man in a white apron just looked at him.

"Your list, do you have your list?" he said in that burbling way, but more severe.

"List?"

"Yes, like this one." He showed Reece a piece of paper with little rectangles. Inside the rectangles were the names of things, and beside each one a check box. Reece's look must have moved him to some sort of pity. He fumbled in a tray and pulled out a blank list and made a check mark beside "Cicken." The list was in duplicate, with a sheet of carbon in the middle. He handed Reece the top sheet. Reece repeated the process for dry goods, then squeaked the buggy back to the register window where he finally paid.

He and Livvy sat in sturdy metal chairs while Hattie finished up her walk through the Victory maze. The manager learned through Livvy that Reece had never had chamomile tea. From somewhere, a few minutes later, he reappeared with two plastic cups, a little square of paper attached to the tea-bag string hanging over the side. The cups were bright orange, the color of traffic pylons. The tall manager, dark and round-faced, was eager for Reece to try the tea. Reece sipped the tea. He was accustomed to the massive sugar content of cold sweet tea, and this tasted flat and floral.

"Mmm, pretty good," he said.

That afternoon, back at the guesthouse, Reece ate three oranges and two of the tiny bananas. The fruit tasted exactly as it should. He made half a mayonnaise-and-cheese sandwich with some thick, homemade white bread that Livvy had made. Against his better judgment, he fished out a container of sugar-free lemonade mix from his food trunk and made a pitcher. Finally, not hungry and anticipating dinner that night with the Watsons, whom he had yet to meet, he retired to his bunk and wrote two letters to Kristin, dating the first as the day before.

He recounted the day's events in great detail and ended by saying how much he missed her, that he loved her, that he was taking photos and would mail film soon. He told her that his visa was only good for thirty days and that a mistake had been made, that Hattie already had her work permit and would head upcountry the next day. He could go once the visa was straightened out and other paperwork taken care of. He felt isolated and told Kristin that he was lonely. He folded the thin, blue, prepaid aerograms into tidy square mailers.

An hour of sitting on a couch passed before dinner was ready at the Watsons. The little ranch house, with a large plate-glass window in the front room, was dim and sparsely furnished. No pictures or art on the walls. No rugs or carpet on the wooden floors. Each footfall echoed in the bareness. A fuzziness, a discontent sat heavy in the rooms, and Reece felt the weight of it. Even Hattie seemed subdued and puzzled. The two young boys, Jeremiah and Nahum, stayed in their room, hardly making any noise. The mother, Betsy, bumped through the house. She did not seem to be cooking. Reece couldn't tell what she was doing. She did not speak and sighed often as she wandered. Reece studied her black, sort of curly hair, her freckled face with a nose that could have been bigger. The moment she left his field of vision, he couldn't remember what she looked like.

Thomas Watson, the man of the house, the business manager, the real missionary of the lot, seemed like none of those. Tall and thin, energetic in a haphazard fashion, he paced inside the house. He spoke on the phone to someone in very loud and slow Amharic. His eyes looked tired behind his thick glasses. His puffy, wiry hair, prematurely balding, gave him a slight Bozo look. He ended the call in an angry tone.

Sitting with a plastic plate, Reece picked at his rice and a piece of fried chicken. There were slices of orange.

"We have plenty of food to give out," Thomas said, wrapping his large hand across his forehead. He devoured his food. Betsy was in the kitchen making coffee, which Thomas seemed eager to have. "But we get all these people out there in the middle of nowhere, and they want plumbing, you know, hot showers, and they complain about the outhouse toilets. But that's the way it is, right?" He didn't wait for Reece or Hattie to answer, stood, and went outside to rummage through the vast piles of junk, looking for spigots.

Showers? Reece didn't realize that by "shower," Thomas meant a barrel with a spigot at the bottom. Wheat and milk powder were plentiful, but spigots were hard to come by.

Betsy let everyone come into the kitchen and pour their own coffee. She struck Reece as ghostlike, not really there. Thomas took his coffee and announced he would be putting the boys to bed, reading them a story. He made it clear that this was a significant ritual, in a cautionary voice, as if his world were steep banks of loose dirt always in danger of collapsing. Reece took an orange mug and spooned in two scoops of sugar. It was his first cup of coffee ever. He had yet to realize that Ethiopia was the mother of all coffee, that in peasant villages, some of the finest coffee in the world was served in tiny Chinese porcelain cups available at the remotest markets.

Thomas did not reappear, and Betsy washed dishes as Hattie and Reece talked in hushed tones. After half an hour of killing time, they excused themselves and wandered back to the guesthouse. Reece was still hungry and decided to make banana bread before settling in for the long evening.

Dr. Guthrie, knocking on the door, woke Reece. Hattie was already up and packing for her flight upcountry to Gundo Meskel. He had heard her showering and gone back to sleep. Each day seemed unplanned, and he fell into the expectation that he would get out of bed, and then nothing would happen. He put on a pair of cutoff scrub pants and a t-shirt. He felt silly being woken, like he should have already been up.

"Wake you?" Dr. Guthrie was freshly showered, ready for action. His shirt was too small.

"No, well, maybe," said Reece. He wanted to brush his teeth.

Dr. Guthrie spied the loaf of banana bread and helped himself. Reece had forgotten to add baking soda to the mix, and the result was a compact, chewy affair.

"Reece made that," said Hattie. "He's a good cook."

Dr. Guthrie grunted. "Hattie, we got to leave here in about thirty minutes for the airport. Keep your papers handy."

"I never did find my Bible," said Hattie. It had been missing since yesterday. Reece worried she thought he had taken it. She mentioned the cleaning lady, Gabra, to Reece. Gabra had washed dishes and changed linens while they were away.

"Well, it's doing good work wherever it is," said Dr. Guthrie. "Tesfaw is going to take you, Reece, down to the immigration office and get your visa straightened out. Make sure you take your passport and an extra photo just in case." Reece had six black-and-white passport-size photos in an envelope. "Once we get all that straightened out, we can see about getting you upcountry."

"I'm still waiting on a trunk that was lost," said Reece.

"Well, they should call us, but don't hold your breath. We've got some other stuff out there we need to check on, too. They're bad about holding videos." Reece remembered the videos in his missing trunk, wrapped in foil.

Reece walked down to the office as Dr. Guthrie suggested. The presses were quiet, but the smell of black ink clung to the interior. He found Tesfaw walking on crutches. One of his legs was withered. He had a serious case of scoliosis, too. There was a heat that surrounded Tesfaw, a shimmering aura. He always wore a full aqua suit inside the stuffy building, sweating. There was a fan, but it was turned off or did not work.

"Your visa, yes, yes." Tesfaw smiled and made a sound, as if the visa itself had been naughty. "We will go together..." a throaty inhalation "...and make it good."

"Should we go now...or later?" Reece had been told that appointments were lighthearted matters in Ethiopia, and he felt strangely liberated being in the hands of an Ethiopian.

Tesfaw spoke to the woman at the desk to his right. She had been very quiet, writing figures in a ledger next to a tall pile of receipts. Then he turned back to Reece. "I think after you have your lunch is good. In three hours, I will pick you," he said.

It was a little after nine o'clock. Reece felt like he was on a small raft, occasionally scraping a sandy bottom, catching and then slowly spinning free.

"Okay," said Reece. "So..." and he wondered if he seemed uptight "...at twelve o'clock." He never used "o'clock." He felt invested in being easy to work with. He adopted Tesfaw's pattern of respiration, much slower than his own, and now he began to feel just the tiniest hint of faintness and took a sudden deep breath, which tickled his throat and made him cough.

"Yes, yes, I will come to you, and you will have your papers, okay?"

"Okay." Reece let the old, wooden screen door slam on his way out. The brightness caught him off guard, and he shielded his eyes. The jagged, white clouds in the bright blue sky seemed one-dimensional, as if they had been pasted there with glue.

Another long day. Isaac swept as much of the drying mud from the clinic as he could with the homemade broom. Emma carried the catch-all bin outside to rinse the day's collection of pus, skin, iodine, and peroxide runoff. One woman had vomited, but Afewerki had managed to get her outside first.

"We need to pray for that baby." Emma felt helpless, hopeless, lonely, inadequate, selfish. Prayer seemed like the best bet.

"The child will die," said Isaac.

"I think so," said Emma.

"The mother is saying there is a ghost in the bones."

"A ghost?"

"She has seen the ghost, like the devil, eating the flesh. He will die."

That idea seemed even more horrible than a poisonous spider bite or fast-moving cancer. "She will come back, right? I want to know what happens. Maybe I don't."

"God will know these things."

"Let's lock up and head home, okay?" Emma put back onto the shelves a crystal-clear bottle of IV fluid, one of the bottles from Iceland. "These bottles are so pretty."

"Yes, very useful."

"I wish that I'd met them, the nurses and doctor from Iceland. They sounded like characters."

"Very hard workers," said Isaac. "Svana is to make me laugh many times." Isaac looked like a mechanic in his brown overalls, much too hot for the weather, but everyone bundled themselves as if expecting an ice storm. It cooled down rapidly at night, though. Seven thousand feet of altitude was nothing to sneeze at.

"Why did they leave?"

"Dr. Guthrie is frighting them. The Icelanders is practicing strange religions, so they must go." Isaac swung the squeaky tin door shut and padlocked it. "They are asking the priests to see the sacred places. They are looking for things that do not belong to them, only to God."

"Weird and weirder." Emma had rolled up the bottoms of her jeans and was stepping with care from stone to stone.

The younger guard with the large afro, who wore a grain sack on his head as protection against the sun, let them through the gate.

"Ciao," said Emma.

"Ciao," said the guard.

The deepening purple sky and setting sun washed the wide, steep path up to living quarters with a cold, blue light. Down the path came Mariam, the soft-spoken team member with the shaved head. He was very shy, especially in Emma's presence.

"Abet?" asked Isaac.

"Isaac, ask about Afewerki," said Emma.

Mariam removed his prized tartan tam-o'-shanter and took Isaac's hand for the walk back uphill. His slacks fit him well and matched his sheer, pink, short-sleeve shirt with a huge pocket, big enough for a small loaf of bread.

Afewerki was indeed in jail. It was not so inconvenient, though, for him. His parents' compound shared a wall with the prison compound. His mother had already passed him dinner over the fence. The primary worry was bedbugs and the mites that caused scabies. There was a murderer inside as well, but he was only guilty of killing for revenge, a common and understood occurrence in the Highlands.

"Ferenj! Ferenj!" Three little boys and a girl shouted from within their fenced compound, bright smiles as big as heaven, covered with flies.

Emma waved.

This was the third time that the Hyena had arrested Afewerki. The arrests always seemed to come on ration days when the Hyena would get drunk, angry, and jealous of the power exerted by so much food and medicine. His better revenge was sending his thugs in to steal from the warehouse at night. A gallon of soybean oil he could sell in Addis Ababa for twenty birr, the equivalent of a peasant farmer's wages for a month.

"Does he want to meet with me, the administrator, the Hyena?" She felt silly calling the man by his nickname, but didn't know his real name.

Mariam made that odd, inspiring sound to indicate yes. "After the sun is up by six hours," said Mariam. He spoke slowly and with care.

"That's lunchtime," said Emma. "Maybe he'll make some finger sandwiches and punch."

Isaac let go of Mariam's hand and looked puzzled. "Fingers sandwich? He is not to punch you. We will die him. God is strong. Hyena is devil."

Emma laughed. "No, well, never mind. He won't lay a finger on me. He's too much of a coward, at least when he's not drinking."

"Ow, he is frighting you," said Mariam.

They topped the steep climb and veered around left and then right to reach the gate of the mission's living quarters, a good half-acre of grassy dirt walled in with corrugated tin nailed to poles. The team members, Isaac, Mariam, and Barra, lived in four adjoining rooms made from traditional stick-and-mud construction, but with the modern touch of the tin roof and inside walls lined with heavy sheets of plastic. Afewerki lived with his parents. There was a cookhouse made of poles with a tin roof as well, uncomfortably close to a plastic-sheathed outhouse or shintabet. Emma's house had been built for her, a tiny, square, whitewashed, stick-and-mud house with a tin roof, mini propane stove and fridge, a gravity-feed water purifier, and a sagging cot beside a wooden table that had seen better days. It was paradise compared to the tent pitched on rocks that she'd first lived in at Gundo Meskel. It looked like the new guy, Rice, would take the empty room between Isaac and Mariam in their "motel."

Arrived, the gate opened to the animated face of Irigit, the guard. He was always laughing, especially at Emma. His round, floppy hat and tight shirts made Emma think of an uncanny lifeguard. Wafts of spiced smoke leaked through the undaubed walls of the cookhouse. Emma's mouth watered, anticipating the fiery meal.

Tesfaw arrived on time. He wore a bulky watch that reminded Reece of the Chunky Bars he ate as a kid.

Tesfaw drove the Toyota van very carefully and slowed to take on a passenger, a young woman with a bright white cloth wrapped around her head on which was balanced a plastic case of empty Coke bottles. The bottling plant was not far away, Reece had been told. When the van stopped on the dirt road, it looked as if several people might pour inside, but Tesfaw jarred them all with a brief but stern flurry of rebukes. The young woman sat in the first row of seats behind them, placing her bottles in her lap.

Tesfaw exchanged pleasantries and information with the woman, then nodded several times as if all was right with the world, and glanced at Reece, smiling. He pointed out a large Orthodox church. After gaining pavement, the van pulled in front of a market, and the woman got out, taking the bottles with her. She covered her face and was gone.

Tesfaw approached Mexico Square, a traffic circle with five streams of vehicles rushing into the endless whirlpool of diesel fumes. Mexico had supported the Ethiopians during the Italian occupation from 1936 to 1941, resulting in this parklike oval tribute, the eye of a small traffic hurricane. Tesfaw pointed out the Wabi Shebele Hotel on the right. They served delicious club sandwiches. Did Reece know about club sandwiches? And past the National Bank and Black Lion Hospital, and then into narrow, crowded streets.

"You like this place?" asked Tesfaw as he parked the van. Two young boys made quite a scene of directing the van into its spot. He ignored them and then smiled at Reece to follow.

"Ferenj, birr," said the taller of the two boys. He wore a brown sweater torn at the shoulder seam. He glanced, nervous, at Tesfaw, who raised a crutch at him and barked. They backed away but did not seem unhappy about it. Reece wanted to give them some money, but he took Tesfaw's lead and followed him inside a squat building past an armed guard into a concrete-block room painted a deep, thick blue.

Tesfaw spoke to the woman behind a small window space in a quiet voice and turned often to nod at Reece. "You wait, okay," he said to Reece and hobbled around a blind corner, leaving him alone in the room, sitting in the only chair. Reece let be what must be and prepared himself for a long wait. His mind wandered down paths of improbability—his immediate deportation, a car crashing through the wall from the street.

There was no clock, and he wore no watch, which had required some explaining. It amazed Tesfaw that he did not wear a watch. Everyone in the city wore a watch, if they could get one, whether it worked or not. No ferenj they had known was ever without a watch.

The woman behind the window, of middle age, with dark brown skin, and an American style to her straightened hair, busied herself with unseen tasks below the window ledge. The guard in front of the cracked glass door stood very still, cradling his AK-47, pointing the barrel to the ground. The curved magazine seemed like a half-smile. On one occasion, he shooed away a small pack of girls and boys as they pressed their faces to the blank window, grinning and waving at Reece. "Ferenj!"

After forty-five minutes, Tesfaw emerged, looking tired. Acquiring the proper visa and work permit was an exercise in patience. Acquiring it within a day or two was an act of calling in favors and open bribery. "It is good, good," he said to Reece. "Come with me."

In the heat of the day, the quiet of the air-conditioned van seemed unreal but welcome. Reece held the idea that he should be "of the people," but instances of separation from the crowds came as respites, little breathing spaces, at least until he acclimated. Tesfaw adjusted the radio to a station playing traditional Amharic music. The yodel-like quality of the vocals, smooth and melodic, frenetic at times, sounded Middle Eastern to Reece. Tesfaw drove as if on a fixed course. Every motion was deliberate, with much head turning and checking of mirrors. He parked half in an alley and half on the busy road. The tall, blank building with a few Amharic letters on the brick façade bordered a wide walkway made of square, yellow bricks.

Tesfaw asked Reece to stay in the van without explanation. He disappeared on his crutches into a double doorway. Reece moved to the back of the van, where the windows were tinted, and he could open the side windows on push-out latches. He was hungry. This is the way things are, he kept telling himself, still distracted but overwhelmed by the strangeness of it all.

Back at the mission compound, Reece organized his suitcase. He watched through the back window as Gabra stood bent at the waist, as if on a hinge, scrubbing his clothes in a metal tub. He felt embarrassed. She would hang them on a long clothesline and then iron them. He didn't know how to tell her not to iron them. He supposed it was her livelihood.

From a stack of tattered paperbacks, Reece pulled a copy of *2001: A Space Odyssey*. He imagined others spending long weeks of complete silence in the guesthouse living room, sitting alone with their backs to the window, reading each of the twenty or so books in succession. At the end of each book, they would perhaps stand and walk to the window to see if anything had changed, pick up another book, and begin to read again in silence. The interior of the guesthouse seemed very much like the inside of the spaceship *Discovery* after Bowman's companions were killed by the ship's personable computer, Hal. That sense of moving at an incredible speed, but without any reference, no trees or billboards whizzing past. Working the night shift in the CCU had been like that. The central nursing station surrounded by a rectangle of twelve intensive-care beds. The bright fluorescent light. No windows. The only sounds being IV pump alarms, the grind of ventilators, and the occasional shaking of a bed rail.

He had promised Kristin that he would call again that day. If there were a private phone, that would be one thing, but he had to ask permission. He yearned to hear her voice, but couldn't face the chore of walking to the Ashberrys or the Watsons. He settled in with *The Martian Chronicles,* which he hadn't read, and promised himself that he would write a long letter to Kristin that evening and to his grandparents as well.

Just about a chapter into the *Martian Chronicles,* Sam Woods came through the front door, wiping his feet. He was in his seventies, had lived all over Africa, and looked tired but fit. His frequent smile seemed to say, "Let's agree to disagree. We can still be friends."

"Your luggage is in. You want to go with me to the airport and get that and a couple of other things?"

"Sure. I'm a little surprised it showed up so fast." He put his book away, washed his face at the sink, and walked out to an older Toyota Land Cruiser.

"You want to drive? Might as well." Sam walked to the passenger side, and Reece slid behind the wheel. He'd paid ten dollars to get an international driver's license from the AAA. He supposed it was valid but didn't see how it possibly could be. In the cab, Reece noticed the four-wheel drive shifter, a separate entity from the regular shifter. He quickly studied the stick's four white diagrams. Would he need to fool with it? The invisible weight on his soul increased.

Sam just smiled at him, letting Reece take the helm. Reece cranked it and glanced at the faded diagram on the ball of the main shifter. The Land Cruiser jerked forward in strong but smooth leaps until he got the hang of it. He pulled around the circle, pausing to let Sam roll down his window and speak with Thomas, who ran in front of them, *loping along,* thought Reece, waving his arms as if stopping an airplane in mid-flight. Thomas spoke in such low, hushed tones that Reece couldn't catch a single word. Sam had to lean out of the window, straining to hear Thomas.

"He's upset," said Sam, offering no further explanation.

"Which way?" asked Reece.

Once through the bewildering maze of lanes in Revolution Square, traffic turned to chaos, cars and trucks bunched along the roadsides. Soldiers lined the streets with machine-guns. "Must be somebody important coming from the airport," said Sam. "Could be Mengistu himself. Just pull over as close as you can and wait."

A soldier with one white glove accosted a large truck, its cargo covered with flapping sheets of plastic. He screamed at the driver, who shrugged his shoulders and threw up his hands.

Within fifteen minutes, a convoy of ten or so outdated but shiny American cars, one a Buick with tailfins, squeezed through the channel constructed for their passage. A comical-looking armored vehicle with a short gun barrel jutting from its turret struggled to keep up with the parade.

"Did that thing scrape that bus?" asked Reece.

"I think it did, but just be ready and don't let anybody go around you," said Sam, annoyed by the whole affair.

It took them a full forty-five minutes to cover the next mile or so to the airport, the entire city seeming to be a cart that had been upset. But instead of righting the cart and picking up the apples, people seemed bent on finding new paths of least resistance, incorporating the traffic jam as if it were a new leg that had grown and needed exercise.

After washing her hands, brushing out her shoulder-length hair, and changing into jeans and a long-sleeve t-shirt, Emma walked into the gloaming dusk, still bright with light, but promising a cool, dark night. Sounds of laughter came from what she called the dining hut, a round thatched tukul, the most traditional of structures in Godo.

"Coming in," said Emma.

Inside, Barra leaped to pull back the plastic flap covering the entrance. "Welcome, my friend." He took her hand as if greeting his most respected elder. "Yes, eat with us. You are very tired. It is a long day."

Emma nodded.

"Sit, please." Isaac stood so that Emma could scoot around to the empty webbed folding chair, the kind of chair her mother would shell beans in beneath the carport back home.

On the low, round table covered with a hand-sewn infant's blanket, a Mennonite creation, sat bottles of water and of birzz, the sweet unfermented honey drink, cloudy and rusty. Clean orange cups draped the mouths of each bottle.

Barra slipped through the flap and called out to the cookhouse for the food. Misrak, the bustier of the two who often cooked topless, breasts swaying above the steaming pots, had gone home to her family, leaving Zenebek, a divorced woman with high cheekbones, a Coptic tattoo on her forehead, and a Hollywood smile, to serve dinner.

"Is coming," Barra announced to everyone. "Yes, is coming." He rubbed his hands together.

The flap opened, and Zenebek, tired of waiting and without her smile, placed the metal pan of enjera on the table, a base layer of two of the round, gray, flat breads to soak up the wot with four portions folded in quarters, one for each of them. She waved her finger in the air, indicating she would be back with the rest. Her dark-blue sweater flashed back through the flap, anticipating the color of the evening sky.

Emma felt drained. She was hungry but knew that whatever spicy wot was about to appear would test her stomach to its limits. She felt she needed a break from the spicy food, that she should eat plain bread for a few days. The food was delicious, but so hot with the powdered red berbere spice used in almost every dish.

She looked around at her compatriots, "the team," as Dr. Guthrie called them. They had wanted her to lead them in Bible study, except for Barra, who did not think it wise for women to be teaching men such things. Emma wondered if this guy Rice, or whatever his real name was, would take over, maybe implement a Bible study for the team. She was a bang-up nurse, especially under pressure, but it was hard being a woman in a land where women bore the brunt of daily life, giving birth, carrying heavy clay pots of water, gathering firewood down canyon where men often lay in wait, cooking, feeding, sewing, selling what could be sold in the markets on Tuesdays and Saturdays, cleaning up livestock dung from the yard and using it to smooth out the breaks and scuffs in the tukul floors. Keeping the fire going, what a chore. It was shameful to let the last ember die, to have to beg an ember from a neighbor and toss it back and forth in blackened hands as a kind of punishment. Women held everything together yet had the status of animals, albeit prized animals.

Zenebek reappeared with an enameled metal bowl smoking with a blood-colored kiyawot in which floated the bits and pieces of a chicken and ten boiled eggs cooked to the consistency of golf balls. Pockets of oil pooled on the surface. Emma's mouth watered, and the top of her head began to itch in anticipation of the hottest of hot dishes.

"Any more news from Afewerki?" asked Emma.

"He will grow fat in the jail," said Barra, laughing. His teeth flashed in the dimming light that would soon be replaced by the hissing kerosene lantern.

Isaac stood and held the bright yellow basin for Emma. She held out her right hand, water pouring from an IV bottle over it. The water felt nice, soothing, but there was nothing on which to dry her hand. He poured for Barra as well, and Barra returned the favor, then poured for Mariam. Now they were ready to eat.

"Isaac, do you think that baby with the missing face will live? Should I have given the baby painkillers?"

"Oh," said Barra, "we must pray now for this food." His voice carried a hint of reprimand. Without further ado, he offered a lengthy soliloquy in Amharic. "Praise to God, Holy Father, and Jesus Christ." Barra ended his prayer in English.

Emma waited for someone to dish the steaming wot into the middle of the enjera so that she could begin the necessary ordeal of eating with an appetite that waned with each passing moment.

The team ate with gusto, and Isaac spoke. "I know good joke," he said. "Is American, Russian, and Ethiopian on boat..."

He stumbled through the story, resorting to Amharic during key moments and ending with, "So we throw Russian over side of boat. We have so many of these." Barra laughed a deep laugh, and Mariam smiled and tried to laugh. Emma didn't get the joke. She had been lost in her thoughts, taking a bit of the spongy enjera soaked in sauce, followed by slow gulps of water. What more could she have done for that child? Maybe she should have gone home with them. But, Isaac had explained to the mother how her husband should take the chloroquine, how she should offer soft eggs and mashed banana to the child, and clean water as well. The child would never make it, and she was powerless to stop his slow, painful death.

After wading through several kids who were eager to guard the Land Cruiser while they were away, Reece followed Sam. The room with his trunk, two other suitcases, and a video camera that Sam was picking up was not a room at all, just a hallway jammed with stuff. But his trunk was there, and a stern lady with razor cheekbones, who inspected every item, confiscated all the foil-wrapped videotapes for evaluation.

"We may never see those again," said Sam.

Reece didn't care, but felt responsible. He wondered how he could have hidden them better.

The inspector held up a blister-packed fingernail clipper and studied it as if memorizing it. Reece felt silly, wanting to tell her what each item was, but she didn't ask. She carefully placed everything back in the trunk and stamped a piece of paper with purple ink. He signed the paper, and she stamped it again. Sam placed a five-birr bill on the counter, and they struggled the load outside where a group of five young boys, all dressed in torn, mismatched clothes with shaved heads, cajoled the trunk and suitcases from them, carrying them with great gusto to the Land Cruiser, the trunk held high over two heads like a blue coffin trimmed in brass. Sam gave the tallest of the bunch a single birr, and a great row ensued among them.

Driving back to the Mission, Reece felt sleepy. Ed chatted a bit about the famine, but it still made no sense to Reece. As Reece chose one of the dozen lanes through Revolution Square—*Long Live International Proletarian-*

ism!—he stared at the black and red billboard of Marx, Lenin, and Engels set up on a scrubby green knoll. The improbability. But there it was, those bushy beards towering over the center of a major African city, little blue-and-white Russian Lada taxis buzzing along like lethal toys beneath their gaze. The Russians were everywhere, and not very well-liked, Reece gathered. The people on the sidewalks and edges of the roads all walked at the same moderate pace, seemingly oblivious to the mantras.

With Hattie gone, Reece had the guesthouse to himself and settled in for a long, slow evening of reading and writing. He decided to put off calling Kristin until the next day, and then felt terrible. He noticed a little pile of mail on his bed, and there was a letter from her. A sickness surged through his stomach, a kind of coldness bordering on fright. He held the letters, smelled them, and put them back on the bed. He wanted to enjoy them, but decided to cook dinner first. The chicken had been thawing in the refrigerator. He would fry it and bake a potato. Her handwriting was expressive, full of loops and curls, but neat at the same time. The letters had been addressed to the Mission's P.O. box. The mail trickled its way through there and then upcountry to the feeding stations, by helicopter, plane, or sometimes in one of the Land Cruisers.

The chicken from the supermarket proved rotten. It smelled so bad he did not even try to cook it. The skin was purple and hard. He nearly threw up looking at it, and he had a pretty strong stomach. Disgusted, he canned the idea of a baked potato and ate bread and cheese and then a mushy banana that clotted his throat. He gagged, remembering a man who had drowned, a patient of his.

For all practical purposes, except for his heart beating, the man had been dead. His waders had filled and pulled him under, where he breathed in copious amounts of warm, green lake water. He was cold, clammy, gray, and purple like the chicken. If he had lived, he probably would have lost his legs from the toxic vasoconstrictors shot into his veins to salvage his blood pressure. "Levophed," the on-call doc said, shaking his head. *Leave 'em dead,* thought Reece, rushing around this giant corpse of a man, his belly rising from his waist like a wheelbarrow on its backside. The drowned man's heart streaked off into half a dozen arrhythmias, one after the other. The ventilator cycled on and off, forcing 100 percent oxygen into his soaked lungs. "Let's get a catheter in him," said the doc, a former airline pilot with neat hair to prove it.

Reece had raised his eyebrows and mentally added it to the thousand and one tasks involved with admitting a new patient, and a drowned one to boot. Every light in the room coalesced, creating an uncanny illusion that sunlight must be nearby for there to be such brightness. Buzzing in and out of the drowned man's room directly across from the nursing station, Reece had that vague sense of flying through space that he felt when working night shift. He had another patient to deal with as well and tried to wrap his mind around what was needed in room three. He should change her IV. The insertion site was red and swollen. The pump had kept beeping, but then the drowned man had dropped in, and Reece was first-admit. No one liked being first-admit.

Standing there with Gary, another nurse, who was

assisting with the catheter, Reece watched a firehose of brown vomit surge from the drowned man's mouth in a stream that, if frozen, would be hard to distinguish from a clay pipe with a diameter of six inches. Simultaneously, Tina, the monitor tech, belted out, "Check eleven!"

"Holy fuck," said Gary.

The man vomited again, this time hurling his stomach contents to the ceiling, splashing the overhead light. The vomit fell back where it came from, creating pools of dark brown acid in the man's deep eye sockets. Reece grabbed a rag and scooped the vomit from the drowned man's eyes. Already, they looked burned, red, cooked by the juices.

"God, what is that? Beef stew?"

"Carrots, peas. Looks like he had a feast," said Gary.

The whole room smelled like vomit on top of death. The ventilator alarm squawked, the IV pump bleeped, and the heart monitor rendered a flat line. The sterile catheter insertion tray sloshed with brown puke.

"He's out," said the doc. "No resuscitation."

The drowned man lay like the corpse he was, and it took Reece and a nursing assistant a good forty-five minutes to clean him up, wrap him, and drag him onto a stretcher for the quiet trip to the morgue.

Gripping the kitchen counter, Reece remembered what he was doing and tore off a hunk of Mrs. Guthrie's home-made white bread like a piece of spiral notebook paper and then opened one of the blue cans of cheese from Australia. The cheese was bright orange, soft, and smelled and tasted of cheddar. *Not bad,* he thought, wondering how well the cheese was received at the feeding stations. He remembered the letters waiting for him and ate slowly, washing his meal down with a Fanta. He had yet to see grape, but there seemed to be plenty of orange Fanta in Ethiopia.

In the red glow of the kerosene lantern, Emma excused herself from the dining hut. Darkness had closed over Godo, the sun snapped shut inside a black change purse. In front of her were the team's rooms. To her left was her little white house, glowing in the brilliant starlight. She looked up and had to stop. The stars outnumbered the stars. There was no room left between them, a breathtaking yet nauseating sight. She looked down to regain her balance. God seemed so far away, the universe much too large, life far too cruel.

Irigit shuffled over, talking nonstop, smiling and smiling. He walked Emma to her door, pushed it open for her. The door scraped the grainy cement floor, shattering the silence. Inside, a mole with a clarinet nose scurried to hide between the plastic and the wall.

"Denadur." She felt for her flashlight and turned it on.

Irigit smiled and closed the door for her.

Once, Irigit had padlocked her door from the outside, thinking it was his job to do so, to keep her safe. Emma listened. She heard his humming as he walked back to his place at the corner of the team's building, just outside of Barra's door.

The tiny fridge's pilot light hissed in the darkness. Emma went to her bed and lit a candle there on the table, a chunky white candle with three wicks. The candle provided enough light by which to read and write. Runs of wrinkled wax sealed the candle in its place. She thought about bathing with a pot of hot water, but didn't feel up to it. Instead, she struggled to tip over one of the forty-gallon plastic jerry cans and fill a small metal pot. A cold face and hand scrub would suffice. She pulled the curtains across the single rough window covered with a piece of rusted screen. A light breeze ruffled the curtain printed with faceless clowns. She could close a shutter across the window from the outside if needed.

"Jesus, my feet smell." She peeled off her socks, collared with dirt at the ankle. She exchanged her dirty jeans for a baggy pair of white scrubs, a "Property of" pair she'd brought from the States. A long-sleeve t-shirt was just right for the cool, minus the bra, which she worked off from beneath. She wanted to look in a mirror, to look at her breasts, to make sure they were still even, to feel that something was in balance.

Beside the candle lay her Bible, open to the book of Second Kings. She was reading the Bible from cover to cover for the first time. The text jumped from battles with Moabites to the familiar story of the woman blessed with ever-multiplying vessels of oil. With the oil, she could pay a debt and keep her two sons from being placed into servitude. And then the miracle of the Shunamite's son, dead, brought back to life by Elisha. Emma read aloud, "And the child sneezed seven times, and the child opened his eyes." So many blessings. So many miracles. And then she read about Naaman, who was cured of leprosy. All he had to do was follow Elisha's advice. Bathe in the Jordan River seven times. Done. Cured. Emma closed her Bible, sheathed in a nylon zippered case. Where was Elisha when you needed him?

Emma lay back on her cot, glanced at the photo of her

mom wearing glasses that dwarfed her thin face. A slow burn crept from her stomach to her throat, and she sat up. She had to pee as well. Tears forced her green eyes and spread to her cheeks.

After the shintabet experience, Emma slept like the dead. She dreamed that dream that she could not share, the one where she woke paralyzed, floating through the air, through the walls, trapped in a cube of light, ascending. Beyond that were the concrete details of place, the table that looked like metal but wasn't. The bronzed light. A contraption that looked like a metal detector. The line of visitors, tall and lanky with large eyes and pear-shaped heads. The eyes had no pupils, just black round things like enormous blackberry drupelets. And then a perfect little brown girl with a huge smile, skipping away.

The noise of doves scooting on the tin roof, purring, fluffing, and scratching their nails, woke Emma. Light flooded the print curtain, pierced the gaps around the door, and fingered through numerous openings between the roof and walls. The clinic opened at eight a.m., which meant two to three hours after the sun had risen in local time. Someone was talking outside near the gate. A rooster squawked a measly crow in the distance. In the year 1270, Yekuno Amlak had become emperor of Ethiopia after eating a rooster's head. The rooster had spoken to the Zagwe, the current ruler, telling him that whoever ate its head would become king. He had the rooster cooked, but the cook threw the head away, and it found its way to Yekuno Amlak's mouth.

First things first, Emma hurried to the outhouse, the

one built at the far end of the compound just for her. She waved at Zenebek, who was dipping a pot of water from the rain barrel, and glimpsed Misrak through the cook-house smoke. The toilet seat was cemented into the floor over the pit. Next, she brushed her teeth, walking behind her house for privacy, spitting the toothpaste onto the ground and rinsing with one of the ubiquitous orange cups. She peered through the fence made of poles and sticks. The government health clinic was there, run by the very capable Atakabura. His primary weaknesses, Emma knew, were a shortage of supplies, only delivered every four months, and an inclination to reuse syringes and needles. People still visited his clinic, even though they had to pay for their treatments, being either wary of the Americanos and their medical wares or perhaps fearful of being treated by a woman.

Dressed in full scrubs, light blue ones, and her hiking boots, which were hot during the day but comfortable, Emma passed the dining hut, smelling oily kiyawot.

Ketow, the daytime guard, met her halfway across the yard. He wore the shabbiest of shabby clothes, ripped and patched army-green shorts with a matching top that looked military. The leg openings of his shorts were wide enough to put tree trunks through. He talked rapidly, pointing in the direction of the village square. Emma understood nothing except when Ketow lowered his voice, took on a serious look, and whispered, "Jeb." Hyena.

Emma knew that she was going to have to deal with the Hyena, but had put it to the back of her mind, hoping that Afewerki would appear as he did every morning. He whistled tunes that she'd learned as a child in Vacation Bible School, which made her smile and shiver at the same time. It all seemed so incongruous, but magical. *Stop! And let me tell you, What the Lord has done for me. Stop! And let me tell you...*

"Ishi, ishi," said Emma. She understood. The team was at the jail. She couldn't tell if Ketow was telling her to get there quickly or to avoid the scene like the plague.

Misrak emerged from the cookhouse and spoke to Ketow. She looked anxious and made a hand-to-mouth motion. "Bel-ow?" *Will she eat?*

"Yellum, for now anyway." Emma loved the Coptic Cross tattooed on Misrak's forehead and the three vertical lines on her chin, all the same dull-green color, subtle against her golden skin. Like Zenebek, when she smiled, her white teeth flashed against gums tattooed an indigo blue.

Emma jogged back to her house for a cable-knit sweater to keep the morning chill at bay. She put the padlock in the hasp, but did not lock it, and headed through the heavy gate to butt heads with the Hyena.

After reading the first letter, Reece felt sick. Sick because Kristin was angry, and sick because he missed her. He closed his bedroom door, threw the letter on the bed, fell to his knees, and cried for several minutes, heaving, as if lamenting the death of a loved one. He was exhausted, too exhausted to read the other letters. He wanted only to sleep, and suddenly there were voices in the common area, the front door opening and closing. He recognized the voice of Dr. Guthrie's wife, and then someone knocked. It must have been six, maybe seven o'clock. Outside, a fading light clung to the sky, coming through the windows as yellow. Reece collected himself in a hurry, puzzled, caught off guard, glad to hear voices but unprepared. He cleared his throat, rubbed his eyes, and said a practice *Hello* before opening the door.

"Hello?"

The room had filled with five women and a man in a gray suit. Folding chairs had appeared. It was Friday. Friday night women's fellowship, and there was a guest speaker, someone from the Foreign Mission Service in Virginia. A coffeemaker burbled. Lemon cookies. Bright light.

"Were you sleeping?" Livvy looked spiffy in her white dress.

"Maybe napping," he said. "Is there a meeting?"

"It's a get-together we do every Friday night with the ladies. Dr. Summiton is in the country, and he's going to be the speaker tonight. Usually, we just discuss a book or something, but he's going to talk about mission work. You want to join us?"

Reece surveyed the room. He watched Dr. Summiton stoop over, listening to Sam's wife, Shirley. They seemed to be old friends. The doctor's coat looked too big for him. "Sure. Do I need to bring something? What do you guys do?"

"Don't worry about that. Just have fun." Livvy seemed tired of being patient and motioned for him to join them in whatever fashion seemed best.

Reece entered the small bathroom, closed the door, and wet his face. He wanted to brush his teeth, but his toothbrush was in his room. He emerged and sat on the couch. No one else seemed interested in sitting there or on the loveseat. Instantly, he knew it was a mistake. He should have stayed in his room or just said, "No thanks," and read *The Martian Chronicles* on his bunkbed.

"I appreciate you all gathering here tonight," said Dr. Summiton. Everyone in the room, except for Reece, knew each other. Reece sensed that Dr. Summiton would have taken greater pleasure if his audience were ladies only. "Who here tonight has a gift?" he said, raising his hand by example.

Oh Lord, thought Reece. No gathering of Baptists could escape the fascination with one's gifts. Reece's mind raced, speeding through the various gifts a Christian might find useful in a world filled with sinners.

"Faith," said a thin, stern woman whom Reece hadn't been introduced to. Her lips were the width of a pencil mark. Her dress was very plain and simple, reminding Reece of the Amish. She hadn't raised her hand, and that seemed to annoy Dr. Summiton.

"Yes, faith, and what else?" he said.

Livvy raised her hand, exposing her soft, pale under-arm. Dr. Summiton smiled and pointed at her.

"I would say patience is my gift." And she laughed a laugh that said her life required patience.

"Yes, patience is a virtue. Can you give us an example?" He took a sip of coffee from an orange plastic cup. His eyes looked tired.

"Well, Norbert, of course..." Lighthearted snickers dotted the bright room. Livvy looked around with an "Oh, you guys" smile. "What I meant to say is that Norbert, Dr. Guthrie, of course, holds these animal clinics just about right in front of the house. And it never fails that one of these poor old farmers lets a goat get loose or a cow starts having her calf, and sooner or later there they go into my flowers or knock into those two lemon trees I planted—"

"So, Livvy, what do you do?" asked Dr. Summiton.

"Well, I just draw back and tell myself that I've got to be patient. That Norbert's clinics are part of God's work. Not that I've always had the gift." She bobbed her head for emphasis.

"What else?" asked Dr. Summiton.

Reece had fixed on mercy as his gift, but he was not about to discuss it. At a youth retreat in Alabama one summer, a whole evening had been given over to exploring one's gifts. Everyone had taken a written test, and Reece's gift had emerged as mercy. At the time, amid the energy and emotion of the gathering, he had embraced the idea, on the verge of tears. No one ever had two or more gifts, though, just the one.

Ben's wife wasn't there, but Betsy, Thomas's wife, was. She sat blankly with her arms folded. "I've never had a specific gift, I don't think." She kept her arms folded.

"And what do other folks think about that?" Dr. Summiton smiled.

Reece knew that a gift was about to be bestowed on Betsy, whether she wanted one or not. She seemed like a shadow.

"Are you thinking what I'm thinking?" Dr. Summiton said to no one in particular. He scanned the room.

Reece wished he were sitting farther away from him.

"Yes, Stephanie." Summiton's eyes sparkled at Stephanie. Stephanie was the journeyman living in the tiny guesthouse to the right. She was twenty-two, had long brown hair and a thick scatter of brown freckles across a broad white face. She wasn't fat but had large hips that screamed to birth babies. Reece knew she would provide the correct answer.

"I'd have to say either humbleness or humility." Stephanie sat up straight and glanced over at Betsy, whose expression took on a look of worry.

"That's exactly right, Stephanie, humility...humility." Dr. Summiton looked to Reece as if he might be getting a cold.

Betsy did manage to raise her eyebrows in a kind of "Well, if that's the way it has to be" manner. Anything Betsy could say or not say would only draw her deeper into her newly assigned gift.

The next morning, Reece knocked on the Ashberrys' door. Inside, he could hear Claude making animal noises. Ben opened the screen door and stood there, his dress shirt untucked from his jeans. He hadn't shaved.

"What's up?" Ben pulled a smile across his face. His voice projected like a radio announcer.

Reece knew other people like him. With no apparent effort to amplify his voice, it emerged loud and deep. "I hate to bother you guys, but I need to use the phone." Reece wanted to add, "And is anyone going to the post office today?"

"Sure, sure, I know how it is, needing a phone."

Reece walked past him into the front room. Claude burst in. His glasses gave him the look of a miniature thinker, but then he crawled under the rug, making a "hiding sound," as Ben called it.

"Claude!" Teresa appeared in the doorway leading to the bedroom. Reece could see a dark areola through her thin, yellow t-shirt. "He thinks he's a snake."

"Phone's back there," said Ben. "Claude get..." and he stopped.

"Kimo's asleep on our bed," said Teresa. "Can you come back later, in an hour or two? I just laid him down."

"Is anybody going to the post office today?" asked Reece. "Sure, I can come back, maybe after lunch. It's like eight or nine now?"

"How's his visa and work permit?" Teresa asked Ben. She put her hands beneath her breasts, raising them as if they were too heavy. Claude lay still, only his feet showing from beneath the rug. Ben stared at him.

"Slow, but Tesfaw thinks only three or four days." Ben put his hands on his hips. Reece now stood directly between them and slipped around an armchair. "We've got a plane going up, though, tomorrow. Reece can go along and see the sights."

Reece nodded, glad to get away from the vacuum of the mission compound. "What time?"

"Be ready by seven. We'll fly up to AK. Dr. Guthrie gets dropped in Gundo."

Reece was up early the next morning, excited about the plane ride upcountry. Finally, the smell of adventure was in the air. He sensed the plane would be old, that it would be crowded, and it was. The previous day had been a bust of sorts, reading and writing Kristin a long letter. He had given Tesfaw several letters and a small package containing the first roll of film to mail back to Kristin. Reece imagined it would be exciting for her to hold the film canister and wonder what was inside. He pictured her running down to the one-hour photo at the mall and waiting for the pictures to be developed.

When he'd gone back to the Ashberrys to call Kristin, she wasn't in. She was working, her father said. And Reece spoke with her father for two or three painful minutes. Whenever Reece hung up the phone, he felt as if that was it, that the complex sequence of events necessary to make the phone ring in Kristin's house would never again be possible. Being consumed with just the act of calling, the chance that he would have to talk occasionally to her father or mother hadn't occurred to him. Now he could add that little unknown into the mix. Her father talked so slowly and carefully. He was the nicest guy in the world, but ended every sentence with a sense of uncertainty, always guessing, *Well, I guess* or *I don't know, but...*

Ben drove the Land Cruiser, and Tesfaw drove the van to the airport. The day charged bright and sunny. A light fog had blanketed the mission until the rising sun burned it off. The vehicles drove behind the airport, passed through a heavily guarded checkpoint where guards scrutinized papers, and pulled within twenty feet of an ancient silver plane with fat turboprops on each wing. Reece wondered where this thing would land. He understood the Highlands to be mountains and ravines and stood around watching the luggage, boxes of veterinary supplies, and cartons of medicines being loaded into the plane's underbelly. He was only going up for a day and would return the next, so he took only a change of underwear, toothbrush/toothpaste, socks, a t-shirt, and his Ricoh 35-millimeter camera.

The plane's engines started without warning, sounding like two machine guns, each of a different caliber. Reece edged away from the plane, wondering if this racket was routine. The engine on the right quit and spun in fits for a few seconds and then kicked back in. The pilots seemed to get them in sync, but only after racing the engines up and down, as if trying to create a mechanical failure. The plane had no markings other than numbers to distinguish it in any way. It belonged to the RRC, the Relief and Rehabilitation Commission, founded by the Derg, the Derg being the Marxist military government. So much money and equipment were pouring into the country that it was hard to tell who was ponying up for what. "Do They Know It's Christmas?" and Bob Geldof's Band Aid had sparked the flood of media attention, which triggered massive pipelines of food, medicine, and equipment into the country.

Most of the goods came through the Red Sea ports located in Eritrea, with whom the Ethiopians were actively fighting.

Reece lingered, put his hands in his back pockets, shifted from hip to hip, waiting, growing weary of the plane's loud engines. Dr. Guthrie, wearing his safari vest of many pockets, motioned for Reece and the others. Ben and Tesfaw weren't going and had left with the vehicles. A couple of Ethiopian officials dressed in blue pants and blue shirts boarded the plane. Dr. Summiton, along with his wife, was with Dr. Guthrie. The Summitons dressed in their Sunday formals as they had at the little gift-bestowing get-together in the guesthouse. Reece hoped the pilots had the gift of flying and wondered who they could be. Two other men whom Reece hadn't met also milled about, both rotund, white, Canadian, and wearing glasses.

Inside the cockpit sat two men, thirties, maybe Americans, surveying the array of switches and dials. The cockpit looked roomy, and the pilots seemed to be cheerful, perhaps even having a good time. The noise inside the plane was even louder than outside. A few seats in the short passenger area had been removed. Reece took a stained window seat that had no aisle seat beside it. Only one row ran down the right side. The large window glass was scratched and milky around the bottom. He looked out over the silver wing to an ascending escarpment in the distance that towered like the inside of a giant gray bowl. The plane vibrated and made a slow *yow, yow, yow*, fading, vibrating in and out. No air moved, and it was cold.

After half an hour, the plane jerked forward, wending its way to a takeoff position. The *yow, yow, yow* segued into a *wuh, wuh, wuh*. It was too loud to talk, but Reece could hear Dr. Guthrie shouting at Dr. Summiton. Dr. Summiton's face looked strained, and he occasionally nodded. The plane gathered speed, and Reece was sure it would never lift from the ground. When it seemed there was no more runway left, the plane hopped into the air and strained for the gift of altitude.

The city beneath peeled away and faded into a vast, wild country from an ancient age. From a few thousand feet above the ground, the topography looked brutal. The terrain rolled from flat-topped mountains and large conical hills to tremendous cliffs and deep valleys. Reece saw isolated hamlets, groupings of tiny, round huts surrounded by patches of cultivated land. The land was brown with vague hints of dirty green. It looked like a handful of Grand Canyons spilled onto the ground. It looked unreal.

By air, about ninety miles separated Addis Ababa from the outpost at Gundo Meskel, the first stop. The trip took roughly forty-five minutes before the plane began to circle an area terraced to one side and with a small village nearby. Reece couldn't see a runway as the plane dropped onto a flattened area of the long mountain. The aircraft came down fast and hit dirt, jouncing, tires hitting stones, clouds of dust trailing behind them. The plane wanted to stand on its nose as it squealed to a stop and swung right. The engines roared with backwash.

From his window, Reece saw a group of men hurrying toward the plane from beyond a fenced area a hundred feet away. A pilot emerged from the cockpit, wrenched open the outer door, and lowered the stairs. Dr. Guthrie was out of his seat, shouting at the other pilot, and then exited the plane. Reece unbuckled his safety belt and wondered what to do. Was he getting off? No one else seemed to be moving.

Through his window, he watched a young woman in a pair of faded blue scrubs approach. She looked like an ICU nurse, with that confident, yet tired, look. Her blonde-brown hair was windblown, hands on hips. He wondered if she was the Jill whose fiancée had committed suicide that Dr. Guthrie had mentioned. He watched her, fascinated that she lived and worked in this place. Loud, bumping noises came from the cargo area of the plane as numerous boxes were unloaded and, balanced on the heads of the young men, were taken away beyond the fence.

The young woman gestured with her hands. Dr. Guthrie listened with his hands in his pockets. He was a few inches taller and looked like he was giving her a pep talk. Dr. Guthrie put his hand on her shoulder and disappeared with her beyond the fence. The plane rumbled and shook.

With Guthrie back on board, the plane jounced to the end of the crude runway. The hulk of a rusted, gutted tank sat awkwardly among large boulders. The plane shot off the top of the mountain, having lifted a few feet from the ground. A vast void opened below, twisting browns with dull swatches of green, an infinite haze supporting the distant skies.

They had dropped into Gundo Meskel for a quick visit. Now they were flying to Alem Ketema, or AK as the missionaries called it. The Mission helicopter was based there, and AK served as a distribution center for the relief stations at Gundo Meskel, Godo, Mehal Meda, Meranya, and Rabel. The ground continued to drop from the plane, browns melding into oranges and blacks.

The snake of a dry riverbed lay in the deepest portion of the vast lowland below. As the plane climbed again and circled, Reece watched the flat-topped mountain with its fall-away cliff, its dark green swath of scrub and small trees scattered below. On the second rush at the mountain, the plane looked as if it would smash into the cliff before it lifted and veered away once again. No one seemed particularly afraid, but Reece gripped his armrest. He had to pee and lifted the seatbelt with his hand to provide some relief from the pressure. The plane rose again, circled out over the vast valley, climbing. Below, dirt roads ran through scatterings of huts and square buildings with corrugated tin roofs. The runway looked like a field of rocks.

The silver plane barreled once more at the mountain and dropped onto the runway with a thud and clatter, skidded sideways for a fraction of a second, and then ground to a shuddering halt in front of vast piles of jagged skull-sized rocks. Dr. Guthrie grinned and looked around the cabin to see if anyone had "peed themselves," as he said later at dinner that night.

Who was in AK? Reece knew that Hattie had gone to Gundo Meskel. She had not appeared, though, when they landed there. And where would he sleep? Was it true that he would visit Godo, the village where he would be living? *How long will I stay in this place?* Every letter and phone call from Kristin asked that question of him. "You can't stay for two years," she had written. "Please tell me that not even a year is what you want."

It took half an hour for a pickup truck and an ancient Toyota "jeep" to show up and carry them to the mission compound at AK. The pilots stepped out of the plane but did not bother to mingle while they waited. Dr. Guthrie held court with the two bespectacled Canadians, who had some hand in the tons of wheat and sorghum pouring into the country. Reece wandered off a short distance among vast heaps of rocks and relieved himself. The plane cut its engines, and a strange, deep silence surrounded by the sounds of wind emerged. The two Ethiopians stood apart from the others. Dr. Summiton and his wife stayed within a few paces of each other, lingering in the shade of the plane's wing. She sat on the hard dirt and pulled her dress over her knees. Old people sitting on the ground drew Reece's attention. There was something uncanny about it. Her face was so thin and severe, yet her skin was tight and youthful. Reece imagined she had lived a life of sacrifice, that she had wanted children. Dr. Summiton looked out of place in his suit. He sneezed and looked miserable.

Reece gravitated toward the Summitons, drawn by their age, their lack of conversation, and the appearance of discomfort. He had lived with his grandparents at their small retirement house beside a mile-long, dammed lake after leaving Texas, after his parents were shot and killed. He had spent several summers with his grandparents as well, growing closer and closer to them as the years passed.

Emma rounded the outside curve of Afewerki's family compound, passed the sentinel fig tree, and walked toward the administrator's compound adjacent to the windowless, square jail with a tin roof. Anyone could escape with ease, except they would be shot with even more ease.

At the crude arched entrance to the Hyena's mud-and-pole offices stood Isaac and Mariam. Inside, two teenage guys milled about with their AK-47s slung like guitars. Their large afros painted them as being from another place.

"All right, what's going on?" asked Emma.

Isaac stuttered. "Is working." He wore his mechanic's coveralls.

Mariam whispered something, dressed in yesterday's pink shirt.

"Have you seen Afewerki this morning? I've got work to do. You've got work to do. This is ridiculous."

"Inside," whispered Mariam.

Emma walked between them beneath the arch. The crude door made of bound poles stood open. Darkness filled the building, beyond the rhomboid of light washing the floor. The two young guards surrounded her, not stopping her but moving with her. One reeked of alcohol. The other had that lazed look of qat. They were about Emma's height.

"Dammit," said Emma. "Get that barrel off me." She pushed against a gun with her shoulder.

A hand grabbed her arm.

"Let go!" Emma made eye contact with the unsteady drunk one. "Jesus loves you, but I do not. Let me go."

"Emma!" said Isaac. "You must wait, be patience. They say Afewerki is thief, but we know it to be a lie. He will arrest you."

Just like she could never hear her basketball coach in high school yelling at her to keep the ball in the last seconds of a game, Emma could not hear Isaac. She pushed a hand from her arm, which went to her breast, lingering for a moment.

Emma turned, backed, and threw an open hand at his face. He must have been sixteen, garbed in military fatigues, gripping his automatic by the barrel tip, an arm up to block Emma's hand. He laughed and then spat. The other guy laughed and spat as well, but the spit clung to his teeth.

"Emma!" Barra rushed from within the dark bowels of the building. He looked rather sheik with a clean white shamma draped around his neck over a light blue, long-sleeve button-down. "No, no. God is helping us. Please to help me, Emma."

"He grabbed me," said Emma. "Where is he? The administrator? What's his real name?" She pitched forward into the doorway. She saw the desk in the dim corner, the spotted hyena's pelt nailed to the wall.

Everyone stood back from Emma. The guards were no longer laughing as the Hyena, a would-be miniature of the Marxist military dictator he served, met Emma face-to-face in the doorway.

"You," said Emma.

The Hyena nudged her backward with his chest. His

eyes glared red and bloodshot. That fruity breath of his made Emma cringe. He held out his hand for her to shake.

Isaac and Mariam came to her side, Isaac speaking to the Hyena in an apologetic tone. Emma let Isaac take her arm and lead her outside.

The Hyena followed her, zombie-like, his hand still extended. She *would* shake his hand. That's what he wanted.

Emma folded her arms across her chest and took a deep breath. She felt her heart beating far too fast. She felt short of breath. The sky was such a brilliant blue. A chicken pecked the dirt.

"Please to shake his hand." Barra was angry, it seemed, at everyone except the Hyena.

"He can shake his own hand," said Emma. "What about Afewerki? I need him in the clinic now. Tell him that." What was there between Barra and this guy, this strange, drunk, mean little man dressed in combat boots?

Barra folded his hands and spoke in a deferential tone, asking when Afewerki would be released.

The Hyena grinned, showing his gold-edged front teeth. "You will see him soon. Perhaps this day, God willing." He laughed, and his minions laughed as well, deflated laughs, not even evil laughs, which made them seem silly to Emma. The Hyena turned and melted into the dank interior of his tiny kingdom.

When the Toyota FJ40 Land Cruiser flopped onto its side jouncing across a patch of bowling ball-sized rocks and then sliding sideways across a long mud hole doing fifty kilometers an hour, the four perched on top, clinging like cicada hulls to the roof rack, and the guy riding the spare tire in back took immediate flight, suffering minor injuries except for one split skull, down to the bone, which bled profusely but then slacked once stuffed with a wad of precious toilet paper destined to be sold in the market at Godo. Inside was a different matter as a hand grenade fashioned to the driver's shirt flew loose. Having lost its pin many years ago, the tape holding down the spoon slipped, and there was a terrific explosion that killed three and seriously injured five. As the jeep-like vehicle held four comfortably, the tight packing of occupants perhaps contributed to the low death toll. As it was only ten kilometers to Godo and sixteen to Alem Ketema, the wounded were being carried toward the closer option.

Emma stood over her fifth diarrhea case of the day, her eleventh patient. Any minute, she was waiting to hear of Afewerki's release. One of the daily laborers, his disintegrating hat in his hands and wrecked clothes barely clinging to his body, ran to the clinic door with the report. He saw Emma and kneeled as he spoke with great urgency. News of the accident on the road had relayed itself ahead of the injured.

"Bucka," said Emma to the young man with diarrhea, a chiseled, handsome face, and a week's growth of beard. "Isaac, what is it?"

"There is an accident on the road. Many have died," said Isaac.

"Where? Here?"

"From beyond the river. Some are coming now for medicine. This man, Omar, is saying to us wait, they are coming for help."

"How far away? Should we go there? I wish we had a

radio. I could call Terry, maybe. Damn."

Isaac spoke with the laborer Omar in rags, who wore the sign of Muslims, the black string around his neck. "He is saying one mule is coming the lady. She is dying and to pray to God."

Emma ran her hands through her hair. Her lips were dry, flaking, hurting, and she needed water. The day was brilliant, beautiful. The weather never better. The mud had dried, creating fudge-like cracks in the ground. She'd forgotten to bring a water bottle but dared not drink from the spigoted water can. To drink the water, one had to have been born and raised there, adapting to the area's multifarious population of intestine-nuking rotaviruses and bacteria.

Omar bowed and ran off to spread his news.

Emma returned to her patient, who looked miserable. She spoke to Isaac. "I guess we'll wait. Any idea when they might arrive?"

"Perhaps soon. Only God is knowing," said Isaac.

Mariam stopped outside the clinic door. He removed his tam-o'-shanter and whispered to Isaac.

At seven thousand feet, the sun beat down especially hard. The light was too bright, no matter which way Reece turned. Heat radiated from the cracked dirt runway. He put himself within speaking distance of the Summitons.

"Is it Rice?" asked Dr. Summiton.

"Close. It's Reece."

"I knew it was an unusual name."

"Are you guys staying here for a while? Traveling around?" asked Reece.

Mrs. Summiton stood and smiled, brushing down her long, thin, dark green dress. Mr. Summiton cleared his throat.

"Just sightseeing is the best way to put it. I'm a regional coordinator for mission offerings in Florida, Alabama, and Georgia, and I like to get around and see things for myself. I'm a retired minister, of course." His eyes looked red and watery.

"I'm Gail." Dr. Summiton's wife introduced herself and put out her hand, which Reece shook.

The prophet among us, thought Reece.

"She's Gail, alright," said Dr. Summiton, chuckling. "Been together how many years? She was fourteen when we met. My friends used to joke that she was Gail bait." He looked off into the distance as if waiting for an echo.

"Stop it, Clark. You haven't missed a meal since we were married."

"Well, course not. Pot pies, TV dinners..." He winked at Reece.

"You might have had a pot pie the day I gave birth...but that was the only day." She looked very sad and almost angry. Dr. Summiton put his hand on her shoulder. Their child had been born dead. The sound of gasoline engines approaching grew louder and louder.

"You're a good woman, and we've had thirty-four fine years together." He lifted his chin as if he meant it. "Here comes our ride."

A maroon pickup followed by an old jeep sidled up to the plane, and six young Ethiopian men piled out with big smiles and warm, enthusiastic greetings, especially for Dr. Guthrie. Two of them, Alene and Daniachew, spoke some English. The two Ethiopian officials on the plane and the Canadians were moving on to the next stop in Wollo to the north, where the plane would refuel.

"This is Rice," said Dr. Guthrie.

In turn, Alene and Daniachew stepped forward and took Reece's right hand, coming in close until their chests nearly touched. They both wore Western clothes. Alene looked like a schoolteacher, a bit harried, a word of wisdom hanging from the tip of his tongue. Daniachew seemed to be merely happy, smiling, relaxed, ready to do nothing or everything. After shaking Reece's hand, Daniachew held onto it as they walked toward the vehicles. He spoke in a slow, broken English. The other four young men were tackling boxes, hefting them to the pickup truck. Having his hand held by Daniachew unnerved Reece, and he felt as if his body might lift from the ground.

"You are from Ah-la-bah-ma like Dr. Guthrie?" asked Daniachew, speaking into Reece's face, his big, brown eyes registering genuine curiosity.

"Yes. Alabama." Reece said Alabama slowly, stressing each syllable. "But I was born in Georgia." His voice sounded foreign to him. Alene walked in front of them, paying close attention to what was being said.

"Zhorzhia," said Daniachew, as if invoking the name of a newly discovered flower that cured hunger.

Alene turned and said, "Jor-ja." He looked at Reece for approval. He then rattled off a few lines of Amharic in an instructive tone. In response, Daniachew's smile only grew wider as if this was the best day of his entire life. Reece began to think the whole exchange funny and coughed away a laugh creeping up the back of his throat. Once that started, he would be helpless to stop, and everyone would think he was either rude or had gone mad. He shifted his train of thought to the ground, the hard, coffee-colored ground laced with inch-wide cracks. It looked as if it had been mud a few hours earlier and then flash-baked.

With all the gear and boxes loaded into the back of the truck, Reece wondered where everyone would sit. He wound up squeezed into the truck cab with Alene, who drove, and a younger guy who did not speak English, although he had said "Good evening" with some difficulty. Even though it was very hot, the windows were rolled up. Daniachew drove the jeep with Dr. Guthrie and the Summitons. The plane was roaring and beginning to move.

The dirt road disappeared down a curvy swath cutting through high, dry grasses. They drove away from the cliffs and inland across a series of small but steep hills. They crawled along, negotiating deep ruts. A long view opened at the top of the next hill. "Alem Ketema," said the guy in the middle, pointing.

"Ahh," said Reece, "AK." He saw a batch of buildings and houses arrayed in some vague order. The variety of browns seemed almost colorful. Alem Ketema was an outpost, the last proper town before the smaller villages that were scattered across the vast highlands to the north, east, and west. AK lay on steep, rolling ground with flat, rocky fields.

As they rounded a bend, a small herd of goats, whipped by a tiny boy no more than five years old, swayed back and forth in front of them, looking like fish chasing one another tail to tail. Alene slowed even slower. He rolled his window down as he passed and yelled at the little boy, whose face twisted with scorn. Alene and the other guy laughed. The little boy wore a patched, knee-length dress of sorts made from stiff, green cloth. His head had been shaved except for a fist-sized tuft right on top, the quntcho.

"Hard work," said Reece, almost as a question.

"Ankara," said Alene, rolling the r. Reece nodded, taking that as an affirmation.

Reece repeated, "Ankara."

"Ow, bataam taruno!" said Alene. Both he and the guy in the middle grinned. Reece did not know what it all meant, but just went with it. He knew that "ow" was yes, and it seemed, at least from his limited experience, that taruno meant good. The truck rocked and bounced.

The trip to the outskirts of AK took only fifteen minutes. Reece wondered where the vehicles refueled. He looked for wildlife. He was not sure what lived in the area, whether he would suddenly see a rhinoceros or not. Thus far, the country limited itself to skulking hyenas at the dump and plane-sized vultures soaring through the skies.

Men and women walked the roads, men wearing baggy short pants and shirt-like tops made of coarse fabric, the women in a variety of dull, dusty, long, and patch-heavy dresses that swept the ground. Older men wore the white shamma around their heads and shoulders. Most men wore a shabby hat, walked with a stick or staff, and wore crude sandals made from old tires. All the women and kids were barefoot.

No other vehicles were in sight, and the two-vehicle convoy moved like a bright light along the roads, drawing everyone's attention. Alene conducted a dozen mini-conversations as he drove, someone always jogging beside the truck, peering in at Reece, grinning, and then peeling off to be replaced by another. Little groups of kids chased along, yelling at them. The distinct "Ferenj!" was the same as in Addis. Everyone was thin, but no one seemed starved or on their last legs. The same concoction of leaning, tired buildings made of poles and corrugated tin roofing, found in the more derelict parts of Addis, dominated the town. Some of the outlying clusters of round huts, or tukuls, were made with pole-and-mud walls with conical roofs of straw. Whether round or square, wisps of whitish smoke trailed from most every home. That smell of wood smoke and the mustiness of clothes rarely washed was becoming to Reece familiar and reliable.

They passed through a crude traffic circle, the center occupied by a low wall of rocks on which several old men sat, passing the time in the intense heat and light. Everyone stopped to look at the vehicles, shielding their eyes with a single raised hand. The kids waved and ran along laughing. "Ferenj!" they shouted. "Caramella! Caramella!"

they cried, meaning candy. Alene had closed his window again and the truck's engine became Reece's focus, providing the background noise to the silent, moving tapestry floating by—a hand-pumping station for fuel, a crude assemblage of spigots, women and young girls crowding to fill clay pots and plastic jerry cans with water piped from deep in the ground. A tiny store, not more than fifteen feet square, little boxes of animal crackers hanging from a piece of wire, packs of nine-volt batteries, a chunk of sugarcane, a few spotted thumb-size bananas, a brown face with wide, dull eyes peering from the open window, nothing more than a stall.

"That is our school," said Alene, pointing downhill at a tin-roofed building made of concrete blocks surrounded by a couple of outbuildings. Reece nodded. The guy in the middle spoke, interjecting with a deep inspiration or two, a sound that reminded Reece of a tire being suddenly inflated.

"This is Tilahun," said Alene.

Tilahun looked at Reece.

"Tenesteling," said Reece, using the general greeting he knew. He figured he would pick up the language as he went along. He understood there would be an interpreter with him in the clinic along with Emma.

The truck climbed, and a very long view emerged, hundreds of miles, Reece imagined, as they rounded a bend and paralleled a cliff not more than fifty feet away. The truck turned toward an open gate, a guard sitting against a rickety shack in the shade. He jumped up, a rifle slung across his shoulder. Inside, the fenced compound spread across a sloping bowl of rugged ground. Up along the ridge sat a haphazard cluster of buildings, mainly living quarters, all constructed of corrugated tin and poles. A warehouse filled with grain and other famine-relief supplies sat on a level but rocky field. Nearby, a blue and white helicopter, the Bell 412, perched atop an elevated helipad made of cement and rocks. Long ropes tethered the machine and rotors to the ground. Strong, steady winds and gusts poured up and over the cliff line from the valley below. The buildings rattled and whistled almost nonstop.

The main event of the day seemed to be the arrival of Reece and the Summitons. Nothing in particular was going on, everyone gathering in the communal kitchen and dining area. There was a propane stove and a propane refrigerator. The fridge held bottles of fizzy Ambo and trays of bovine vaccines. A long, homemade table filled the room, sitting on a rough cement floor. Plastic sheets lined the inside walls, which puffed in and out with the wind. The pitched ceiling was open, revealing the underside of the tin roofing. Light came through a window at each end, covered with plastic, and through four pieces of corrugated, white fiberglass, interspersed with the tin roofing as skylights.

A large bowl of oranges sat on the table, and Reece helped himself to one, then two, and they were very sweet and good. Food appeared when needed, but he found it disconcerting that he couldn't snack whenever he wanted. Dr. Guthrie was out and about, leaving Reece and the Summitons together, along with a young Canadian woman nicknamed "Duckie." She struck Reece as interesting, and he wanted to ask her a thousand questions, but she seemed shy, and after the initial hellos, she settled back to writing in her journal. The Summitons each had an orange as well and decided to go for a walk. They had been there before and knew where the guest rooms were. Reece lingered for a few minutes, trying to get up the courage to ask Duckie about her work. He wondered what had happened to Alene and the others. They had been unloading the truck when Reece entered the dining hut. He went back outside through the door at the other end, where Duckie sat with her pen and notebook. She had brown hair pulled back in a ponytail and very clear, tan skin. Her eyes seemed to be coffee colored, and she was beautiful in a very simple and plain way. Reece felt as if he was about to make a mistake.

"Who flies the helicopter?" he said, continuing toward the door in case she did not hear him.

She looked up, and her gaze did not seem to pass directly his way. "Not me," she said as if that were her final word. "That would be Terry. Terry and Lisa. Have you met them?" She returned to her journal.

"No, maybe they're around. I'll introduce myself." Reece passed through the door, the tin scraping the wooden post. He imagined that Duckie was his age, doing similar things. Maybe she was a nurse. A surge of despair settled in his stomach. And as he walked toward the helipad without really paying attention, suddenly he saw a woman wrapped in a towel emerge from one small building and enter the door of an adjacent building. What had he seen? A tan woman wrapped in a white towel with wet hair, as if she had stepped out of a shower. And she had waved at him. And did he wave back?

A stiff breeze blew across the compound, the sun on

its way down from the touch-me sky. He walked toward the gate and had what was becoming a familiar routine with the guards. This guard was older with a stubble of gray beard, his thin body clothed in large-legged farmer shorts, a shamma on his shoulders. He sat on a stool made of twisted wood, the seat fashioned from particleboard, a relic of grain drops by the Polish Army. He was barefoot, holding a long bolt-action rifle on its end between his skinny, muscular legs. The man stood and made a kind of bowing motion with his head. Reece pointed toward the road, and the guard spoke as if in warning. Reece supposed he should register a look of concern, and he did, continuing through the gate onto the empty, dusty road.

Reece looked over the vast emptiness filled with the outlines of the flat-topped ambas in the distance. Fifteen feet from the road, a jagged, terraced cliff dropped away fifty feet, leveled briefly, and then spun down for what seemed like miles. He could see the outline of a river snaking its way deep and far away. The wind whipped his shirt and felt good in the heat. From nowhere, a child appeared, then another, and then another, all boys, the oldest perhaps twelve. They smiled and laughed, and the oldest said, "Ferenj," hesitating as if testing the word for soundness.

Mariam left to find an umbrella to protect Afewerki from the sun, leaving Isaac to tell Emma the news of Afewerki.

"What?" Emma's eyes flashed. She swatted at the half-dozen flies swarming her face. One flew into her mouth, and she spat it out. The fly staggered on the floor and flew into a corner to rest for the next attack.

"He is tied in the sun as a punishment for stealing," said Isaac. "To shame him and shame his father."

"Jesus, we got a carload of accident victims about to drop in on us, a line of sick folks here, and now I have to go and deal with this. Tied up?" Emma felt her blood boiling, a tightness in her chest. She needed, wanted help. If the new guy, Rice, were here, they could divide and conquer, but this was ridiculous.

"Please to be patient," said Isaac. "We are praying to God."

Emma turned to her current patient, the handsome young man with diarrhea. "Let's give him oral rehydration solution, six packs. He says he doesn't have blood or mucus in his stool. I think maybe it's just a virus. Let's mix him a cup now and have him drink another in an hour. He looks pretty strong."

"He wants injection, murphy," said Isaac.

Emma looked irritated. "He doesn't need an injection. This *will* help you." She held out the packets to the man.

The man looked at Isaac, puzzled. .

"We're done. Let's check outside and see if anyone is critical. I need to go and see about Afewerki. I'll cut him loose myself if I have to."

"No, no, that is a bad thing."

"So is being tied up and humiliated." Emma walked outside. She surveyed the ten patients sitting against the clinic wall. A few shimogeles, a.k.a. old men, a priest among them, flapped their oxtail swatters. The rest, women with children. Emma walked to the closed gate and pushed it open. The clinic line stretched up the hill, patients squatting in the sun, a few with large, black, sun-bleached umbrellas. She counted about forty souls sitting on rocks, leaning into the stick fence. Little kids sitting in the dirt. A bright, hot sun providing too much clarity, shadows running to the right. No one seemed prostrate. A woman with a cantaloupe-sized goiter and a large child clinging to her back looked rather pitiful.

"Isaac, keep that line moving. Treat the stuff you know how to treat, like worms and diarrhea that don't require antibiotics. Got it?"

"Yes, Emma. You are going the Hyena? You must be careful."

"I'll be back as soon as possible. Have the guard pass out some biscuits to anyone who wants a packet."

"Ishi," said Isaac.

She took off up the hill, a clot of dread in her chest.

Shouts of "Ferenj!" from a group of children, and Emma found a child attached to each of her hands. She let them hang on and noticed a little boy sitting alone near a mud puddle. He was beyond filthy. Hundreds of flies swarmed his face, clotting his eyes and feasting on the snot running from his nose. She walked over to the little boy who was dressed in a long top made from coarse cloth. He wore no pants or shoes, and must have been four or five. Emma squatted and tried to wave the flies away, but they weren't budging.

"Wuha," she said aloud. She wanted water to wash his face.

The little boy sat there resigned to his fate. The other children gathered and smiled at Emma.

"Emma." Mariam jogged up, having just left Afewerki.

"Thank God. Mariam, we need a bottle of water and some eye ointment for this little boy. Do you know who the mother is?"

Mariam inspired deeply. "Ow, yes, mother is died. I go."

"There's an old wine bottle there you can put the water in. How is Afewerki?"

"He is strong. I find jentilla, umbrella, for him, to cover him."

"Hurry with the eye ointment and the water. I need to get up there. And bring some gauze pads, too."

"Ishi," and Mariam jogged around the path's corner and down the hill.

Emma spoke to the little boy and gagged at the briquettes of flies crowding his eye sockets, mucking their insect feet in yellow discharge. She made another futile attempt to frighten them away, fanning the air around his face with her hand. The few that took flight zoomed right back into the custard. One, though, drilled straight into her nose, and she cursed. She blocked her nostril on the opposite side and blew as hard as she could. The fly was stubborn. She could feel it resisting as it sucked up moisture with its proboscis. She blew hard again. The children gathered around her laughed, and then cheered when the fly shot out, taking flight into the ether.

Mariam returned in less time than it would take to order at a fast-food drive-thru. He looked concerned as he trotted up with the water and ointment. Sweat beaded above his thin eyebrows. A man, swaying, had joined Emma and was lecturing her. His red eyes looked torched and swollen.

Mariam told Emma that the man was the little boy's uncle.

"Well, what is he saying? Tell him I'm trying to help his nephew. For God's sake, the kid's going to go blind if he's not taken care of." Emma took the bottle of water from Mariam and had him open a gauze four-by-four. She'd forgotten to ask for gloves.

The uncle, dressed in tattered shorts held up with a rope made from grain bags, barked at the little boy, telling him to get home. He scowled at Emma. His head was enormous, with patchy gray hair. He was drunk, Mariam told her, fresh from a morning of drinking tejj, the honey liquor.

Emma made a *Grrr* and squatted again to tend to the little boy who sat with legs splayed, inert. He looked like a marionette at the end of limp strings. She soaked a pad and handed the bottle to Mariam. The flies moved, like mud being pushed aside as she wiped from the inner canthus to the outer. Great streaks of filth and crusted yellow matter clung to the pad. She tended the other eye as the flies, confused and alarmed, darted back and forth from eye to eye, some being squashed.

The uncle sat on a rock, clutching his doolah, a strong, short stick wrapped with lead on one end, a mesmerized look on his large, oily face, and he muttered to himself.

"Here we go, mamoosh." Emma leaned his head back. "Mariam, pour."

"Aiyee!" the little boy cried thinly as the cool water splattered his eyes and cheeks.

Emma continued to wipe his eyes until only light streaks of blood blotted the pads. The uncle seemed to be asleep on the rock he had taken as a seat. The flies had scattered to the other children but still zoomed back to this boy's face for a quick meal.

"He needs to move," said Emma. "Can you move, little one?"

The little boy sat there, glued to his spot by the mud puddle.

"He cannot walk," said Mariam, taking a deep breath.

"For God's sake, let's get him out of the sun and into some shade. The flies have him pegged to this spot. You take care of him, okay? I need to check on Afewerki."

"Okay, Emma," said Mariam. He shook the drunk uncle to wake him.

The kids must have sensed Reece's desire to climb down the cliff face. He could see a small cave or what looked like a cave below, twenty feet down. He tested the rocks one by one as he worked his way down. The kids did not follow him, at first preferring to watch, as if gazing at a TV. He backed his way to a small ledge and swung his feet over. The ground opened on either side, a narrow grassy slice of dirt and grayish rock. Two of the boys appeared at his side, staring at him, indicating it was his move. Reece watched as the little one wearing an oversized plaid shirt scampered back up the narrow chute barefoot.

Reece looked down and to his left. Below lay a fall of a few hundred feet, and then the final fall to the valley far, far below. He wore a pair of Italian hiking boots that had looked better than all the other boots in the outdoor store back home. They hadn't had his size, and he had bought the pair they had, a size too small. His feet hurt, and he felt ill at his impatience, then, and now felt silly watching the barefooted boys. He turned his gaze toward what he imagined was north, where lay Godo and adventure beyond imagination.

Getting down to what had become a cave in his mind, Reece tested a couple of different approaches. Neither seemed satisfactory, but he chose the simplest route to the side of the lip in front of the cave. His feet wouldn't have to dangle at any point. Once down to the level of the foot-wide purchase, he felt the tug of gravity and panicked. He turned, grabbed a knob in the rock, stood, and hugged the wall in front of him, sliding sideways. He stopped, scooted, then stepped inside a foot or so, stooping to avoid banging his head. The cave turned out to be a shallow hole in the cliff, not a real cave at all. The fine dirt beneath his feet was smooth and powdery. There was no sound, no bones, no cave art, just a jagged hole of light in front where lay the rest of everything.

Reece sat, inching closer to the edge. A clutch of rock on his right gave him something to hold onto as he dangled his legs over the edge. Looking down made him sick, and he wondered why he was there. He looked up and glimpsed a face looking upside down at him, puzzled. He worried that the boy might fall and waved him away. A thousand thoughts streamed into the hole with him, and he began to ponder his way out. The way in had seemed easy enough, but had proven nerve-wracking. He stood, teetered, and, holding as long as he could to the wall beside him, put his right hand over the edge above him and pushed his head up for a look. His chest hit rock, keeping him just shy of being erect. There was no way he could lift himself up and over.

The light was dimming, and a spray of coolness touched the wind. The boy stuck his head over again and said something, which Reece couldn't understand. "Don't worry," said Reece, but the dizzying height would not go away.

He scooted to the edge again, facing the inside of the hole, on his knees, reached up his right hand, dug his fingertips into a groove, and pulled as he stood, hugging the rock. His head hit the lip, and an electric shock bolted through his body. He sank back to his knees and inhaled.

He strained his neck back to see where he had made his mistake and then pulled up again, feeling he would be thrown backward, flailing, into the abyss. Once standing and cowering over his available purchase like a starfish on a beachball, he looked down at his feet and, mindful of his hands and feet, worked sideways until the earth slanted inward. He bolted forward. Midway up the chute, heart pounding, he stopped and looked back down one last time before scrambling to the top.

The wind continued to blow, gusting, growing ever cooler as the giant pink sun set to the west. Reece felt that he'd had an adventure and was glad that no adults had been there to point out his folly. Two of the boys followed him back to the gate but ran when the guard appeared.

No one had missed Reece, but Dr. Guthrie did ask him what he'd been up to. Reece said he had been exploring, walking around. Mrs. Summiton was busy at the stove. There was more fruit on the tables, which now had white tablecloths on them. Duckie peeled potatoes. Dr. Guthrie opened a can of cheese. And then the tan woman with dark hair walked in, wearing a long, strapless dress. Her flip-flops made flip-flop sounds. Reece watched all of this from an aluminum folding chair, the kind his grandparents kept out by the metal swing. He couldn't decide what to do and almost stood, but then wondered what he would do if he stood, so stayed put. But the tan woman with the dark flowing hair walked toward him as if she knew him. She seemed larger than he thought from his first glimpse, firmer. He stood and shook her hand.

"You must be Reece," she said. She seemed to Reece to be the first person truly glad to see him. He knew what she would say next and wanted to hear it. "I'm glad you're here with us."

"Really?" asked Reece.

"Yes, really, I've heard good things about you. We'll have to talk sometime. My husband, Terry, is the pilot." She touched Reece on the shoulder.

"Is he around? And what's your name?"

"He'll wait until everyone is finished, not very social. He's got a busy day tomorrow, dropping supplies. I'm Lisa."

"I think I'm supposed to fly over to Godo for a visit, where I'm to be stationed. Tomorrow." The room buzzed with activity, and he had a sudden vision of the structure being picked up by the wind and thrown from the cliff.

"Well, if that's the case, Terry will take you." She touched his shoulder again and turned. "Let me walk back and get something from the house. Be right back." She left the same way she came in.

Reece watched her leave, gripping the armrests of his chair.

Emma continued uphill in the blazing sun. Low, puffy, white clouds dragged shadows across the rocky path. She turned and passed Afewerki's home compound. Just beyond was the shady fig tree with the administrative compound and jail off to the right. Beyond the tree was open, dusty ground filled on market days with farmers selling chickens, sugar cane, berbere, lemons, tire sandals, and tins of concentrated permethrin, guaranteed to kill anything with six legs and sometimes two.

Emma's jaw dropped. In the middle of the empty market, tied to a chair with parachute cord, was Afewerki. A sign, written in Amharic and tied to the back of the chair, announced that he was a thief.

"Untie him right now!" said Emma to no one, anyone.

"No, no, Emma. It is okay," said Afewerki. Sweat drained down his face. "My father is with him, the Hyena, begging to release. He is needing some teff."

"He wants a bribe? Doesn't he steal enough from us as it is?"

"He is too hungry," said Afewerki.

"Hungry my foot," said Emma. "Do you need some water? You need some water. This is just plain crazy."

A group of curious children lingered near the fig tree. "Ferenj!" The sight of Afewerki bound to the homemade chair, lashed with ox hide, seemed of little interest to them. A rogue dog skulked through the open space. A rock followed him, spiffing the dust.

"Here, let me get some water from somewhere." She

looked around, hoping someone would appear with a cool bottle of water. A line of sweat rolled down her nose. Black flies darted in and out for a taste.

Afewerki's mother crested the steep hill coming from the west where she'd been gathering firewood. The pile of hard sticks secured by rope to her shoulders stood three feet above her head. Some of the wood she would sell. A terrific gunshot split the heat. Afewerki managed to stand with the chair clinging to his backside and saw his mother stumble as she released the load of wood onto the ground. Shouting came from the Hyena's office. Afewerki's father, Nigussie, flew through the doorway and fell to the stony dirt, followed by the Hyena's stooges, AK-47s drawn and beaded.

The Hyena emerged holding Nigussie's vintage Preduzece bolt-action rifle and threw it on the ground. He laughed and then cursed. Nigussie had fired a shot through the tin roof in anger. To have his son accused of being a thief, tied in the sun like a donkey, was a great shame.

Afewerki's mother ran to Nigussie and rubbed his head with tears in her eyes. She waited for her husband to get up, but he was dazed from the club to his head and groaning.

Emma ran to Nigussie to see if he had been shot. There was no blood, though, just a large knot on the back of his head where he'd been hit with the rifle butt. He came to his knees, and rifle shells fell into the dirt from his pocket. He shook his head and staggered to his feet with Emma's help, gathering the precious shells. Mariam appeared, running after hearing the gunshot. A small crowd of finger-biting onlookers had gathered, murmuring. Through the Hyena's door stepped Barra with a worried smile.

Barra eased over to Emma, who held onto Nigussie. His wife held his other side. A crisp, ironed breeze moved through the chaos, fluttering sleeves. "He is lucky man," said Barra with his brilliant white teeth.

Emma grunted. "He needs to lie down for a while. Can you help walk him home? As soon as Afewerki is set free here, which I hope is in a hot minute, I'll be down."

Nigussie cursed under his breath and leaned on Barra. His gaze met Afewerki's, an apology to his son. Barra reassured him that Afewerki would be released soon, not to worry. The Hyena wanted twenty liters of soybean oil or a quintal of teff for his release.

Isaac, in sweat-stained overalls, trotted into the muddle with an umbrella and announced that the first accident victim had arrived, a man with the back of his head gashed to the bone, thrown from the back of the jeep, where he had been riding on the spare tire.

"Damn," said Emma. "Mariam, you stay with Afewerki." The sun weighted the scene with clarity and hotness.

Isaac handed Mariam the umbrella. Mariam nodded. "Ishi."

The Hyena had disappeared back into his lair, but his henchmen with rifles drawn remained outside the gate, leering with ugly looks.

Emma called after Barra. "Barra. Tell me exactly what happened in there, but later. We have to get Afewerki untied and back to the clinic. We need him. There's been an accident—"

"Yes, the accident," said Barra. "You must go to clinic and take care. I will take care."

"Good. Isaac, get Afewerki some water, okay?"

"Yes, Emma," said Isaac. "Wuha!" he called to Afewerki's mother as she helped lead Nigussie away.

Emma surveyed the scene, the dusty ground. Afewerki tied to a chair and wearing a long-sleeve, V-necked sweater, for God's sake. Mariam held the ancient umbrella over him, streams of sweat coursing down their faces. There were so many rocks underfoot, so many cuts on her hands from all the rough surfaces in Godo.

Emma slowed her walk down the steep incline to the clinic. The line of patients outside the gate had grown. An old woman, plopped on the ground at the end of the line, stared at her with dim eyes, rubbing her head of short gray hair. She had a few teeth left and the look of one accustomed to waiting with poor results.

Emma ducked into the compound, her scrub top sticking to her back. Thank God it wasn't a ration day. What else could happen? In answer, a fifty-foot dirt devil erupted in the far corner of the compound. The tail whirled, reached into the dust, and colored itself a dusty brown. It advanced in jumps, the tail whipping to find purchase. The tarps, held with rocks over stacks of soybean oil, tore loose and shot skyward, then outward. Wending toward the warehouse, the funnel disintegrated into a wisp.

The man with the head gash, sitting outside, drinking a cup of water, had walked roughly ten miles. Blood caked the back of his AC/DC t-shirt. The fleshy edges of the open wound glistened like a bloody oyster. His eyes were a little glassy, but he seemed to be in good spirits. Emma had never been trained to suture and had learned on the job back in Gundo Meskel. She knew from experience not to suture the wound shut until any infection had been cleared.

"Okay, Isaac. Ready to help?" Isaac's primary job was to run the warehouse, not to work with patients.

Isaac lit one of his ingenious smiles that seemed to accept all hilarity, whether it be obscene or merely mortal. "Yes, Emma. I will help. He needs some threads?"

"He needs threads in his head and a new shirt. Get that one off of him for now. Let's stay outside where the light is better." She patted the stocky, short man's shoulder and went inside to gather a suture kit, peroxide, a razor to shave the hair from the gash, and some gauze pads. She felt sick.

Reece noticed that Duckie had finished peeling potatoes and walked over to volunteer to do something. He was not a cook, but knew the fundamentals.

"Can I do anything?" Reece asked Mrs. Summiton, her hair knotted tightly. She was slicing small round loaves of dark bread. Dinner would be simple. Water for the potatoes steamed on the gas stove.

"Well, let's see." She sliced the bread very carefully. "I think we'll do fine, if you just want to rest," which he took as *Sit down and wait.* He left her there, arranging the bread, and walked past Duckie, dropping handfuls of potatoes into the boiling water.

"Need any help?" he said. She turned his way, and he decided that she was blind in her right eye, and she was.

"Oh, no."

Duckie let a double handful slide into the water and then rinsed her hands beneath a small barrel with a brass spigot that drained into a tall, green tin container.

"Maybe half an hour?" Reece stood with his hand on the screen door. The breeze pushed against it. A dozen flies stood ready to swoop in.

"Sooner," said Duckie. Her dark hair seemed too healthy for a famine. He had imagined that everyone would be compromised with bad haircuts, sunburns, and bruises.

"Okay." His eyes lingered over the interior scene, a still from a movie that he would play over and over again.

Outside, he walked in a circle across the rough ground.

He saw a bearded man on top of the Bell 412 helicopter with a wrench as long as his leg. A panel hung open. The man took no notice of Reece. Reece glimpsed a cat, which took off. Overhead, thick, puffy clouds scurried in the mudding twilight. Reece could have used a jacket.

He was about to say Hi when Terry relaxed and spoke first. The huge wrench was the largest Reece had ever seen. "You must be Reece," he said, just like his wife Lisa. They were both Canadian and spoke in a clean, polished English. There was something of an accent, but primarily it was the lack of a Southern accent that framed their speech.

"Need any help?" Reece said. The copter was bigger up close.

"You know about helicopters?" Terry asked, resting on top of his machine as if it were a giant motorcycle.

"I can't remember if I invented them or not," he said. "Oh, wait, no, I invented the artificial heart, sorry."

"Same thing," Terry said, making a move to clamber down the opposite side where the large cargo door stood open.

Reece walked around and watched Terry slip to the ground, fold a bundle of straps inside, and secure the cargo door. Reece noticed what looked like a huge blue waterbed mattress, hidden behind the shed near the pad. It quivered in the wind. "Fuel in there?"

"Yep."

"Nice machine...Are you the main guy?"

"I'm the only guy." Terry walked around the helicopter, touching and looking at things Reece couldn't discern.

Reece had already developed a romantic notion of helicopters, especially the air-splitting sound, like wood being chopped far away, the sound faint, then clear, then louder and louder until it consumed everything.

They chatted for a minute or two, and Terry walked back to his house, a two-room tin shack with a cement floor that he shared with Lisa. Reece trotted to the dining house. He pushed inside, glad to be out of the wind, and closed the heavy door. The wind whistled through the pole rafters, but it was much warmer inside. Everyone except Mrs. Summiton had spaced themselves evenly along the benches. The obvious place to go was at the end of the nearest table to where his folding chair had been moved. Duckie sat to one side and Lisa on the other. On the table were the canned cheese, sliced bread, oranges, and bananas.

A woman he hadn't noticed before motioned for him to come and sit beside her. He wondered if the prayer had been said as he walked to the second table and eased into the space made by the older lady with flowing silver hair. She seemed very old, he thought, but very healthy too. She had a broad smile and large white teeth that looked like dentures. He imagined she had been in Africa most of her life. Could she be seventy, maybe eighty?

"I'm Reece," he said.

Dr. Summiton sat to his left. He had been speaking with the woman before Reece sat down and moved over in a series of small scoots.

"I'm Lenore Thurmond," she said. "My husband is Dr. John Thurmond. He's in Nairobi for a couple of weeks." She spoke softly and precisely. She was from the South, but he couldn't quite place her, maybe South Carolina?

She seemed sincere, long-suffering, but an edge of privilege dallied around her face. She was a nurse, she explained, retired in theory, but like most retired missionaries, found life back home dull.

Mrs. Summiton placed big bowls of boiled potatoes in broth on the tables. There was no salt or pepper. Reece put a slice of bread on the bottom of his cracked bowl. Growing up, he liked potato broth on bread. The cheese was good. He was hungry. Dr. Guthrie and Alene sat across from him. Alene made stabs at small talk with the two doctors, ignoring Reece. Alene was thin with a long neck, golden skin, and a neat, squarish haircut. In the right clothes, he could have walked onto the set of an old *Happy Days* rerun and fit right in. Reece pushed a few potatoes around his bowl as if facing a dose of medicine. Dr. Guthrie dominated the table with his loud voice and guffaws. Dr. Summiton seemed to be his straight man. The conversation revolved not around famines or disease, but *Andy Griffith* reruns and the intricacies of apple cider.

Terry walked in and grabbed Alene by the shoulder. Alene tried to stand but sat back down. Terry had placed a bottle on the table, which drew everyone's attention. From across the room, Lisa yelled, "Don't do it!"

After shaving a bald patch around the five-inch open wound, Emma soaked the split skin with peroxide. An angry foam grew into a bubbly meringue. She lathered on Betadine, dotting out bits of gravel with the gauze. The man whispered to Isaac.

"He is wanting murphy," said Isaac. "He is to fear infection."

"Oh, Lord," said Emma. "Don't worry, he'll get his murphy."

Isaac reassured the patient that his injection was forthcoming. The man whispered his thanks and smiled.

"We'll have this one wrapped up in a jiffy," said Emma. "There's an old woman at the back of the line—"

The sound of grinding gears, shouts of a herd boy, and goats bleating came from beyond the fence. An old jeep carrying three more patients parted the herd of goats. The lady on the mule had died and was being taken to AK, where she was from. The other dead were from towns between AK and Addis, Lemi and Mookaturi, and the bodies would have to find their way back as best they could. A few had brushed themselves off and continued on foot. A jeep traveled the tortuous road from Alem Ketema that ended in Godo every few days, ferrying people to and from the outpost bus stop in AK, which was as far as the buses from Addis could travel due to roads and fuel. The twenty-six-mile ride between AK and Godo cost twenty birr one way and was quite the luxury, being the cost of a small sheep.

Emma was hungry. "Isaac, can you get me a famine

biscuit?" UNICEF donated the high-protein, high-carb crackers. The gate guard brought the news, just as Emma opened the suture kit.

"Tell them to come on in," said Emma. "Can they walk?" She took a packet of famine biscuits from Isaac. "See if you can help the others while I finish here." One thing was positive. Flies did not care for the Betadine, a syrupy, brown iodine solution. "First, though, open another four-by-four for me."

In came the first victim, a woman of thirty-five in a bright print dress. Her cheek was bloody, having dripped and dried on her neck, and she held an arm close to her body. The patients waiting in the sun murmured, half in wonder and half from worry that their spots in line were slipping away.

Emma finished cleaning the man's wound and glanced over her shoulder. "Dammit, I need Afewerki." She wondered when this new guy Rice was coming. This would have been a great welcome for him. Without lidocaine to deaden the suture area, she dipped the curved needle into the skin and got to work. "Isaac, just sit her in the best shade we have. She'll have to wait. Let's see what the other two look like. Lord, have mercy..."

Through the gate hopped a man without pants. From twenty feet away, Emma could tell that a loop of his intestine had forced its way into his scrotum. His golden skin looked very pale. He held on to the driver of the Land Cruiser for dear life, as if they were connected. He moaned with each step.

"Jesus."

Emma let Isaac take charge for a few minutes and

focused on the job in front of her. The third accident victim had flash burns to his hands and chest and walked zombie-like into the growing melee of human suffering. He sat on a biscuit tin and held his hands out in front of him, still in disbelief.

With the clinic stabilized, but still with a long line of patients to care for, Emma caught her breath, ate another famine biscuit, and drank some filtered water she had brought in one of the Icelandic IV bottles. Above Godo, hooded vultures soared the great currents from the valley below. There was always a goat or sheep carcass somewhere to pick, having become lost and ripped apart by hyenas the previous night.

The poor guy with his intestine crowding his testicles would be on standby for the next helicopter flight out. It could be a two-day wait at most until Terry returned, or a bouncing ride back to AK in a jeep. The Mission frowned on the nurses sending patients to Addis, but there was nothing she could do for the man. The danger was that the extreme herniation would constrict and kill off a loop of gut. The intervention required was surgical. The man with powder and flesh burns was treated with Silvadene and antibiotics. He would be okay, but his hands would be useless for perhaps weeks. Despite the urgency of the accident and its casualties, Emma was eager to get to the old woman with the long-suffering face. She looked ancient, but Emma guessed she was only in her early sixties.

While Emma hurried among the sick and wounded, Barra had one of the daily laborers fetch four of the gallon cans of soybean oil, which lay stacked in a pile between the helipad and the warehouse. It was indeed a ransom for Afewerki, but Barra knew it was the most expedient course. He knew Emma would disapprove.

Mariam was still with Afewerki, shielding him with the umbrella, having been given a short break by Afewerki's mother. Afewerki's father, Nigussie, was at home, recovering beneath the thatched roof, lying on his bed, sipping homemade katikala, an Ethiopian vodka. He always slept outside the hut with the Preduzece rifle, watching over the compound, protecting it from thieves and warding off possible attacks by hyenas on the animals penned at night.

Emma took a deep breath and looked around, just to make sure there was not some human fire that needed extinguishing. She pressed her hand to the wall and arched to relieve the stress in her lower back. Lunch had come and gone, but there was plenty of work left to do before dinner. "Isaac, go outside and bring the old woman at the end of the line inside." She walked with him to the gate and pointed her out. She counted the short line inside the gate, eight, and then eighteen more outside, stretching up the hill. Large rocks had been moved close to the fence as seating. The path was wide, but there was no shade as the sun was beginning its descent into the west.

While Isaac helped the old woman to stand, Emma untucked her scrub top and filled it with packets of famine biscuits. She went down the line, handing them to pairs of grateful hands. Some would be eaten, others sold at market. She noticed one of the mothers looking at her feet. She looked nauseous, perhaps dehydrated from waiting in the sun. While the old woman made her way ever so slowly, Emma ran and gave a cup of water to the faint mother, her child hiding, sleeping on her back beneath a swath of cloth.

"Amenseganolo," she said.

"You're welcome," said Emma.

Afewerki walked into the compound, a weary look on his face.

"Afewerki!"

Mariam followed him, smiling his shy smile.

"You're free. How did you do it?" She took the old woman by the arm and helped her into the clinic.

"It is God's will for me to be free."

"Well, whatever works," said Emma. "We've had a heck of a day, and I need you to go down the line and see who needs worm meds, who has diarrhea, and if anyone needs my attention right away. Okay?"

"Yes, Emma. You have been working hard, but this line is always the same. Some are coming just to sit so they do not have to work."

"I know you say that, but I still have to see everyone. I can't turn them away."

"Some are taking advantage."

Emma stood over the old, stooped woman who was busy smoothing down her dress with frail hands charred black in patches from handling hot coals. She smelled of smoke and pepper spice. "Mendeno, mama?" she asked the old woman.

"It is her tooth," said Afewerki.

Emma noticed the swelling below her ear. "Ugh, teeth." Emma opened her mouth wide and motioned for the woman to do the same.

The dry mouth opened just enough for Emma to glimpse inside. A foul odor caught her breath. "Whew!"

Afewerki fanned the air and gagged. "Oh, my goodness! Such a smell."

The old woman tried to laugh but then winced. A tear escaped the corner of her eye. Flies darted among the folds of her clothing.

"Alene loves it," Terry said of the hot pepper concoction in the bottle. It was his take on the local berbere mix, the spice that flooded all dishes and made the top of Reece's head sweat. Terry mixed it with water, soybean oil, salt, and garlic.

"He can't eat these plain potatoes. Or what do you call them, Dr. Guthrie..." Terry looked at Dr. Guthrie. "...taters?" He laughed and left the sauce, which was in a re-used Merti ketchup bottle.

A gust of wind slammed something into the side of the building. Lenore jumped. The light had faded enough to light two kerosene lanterns, which hissed and chased the darkness into the corners with a reddish light. Dr. Guthrie took the hot sauce and sprinkled a few drops on his potatoes like blood. He handed it to Alene with a knowing look as Dr. Summiton proclaimed his wholehearted disinterest. He mentioned that tolerating hot sauce was not one of his gifts.

Dr. Guthrie looked at Reece, "Set you on fire, son."

Alene focused on the bottle and his potatoes, pouring what Reece thought was deadly into the bowl. Reece's mouth winced just thinking about it. The potatoes on bread were a bit bland, but tasted good. Alene made approving noises, looking at Terry after each bite to assure him that a good deed had been done. Alene proffered the bottle his way, and Reece took it, looking at the label, interested in what it used to be.

"That's a ketchup bottle, Ethiopian ketchup if you can

believe it," said Dr. Guthrie.

Reece nodded and leaked the sauce on his potatoes, somewhere between Dr. Guthrie's dribbles and Alene's globs. The pepper left the potatoes and wafted toward Reece, swaddling his head in a cloud of spice. His mouth watered, and he ate a piece of cheese. He realized he had no cup and asked Lenore to pass him one of the orange plastic mugs. He filled it with water from a plastic pitcher and took a bite of potato. The taste was plain at first, but then spread like a chemical burn around his tongue. His eyebrows took a few seconds to fill with sweat. "Wow."

It came up that Duckie had lost an eye, that she had a glass eye. Reece wished he were sitting at the other table, having never met a one-eyed Canadian named Duckie. He answered all of Lenore's questions about where he was from, what he thought so far, and so on. She was very nice, grandmotherly, and he detected that undercurrent of Christ-centered worshipfulness that possessed the more devout among them. He imagined she began and ended her day with scripture and prayer, that she kept a prayer list more extensive than his own.

Lisa and Terry left first. When Terry opened the door, a gush of wind cleared out the accumulated warmth. The lanterns swayed, casting a chaos of shadows around the room. Duckie left next, calling out goodnight to everyone. Reece decided it would be best to find his room, collect his thoughts, and write a letter to Kristin.

"Any idea where I will sleep?" Reece directed his question at Dr. Guthrie, who was standing.

"Yep," he replied. "Alene, can you show Reece here to one of the beds?" Mrs. Summiton was boiling water for tea on the stove.

"Oh yes," said Alene in a bubbly way. "You going now?"

"Yeah, if that's okay," said Reece, standing, stretching. He wondered how he would cut his hair, and who cut Alene's hair. He imagined Dr. Guthrie's wife, Livvy, cut his hair, and she did.

The outhouse, the shintabet, stood leaning into the wind, off by itself down the hill from the main cluster of buildings. A well-worn path led there through the scudding darkness, weirdly coming and going as thick clouds passed between the earth and a sliver of moon. The sky was heavy with stars. He felt one would squeeze out and fall cold and brilliant into his hands. There was no toilet paper in the outhouse, but he would learn to bring his own. The narrow, closet-like space, shrouded in corrugated tin with a slanted tin roof, groaned in the cold, dry wind. A toilet seat had been glued, nailed, cemented, he couldn't tell, into a bench with a hole in it. The smell of human waste was godawful and kept his visit to a minimum. He imagined scorpions and millipedes sifting through the mess below. From stories told by his grandfather, he knew that black widow spiders liked to gather around the toilet seats of the old country outhouses and bite unsuspecting genitals. He just held it and only urinated, hoping he could find his way back to his small but clean room with the narrow bed and a stack of Mennonite blankets on a table.

Despite a nagging headache and the sensation of food solidifying in his stomach, Reece slept well until sunrise. He could hear an occasional rooster crying in the distance, thought he heard the sounds of cattle lowing as well, and peeled the colorful blankets to the foot of the springy bed. Odds and ends of sound he did not recognize worked on his imagination, occasional banging sounds, animal sounds, the squeak of metal against metal. A group of birds landed on the tin roof, their little toenails scratching and scritching. He heard cooing sounds and figured they were doves. Reece had to pee again and dreaded lumbering down to the toilet. He looked around for an alternative but couldn't think of anything. A bottle of water with a dull red stopper sat on the wooden stool beside his bed. He tilted his head back and examined the simple headboard. Lines of wax from candles past ran down the veneered wood. He had meant to read a Bible passage, but the letter to Kristin had exhausted him.

Reece turned on his side, drawing his knees to his chest to relieve the pressure on his bladder. The wall looked like mud that had been painted white. Tin roofing sheathed the outside walls. His drawstring overnight bag sat on the rough cement floor. He wondered about bathing. He felt he needed to do something, at least brush his teeth, throw some water on his face. Everyone else seemed so well-groomed, except maybe for Terry. He thought he could hear voices and grunting and turned over.

He managed that for another forty-five minutes and couldn't bear it any longer. He had to get up and do something. What it was, he wasn't exactly sure. Maybe breakfast would be cooking. Maybe Terry would be working on the helicopter. He was supposed to go to Godo, right? How would that turn out? What was Emma like? Who would go with him? Would he spend the night? But his work permit hadn't yet been finalized, right? He hastily made up the bed, folded the blankets as he had found them. Each one had a small hand-sewn label, "A gift from Mennonite Missions, Manitoba, Ontario, Canada." Thus far, the Canadians were giving the Southern Baptists a run for their money, he thought.

Breakfast was biscuits, pretty good biscuits, but flat due to the altitude. A gravy, though, made from stew powder shipped from Ireland, turned the biscuits into a real meal. Reece examined a clear plastic bag of the powder, just flour, salt, seasoning, a few dried peas in there. The people didn't quite know what to do with it, Dr. Guthrie explained, as half the group from the night before ate biscuits and drank tiny glasses of fresh squeezed lemonade.

"The Polish have been helping out?" asked Reece. Where the plane had landed was called the Polish Airfield.

"They were here at the beginning," said Dr. Guthrie. "They left about six months ago, moved their operations up country, and have a large base near the old airport in Addis." He insinuated that perhaps a few children with Polish blood would soon be found scampering around the town.

Poland was as much of a mystery to Reece as Ethiopia or Iceland. He imagined thin soldiers with wispy blond hair, speaking broken English, wearing old glasses, carting around thick history books.

Duckie never reappeared. She was working with a Canadian relief group, Reece learned, and would be leaving for parts unknown that day. The Spanglers, Terry and Lisa, did not work directly for the Baptists. Terry was a freelance pilot contracted through the RRC network to work with the Baptists. His sole job was to take supplies from AK to the five Baptist relief centers in the area. He also flew passengers from AK to Addis and to the stations. AK had one of the few "hospitals" in the area. The Mission provided the four-bed ward with medical supplies. Terry waltzed in and took a plastic cup, filled it with biscuit and gravy, and went back out.

"Make sure you have your stuff ready to go, although it may be around noon before he's ready," said Dr. Guthrie, referring to Terry. "You'll meet the whole group in Godo, a good group of guys working with Emma. She's a pistol."

"How long will I be there?" Reece felt bloated. A patch of dry skin floated on the end of Dr. Guthrie's sunburned nose. This Emma was attaining legendary status as the days went by.

"As long as it takes Terry to fly back, pick up a load, and then come back to get you. Maybe a couple of hours, three, maybe four." Dr. Guthrie had a cattle clinic scheduled in a nearby field, and a jeep was being loaded with supplies for him. He belched and wished Reece good luck.

On October 16, 1980, George Hennard drove a Ford Ranger pickup into the dining room of a Luby's restaurant in Killeen, Texas. He killed twenty-three people with a couple of pistols and then shot himself in the head, all about half a mile from the little, pink brick house Reece Myers lived in during high school.

With a tongue depressor and flashlight, Emma got a better look at the old woman's rotting molar. It looked brown and pulpy on top with a black stripe down the side where it had cracked. The surrounding gum was red and swollen.

"Yikes," said Emma. "Ask her if it's loose."

Afewerki interpreted. "Yes, it will come out soon, she is saying, but the pain is too much for her."

"Do you think we should try to pull it out?"

"Perhaps it would be best if a dentist—"

"But there is no dentist. Ask her if I can touch it." She palpated the woman's neck. "Lymph nodes as big as quail eggs on this side."

The old woman nodded and grimaced, preparing for the bolt of pain that would ensue. "She is ready," said Afewerki. "Careful, she does not bite you."

Emma leaned over the woman and motioned for her to open wide, and looked again. "I'm going to give it a go. I can get a pretty good grip." She pulled a pair of latex gloves from a box and snapped them on. Sunlight-filtered dust rained down from insects burrowing into the rafter poles. A couple of curious onlookers peered through the door, eager to see what would happen next. "Open up a gauze pad for me." She took a deep breath. The woman's breath smelled like a clogged drain.

Emma took the gauze pad and opened her mouth wide. The old woman laughed for a moment and then followed suit. Her eyes crinkled, anticipating the gunshot in her mouth. Emma reached in, and the woman's front teeth closed on her fingers. "Dang!"

Afewerki's brow beaded with sweat. "You must put something between her teeth," he said. "To keep her from biting. She is biting you." He laughed.

"Can they pull teeth in the government clinic?"

"Oh yes. Atakabura pulls many teeth," said Afewerki

The old woman moaned and put her hand to her swollen jaw.

Emma wadded five gauze pads and made a wedge to hold open the woman's jaw. "This should help."

The woman gagged and turned her head. Tears came to her eyes.

"It's okay, Mama. It's okay." Emma slid her fingers, gripping the pad inside. An odor of rotting meat flushed her face. She pinched the tooth with the gauze, and the woman croaked a scream. "Holy cow." Emma held the tooth, roots and all, dripping with thick yellow pus for Afewerki to see. "Damn. Excuse me."

The old woman spat on the floor, blood and pus, wiping her mouth with a gentle touch. She muttered, "Xavier meskin," and lifted her eyes toward the great unknown in thanks.

"She is thanking God," said Afewerki.

"I am, too," said Emma. "It felt like pulling a piece of chalk out of mud. Lord, now we have to get her to rinse with some saline and get her on antibiotics. I'm sure she wants a murphy. I can feel it."

"Oh yes, that will make her very happy," said Afewerki.

Many heads buzzing with flies and crowding the doorway smiled as if in agreement.

After finishing with her last patient around six p.m., Emma made a trip to the shelter filled with moms and kids recovering from a variety of ailments. Most were merely homeless, husbandless, stragglers from the north who had arrived on the brink of starvation. The poor man with his intestine draped into his scrotum was staying there, huddled by himself, sitting on a stone. The pit toilets stunk to high heaven, but everyone was doing the best they could. Emma made her rounds, fascinated by the little community knit together by two long, tin-roofed buildings with dirt floors. Mothers nursed. Kids romped naked. A fire in the cookhouse billowed smoke through the door. Emma's stomach rumbled, and she wound her way back downhill past the Orthodox church and to living quarters.

Dinner was celebratory, with Afewerki's night in jail being the subject of conversation. There were no cells there, just an open dirt-floored room with grain bags to sleep on. A single chamber pot served the inmates, whether they were two or twenty, lending the large room, by virtue of repeated spillage, a rank air of human waste. His mother had passed food over the fence to his jailers, so no meals were missed, but he'd had to share it with the other two men awaiting trials in AK. One had murdered a man, shot him to death in revenge for killing his brother over a stolen donkey. The other had been charged with stealing, just as Afewerki had been. The jail door was nothing more than corrugated tin on hinges, but it was the armed guard and his orders to shoot that kept prisoners at bay.

Back inside her little one-room house, with a belly full of peppery, fried goat meat, Emma boiled a pot of water to wash with. The extreme darkness gave a single candle the power to fill a corner with light sufficient to bathe and prepare for sleep. In the night chill, she undressed and ran the hot washcloth across her body. The warmth was luxurious, and she felt as if indulging a secret pleasure.

Scratching, scurrying noises came from between the plastic and the walls. She had glimpsed the creature, a sleek mouse or mole with a long proboscis like a miniature elephant trunk. It sometimes woke her at night, scuffling in and around her cot, but she couldn't imagine that it would bite her, plus it was cute.

She slipped into a clean pair of scrubs and put another pot of water on to boil. Every night, she made a cup of hot tea for Irigit to help him ease into the dark watch over the compound. She liked his cheerfulness. She could hear him humming in his spot near the gate.

She stubbed her toe on the small table. "Ah!" Hot wax from the candle dripped onto her foot. "Oh!"

"Abet?" Irigit was outside her door in an instant. He rattled off a long passage of concern in Amharic.

"I'm okay. Ishi. No worries. I'll have your tea in a minute." Soon, she opened the door. Irigit wore his funny little hat, a round, floppy affair stitched together from scraps. His teeth flashed white, a wrap around his shoulders and chin.

She poured the hot water into an orange cup, filled the bottom with half an inch of yellow sugar, and dropped in a bag of Ethiopian black shai. Steam whispered from the cup in her hands. "Here you go. Shai. Hot. Hot."

Irigit received the tea and bowed his head. "Amenseganolo," he said.

"Good night."

Emma closed the door, latched the latch, and decided to read before attempting to write a letter to her mom. The mouse with the long nose rustled in the wall. Her cot springs squeaked. The candle flame wavered in slow motion, casting bulbous shadows onto the walls.

Mrs. Summiton stepped out to the rain barrel for water to heat and wash dishes. Her husband lounged outside in a chair, soaking up the early morning sun, wearing a big straw hat and blue jeans. Reece helped tidy up, scraping food into a small metal bucket and stacking dishes for Mrs. Summiton. She smiled but said nothing, so Reece wandered outside, his mind on the dreadful shintabet. He walked that way and saw Lenore coming out, looking fresh and "light" as his grandfather would say. He wondered how his grandparents were doing, what they were up to. Horace had grown up half-starved during the Great Depression and spent his whole life running from poverty. Dora had too, but she seemed to have forgotten it, unlike Horace. If she kept anything from her days of hardship, it was a cutting, no-nonsense sense of humor. "Well, you've gained some weight," she'd said to his fiancée Kristin more than once.

Reece lingered a minute or two, allowing Lenore her privacy and space, and then walked stiffly toward the shack-like apparition. Growing up, he'd had no brothers or sisters to fight with over a toilet, tub, or sink, and as an only child, his wall of privacy rivaled that of God. During high school, he never, not once, entered the restrooms there. As he reached for the crude handle, he remembered again that he had no toilet paper. Inside—flies clinging and jumping along the flimsy metal walls like tiny black magnets—he cursed himself and took solace that he only had to pee. His whole body felt bloated. He heard the helicopter, long blades swiping the air.

To his room he walked, feeling "blah" as he would write Kristin that night. He couldn't remember if he needed to take his overnight bag to Godo, then remembered that he didn't. He wondered if he needed money or bottled water. Should he take his passport? The helicopter's engine took on a sound of readiness, the surrounding air pressurized, and he felt a mild panic as he hurried to the helipad. Carrying hundred-pound bags of grain from the warehouse, a group of five laborers in tattered farmers' clothes dropped their heavy loads on top of a large cargo net sprawled on the ground. Terry idled the helicopter back to something less urgent and jumped out, leaving the cockpit empty. Reece guessed there were forty bags of grain in the net, along with an assortment of tins and boxes.

"You ready?" asked Terry.

Reece wondered what Terry's wife, Lisa, did all day. "Yeah." Reece stood there waiting for further instructions.

"Okay, maybe five minutes." Terry grabbed a hook from the helipad shack and crawled beneath the trembling helicopter.

Reece walked around the perimeter, watching the workers strain beneath their loads, getting a second cargo net ready. The men were hard workers, good-humored, talked loudly among themselves, and helped one another hoist the heavy bags. Their skinny legs burst with pure muscle under the weight, all of them shouldering two bags for the 150-foot journey from the warehouse. Sweat drenched their faces, which fascinated Reece. They were looks of hardship, but not bitterness, a kind of "bring it on" practicality without the chutzpah. They ignored Reece. He wanted to feel the weight of the bags. He loved to labor and sweat. Most people thought him skinny, although he felt soft and fat among the Ethiopians, especially these tough country farmers.

Friday was ration day, and among the first patients of the day was the man with burned hands, returning for his first dressing change. Emma unwound the dirty gauze impregnated with silver sulfadiazine. The denuded skin was pink and marbled where the outer layers had peeled away, a thorough second-degree burn. He held his hands out like wooden claws as she applied more of the ointment with a clean tongue depressor. He spoke to Afewerki, who interpreted for Emma as she re-wrapped his hands.

"He is worried for his crops. It is the time of the rains, and he is to sow his crops of teff and corn. But how can he with his hands becoming useless?"

"The skin should be back in a month or so. Can he wait that long?"

"He must plow very soon. Perhaps he will hire someone. He has no son, only daughters who fetch the water and care for the chickens."

The man lowered his eyes and rattled off an "*Ai yi yi.*"

"In a week or so, we'll switch from the silver sulfadiazine to something that'll help the skin to granulate and grow back. We have tubes of Preparation H, which is perfect. Good for hemorrhoids and burns. Works miracles on burns."

Afewerki nodded, translating for the man. "He is thankful to God. He thinks there must be some evil spirit that is troubling his life."

"The devil," said Emma.

"Yes, the devil."

"Always the devil. We'll see him back here again tomorrow, tell him. Make sure he knows we're only here before lunch, though."

The man took off his tattered hat and bowed his head in appreciation. Big drops of rain fell on the tin roof for forty seconds and then stopped. An instant aroma of humid, earthy steam rose from the hot ground and swaddled the clinic.

"He is saying he will bring you something," said Afewerki. "A gift."

"Tell him, no gifts. This is my job."

The man gestured with his bandaged hands, thumbs protruding. He must bring the gift, he insisted, a special gift for Emma.

"If he has to," said Emma. "I'm sure we can use whatever it is."

The man bowed again and stepped down from the clinic, bare feet to the rocky dirt pocked with the brief splashes of water from the sky. As quickly as he exited, in came the next patient, a woman with a small child. The child had yellow diarrhea. Emma sighed. Diarrhea that still had some color to it was usually a good sign. There had been an outbreak of cholera in Godo the previous year. Afewerki had described many people dying, as many as one hundred. Death by diarrhea and vomiting. The rocky mounds of the mass graves could be seen downhill from the clinic compound. Rumors that the outbreak had been caused by the sexual trespasses of the Icelandic team had contributed to their departure, that and their extreme curiosity in religious artifacts held in the churches and caves in the area.

The vague strum of the helicopter announced that Terry would be there soon. Isaac sent out the call for his team of daily laborers. Mariam made his way to the clinic from the market area. Barra brushed his teeth, rinsed noisily, stuck his head into the cooking house, and barked at Misrak to make sure that lunch was ready on time.

"Jump in!" said Terry.

Reece kept his head low as the warning decal suggested, a simple diagram showing a blade against the neck of a stick man. He internalized the *whumping* sound and sensation of the rotor against the thin, dry air, memorizing it.

The inside seemed smaller than it should be, very cramped. But the forward view, looking slightly up, was much better than that of a small airplane. The view to his side was ample. Below his right foot, through a curved panel of Plexiglas, he could see the gravelly surface of the helipad. Terry dropped a headset in his lap. A button on the floor, foot-controlled, allowed him to talk to Terry, but everything seemed to be one big static and rumble. Terry's voice sounded like it was being shot from a can of shaving cream.

Terry fiddled with switches and performed what Reece assumed was a preflight check. Even sitting still, with the sensation of a Mexican jumping bean vibrating on the hot hood of a muscle car, the copter felt to him like it was under the spell of an invisible gyro. He liked it and took it as a sign that his real adventure would start there in the helicopter. He felt suddenly as if nothing interesting had ever happened to him until then.

Dr. Guthrie was waving and approached, bent over, carrying a sack. Terry swung his door open and reached out for the bag, which contained mail for Godo. Terry handed the bag to Reece, indicating that he should throw it behind them, and he did, straining his shoulder.

The engine climaxed, and the machine eased into the air, turning on a dime. Reece couldn't see Alene standing on top of the grain bags wrapped in the cargo net. Terry hovered over the pile of food, and Alene attached the net to the hook dangling from the copter. Reece watched Terry give a thumbs up and felt the machine rise and struggle with the weight. Within seconds, they were out over the vast valley bottom, the distance from the ground shooting from a hundred feet to over four thousand. Reece heard Terry's garbled voice in his headset. It took Reece a few tries before he mastered the speaking button on the floor.

"How long you here for?" Terry said.

"I don't know."

Terry nodded.

And then Reece imagined Terry said something in regard to Emma. "Emma can't wait to meet you" is what he said. The light blue sky seemed limitless. A tiny white cloud floated far away, like a used cotton ball.

"And of thy mercy cut off mine enemies, and destroy all them that afflict my soul: for I am thy servant." Psalms 143:12

Below, a hazy patchwork of tans, browns, and dull greens, and a riverbed snaked, dry in most places. The helicopter jerked forward through the air. Reece could feel the gravity. The land below was a movie. His life was a movie. Emma was a character in a movie. This was a dream, a dream in which he watched a movie.

He looked at Terry, silent now. "Is she at Godo?" he said. He felt silly saying Godo like it was a Hobbit village.

It seemed made up.

"Yeah, Godo."

A long silence as they hummed across the massive void below. Reece felt like a plastic football player being propelled along a vibrating piece of thin steel painted to resemble a football field. The game had made no sense to him, even as a child. What was the point? You lined up the plastic players and then turned the little switch to make the playing field vibrate, hum, and buzz. The weighted figures dispersed, going in all directions, some falling over.

"I can't wait to meet her," Reece said.

The thirty-minute flight continued in relative silence, with a few sights pointed out by Terry, the unseen feeding stations at Rabel in one direction, the feeding station at Meranya in another. Reece's stomach burned. His headache bordered on bad. The land dropped as they crossed two small rivers in succession, both with water pooled in scattered bends and hollows. Fenced compounds of five and six thatched huts appeared here and there, the land worked into rhomboids around them. Reece felt an ancient orderliness, a dormant spirit ready to reach out and slap them from the sky should the need arise. A road below, people on the road, a mule or a horse, a flock of small animals scattering like rings of a rock into a still pond.

In the near distance, on the brow of a yellowish slope, some green splotches, a ridge maybe, the low profile of a village, a town. "Godo," Reece heard Terry say. As the distance between the ground and the blades diminished, the machine seemed to breathe harder as it struggled forward. Reece tried to take it all in, rocks everywhere, a group of people gathering in front of what looked to be another warehouse constructed of hundreds of sheets of corrugated tin roofing. Dirt lanes, footpaths, thatched roofs, tin roofs, the dryness of it all, the dust rising to meet them as the machine twirled down, hovering as someone below disengaged the cargo net. They shot into the air and circled back around to a crude version of the helipad in AK. They were in a large, fenced compound on a steep, rocky slope.

Terry stayed in the helicopter. A line of laborers was making short order of the pile of grain bags, disappearing with their loads into the dark mouth of the leaning warehouse, backs stooped, calves straining. The clinic, a shorter, lower, tin-roofed building made of poles and large sticks, but without the mud chinking, sat to the right of the warehouse. In a clearing, a chaos of barrels and large olive-drab tins and black plastic sheeting lay as if wadded in a giant fist. Four young men were approaching the helicopter. Terry was saying something. He imitated how Reece should open his door, but first Reece had to disentangle himself from the seat's shoulder and lap belt matrix.

"Be back in two hours, three maybe," Terry shouted at Reece, holding up his fingers.

Emma glanced out the door at the hubbub. The child with diarrhea also had tapeworms. She saw a lanky guy about her age jump down from the copter. *Rice.* Afewerki stepped outside.

Reece ducked, hunched, walked to the edge of the warm rocky platform, and hopped down the foot or so onto the ground. He walked into a semicircle of four young men, all with wide smiles. The gasoline-infused backwash from the helicopter whipped their clothes as the group made its way to level ground near the clinic. Inside the doorway stood Emma. The first thing Reece noticed was her mischievous, lopsided smile. She waved at him. He waved back. One from the group ran to the helicopter, and everyone watched as Terry threw the mailbag out of the door. Isaac, thin, fuzzy beard, and wide-set eyes, grabbed it.

What these cheerful young men knew about him, Reece hadn't a clue. The sounds of the place came into focus as the helicopter faded into the distance. The workers hefting grain were distracted by Reece, watching him. Reece heard bells, tinkling bells, a rooster crowing, the warehouse roof groaning and popping in the heat, people murmuring, something like a gunshot in the distance.

"We are welcoming you," said Isaac in his slow English. He wore his jumpsuit and a pair of wire-frame glasses, like a studious mechanic might wear, and held the mailbag.

"Are you resting?" asked Mariam, tall and close-shaven. He was very shy but neatly dressed in a button-up, short-sleeve shirt, slacks, and Western sandals.

Emma watched the boy chew and swallow his niclosamide, then stepped down from the clinic door. "Rice!" she said, and a hug of some sort passed between them. "Is your name really Rice?" Emma suspected it was one of those misunderstandings, like the toilet seat that was cemented into the floor of her personal outhouse.

Reece shook hands with a small, very dark man with wide-open eyes. He was Barra, he said, and grinned, laughing. Reece turned his attention back to Emma. "It's Reece, like the peanut butter cup."

"Aha," said Emma. "I should have known."

The smells impressed themselves on Reece. Body odor. A sweet smell—*Someone must be wearing cologne.* The smell of leather, dust, hot metal. A vague vomit smell from somewhere. Reece could still hear the helicopter throbbing in the sky.

A short, stocky young man, about Reece's age, with a small mustache, approached. He seemed very excited and grabbed Reece's hand with vigor. "You have come!" He spoke with enthusiasm.

"I'm Reece," he said and gazed at his new friend.

"Oh, I am Afewerki."

Reece nodded, not sure what to do next. There was work to be done, he sensed, and after ten minutes of sincere pleasantries, the little party in the sun dispersed, leaving Reece with Afewerki and Emma. "Ferenj!" said a little boy peeking from beneath his mother's leather carrier.

Reece followed Emma and put his head in the clinic, drawing a look of surprise from a young mother holding a baby boy naked from the waist down. The room smelled of milk and smoke. A leather carrier sewn with dozens of small bells hung from her waist. Crooked shelves with a variety of bottles and tins. Benches made from rough boards laid across large rectangular steel cans. No lights, just the light filtering through the walls and a piece of corrugated, green fiberglass placed on the roof.

"What do you think?" Emma pulled back her dirty-blonde hair and gave it a fluff, making it look wild.

"Wow." Reece was speechless. He would be working with Emma in this clinic, caring for the sick and wounded. "I've heard a lot about you."

"How long are you here for? I had no idea you were coming today. Otherwise, I would have been ready, maybe to take you on a little tour. The line out there is jacked up to Jesus like usual."

Reece laughed. "How many patients per day?" He gazed at the mother and child in awe. The people were real. This was where the work started. They looked thin but not starved. But the worst was over, he had come to understand.

"Depends. Forty on a slim day, a hundred on ration days."

Afewerki smiled, nodding at the magnitude of work to be done each day.

"Wow." Working in hospitals, he had been responsible for only one or two critically ill patients at a time.

"Why don't I let the guys show you around. How long are you here for?"

"Terry said two to three hours. I don't have a watch, though."

"Don't worry about that, just listen for the helicopter and come back when you hear it." She asked Afewerki,

Isaac, and Barra to take him to see the living quarters. Mariam would stay and translate for her. His English was the weakest, but passable.

Reece followed his guides through the heavy, wooden door framed into the fence built of poles and tin sheeting. Downhill, a rough and wide dirt road curved and disappeared. Within seconds, a pack of children gathered, all dressed in rags, smiling, flies clinging to their eyes and noses. "Ferenj! Ferenj!" they shouted over and over. Afewerki said something to them in a growly voice, but they paid him no mind. Barra, though, stiffened and hurled a few stern words at them. The kids bought it, briefly, losing their smiles and skirting away, but within seconds were back at their happy dance.

Up the hill stretched the clinic line of thirty deep. The sick and wounded squatted on their haunches, shading their eyes from the sun. An old man shielded himself with an ancient umbrella. Old and young women sat with children strapped to their backs or in their laps. A young man with blank eyes. *First come, first served,* thought Reece. The hot sun focused on top of his head, pushing him down as he walked up a very steep hill. Family compounds, walled in one way or another, lined the wide dirt path.

"You have come from Ah-la-ba-ma? Dr. Guthrie is from Ah-la-ba-ma." Isaac spoke deliberately, almost slurring his words.

"Yes, Alabama," Reece replied.

"Ah-la-ba-ma," Isaac said, and Reece nodded. The three Ethiopians all watched Reece as they plodded uphill, as if he might fall over, the path narrowing to the width of an alley.

Reece took in the sights, but nothing seemed particularly real. Alem Ketema was rural, but Godo was very rural. He was catching the surface of things, and the images slid without meaning into the cracks and pockets of his brain. He felt as if he were at an amusement park, in an endless line, inching his way toward a ride that spins and jerks.

They topped the incline. There were more children, and they seemed to know he was coming. Several grabbed his hand, but Barra shooed them away, scolding them harshly. "Get away, you little brat. Your hands are filthy!" he seemed to say.

"We are working together!" Afewerki spoke with relish and laughed.

"Are you a nurse, too?" asked Reece. Afewerki was short, maybe five-five, but proportioned, thin. He had a quick smile.

"Oh, no, no, no," he said, shaking his head. "I am your interpreter. Emma's interpreter."

"Well, glad to meet you." He stopped and shook Afewerki's hand, wondering why he was doing that. Afewerki's English was good, stilted in a musical way. His hair was closely cut, almost shaved. "Well, you will have to teach me many things," he told Afewerki.

"Yes, yes, and I will have many questions." His voice had dropped in volume and taken on a dreamlike quality.

Many people passed them on the path as they followed a high wall made of tin roofing nailed to poles driven into the ground. Tall, thin men with tightly muscled black legs. Reece's companions murmured greetings to everyone they met. Unaware of the complexity of greetings regarding gender and age, Reece made do with the generic "Tenesteling" for hello and the Italian "Ciao" for goodbye.

The gate squawked and screeched as it opened inward to the tug of the guard inside. It was Ketow, and he grinned broadly. He usually took Irigit's place in the daytime. He wore the tattered farmer's clothes and a small, round canvas hat with a short floppy brim. Barefoot and armed with a gleaming rifle, he leaned the gun against the crude wall of the compound's cooking hut. Inside the single smoky room, two women, one with the top of her dress pulled off her shoulders and swathed to her waist, were busy cooking the team's lunch, preparing the large round flat sheets of enjera and a spicy wot. A smell of smoke and butter and meat and onion. The women, who cooked and cleaned for the team of four young Ethiopian men and Emma, looked shocked to see Reece standing there, peering in at them. They laughed and clutched one another, covered their mouths, and made loud noises of surprise, the topless one with large golden breasts swinging. He didn't catch their names, and the group moved on.

The grassy compound held five structures. Isaac, Mariam, and Barra each had a single room in the long, narrow, tin-roofed building. Catty-cornered to that was Emma's tiny white house. A small, round "dining hut" stood in the center of the compound. In the far corner was the rickety outhouse constructed solely for Emma. Next to the cooking shed, perhaps too close, was a plastic-draped shint-abet, a hole over a six-foot-deep pit filled with feces and covered with poles.

"I will live here?" asked Reece. He pointed at Emma's simple house.

"No, that is Emma. You will live with us. Here." He pointed at the second door of the four-room "motel." "We have been waiting for you," said Isaac.

Reece surveyed Emma's house. From the front, it was a square of mud and poles for walls, whitewashed, giving it a smooth but lumpy look. It had a tin roof and a small window. A homemade door stood to the right like the last tooth of an old man. A rain barrel caught water off the roof. They walked around the house, and then Ketow, with the unrequited smile and a small stick in his mouth, produced the key to the padlock on the door.

"You want to see?" asked Barra.

"Sure."

It took a few jerks, but the door swung out. Everyone crowded in, except for Ketow, who could gain and lose interest in a subject with amazing speed. The cement floor and the whitewash made it relatively cool inside. Reece gazed up at the crooked poles. Things he did not expect to see crowded the room. Someone had constructed crude sagging shelves on which sat cans of Italian tomato paste, a box of Knorr bouillon cubes, and unmarked foil packets. A crude wooden table contained a mishmash of pots and pans and plasticware, plain coffee cups, and a few of the orange plastic cups that Reece thought of now as famine cups.

Isaac pointed out the two-burner propane stove and the chest-high propane fridge, which Reece opened and discovered was filled with the Icelandic IV bottles. *She must use them for drinking as well.* A large water filtration device with a ceramic, gravity-flow filter. A small springy fold-up cot where Emma slept. Reece felt like he was intruding.

One wooden chair. Reece was disappointed because he had imagined that the urgency of famine wouldn't allow for such comforts, that he would sleep on the ground, maybe inside a tent if he was lucky. He had had no expectations, other than hardship, and these initial creature comforts disappointed him.

They all stood there in the house, no one sitting, taking turns asking questions.

"Are you guys from Addis?"

Yes, they explained, except for Afewerki, who was from Godo and lived just a compound or two away with his parents and two younger brothers. And Barra, who was from the south.

"Do you like our country?" asked Isaac.

"Yes." Reece said it was stunning and that the people seemed very nice. He wondered if they would show him his room. "How many days a week does everyone work?"

Barra spoke. "Each day except for Sunday, the day of rest, and the special days, and when you are sick, and when you are away, or when there may be a trouble of some sort."

"You are married?" asked Isaac.

"No, not yet. I am engaged." Reece could tell they did not understand "engaged" but felt at a loss for words to explain. He thought he heard the helicopter, and then he didn't. Finally, Isaac suggested they go outside, and then Afewerki insisted they visit the shelter. Barra took leave, saying he had to go.

The path narrowed and continued to climb. Many goats, many roosters—bleating, pleading, crowing, scratching. Reece paused at a large, round thatched building, the town's Orthodox church. No one was there. The church sat amid a slope of large, flat, scattered rocks. At the top of what seemed to be a rounded ridge, two long tin buildings appeared. A few women ran inside. Women inside ran to the doors to peer at the entourage. A smell of urine and feces and smoke. A dozen toddlers and small kids in small groups stared. Some went back to their games, others gravitated toward Reece with large, fly-encrusted smiles. A single guard with a rifle teetered on his feet, chewing qat leaves, smiling sleepily.

Reece failed to ask what the shelter was for, who lived there, for how long, who paid for what, why it smelled so bad, and so on. He stepped around little piles of human waste, nodding and looking out toward the vast valley he had flown across in the helicopter. Everyone seemed to be in good spirits, although he noted a specific lull on the women's faces, as if they had escaped one fire and now could examine their lives for a few moments while God dreamed up their next fiasco.

The group headed back, wandering through small byways, Reece already feeling as if he had lived there all his life, incapable of asking a single pertinent question, just nodding his approval or noting his interest in an old woman loaded down with firewood stacked above her shoulders or a small boy sitting in what probably was mud yesterday, his eyes a mask of flies that moved and wiggled like an animated pair of sunglasses. *God Almighty,* he thought over and over. He was very thirsty.

Reece learned that twice a week, on Wednesday and Friday, the people in the area with ration cards came and stood in long lines to sample the famine relief buffet:

wheat for bread, sorghum for enjera, milk powder to eat like candy, soybean oil for wots, famine biscuits to eat like snack crackers, and then the assorted other foods such as canned cheeses, dried cod, and tomato paste that no one really wanted but took anyway to perhaps sell or barter with. In addition to food, they were entitled to a clinic visit, a second line to navigate in a land where lines had never before existed except for coffins and airline tickets out of the country. The team, as they liked to be called, took care of the details for Emma. She was in charge, but her primary duty was the clinic. Reece would be working alongside her, loaning his knowledge and skill to a worthy cause. He also learned of the team's desire for him to be a spiritual leader of sorts; a Bible study would be nice, Isaac suggested. They liked to sing and, to demonstrate that, sang a rousing Amharic version of a hymn that he knew but to which he couldn't remember the lyrics.

The group wended their way back to the warehouse/clinic compound, rejoining Barra and his flashy smile. The group touted Barra as the singer of singers, and he did indeed seem to flout whatever laws of physics could be involved with quavering one's voice mellifluously. Reece assured them he would prepare some regular study sessions and that, off the top of his head, the Book of the Apostle James should do. They nodded in general agreement but seemed still unused to the idea of the New Testament as a source of comfort, the Christian Orthodoxy having run smoothly on the back of the Old Testament since the fourth century AD.

He poked his head into the clinic. Emma and Mariam were bent over a little girl, attending to her ear, which was infected. "How was it? Make some new friends?" Emma noticed that Reece's jeans were a little tight in the legs. A week or two upcountry would fix that.

"I saw your house, went inside. I hope you don't mind. It's more than I expected. The paths are so steep."

"Yep," said Emma. Peroxide bubbled from the girl's ear.

"Saw the shelter. I didn't realize you had shelters."

"It stays full, mostly moms and kids, a half dozen orphans. I make the rounds up there once a day after clinic is over. If they're sick, they'll come down to the clinic, usually."

Fascinated with the whole shebang, but thirsty, legs aching, head throbbing, a persistent annoying cough tickling his throat, and constipated, Reece willed the helicopter to come, and it did, slowly backing down from the sky with another nest of grain.

"We'll have to catch up when you move in for good." Emma brushed back her hair.

Terry had the copter running. With handshakes all around, Reece stepped onto the runner and opened the passenger door. The downwash felt good, pressing his shirt and parting his hair. Head down, Afewerki handed him a mailbag filled with letters to the team's families and letters from Emma to her mother and her church pastor. Terry gave Reece a thumbs up and handed him three letters, letters from Kristin that had been following him for the past two days. With only an empty net in the cargo bay and a net below swinging a hundred, empty, five-gallon soybean oil cans to be recycled in Addis, Reece and Terry sped across the valley, the helicopter's engine chopping the air.

"Get an eyeful?" asked Terry.

"Enough for now." Reece had no idea really of what had filled his eyes, but they did seem to be full. What seemed real to him most at that moment were the six thousand feet between his feet and the incredible otherworldly earth carving below.

"You'll get used to it," Terry said, static ripping the words apart like cotton candy.

Reece imagined it was his guy way of saying, *Hang in there.* He nodded his head, forgetting to speak.

"What do you think of Emma?"

Reece's head felt like an orange pushed into a glass. "She seems like she knows what she's doing. Not someone to mess with."

Terry nodded, scanning the horizon around them. "Everybody loves her. Dr. Guthrie, especially. She's a hard worker and not bad looking either. But I'm married. What about you?"

For a split second, Reece couldn't remember. "I'm engaged. Got engaged just before I came over here. She's a nurse, too."

Terry gave Reece a too-bad-for-you look. There had been much speculation on how Reece and Emma might hit it off. No one had known he was engaged until he arrived in the country, dismaying a few, including Emma.

For the rest of the day, Reece stayed in his room and read—*Hind's Feet on High Places,* a gift from his church—then walked a stretch inside the compound. The letters from Kristin lay on the bed in his small room. He ran his middle finger over the bridge of his nose carefully, discreetly feeling out a stiff hair. He'd felt one earlier and now verified it. He told himself to wait, to be patient, that it would be impossible without tweezers.

Terry's wife Lisa made a cheese pizza for dinner, of which Reece was allocated a slice. In the quiet following the nearly silent eating of the pizza, Reece mortified himself by farting. No one said anything. His intestines felt like rocks.

"That was delicious pizza," he told Lisa. He then spent a miserable night reading Kristin's letters out of order, by accident, first hearing how she named her new puppy and then how she bought her new puppy and then how a friend from work's Cocker Spaniel had had puppies and how precious they were and how lonely she was and when would he be coming home? She called the puppy Stones, and did he approve? Because it was their puppy. He felt a wave of despair. He thought that maybe she would explain why she had chosen Stones as a name, and then decided she would mention it in the next batch of letters or that she would reveal another name more suited to a puppy.

The plane landed around noon the next day, throwing up great clouds of dust, nearly depleting the runway before swinging around sharply. Reece thought the right wing touched the ground and said so, but Dr. Guthrie said otherwise. He and Dr. Guthrie and the Summitons had stood in a field of rocks for nearly two hours waiting for the plane. Reece felt that a lot had been accomplished, that he had in effect crossed a great divide in terms of understanding his place in the famine, even though the violent darkness he had imagined seemed more like a muddy headlight. A vision of Emma lodged in his mind.

The pilots were the same. They never spoke or even seemed to know that anyone was on board. The two Ethiopian men in suits were back on board as well, although looking dehydrated with pinched expressions. Loaded, the plane felt like it was being pulled by a small car as it lumbered toward the cliff edge, suddenly accelerating as if the tires had found purchase, tossing itself off the massive cliff face a bit sideways before arcing south toward Addis Ababa.

Between patients, Emma took a long drink from her re-cycled Icelandic IV bottle and plugged the red stopper. Afewerki stood in the door, gazing into space. Emma felt like having some of the Australian cheese, but didn't have an opener in the clinic. She didn't quite know what to make of Reece. He was cute but seemed very shy. How well would he work with patients? Could he take the stress of long, hot days seeing patient after patient—tapeworms, diarrhea, anemia, ear infections, leg wounds? Could he stand up to the Hyena? It was only a matter of time before there was another run-in. She thought about market the next day and went over a list of foods she wanted: lemons for lemonade, bananas for breakfast, maybe some eggs.

"Who's next, my brother?" she said.

"Oh, many, many complainers," said Afewerki.

"It's what we do."

"But, we are not complaining."

"No, I mean we fix the complaints."

"Yes, we are fixing these things." He looked bored as he extended his hand to an old woman with a leathered, wrinkled face. "She is very old."

Emma helped the woman settle on the bench. Her rag-ged dress gave off a puff of dust. Her fingers seemed carved from wood, the nails ridged and creamy brown. She had a few teeth left, four or five, one lone tooth in the front. Her personal collection of flies walked calmly about her face, as if taking a stroll in the park.

"Endemin-nesh?" asked Afewerki. He spoke with a faraway look in his eye.

The old woman twisted her fingers and moved her lips, barely audible.

"What is it?" asked Emma.

"She says she is weak. She needs energy."

Emma squatted and gently pulled down the lower lid of the woman's eye. The lining was pale, indicating anemia. "Does she eat meat or eggs?"

"No, she is very poor. Sometimes she can drink a little milk when her daughter brings it to her."

"Well, let's dose her up with a month's supply of vitamins and some famine biscuits. Does she get enough to eat?" Emma pulled up the old woman's dress and squeezed her bony thigh. "I guess maybe not."

"Her third husband is died. She is living with her daughter, who has no husband."

"We could take her to the shelter for a while, get her fat, and send her home."

Afewerki explained this to the old woman. Her eyes seemed to float in liquid. She mumbled.

"She cannot leave her daughter's house as she is nursing three children, one boy and two girls."

"What? Nursing her daughter's kids? Holy cow, no wonder she's emaciated. Are you sure?"

"Yes. She is telling the truth."

Emma thought for a minute and sent the old woman home with a big can of Nido powder. She should drink three cups a day, in addition to her meals. "Plus, let's make sure her daughter gets a bag of milled flour. She can at least eat some dabo, if her daughter will bake it for her."

"Her daughter will keep the Nido and sell it," said Afewerki.

"Maybe not. Let's try anyway."

Afewerki frowned and relayed Emma's treatment plan. The old woman held her hands out toward Emma and touched her face, smiling, showing off a brown tooth.

Making her rounds with Afewerki at the shelter before dinner, Emma realized that she should have sent the man with his gut in his scrotum with Terry and Reece. Terry, though, should be back again the following day. The man, dignified with his mesh ballcap and wide-legged trousers, had little shyness about his condition and eagerly dropped his pants for Emma to see. He had been to the bathroom, he said, passing only gas, but Emma took that as a good sign that the loop of intestine was not strangulating. It just looked godawful and made her squirm to look at it. Afewerki uttered a *tsk, tsk, tsk,* feeling the man's pain.

A couple of young moms sat on stones set against the side of the shelter in the shade, weaving colorful straw baskets for Emma. One had placed a piece of lemon peel in her nose to combat the odors. Emma stopped to watch for a moment. The women wove colorful dyed straw into and around coils of plain straw to make baskets designed to hold seeds and grains. "Bataam taruno," said Emma. The women nodded, shielding their eyes.

A shout, and a woman screamed. Pantsless boys stopped their romping. Emma saw the two dogs standing just below a turn in the path that led past the church. They were thin and skulked, pointed shoulder blades sliding up and down. The guard emerged from his tiny three-sided shelter and shouted. He picked up a hefty rock, and the dogs shot away before he could throw it. One of the most disturbing sounds to Emma was the vicious dog fighting at night. The noise was almost unbearable at times, the gnashing and yelping sending a chill down her body. They sounded as if they were ripping each other apart, and they were.

With the dogs gone, play resumed among the children, basket weaving continued, and little girls braided each other's hair. The smell and copious amounts of snot and flies on the kids' faces made Emma uncomfortable, but she was doing what she could. She didn't think she would ever get used to the crusty, fly-soaked faces, but her horror had attenuated to something less alarmed. She refocused and took heart in the fragrant wood smoke coming from the cookhouse where a middle-aged woman with tiny breasts tended a bubbling pot of shurowot. Fresh rounds of spongy teff enjera lay in a clean basket. A fly shot straight into Emma's ear, breaking the reverie, buzzing in the canal, driving toward her brain, erasing the brief moment of peace.

"Hell!"

Afewerki laughed, frowned, then offered to help.

"It's stuck. It's stuck in my ear," said Emma. She tilted her head up and then down, tugging on her earlobe.

"I will look," said Afewerki.

All of the women stopped what they were doing and murmured, covering their mouths.

The fly burrowed deeper. Emma wanted to pluck it out, but feared pushing it beyond reach. She turned her back to the incline and looked out toward the hills and vast valley beyond. The view was stunning. "Afewerki, see what you can do." She sat on a rock and tilted her head.

He knew that one way to draw the fly out was to spit into the ear, but he knew Emma would not approve. "We must get the pliers." He called the long-nosed hemostats in the clinic pliers.

"Tweezers would work too. This is driving me crazy. Let's go back to the house. I have tweezers there." The fly's roaring buzz diminished as it wedged itself deeper.

"Okay, let us go." Afewerki was hungry and ready to leave.

"If it's not one thing, it's another," said Emma.

"Yes, the devil is working among us. These flies are devils."

Emma agreed.

The stove magneto ticked, and a whoosh of blue flame leapt from beneath the pressure cooker. Staying at the guesthouse while waiting for his work visa entailed boiling water and then pouring it into the dozen or so glass bottles with red rubber stoppers, the used Icelandic IV bottles. Soft drinks and the fizzy Ambo were safe—alcoholic beverages being the safest but not part of the Baptist discussion—but all other water sources, whether bottled, iced, from the tap, or falling from the sky, were one-way tickets to fever, diarrhea, vomiting, and sometimes worse. After cooling in the fridge, the cold bottles of water tasted great.

The Summitons had departed, and Reece saw Ben and Dr. Guthrie here and there, but never Thomas Watson. In the few more days, five to be exact, that it took to secure his work visa, Reece viewed Teresa's nipples on two more occasions as she breastfed Kimo outside on the porch.

The first phone call that week to Kristin involved a detailed accounting of the acts and manners of Stones, the new puppy. She sounded very sad and made it clear that Stones was helping her through the most challenging period of her life thus far.

"Why did you name him Stones?" His voice echoed as it traversed the earth.

"You said there were lots of stones in Ethiopia." Her voice sounded weak in addition to being faint. Every few seconds, a beep and sometimes a little blank space.

"Yes, I did say that, didn't I? It's true, too. Rocks everywhere." And he supposed it made sense now, except he would have named the dog Rocks.

The second phone call, the day before he was scheduled to ride in a jeep upcountry back to AK, recounted the changing of Stones' name. She felt it wasn't a real name, like Billy, and that it hadn't been fair that Reece didn't have a say in giving their dog a name. He had thought of a dozen names but had forgotten them.

"Did you have another idea?" he said, wondering again who would pay for the call. Would they deduct it from the tiny stipend deposited each month in his US bank account? He hadn't relished the idea of establishing an account in Ethiopia, and everyone said it would be a big hassle, suggesting it would be easier to have someone from home send cash through the mail, which he arranged with his grandparents.

"My mom likes Walter as a name," she said. He could tell that her mom was in the same room with her. He could see them making a face at one another. He felt relieved that the issue was settled.

"Walter's good," Reece said. "I've never really known a Walter."

They simultaneously sensed that the last phone call in a while was drawing to a close, and knots in throats and hot tears bloomed for the final thirty seconds. Reece hoped Kristin didn't hear him stifle a brief blubbering. He mumbled, "I love you," wiping the tears from his eyes. Kristin responded that she loved him more. Claude had opened and closed the door twice in the past fifteen minutes, and he stood there again staring at Reece with his magnified tiger eyes.

Dr. Guthrie's wife, Livvy, invited Reece over for lunch. She didn't make him uncomfortable like Teresa. Livvy's sexuality had long departed on some bus or train headed to a faraway beach or mountain. She exuded pure wholesome function, and to Dr. Guthrie, she was critical. She picked up Reece, even though he could have walked over. The van moved through the people and donkeys and goats like a ping-pong ball stuck in a river of warm, thick syrup. Dr. Guthrie stood in the large front yard, a working place, surrounded by a small herd of humped velvety brown cows. He leaned sideways into the back end of a cow held by two men, his arm invisible, deep inside the animal's trembling thighs. Reece knew that Dr. Guthrie had been trained to feel slippery things hidden deep in the bowels of animals. Reece waved, and Dr. Guthrie gritted his teeth.

Inside the Guthries' home, Reece felt he was back in a Birmingham suburb. A smell of bread baking. Although it was only eleven and a Friday, the house felt like three on a Tuesday. A clock ticked loudly in the dim living room, a recliner and a TV. A wall of videos. A lamp. A rug. Photos of three brown-haired boys, all with freckles and blank faces. He followed Livvy to the kitchen and sat at a small table while she busied herself, chatting in spurts.

"Today, you're leaving us for good," she said. She gave him the proud but tired look of a mother whose toddler has managed to turn a doorknob.

"It'll be good to get started," he said and believed it. He could see the road before him. Although he couldn't grasp the details, he could see the road.

"How's your stomach?" Each time she spoke, she made a point of stopping and turning toward him. She pulled a tray from the wall-mounted oven, gripping the tray with an oven mitt. The question surprised Reece. Did she mean in general, or did she know something?

"My stomach?" He saw she had made what looked like homemade crackers, and his mouth watered at the sight and smell. His stomach had been dead for days. But the night after returning from his visit to Godo, still at AK, he'd been called from a deep, deep sleep. Reece sat up in bed, first thinking he would vomit, and then knowing he would soil himself if he did not hurry. He couldn't find the flashlight and stumbled into the tin door, probably waking everyone for half a mile around. He found the latch and then remembered his bare feet and the rocks and the walk downhill and the filth and smell and nearly falling jammed his feet into his too-small boots and half pushed the laces into the sides, stumbling into the night, a night brightly lit by all the stars in the universe, and he had wished it were darker. The guard ran over, draped in a plaid blanket and pointing his rifle here and there, and shouted, "Mendeno!" Reece did not look at him and picked his way downhill to the shintabet shining in the starlight, a starlight that cast shadows and gave the rocky ground the look and feel of waist-high walls in places and black holes in the ground in others. He hadn't taken paper, and now he supposed that his fear of the adventure becoming narrative had materialized after all.

"The water here is pretty rough on newcomers," said Livvy. "I didn't know if maybe you were having problems. Of course, you're a nurse." She made a point of making eye contact with him. "I am the mother of three children," she said.

The crackers paired with slices of cheese, followed by homemade pecan sandies, sat very well with Reece and his shocked insides. He felt a kind of love for Livvy, reaching for crackers until they were gone. The lemonade was terrific as well, and he felt a great loss when Dr. Guthrie came into the house and announced that the jeep should leave within the hour and that Reece should return to the main compound. As Reece rose to leave, Livvy pulled a fresh tray of crackers from the oven, and he felt his dismay cinch a notch or two.

With a purple-stamped wad of papers in the glovebox and his things in the back of the oldest of the Toyota Land Cruisers, a dusty light-blue 1970s box on wheels, the tightly sprung jeep began its endless bounce to Alem Ketema, a kind of mechanized seizure that made seat belts more chafing and choking than useful.

Reece looked ahead through the rectangular windshield, a sizable crack running like lightning through his side of the glass. The front view wasn't as bad as in the helicopter, but the tall hood and short glass hid twenty feet or so of road directly in front of them, as if that part of the world did not matter. A makeshift mailbag lay in the seatless back bouncing around with his suitcase, two trunks, and Craig's stuff jammed into a dark blue duffel bag. A rusty, steel, ten-gallon jerry can of gasoline infused the cab, but the windows would remain down the entire trip. Craig was an engineer, and he and his wife Eve lived in Meranya, northeast of AK, an hour's copter ride from Godo.

Along the Gojjam Road, they traveled toward the

mountaintops, winding up, up, up into the mountains. Goats and women like zombies, stacked with arm-sized branches from the eucalyptus trees, ambled along. And mini-buses packed with black and golden people, the tops piled with cargo and an occasional open-air passenger, the roads narrowing, Russian tanks blown apart and left as road art.

Craig did not speak much, being consumed with managing the gears. The black shiny steering column shot out from beneath the metal dash like a heavy gun barrel. The jeep's roaring engine never rested, rushing from a crawl in low to sudden jerks around tight uphill curves.

Reece noticed that Craig's arms were very smooth and that his face was very smooth. The little cap of black hair on his head seemed isolated and foreign. From the side, Craig looked younger than he probably was, and he harbored a faint hint of dissatisfaction in the corner of his eye.

"How long is the drive?" asked Reece.

Craig thought for a moment. "Five or six hours if all goes well." He wrestled the steering wheel.

Reece thought of flats, engine failure, running out of fuel, a broken axle, hijacking, getting lost, falling from a cliff, and wondered if there was anything else that could happen within reason. He added "wreck" to his mental list and then added "stuck in mud or gravel."

"What do you do here?" he said.

"I'm an engineer," said Craig. He had to oversteer to keep the jeep on track.

Reece thought for a moment, not sure of the length and breadth of the possibilities of being an engineer. A few drops of rain the size of small water balloons burst on the windshield. "What kind?" asked Reece, his back already beginning to register a minor complaint. Church affected him that way, too, but in his neck as much as his lower back. As soon as he sat down in church, he felt compelled to stretch out at least one arm along the back of the pew. And then his neck would begin to stiffen so that he had to look up and then down and from side to side, feeling conspicuous, thinking that others were registering his craning as veiled attempts to look their way.

"Civil engineer," said Craig.

"Roads?"

"Mostly bridges and water diversion, but roads too," he said, never taking his eyes from the rough track. His head protruded slightly forward, giving him a mild turtle look.

Ragged white clouds raced across the sky as the heat of the day peaked. Reece wondered why they had waited until noon to leave. The jeep attained a more level section of narrow road, passing clumps of eucalyptus trees planted a hundred years ago. Burros loaded with wood and charcoal tromped down the road. The tall straight trees were bare for the first ten feet, the limbs harvested for firewood. The first checkpoint at Entoto, the capital of Ethiopia before Addis Ababa, was approaching, where one left the city proper and all of God's fury lay waiting beyond.

"Try not to make eye contact," said Craig.

Within a few minutes, with the greenery rising on either side as the jeep climbed, two very young men in green fatigues lingered beside a crude metal building, cradling AK-47s like guitars. A long pole painted white and studded at the end with a heavy metal weight blocked the road. A green and white mini-bus and another larger orange bus sat a hundred feet away on the other side of the barrier, all of the passengers standing uneasily in the grass along the edge of the road. Some were eating, most just standing with arms folded.

Looking straight ahead and resisting the urge to push his glasses onto his nose, Reece willed an extreme calm to flood his body. A movie played in his head, a soldier pushing the butt of a gun into his stomach. He felt blows to his head. He imagined turning a warm gun barrel so that it pointed at his captor's head. He wondered how long he could survive in the bush without food. He was certain there would be snakes, but could he catch them? Would he eat them? He let his head tilt sideways toward the young man approaching the driver's side of the jeep. And then the barrier rose magically, and they were on their way, the jeep lurching. A young girl sold wheat rolls as they passed through to the other side. And she had a teakettle.

"That's why we can't let locals ride with us," Craig said.

Reece didn't quite understand what he meant, thinking of Stones, not Stones, but Werther, not Werther. *Werther's is a type of caramel candy, the color of Cocker Spaniels. Walter. Walter* and he whispered, "Walter." A power line ran along the road for a while and then disappeared. Men carrying long plows wanted rides, but Craig did not slow.

The terrain spread wide and flat, and felt wide and flat, field after field, an occasional cluster of thatched huts in sight. Traffic on the road was very light: a truckload of young men in fatigues and two or three large flatbed trucks, one empty and heading south toward Addis. The view ahead loomed distant and promised many things as the road began to wind and descend. The sun, being directly overhead, beat down on the jeep.

"Your wife lives in Meranya?" He wondered if Craig suffered from sort of hormonal imbalance.

"Yes, she can't wait for me to get back," said Craig. He said it as if that were just a general rule. He was from Virginia, his wife Eve from Toronto. Reece thought Craig's last name was Zilch and decided not to ask. Craig's arms and hands were so smooth. Reece stole a long look at Craig's nose and upper lip. It looked as fluid as a ceramic bowl. And then, like a pickup truck dropping into a swimming pool, he realized that Craig had no eyebrows, no eyelashes, and that the hair on his head was fake.

With the fly dying in her ear, Emma and Afewerki descended to living quarters. The large swinging gate was open, not a good sign. It only opened to let people in and out. Compounds in general were secure spaces protected with fences and gates. The poorest of the poor lived in isolated shanty huts without fences, with ghosts and wind blowing through their thin and undaubed walls at night.

It was the Hyena and his AK-47-toting bodyguards. He was very drunk, eyes blazing red from a daylong bout of drinking tejj. Isaac, Mariam, and Barra stood in the shade of the cookhouse. Zenebek emerged to dip a pot of water from the barrel and disappeared back into the smoke.

"Great. What's he doing here?" asked Emma.

Three sheets to the wind, the Hyena smiled, showing his two gold-edged front teeth. He stumbled toward Emma and Afewerki. His two cohorts mulled chewing sticks and looked nervous. Long slanting rays of sun reached across the village, a call for a peaceful end to a quiet day.

"I've got a damn fly in my ear headed to my brain, and I'll be back in a minute," said Emma. She jaunted to her little house. The padlock was locked. "Ketow!"

Ketow came running with the little key on a string around his neck. Afewerki hung back and explained to the Hyena about the fly in Emma's ear.

There was a titter among the team, and the Hyena laughed, then howled, throwing his bean-shaped head backward. His body followed, and he piled into a heap on the ground. No one made a move to help him.

Emma opened her door. She found her tweezers, came out into the light, and had Afewerki begin the extrication. The fly still hummed in short bursts. Afewerki stood back, afraid to begin. Up behind him came the team and then the Hyena, assisted by one of his minions. Emma tilted her head to the side. Barra spoke in hushed tones, narrating the event for the group. Misrak and Zenebek emerged from the cooking hut, piqued. The gate remained open, and a small group of children had gathered, peering in. Behind them, adults had stopped, a farmer with a heavy plow on his shoulders, a young boy leading an ox by the nose. Emma could feel the eyes on her, but didn't care.

"Afewerki!"

Coming out of his indecision, he maneuvered the tweezers into her ear. He could see black, the back end of the fly, its legs wriggling in desperation.

"I can't hold my head like this all day." Head sideways to the ground, she imagined the crowd around her could not be as large as it seemed to be.

A stillness fell. Even the Hyena seemed to be holding his breath. "Ferenj!" shouted a little boy.

Afewerki yelled in the direction of the little boy. Told him to get home.

"Hey," said Emma. She sounded hopeful.

Zenebek and Misrak carried the enjera and wots into the cooking hut, walking slowly, waiting for something to happen.

Afewerki pulled off one of the fly's legs. "Shoot!" he said, imitating Dr. Guthrie. He went a little deeper, pinched, and out came the fly minus one wing. He held it up for all to see. A collective sigh of relief and cheerful murmuring broke out among the crowd.

There was no more to the show, and Barra barked for the sightseers to move along, to be on their way. "Shoo, shoo," he said to the children, who fled with excited squeals.

The Hyena slapped Afewerki on the back, kneaded his shoulder, and kept squeezing. "You are a brave, brave soldier," he said several times in succession. "Let us eat together. You will be my guest tonight. I will kill a goat, and we will have a feast tonight!"

Afewerki interpreted for Emma.

"No way. He's drunk, and our dinner is ready here. Tell him thanks, but another time."

"Perhaps we should invite to eat with us," said Barra.

"I don't think so," said Emma.

Afewerki was shaking his head, No, No. He feared the Hyena.

The Hyena's eyes narrowed, and he spat on the ground, understanding that his invitation was not welcome. His eyes widened, bleary and red, a light-yellow cast to them.

Something like a small town in the middle of nowhere appeared, rose in the distance like tiny brown transistors. No one seemed to be out. Clusters of huts, a thin, interrupted smoke rising from each.

"Mookaturi," said Craig as he turned onto a dirt road.

"Checkpoint?" asked Reece.

"Yep," said Craig.

"Same deal," said Reece.

"Yep," said Craig. "Want to stop and eat?"

"No," said Reece.

"Okay," said Craig.

This time, the barrier was up, and the men standing there just waved as if they wanted them out of their sight as soon as possible. The jeep passed through a small, dusty town square, everyone staring but not stopping, not interrupting their slow journeys to buy tea leaves or have a sack of sorghum crushed into flour.

"Gas is fine," said Craig.

Reece wanted to say, Oil pressure? Tires? "What's your wife's name again?"

"Eve." Craig tilted his head as if imagining the first time he saw her.

"Children?" asked Reece.

"Can't," said Craig, bouncing up and down more than ever.

"Oh," said Reece, and he wondered if Craig's smoothness had anything to do with it.

"You have perfect skin," and Reece mentally retracted

the statement, not sure if he had even said it.

Craig laughed and adjusted his short pants, pulling at the crotch as he drove with one hand. Reece did the same with his jeans. "I'm a hairless man," he said with a sigh.

Reece pondered what to say and came up short of words. The jeep jounced along, the packed dirt road leading them to a little town called Lemi, beyond which Craig said Reece might want to close his eyes. Reece tried not to look at Craig's toupee, which looked more and more like a little flat hat of black hair.

The road swung west toward Lemi, a magical name to Reece. A tall, thin figure with a staff, doolah, or rifle would turn, stop, and watch as they passed. One or two hailed them to pull over for a ride or something more sinister, as suggested by Craig. The nooks and crannies of Ethiopia were famous for shifta—bandits, loners, small groups of wandering robbers. Everyone feared the shifta, including the Baptist Mission. Reece wondered if the shifta were like the famine. Everyone had something to say about them, but where were they exactly?

Although he couldn't see it, Lemi lay on top of a necked bit of the flat amba at 8,500 feet, across which the jeep was pushing. In all directions, except the narrow isthmus of land leading to the floating island, the earth grew skittish and withdrew vertically for nearly a mile into a vast, gnarled abyss. In Lemi, there were no mosquitoes, and the nights were cold. Once or twice a week, a tired bus from Addis Ababa stopped there, readying itself and its passengers for the punishing and bowel-gouging zigzag down the cliffs. One could get a fresh wheat bun there for a penny. A hot meal of spicy lentils and sorghum enjera cost twenty-five cents. If one had the stomach, a thick cup of curdled milk swimming with red pepper.

The clouds seemed dazed, even though a steady breeze whipped, as the jeep twisted through Lemi. Craig was looking for something, slowing then leaping the jeep forward in low so that it recoiled a foot for every two feet forward. Reece watched a young girl, her face covered with a colorful scarf. Her impassive stare leapt from the loose gap around her eyes, the cloth moving with the wind. In open doors, he saw small children squatting on dirt floors. Those who spotted him yelled, "Ferenj!" before their reflexes could propel them outside for a better look. The little boys had that patch of hair on top of their heads, shaved down to just a handful so that the angels could save them from falling into fires, plunging off cliffs, diving beneath trucks, stepping on land mines, walking behind bulls, becoming lost after dark. Girls of the same age most often had shaved heads or very short hair. Reece was thirsty and decided to drink his Fanta, a grape one.

Blowing clouds of dust, goats tap dancing through town, old men, men like human clothes racks for rags, a burro, the square jaws of large black mules, and flies, flies, flies. The sun, lilting now, dragged itself down as the potholed dirt lanes fed into the narrow, packed road that paralleled the chasm, a bronze affair, slopes stained dark green in the distance, boulders the size of bulldozers poised to tip and fall. Below was a river valley, through which flowed the Jemma on its way to its confluence with the mighty Blue Nile.

The road took its first serious dip and narrowed to barely nothing. It had taken them three hours to attain Lemi and would take an hour to tumble to the comfort of the bottom below. Magnificent basalt cliffs. This side of the river, Reece could see a patchwork of farmland and villages shrouded in juniper. With the river valley below, gravel and rocks crunched and knocked beneath the jeep. Reece thought if he were ever to mine a road, this would be the one, and he would film it. Preferably, it would be a Soviet tank filled with very bad people, hand grenades dangling from their chests. The landmine, perhaps homemade and not so powerful, but powerful enough, explodes and the tank being so heavy does not budge, but the road beneath disappears, just a chunk, and as the tank's only working track spins, spewing a river of dirt into the sky, the tank slips without hesitation from the cliff. The cannon gunnery mate inside sends a shell rocketing into the sky. The kick from the firing accelerates the tank away from the cliff into a slow-motion free fall. The shell arcs upward for three thousand feet before falling back to Earth and exploding.

Craig looked artificial. Reece felt the jeep skidding more than anything. There was no room to cough. No one walked here, along this road cut and scraped and cobbled. Huge ruts hugged the inside curves. Buses got stuck here, Craig said, and one had fallen and only a chicken had survived. An animal sometimes fell, frightened by buses, pushed off into the oblivion, legs splayed against the fall. And down the jeep twisted, jerking, stopping occasionally to back up *errrah! errrah!* and take a more inside stab at a particularly treacherous spot. The constant presence of vast air, a concave bowl painted on its bottom with organic patterns, fractals, a pudding, a snow globe. Craig did not look real, and Reece thought that maybe he was not real and that he was dreaming, but he shook his head at the neat wad of straight black hair glued to Craig's head. He looked alien now, of another race, another species.

"Do you know Lisa and Terry at AK?" asked Reece.

"Sure. Canadians."

He wondered how Craig kept from sunburn. His skin was so fair and so smooth. The farther they twisted down, the less hazy and less distant the broad view became. Reece imagined he could see things moving across the valley floor, which reminded him not so much of a desert but of an arid place.

Each time Reece thought they were finally at the bottom, four times, the road lurched down again, and the valley slid away once more. But then the bottom came up to meet them, and the road took on a couple of fantastic, straight, but hilly sections. The speed seemed miraculous, and Reece thought about asking Craig to let him drive. He looked in the back at the mailbag quivering there. The jeep slowed, pulling off the road near an outcrop of boulders, boulders that had perhaps leaped from the cliffs of Lemi and sailed for miles into the valley. The jeep sidled to a stop on a tilted, cracked pan of dried clay covered with silt and small pebbles.

"Bathroom break," said Craig, and Reece suddenly had to go as well.

Perhaps too drunk to argue with effect and waning, the Hyena departed under his own power, staggering from side to side between his bodyguards. Ketow closed the gate.

Dinner was alicha, a stew of potatoes and cabbage, and sheets of enjera to soak up the juices. The guys spoke among themselves in Amharic, occasionally lapsing into English for Emma's benefit. Even though they were eating together, the language barrier made her feel distant, as if she were skimming random topics. Barra provided a few snatches of song as usual, the team clapping along with him. He was an excellent singer, and Emma couldn't help but feel her heart lift with the music. She was exhausted.

"Is this Rice good man, you think?" asked Isaac. "I think he is good man."

Emma paused between bites. She drank some cool water from her bottle. Alicha was one of the least spicy dishes, but it still made her brow sweat. She thought of Reece's legs, how nice they had looked in his shorts. She craved to have someone touch her, to massage her neck and whisper into her ear. The only men she came into regular contact with were the team, but the Mission discouraged dating the locals, even though they had no official policy against it.

"He seems nice enough," said Emma. "Should make us able to spend less time in the clinic."

She didn't know he was engaged. There had been a lot of kidding between her and Lisa, Terry's wife, about the possibility of a great African romance in the highlands of Ethiopia. But men could be liabilities. Jill's boyfriend in the States had worried the dickens out of her and then killed himself. Maybe it would be best to try to hook Jill up with Reece, but that would entail trips to Gundo Meskel. Rarely did the nurses from the feeding stations all get together, being scattered across the vast, rugged terrain of Shewa Province.

Barra spoke. "He will lead us to study the Word of God, I think." He looked at Emma, a matter-of-fact gaze that indicated she was lacking in the realm of spiritual authority.

"If you want Bible study, I've suggested we do that each morning. I'd be glad to contribute."

The team nodded. "Perhaps we shall wait until Mr. Rice is with us," said Barra.

"Fine by me," said Emma.

Zenebek pushed the door flap aside. She asked if they needed more enjera. She was always in a hurry to get home to her kids and cook for them. Zenebek was divorced, as were half the women in the village, which had been quite an eye-opener for Emma.

"Are there any women priests in Ethiopia?" asked Emma.

Mariam laughed, followed by Barra, and then Isaac.

"The Bible does not allow such things," said Afewerki.

Emma knew he was technically correct, that the Bible touted men as religious leaders—Moses, Abraham, Jesus, the Old Testament prophets, the New Testament disciples. Ruth, only one of two books of the Bible's sixty-six named after a woman, had spent most of her time gathering grain and raising children, much like the women of Godo.

"Reece is a nurse just like me," she said. "Right?" She pushed her webbed folding chair back to excuse herself. It had been an endless day.

"But he is a man," said Barra.

"We'll see about that," said Emma.

"You are finished?" asked Afewerki.

"Bucka," she said, meaning she'd had enough.

Emma awoke to the scrabble of doves on the tin roof. A rooster crowed from a neighboring compound. She'd decided that she would get a couple of chickens for eggs, but not a rooster. The roosters in Godo were skinny, ugly brutes that never stood still, always crowing, running from their shadows like the scared chickens they were. She glanced at the pictures of her mother, of her oldest sister on the makeshift particleboard bedside table, a group photo of herself with members from her church on the day they had dedicated her life to God's work. Two fierce flies tumbled through the air, perhaps mating, buzzing like mad.

It was Saturday, market day, much grander than market days on Tuesday. Peddlers, farmers, sandal makers, toolmakers, and basket weavers from miles around were there. Walking among the vendors in the village center was like walking a twisted tightrope.

Emma brushed back her tousled hair with her hand. She only had to work half days on Saturday, but it would be busy, and you could never tell what would walk through the door. The curtain fluttered, and she smelled the ubiquitous smoke of a cooking fire. Irigit sang near the gate. The singing stopped, and she could tell that the gate to the compound had swung open. There was the sound of a surprised voice, something out of the ordinary. She wondered what it could be. She hoped the Hyena would leave them alone for a while. It would be unusual for him to show up twice in two days, though.

"Ai yi yi," she heard Irigit say. He was laughing. She was afraid to look out the door just yet. She wasn't dressed. She wasn't ready to deliver a baby or stitch up a head wound. When the new guy Reece arrived, he could take care of half the unexpected events and emergencies that inevitably cropped up. Now she could hear Barra. So now he was involved.

"Emma!" A sound of someone coming up to her door and knocking.

"Hold on." Emma pulled on a pair of loose jeans and slid into a scrub top. She needed to brush her teeth. Lively chatter in Amharic continued from outside. Afewerki had arrived. She let water from the gravity-feed filter wet her hands. She dabbed her face and wiped it with a washcloth. She opened her door to bright sunshine. The grass was getting high inside the compound.

It was the man with burned hands and a young boy. The boy was holding a monkey.

"Is a gift for you, Emma," said Barra, walking over. "Come to see."

In bare feet, she walked toward the gate. The man with bandaged hands was grinning and speaking, pointing to the gray monkey with a black mask on its face, framed in tufts of white, then gray. It had a long gray tail and lay in the boy's arms like a baby, pooching its lips. Isaac and Mariam looked on in amusement

"A gift? I can't take gifts," said Emma. "Especially not a

monkey. It's cute, though."

The boy held it out for Emma to take. It was wiry but soft and had the mannerisms of a child. Its eyes looked from face to face with mild distrust, waiting for something untoward to happen.

"My word," said Emma. The monkey came to her and clutched at her chest. It moved nimbly, its little paws like tiny human hands.

The man with bandaged hands looked on with approval. He spoke.

"He says you have saved his life, and you must take this gift," said Afewerki.

"I don't think I saved his life," said Emma. "It's my job. Where would we keep a monkey?"

"This will not be good," said Afewerki. "It is like a child. The monkey is nasty."

The monkey perched on Emma's shoulder and began to pick through her hair, grooming her. "Oh Lord, we're bonding. Is it a boy monkey?"

"Yes, a boy monkey," said Barra. "You cannot to refuse the gift. It will be hurtful."

Emma peeled the monkey from her shoulder and dropped it to the ground. It sat on its haunches and then grabbed her leg, hugging her. Its little eyes darted from person to person. "What does it eat? Bananas."

"Yes, mooze, bananas. Some fruits," said Barra. "You will keep?"

Emma thought for a moment. She looked at the man's bandaged hands. The gauze was filthy and would need to be changed. She could get Reece to help take care of the monkey. Barra seemed pretty interested as well. "Well, it's cute. I never thought I would have a monkey. Ask him if it's okay to keep it for a week, to see how well it goes."

"No, you must take it," said Barra.

"You must give it back," said Afewerki.

Misrak and Zenebek peered from the cooking hut with looks of horror.

"What about this? I'll keep it for a week, see what happens. If it doesn't work out, we'll figure it out then."

Barra translated for the man with bandaged hands, who seemed satisfied, and excused himself to get in line at the clinic.

"This is very bad," said Afewerki. He wagged his finger at the monkey.

The monkey with the masked face didn't know its new home, so Emma locked it inside her house, hoping for the best. She asked Irigit to open the door and check on it every hour or so while she was at the clinic. "Yes, yes," he had replied, using the only English he knew.

Pedestrians and donkeys, piled with goods, busied the paths. Emma saw a donkey with a football-sized open sore on its back, a common sight. The donkey wasn't moving. Its owner shouted and swung a heavy stick onto its hind end. The donkey didn't budge. Emma's heart sank. She started toward the tall, skinny man with a cloth folded on top of his head.

"Hey!"

Afewerki pulled her back. "No, you must not."

The man gazed at Emma as if she were a fly. She stared back, lips pursed, ready to annihilate him with words.

"Emma, come." Afewerki pulled her after him. Donkeys led tough lives, and there was little she could do.

"That makes me so mad, I can't stand it."

"The donkey is very stubborn."

"So am I."

They rounded the bend to head down to the clinic. A vast blue sky, ribbed with wispy clouds, framed the view of the lively scene. From feet and hooves, the stony, hot ground rattled like pebbles shaken in a box. Only ten or so patients sat outside the clinic, a relief and a curiosity. *Why so few?* She checked her watch; it was ten minutes till nine. The gate opened, and they stepped through. The guard informed Afewerki that they had been robbed during the night of eight containers of soybean oil.

"Do they know who it was? The same people?" Emma could feel her heart rate rise and her face flush.

Afewerki spoke at length with the guard, who showed him how the thieves had climbed over the fence. One had had an AK-47 and stood watch as his partner handed the oil over the fence to waiting hands. The Mission's guards only had old bolt-action rifles and were to shoot only if their life was threatened.

"Grrr," said Emma as Afewerki unlocked the clinic door. At least they weren't after the drugs.

The first patient was a young woman, a child really, with two kids. She staggered under the weight of a three-year-old boy on her back. The younger one, a girl, she struggled to hold in her arms. She had so many layers of cloth with the leather carrier on her back that it took Emma a while to unwind her and see what she had. The mother's lips parted, thin, dry lips sticking to her teeth, tight skin across her face, a wild, serene look in her eyes. Her hair stuck out this way and that. The women were very careful with their hair, and it was a bad sign to see a young woman with crazy hair. Emma pulled her lower eyelids down, and they were white as sheets. The skin on the back of her hand pinched into a little tent and stayed that way. She whispered the whole time, fidgeting with her shawl and bouncing the little one. The little boy, out of his carrier, hovered between her legs, looking back every five seconds like the end was near.

Afewerki gradually made sense of what she was saying, that her husband was dead, robbed and killed by shifta. They had raped her but didn't kill her. This was over two weeks ago. She was traveling back to AK to live with relatives. She said she could feel a devil growing in her womb and wanted Emma to get it out. Afewerki mentioned the shelter to Emma. She agreed they should let the young mother stay there while she regained her strength. The woman sipped ORS from an orange cup and shared it with her son. Afewerki gave them each a famine biscuit. The little boy took it with wide eyes and just held it, looking at it like it was a petrified snake.

Emma felt sick. She could do a vaginal exam on the woman, but what would that accomplish? She looked out onto the compound grounds to see if Isaac or Mariam were about, but did not see them and remembered that it was market day. "Have one of the guards walk her up to the shelter, okay?"

"Ishi."

Emma thought about her mother. She thought about the new guy, Reece. He should be back in a few days. She remembered the monkey. Life was cruel, insane at times, but wasn't there a purpose behind it all? God's will and so forth?

Craig wandered off, entirely out of sight. The hot air was light yet leaden. The jeep creaked and popped, small swallows flitting among the rocks. Reece could hear the earth beneath him contracting. He imagined that if it rained, the water would suck noisily into the network of inch-wide cracks. The cracks looked like miniature chasms, crevasses hundreds of feet deep. He spied a small smooth stone, the color of the bevel of a fine watch, and walked toward it. Craig reappeared, and Reece thought he was the strangest sight in the world at that moment, sliding from behind a small mountain of rock, his skin alabaster and briefly translucent, hairless.

"Ready?" asked Craig.

Reece made an I-forgot-to-pee face and scurried toward the nearest spot that suited his purpose and wondered at the heat of his urine.

"Sorry about that." Reece spied the metallic stone again and picked it up. A kind of deadness spirited between him and the stone, and he stood, thinking better of it. He thought about the boy selling what looked like lemons near the bottom of the escarpment. Craig hadn't said anything and never slowed. Although a few miles distant, he could see the mountains clearly, darkly splotched amid a bluish aura, the land climbing beyond the river, and he knew that somehow the jeep would find its way up and to Alem Ketema. Large birds, vultures, he thought, circled high overhead.

"What does your wife do?" asked Reece. The jeep

hummed along, taking curves with occasional sliding.

"She takes care of me," said Craig.

Reece glanced over to see if he was joking, and he wasn't. "That sounds nice."

"She misses me. I'll spend the night in AK and get home tomorrow afternoon."

An image of Craig's wife Eve assembled itself. Reece thought about mentioning Kristin, but did not. He wondered if there was a letter from Kristin in the mailbag behind him. At least half of her letters were devoted to the rhetoric of longing. Just thinking about it made him feel a bit sick.

"Where is your wife from?"

"Canada."

"Oh. What part?"

"Vancouver."

"Wow."

Wow seemed sufficient. He refrained from asking if it got cold in the winter and wondered what had happened to his boxes of maps. He had always loved maps and plastered his bedroom with maps, but during high school, collecting maps had become an obsession. He remembered writing for maps of Canada. The maps he received, along with diverse travel literature, impressed him as being of high quality. A packet of maps would arrive in the mail, and he would look at each one, open it, and then fold it carefully. He kept the maps in cardboard boxes in his closet. One day, he received a packet of maps and a typed letter that read, "We hope that with this mailing your need for maps of Canada will have been satisfied." And someone had signed it. He stopped writing away for maps after that and focused on aquariums, going so far as to subscribe to *Aquarium* magazine and check out all the aquarium, tropical fish, and Jacques Cousteau books in his high-school library.

Over a series of rises, the river appeared and then disappeared. The rains had returned to Ethiopia, but were still sparse. Crops of sorghum and teff had been planted except where seed was still not available, having been eaten long ago. The long meher rains wouldn't begin until June. The river at low levels worked itself into a braid, occasionally joining into a single watercourse.

A single-lane bridge spanned the river. Created from prefab steel trusses, Craig noted that it was a Bailey bridge and that it was less than a year old. "Doesn't require cranes to build," said Craig as the jeep inched across thick planks.

Upstream, Reece could see a few giant fig trees almost as broad as they were high. The pockets of green towering on the slopes above contained a variety of hardwoods, including clusters of zegba, *Podocarpus falcatus*.

The jeep's higher-pitched growls of resisting the downhill tug shifted to less frantic but deeper whines as Craig fiddled with the four-wheel drive on the floor. Reece imagined it would be quite easy to spill over backward or sideways. The jeep crunched its way up over millions of years of crocodile vertebrae, shark teeth, and turtle shells. Limestone, then mudstone from ancient seas, and siltstone from ages of meandering rivers below sandstone and conglomerates. Jurassic vertebrates. Mesozoic vertebrates, small mammals. Crunching, crunching, the forever sound and sensation of crunching as they climbed, as the shadows began to lengthen and deepen from left to right. The jeep should have two gallons of gas left when they reached AK, Craig said.

Soon, the jeep puttered into town. AK was sizable for the middle of nowhere, but barren. It was still hot, but the promise of cool lay in the breezes. The gate to the compound was closed, then opened before Craig could get out. The guard hailed them heartily as if they had journeyed from afar, and they had. He took Craig's hand and spoke at length, to which Craig only supplied a few halting words. Reece uttered "Tenesteling," but it sounded so unreal coming from his mouth, and he wanted to kick himself. The guard waved them through, talking to them the whole time.

Out behind the helipad shed, Lisa crouched beside a bed of lettuce greens, picking arugula for a salad. She stood and put her hand to her forehead like a visor and then waved. She wore a brightly colored cloth wrapped around a single braid of her long, dark hair. Three young Ethiopians in their late teens appeared, smiling and absorbing them. Lisa was beautiful standing there amid the sharpness, the starkness of it all. Terry appeared, and then Sam.

Dinner that night was pizza à la Lisa, accompanied by salad. Reece thought the pizza quite good, even with the garlic and spinach, and said so. He hadn't yet acquired a taste for salad, and no one pushed it on him. The spinach was a stretch for him, but surprisingly innocuous, maybe even good. He wasn't sure. The salty pizza was especially tasty with the cold, sweet lemonade.

Lenore walked in as they were finishing. She was spending a couple of weeks in AK, doing what Reece did not know. Her long, white hair looked soft and puffy. She had that youthful sparkle in her eye, but her skin was brown and wrinkled. She was somebody's grandmother somewhere. She looked as if she had just emerged from an intense devotional. He imagined her at her table of inwardness, seated, a candle, Jesus on the other side listening, nodding as Lenore confessed her deepest longings, her needs as a woman, her needs as a wife, as a grandmother, as a disciple of Christ. Christ reaches over and covers her hand with his. *That's what I get for reading Calvin Miller.*

"Well, Lisa, I thought I was going to be early and here I am late," said Lenore. There was some salad left, with oil and vinegar, some bread, but the pizza was gone.

Lisa had forgotten about Lenore. She glanced at Terry, wondering why he had let her forget. Shouldn't Sam have said something?

"Oh heck, Lenore, you snuck up on us again." Sam stood and motioned for Lenore to come over. He laughed a good-hearted laugh, the kind that says forgive me, laugh with me, and for goodness' sake, we're all in the same boat, aren't we?

"Craig, did you have a nice trip?" Lenore sat at the end of the table in a chair that Sam pulled up. She busied herself making do with what was left. "Pass the salt and pepper, please."

Reece looked at Craig, and Craig looked at his plate. "Not too bad. No flats," and he laughed. That was the first laugh from Craig that Reece had heard, and it was an odd laugh, like a cough, but after cough syrup.

Lenore took her time arranging her salad on a flat white plate. All the dishes and cups and silverware were mismatched, a jumble of colors and styles. Craig stood and excused himself to unpack his things for the night. He would be driving to Meranya the next day, alone in the jeep. When Craig stood, Reece imagined him as a birthday cake candle that had been blown out.

"How's Eve?" asked Lenore. She ate her salad slowly, leaf by leaf, eating a slice of buttered bread between bites.

"Yeah, how's Eve?" added Sam. He seemed always ready to arbitrate or negotiate, to settle a boundary dispute, a stolen toothbrush.

Craig stopped in his tracks, picked up his plate, and walked it to the sink. Reece held his breath. "She misses me," he said. Someone kicked someone under the table, Reece could tell. "She gets lonely...You know how it is."

"She should have come with you," said Lenore.

"She hates that jeep," said Sam.

"Yeah, she'd just rather not bother. Anyway, good night, all." The door screeched, and the wind pushed it shut with a bang.

"Reece, how was the thrill ride?" asked Sam. He held a toothpick.

Reece had finished long before everyone else and was still hungry. He had his eye on the last of the bread, but worried that Lenore might want it. Terry excused himself and kissed Lisa on top of her head. "Don't keep her up too late." He looked tired and walked away.

"Pretty amazing road," said Reece. The dynamic in the eating shed, as he now thought of it, shifted perceptibly with each entrance or exit. It was somewhat balanced now: two men, two women, one older, one younger of each. "Kind of like a movie."

"It is," said Sam.

Reece wound up helping Lisa and Lenore wash dishes. He enjoyed washing dishes and mopping floors. He had never had a dishwasher in the house growing up, and never used the dishwasher in the only apartment he had lived in for a few months. He felt it took longer to use the dishwasher. Washing by hand, he would always go ahead and dry and then put the dishes away. Using the dishwasher entailed waiting until the next day to unload the dishes, which seemed to double the work. Lisa left next, and then Reece, leaving Sam and Lenore as she boiled some hot tea for the night guards.

Reece found what he thought was a chamber pot in his room and gladly used it twice during the night, but pondered how to get it to the outhouse without drawing attention to himself. He supposed it was a matter of routine. He passed the end of his building, four guest rooms, and there was Lenore in a worshipful pose. He nodded and hoped she would just let him pass without conversation. He could have sworn that she'd had her arms outstretched toward the sky. Maybe she was exercising.

"Sleep well?" asked Lenore from a dozen feet away. She wore a floppy blue jean hat on her head.

"Pretty good," he said over his shoulder, remembering to look down at the rocky ground. He knocked on the ragged corrugated steel door.

"Hold your horses!" It was Terry.

"Sorry about that."

Reece walked behind the little building and stood at the bottom of a slope of rocky, grassy ground. He could hear sounds from the road on the other side of the fence and set the glazed pot on the ground. He'd left the lid in the room, which he viewed as a minor positive. At least it didn't look like he was carrying his feces. He'd left the lid in the room for that very reason. He could hear Terry bumping around inside the shintabet and moved farther away to sit on an empty biscuit tin.

Terry lumbered out and disappeared up the hill. Reece hurried in, dumped, and then went back to his room with the empty pot. There was no easy way to wash his hands. He packed his stuff sack, put his Bible away, and set off to brush his teeth.

The door to the dining shed was open. Inside, Lisa stirred a big pot of oatmeal. Reece walked in and said, "Hi."

"Everybody likes oatmeal," said Lisa, putting on a pot of water to heat for washing dishes.

Reece wondered if there was sugar. "I think I'm losing weight."

"I'm not losing," and she held up her arms as if that were proof. She laughed.

"Oh, get out of Dodge," he said, and if he had been looking in a mirror at that moment, he most likely would have seen someone he did not recognize.

Lisa laughed, and Terry came in with Sam. "Here comes some more hungry boys," she said, stirring the oats.

Clinic was going so-so. The last patient before lunch, an elderly man with an infected toe, had ended the day with little drama, although his toe was a mess and made Emma's stomach turn. *The monkey!* She remembered the monkey and hurried with Afewerki up the hill. She felt like she had accidentally left a newborn in a hot car. The inside of her tin-roofed house could be stifling during the day. She had to keep the door closed to keep the flies out, and the lone, screened window admitted only a slight breeze. What would she name the monkey? Maybe Reece would have an idea.

The gate swung inward, screaming on its hinges. Irigit was babbling to Afewerki, pointing at the house, gesturing with his hands.

"What's wrong?" asked Emma.

"The monkey has escaped. He goes to visit the government clinic, and Atakabura is angry."

"Dang, where is it now?"

Afewerki motioned her to follow him. Beneath the small eucalyptus tree in the center of the compound was a biscuit tin. "He is inside. Irigit put him inside."

"What?"

The biscuit tins held the equivalent of four loaves of bread, hardly space for a monkey. She maneuvered the lid, prying it off. The monkey seemed dead, then leaped from the container to the top of Emma's head and then into the tree, pulling back its lips, speechless but rattled. Squatting on its hind end in the tree, it looked very human, with a thoughtful but frightened look.

"Jeez," said Emma. "Could've suffocated in there. Lucky."

"We must tie the monkey so that he cannot escape. He will bite," said Afewerki. "Oh, is very bad."

Emma couldn't imagine tying the monkey like a dog. It had fingers and a thumb. "Let's give him some space. Maybe he'll learn to stay in the compound. It'll take time."

"He will bother," said Afewerki.

"Let's just see. He's pretty cute. I think I'll call him Marvin,"

"Mar-vin," said Afewerki.

"Mar-vin," said Irigit.

"Yep, Marvin. Marvin the Monkey."

Marvin looked down at them, pinching his face into a scowl. He moved from limb to limb, restless.

"Come here, boy. Marvin," said Emma.

Marvin didn't budge.

"Let's go get some fruit."

"We are to be eating, Emma," said Afewerki. He pointed to the dining hut where Misrak had left enjera and a wot covered with cloth to keep off the flies.

"Right," said Emma. "Let me wash up first."

Afewerki grumbled, watching Marvin creep about in the tree branches. He walked to the water barrel, removed the lid, and dipped a can to pour over his right hand. Everyone was out and about except for him and Emma. He stooped, entered the dining hut, and let the plastic flap fall behind him. He enjoyed Emma's company. This Marvin seemed like such a bad idea. Monkeys were unclean.

"What's for lunch?" Emma brushed under the plastic

flap. "I hope it's not a monkey."

Afewerki grimaced and put his hand to his mouth. "God forbids it," he said.

"So do I."

Afewerki pulled the cloth back from the folded quarters of spongy enjera. In the pot was dorowot with six boiled eggs floating in the oily, red sauce.

"Lord," said Emma. Doro wot was so spicy. It always gave her heartburn.

"You want to pray for this food?" asked Afewerki.

Emma looked surprised. No one ever asked her to pray. It was a man's job to bless the food. "Sure." She bowed her head and said a short prayer, asking forgiveness for their sins. She mentioned Reece, asking God to prepare him for the good work in Godo. She considered praying for Marvin's health, but did not. "Amen."

"Ah-men."

The flap rustled. Marvin held up a corner and peered in like a tiny little man.

Emma said, "Marvin!"

"No!" said Afewerki.

Breakfast was very pleasant, with the sunlight filtering in from all sides. The oatmeal felt good in Reece's stomach. Terry would drop him in Godo on his second run, his first flight being to the station in Rabel. He would have taken Reece along for the ride, but that would have cut into his maximum load. Lenore mentioned she would be headed to Rabel to oversee the operations and work the clinic while the husband and wife living there took a leave of absence.

"Reece," said Sam. "Are you ready?"

"I'm always ready," said Reece.

With the helicopter chugging, the waiting net filled with grain, Alene looked too young and urbane to supervise the crew of sweating farmers. Reece felt that here was a genuine moment. He paused to soak it in, wondering how these things had come together. He felt the same way when looking at the stars or when someone pumped gas facing him. Terry loaded his trunks and suitcase. Reece worried he would lose his glasses. And to reinforce that notion, his thumb jerked them off his face onto the rocks of the helipad.

He was glad to be going to Godo for good. It seemed like he had been waiting for this moment for the last six months. The famine would open up to him now and embrace him. He imagined the last door inside a prison clanging shut behind him, but that was not the image he wanted. Reece felt incomplete, as if his arrival had been a photograph that had lost its frame. He would write Kristin that night, a long letter, and he would feel better, he thought.

The flight over was much the same as his previous flight. Not much was said, and Reece watched the endless patchwork of browns and greens below. The helicopter seemed to be stationary, hovering and trembling. The distant haze layered itself into mists. The haze seemed ancient, as ancient as the jagged cliff lines topped with house-sized boulders that defined the ambas. He thought himself lucky. Whether it was the luck of seeing something new or of simply being alive, he couldn't tell. Maybe it was both, but that was too easy. When he was living with his parents, moving from military base to military base, he had developed a mechanism of being simultaneously relieved and horrified with each move. Whatever problems had accumulated over the previous six to twelve months would just disappear, but then there was the specter of having to do it all over again: changing schools and trying to make new friends.

It had been like that at Fort Knox. He'd had a miserable day at school, had gouged his nose to make it bleed so that he could pretend to go to the bathroom. He despised riding the school bus. Almost every day, there was a fight or the threat of a fight. Reece didn't like to create ripples, but would gladly start swinging if someone else rocked the boat. The fights enraged him. He had hated his classmates, the whole lot.

And, it got cold in the winter, and the heat blew into the tiny apartment through a single vent located near the ceiling above a dingy, gold armchair. To get warm, he had stood on the back of the chair to catch the warm air inside his coat. And, it was a cold day like that. His sneakers were wet, had been all day, from the snow, his feet cold and itching. A punk from eighth grade thumped him twice on the head on the bus. On the second thump, Reece reached under the seat and grabbed the kid's leg, trying to break it, but ended up with the punk's shoe instead, which he slammed down on the boy's head as hard as he could. The bus stopped, and Reece was ordered off by the driver, with whom Reece often experimented, sending him telepathic messages. He knew that adults communicated telepathically and that he had the power to interfere with their messages. He stared at the driver, sending him a death message, and stepped onto the road.

Fort Knox. Reece walked the few blocks to his apartment row and pushed inside. It was dim as usual. His mother was home, and she didn't say anything. He had thought there was one foil-wrapped Hostess Ho Ho left, but the box was empty. He looked out the back door at the slop of snow in their postage-stamp yard. A steel garbage can strapped to a steel post cemented in the ground. He went upstairs to read, closed his door, and when his father came home, he brought news of the next move. It would be yet another December transfer. After dinner, Reece read *Shardik* until they told him to cut off the light. Once again, everything was on fire.

Terry lowered the helicopter onto the pad with ease. It was ration day, and the clinic compound buzzed like cicadas on fire. Long lines of men and women waited to have their ration cards checked and children weighed before loading up with grain and milk powder. The line for the clinic stretched from the door to the fence and up the steep, rocky hill. The woman measuring out giant scoops of dried milk powder into empty grain bags looked white. Occasionally, a puff of wind carried a tornadic cloud of the powder into the air.

Mules and burros and men lingered outside the walls of the compound. Children were playing, and the entire team was there to greet Reece, to welcome him into the mix. This was the famine, or what was left of it, the worst having passed, the tail end of things now. It felt like a Sunday afternoon. He sensed the exactness of his position in time and space and felt secure, although mildly bewildered from moment to moment as the ingenuity of it all washed over him. But it was there in the eyes of the people, the forces of good and evil, slowly aligning as the days passed one by one.

"Your face is good to see," said Isaac. "How are you, my friend?" His words slow, but his eyes bright.

"I am well. Good to see you again...Isaac?"

"Yes, it is Isaac. You are remembering our names."

Emma peered from the clinic and then resumed her work. Reece turned to scan the line of squatting people waiting for treatment. The sameness and raggedness of the clothes struck him again. Long, thick, dark green dresses for women. Baggy and torn shorts with wide leg openings and shirts of that same dark green material for men. The women inevitably with a child on their backs, peeking out from beneath a gauzy covering of dirty cotton. The men sat on their haunches with a staff or lead-wrapped doolah propped on the ground between their legs. They all looked up at Reece, and he sensed that if he maintained eye contact for too long, they would stand. Just inside the gate, a woman older than time itself sat on the ground, draped in rags. She seemed blind. Her face looked square and mummified.

Four sturdy laborers were already moving out of the compound and up the hill with his bags. Reece held half a dozen letters in his hand, three from Kristin, two from his grandparents, and one from a friend. Barra distributed the other letters to the team. The letters with brightly colored animal stamps disappeared into pockets.

"Hey, Emma." Reece shook Afewerki's hand.

"Hey, yourself. Ready to get started? We're ready for you." She smiled a half smile.

"He must go and get rest for today," Afewerki told her.

"Rest?" said Emma.

Smoke streamed from the cookhouse inside the living compound. "We have a special dinner," said Afewerki, carrying Reece's stuff sack and a bag of oranges sent by Lisa.

"You like tibs?" asked Isaac. Mariam towered over him from behind, smiling.

"Tibs?"

"The meat of the goat. It is very delicious," said Isaac, and Afewerki and Mariam agreed. Barra was off negotiating the price of a bag of teff.

Outside the cookhouse, Irigit was carving a large, skinned goat that had been butchered within the hour. The head was nowhere to be seen. Five young men, two dressed Western style and the others not, hovered around a large pot just inside the door, pulling out chunks of liver and other entrails that had been boiled on the spot. Greasy water streamed down their right hands and from their mouths that glistened with the feast. Isaac introduced him to the two in Western attire, and Reece immediately forgot their names. Only one of the women he had seen cooking before was there. She spoke to him in rapid Amharic, and Reece said, "Taruno." The word charged from his feet, leaving a trail of breathlessness through his body. She laughed at him, and he sensed that it was a good laugh. The hut smelled of iron and smoke.

Reece's luggage sat in a pile in front of the little whitewashed "motel." Isaac opened a door. Reece peeked into his narrow room and felt tired. A rooster crowed. Afewerki told Reece about the government clinic and pointed to the building on the other side of the fence behind Emma's little house. They should visit the doctor there soon, Atakabura, who was not really a doctor.

Lunch was the pressing issue, and the team retired to the dining hut, waiting for Barra to return from his errand and Emma to come up from the clinic. Inside, the air did not move, and sweat trickled down Reece's forehead, gathering in his eyebrows and forming little streams that ran behind his ears onto his neck. After a few minutes, Barra joined them, the darkest of them all, and small and thin. His round face stretched into a broad smile, his teeth like large white bones. He was the snazziest dresser, wearing jeans that looked new.

It became evident that Emma would be later than planned, and Barra suggested they go ahead and eat.

"Are you sure? I can wait," said Reece.

Barra pushed his head beyond the plastic covering the door and shouted. He had a very distinctive voice, penetrating, a radio quality. The other man who had been cutting up the goat with Irigit, Ketow, slid inside holding a plastic basin, a pitcher of water, and a ragged bar of soap. He first poured a little water over Barra's right hand. Barra soaped it lightly, then rinsed his hand, catching the water in the basin. Ketow continued around the table, and with their clean right hands, all were ready for lunch. Afewerki asked Ketow something, and he exited the hut, but soon returned, mumbling to himself. Barra pulled the key to Emma's house from his pocket and handed it to him. Ketow soon returned, clutching five liter bottles of water, laughing to himself. Reece understood that the bottles were very cold.

"From Emma's refriger-a-tor," said Isaac.

Reece watched the cold from the bottles coalesce into droplets and run down the sides. Each bottle was capped with a red stopper, the same as the bottle in the guesthouse fridge back in Addis, the Icelandic IV bottles.

"Cold," said Reece, putting his hand around a bottle. It had been only three days or so since he'd had cold water, but already it seemed exotic. In a way, he didn't want cold water, access to a refrigerator, or a stove. He felt cheated somehow. The famine had already begun to wind down, and now these comforts. But he let the notions pass and considered how interesting it all was.

Ketow carried a large, flat plate piled thick with layers of the round, grayish enjera, followed by Misrak, the cook with the happy face. She looked more businesslike now, though, and hurried out of the hut. She had spooned large portions of what Reece assumed were strips of the sautéed goat meat on top of the enjera. Reece could see little bits of chopped green pepper and braced himself. In the middle of the tray, she had poured out cubed boiled potatoes in a thick yellow sauce. The smells were terrific, and Reece's mouth watered. Everyone pulled chairs close to the small round table. Isaac asked Barra to pray, and he did so in Amharic, but Reece felt that he could follow along, that he was thanking God for the day, for the food. Barra spoke softly as he prayed, and everyone said, "Ah-men."

The eating began fast and furious, as if there really was a famine. Reece knew the basics but watched the others. He worried most about touching the food with his left hand, the unclean one, and kept it under the table. Before he could tear off a corner of enjera and wrap it around a bite of the goat meat, Barra, who was across from him, stood and walked around with a large, prepackaged morsel. He moved it toward Reece's mouth, explaining that this was the custom of gursha, and Reece took the huge bite and chewed, his eyes probably larger than he wanted.

The tastes were not even tastes but more like life forces. He wanted to untangle the various flavors, which struck him as strange and pleasant. The enjera was fresh and warm and chewy and tangy. The tibs, the chunks of goat, were at first bland and almost tough, but when chewed released a flood of juices, a bold, meaty flavor, strong but tempered with spices and the crunchy hotness of the green pepper. It took a while to chew and swallow that first bite, and all eyes were on him as he removed the stopper from his bottle of water and took a large swallow. He almost said "taruno" again, but felt it was too soon and instead said, "I like it. Very nice." Murmurs and smiles passed around the table, and within ten minutes, all that was left was a single layer of soaked enjera on the bottom of the pan.

Misrak reappeared with her pot and three more soft folded enjeras with crispy edges, which she placed on the tray, pouring another steaming pot of tibs into the middle, and that was eaten within five minutes. Reece had finished his bottle of water early in the meal, and the top of his head tingled as a showerhead seemed to open up beneath his scalp, streaming, not sweat, but pure water down his face and the sides of his head.

"Are you satisfied?" asked Isaac.

There was general conversation around the table, mostly Amharic, but Reece felt a part of things, yet oblivious to what he was part of.

"Oh yes, very full," and he patted his stomach, which brought ohs of approval from the group. He felt an urge to take a nap, but it didn't seem right. Emma was working in the clinic, *skipping lunch?* He felt as if he were on an exotic vacation and that long naps in the heat of the day probably cost extra. His right hand was very sticky, and he could feel and see enjera pushed under his fingernails. The others seemed to have perfectly tidy hands and nails.

Emma entered, wearing blue scrubs, and she looked very tired.

"Is it always so busy?" Reece said.

Barra stood and shepherded Emma to her seat, talking in a concerned voice. *There, there, it's okay, take a rest and have some food,* he seemed to be saying. Emma's complexion was flawless. She had big brown eyes and a serene look. Her lopsided smile was killer.

"Oh yeah, on ration day, it gets hectic," she said. "But today, maybe a hundred? Still, people lined up, so I have to be quick, but I was starving. I think maybe they heard you were coming," and she laughed. She looked at Barra, then Isaac. "Where's the monkey? Marvin? Is he in my house?"

Barra looked alarmed. "He is gone from here. I am sorry. I have send Irigit to look."

Afewerki said, "Tsk, tsk, tsk."

"A monkey?" asked Reece.

Emma explained the arrival of Marvin and his disappearance. Perhaps he had seven lives like a cat.

Misrak had left to tend to her children at her house, which was close by, but Ketow trundled in yet another plate of tibs with fresh enjera folded in quarters. Isaac murmured, and Ketow dashed back outside. Mariam left, excusing himself. Ketow burst back in and handed Isaac a small dish with red berbere powder in it.

"I'll put my things away and come to the clinic." Reece rubbed the fingers of his right hand against one another. The pepper had gotten into a slight cut on his thumb and burned. He had a flashback: had he touched the enjera basket with his left hand? A dozen black flies buzzed inside the hut. Isaac snatched one from the air, shook it vigorously, threw the dazed fly to the ground, and stomped it with his heavy leather boot.

Emma took a few seconds to chew and swallow. "Oh no. That's okay. You need to get organized, rest up. Tomorrow, you can work." She tossed back her hair, chewing a big bite of meat wrapped in enjera.

The words *I insist* formed on Reece's lips but stayed there. He wanted to unpack and arrange his room, but felt he should push the issue out of politeness, to seem like a hard worker eager to dive in.

"Let me unpack a few things, and I'll come down." Afewerki hung onto Reece's every word. Reece wondered about Afewerki's birth order, where he lived, what his parents were like, and had he lived here all his life? Was there enough room for the three of them in the tiny clinic?

"No, just take it easy," and Emma fixed a maternal scowl on her face.

Reece's mind wandered. He wondered if there was a dump. What did people do with their garbage?

"Well, let me do this. I'll unpack, rest a bit, and then come down just to watch, get the feel of the clinic."

Emma laughed, and that made Reece relax. "Okay, that sounds good. These people will be back tomorrow and the next day."

The group meal dissolved, and Reece and Afewerki left Emma with Barra, who had broken into song at one point. "He is famous singer," said Isaac, grinning his wide smile.

Afewerki followed Reece to his lodgings. Through the unlocked door, they carried his stuff inside. The single room looked more disorganized than he remembered. Little clouds of dust puffed on the rough cement floor. The tin roof creaked and popped as if alive or dying. Reece sensed Afewerki was waiting for him to direct him in some manner. He wondered why Afewerki was wearing a coat. *It must be at least eighty or ninety degrees.*

"Maybe we can go to the clinic in one hour," said Reece.

Afewerki looked at his watch, a woman's watch, but it worked. The nurse from Iceland, Eydis, had given it to him. Reece wondered at the mention of Iceland again. A mythical place until now. *How long had the Icelanders lived there? Why did they leave?*

"I will go to my home and wait," said Afewerki.

"Okay, shall I come there?"

"No," he said. "I will come for you. You open your door when I am here."

"Okay, sounds good." Reece wondered if "sounds good" meant anything in Godo. He wondered if Afewerki would knock on the door or if he should leave it open.

"You must keep the door closed for the flies," said Afewerki, shutting the door on his way out. Flies zoomed through the space, zipping about and landing with breakneck speed. While walking up the steep path to the compound, a fly had driven straight into Reece's nostril. It had wanted to claw its way to his brain, and he'd had to pinch off the other nostril and blow the fly out. The group had paused around him, frowning, but what else could he do?

Reece gazed around the room, about eighty square feet, and felt that he could do it. His things were there. He was there. The place seemed to be rising, presenting itself as possible. He put his hands on his hips. He needed to shave. He wanted to brush his teeth and puzzled through scenarios of how best to do those things. He could heat water, maybe on Emma's stove, for shaving. After lunch, he had seen Barra brushing his teeth outside and spitting into the grass. He could do that as well. His trunk, packed with food from home, scraped cement as he dragged it into a clear spot near the wall. He pulled the other one to the foot of the bed. The floor canted slightly from back to front, just like the clinic.

Someone knocked on the door, and it was Mariam. He held a full water bottle.

"I bring water bottle," he said. "Okay?"

"Sure." Reece stepped away from the door.

Mariam inspired sharply, the affirmative breathing sound that Reece found so interesting, and then a clipped "Yes" as if the e did not exist. Behind him, Irigit, the night guard, spoke rapidly. Reece had no idea what he was saying, and Mariam did not respond. Irigit seemed to be telling himself a joke, laughing at his punch lines.

"Amenseganolo," said Mariam as he and Irigit departed. From his doorway, Reece could see over the compound. To the left were the cockeyed gate and the cookhouse next to the big outhouse. In the far-left corner of the oblong compound was Emma's shintabet, a phone booth–like toilet made of crooked poles and corrugated roofing. Between the house and the toilet sat the conical, thatched dining hut. He could see over the tall fence here and there, just glimpses. Nearby, two women shouted at one another across compounds, a family-to-family conversation. The sentences rose rapidly like buckets hauled quickly from a deep well, the endings dropping off sharply, intoned as questions. He thought he heard a gunshot in the distance.

He scooted things around. He put his Bible and daily devotional book on the tiny particleboard table by his bed, along with a big white candle and two smaller candles. He had a flashlight and a lighter, but no clock. Terry had said it was impossible to sleep for the roosters and not to worry. Besides, everyone operated on what Terry called "farmer time." In the country, he explained that time was measured in terms of how many hours the sun had been up. Five o'clock meant five hours after sunrise and so on. Reece sat on the narrow, squeaky cot and lay back. The thin mattress sagged in the middle, but it was comfortable. He could have gone to sleep. The metal roof popped, and occasionally a bird or two skittered and scratched across it. He began to hear Kristin's voice, her melodious laugh. She seemed indestructible somehow, yet unreal across this distance of eight thousand miles.

Reece and Kristin had ridden bikes from Atmore, Alabama, to Gulf Shores, leaving his white Chevy Citation in the far corner of a small hospital parking lot. Reece had a decent road bike, but when he had picked her up, she pushed an old granny three-speed out of her parents' garage. It had a metal basket on the front and a rack in the back and looked to weigh a hundred pounds.

They must have looked awkward and silly to a lot of folks. Reece wore a fully loaded backpack and had a small blue bag mounted on the front handlebar. Kristin carried a smaller backpack and had stuff jammed in her basket and tied to the rack with cord. Neither one had a mirror, and after leaving the hospital parking lot, they kept their eyes open for a hardware store. She wanted a mirror, and Reece went along with it even though he felt time was slipping away.

They were still riding when it got dark, a little bit lost, and both suffering from sunburn and raw tailbones. After they collided in what could only have been a fit of exhaustion, as the little .22 caliber pistol he had brought went skidding out into the middle of a newly paved road, oozing the day's heat back into the night, they agreed to stop at the next decent spot and camp out. The two-lane was quiet except for the occasional big rig bearing down on them. Reece had a light on the front of his bike, but both only had reflectors in the back.

A car behind them slowed, trailed them a bit, and then blue lights. The trooper said some truckers had called in complaining about them being on the road. Reece thought the truckers should mind their own business, but did not say anything. The trooper, whose face he could never see because of the lights, asked if he could give them a lift somewhere, maybe the truck stop down the road.

"Truck stop?" asked Reece. He quizzed Kristin and told the trooper they would decline his offer and ride on carefully to the truck stop. He made Reece promise that he would do as he said, and Reece said he would. The trooper said he would be in the area and to stay put until daylight. They said they certainly would do that. A large, bright moon was rising. They pedaled in silence, the tires humming on the road. Up ahead, the neon sign for Paul's Flying K cracked open the floodlit darkness, and beyond that, an overpass.

"You want to keep going?" asked Reece. From a distance, the restaurant and store looked like an abandoned manor house in a swamp, but without the swamp. He thought his tailbone was cracked and glanced around the gravel parking lot filled with diesel rigs. There were very few lights outside, and the inside lights blared outward.

"No!" Kristin said. "We're stopping like we promised."

They rode onto the gravel and dismounted, dazed, butts screaming, legs like lead. Half a dozen rigs idled, sleepy engine rumbles. It was midnight. Reece had figured they wouldn't need bike locks, but now thought better of it. They stood their rides near some waist-high holly bushes, hoping to be able to see them from inside. Kristin's wanted to fall over, and it took a little finagling to make it stand. Looking as unlike truckers as anyone could, they pushed through the first set of heavy, dingy glass doors, paused, and then the second set, being careful with their packs.

"Jesus," said Reece.

The carpeted inside smelled like stale lard. A tall ladder and a circular saw attached to a long extension cord sat in the middle of the room behind a row of swivel barstools. Formica-laminated booths with puffy brown seats lined the seating area, with a few tables and chairs in the open. It looked like one waitress was in the house, and she glared at them, stopped, and put her hands on her hips. Three customers turned and stared, expressionless.

"I'm going to the restroom." Kristin slid her backpack, really a rucksack, into the booth. Reece's leaned against the booth divider. He felt that it radiated signals, signals indicating that here was a stranger.

The restaurant was quiet, with just the occasional cackle generated between a hunched-over customer and the waitress. She was short and plump, with shaggy blonde hair pulled back by a hairband. Her uniform was straight out of a restaurant supply catalog, with pockets up front and a bow that tied in back, giving her the appearance of wearing an apron. The double doors into the kitchen looked heavy and wavered, almost not closing, as she passed back and forth. A dull light came from the service slit behind the counter. No one sat at the register up front, and the convenience store, accessed through another glass door, was dark and empty.

Reece looked out the window toward the bikes. He could see where the bikes were, but not the actual bikes. He lifted a bit and thought he could see a seat or a handlebar. A man with a brown beard and big belly and black shoes came in. The waitress shouted to him by name. The man doffed his cap in response and went into the men's room. Kristin had been gone five minutes or so, and the waitress hadn't bothered to come over yet. He began to worry about Kristin. He mulled over the day's ride, the frequent stops for water, drinks, and food.

Another five minutes passed, and no waitress or Kristin. He thought that maybe the waitress was being polite, waiting for Kristin. He couldn't decide if the waitress went to church or not. Another five minutes went by, and Reece stood, looked at the packs, and walked to the restrooms. He lingered outside the women's room for a few seconds, listening for the sounds of struggle, screams, bumping noises. The door opened.

Kristin laughed.

"I was worried," said Reece. "I'll be right out." He stepped into the men's room, a cold, urine-stained tile room, kind of baby blue. The urinals had floor-to-ceiling dividers between them. A hand-painted sign pointed to showers around a narrow corner, and he could hear water dripping.

"What were you doing?" Reece slipped back into the booth, lowering onto his abused tailbone.

"I took a bath."

Reece looked at her, and she did seem spiffed up.

"A bath or a shower?"

"I just got naked in front of the sink and washed off." She smiled her warm smile and laughed. "That lady came in and just about screamed, I think."

"The waitress? She hasn't said a word to me. What did she say?"

"She asked what we were doing, and I told her."

"What did she say?"

"She said I was crazy. She didn't even use the restroom."

"She was checking on you. I didn't even see her go back that way."

"What are you gonna order?" asked Kristin.

"I'm not even hungry, but am really thirsty."

"Maybe I'll get eggs and toast and some bacon."

"When the heck is she gonna get over here?" Reece was too tired to get angry. They had entered another world under false pretenses, and the rules did not apply to them. Kristin looked beautiful. She had combed back her wet curly hair, accenting her cheekbones. She looked fearless.

Ten very long minutes went by. The waitress was actively avoiding them now, whispering to the other customers, then laughing. Reece and Kristin discussed the day, what the next day might be like, how freaking sore their butt muscles were. They hadn't mentioned it yet, but Reece had only brought one tent. They hadn't even kissed yet.

"Y'all ready?" The waitress said her name was Lisa. She didn't have her pad and pen out, like she didn't expect them to order.

Lots of things went through Reece's head. "You ready?" He looked at Kristin.

"I'd like the eggs, bacon, and toast with juice and a glass of water."

Lisa dragged her pad from her front pocket and clicked her pen a few times. "Orange juice? That's all we got."

"That's good."

"I'd like my eggs scrambled," Kristin added.

Lisa frowned. "What'll you have?" She looked at Reece like he was cancer.

"I'd just like a boiled egg and some juice and water, please."

Lisa reared back on one hip. "Nadine don't boil just one egg!" She was just shy of shouting at Reece, looking like he had reached under her skirt or killed her cat.

Reece pondered her comeback for a good ten seconds, caught off guard. He wanted to say, "Well, just have Nadine boil a dozen and bring me one." To save time, he changed his order to a piece of toast with a fried egg and juice. He figured that would be double the work for Nadine, but she would have Lisa to thank for it.

"And can I have a *big* glass of juice?" asked Kristin.

Lisa nodded, smirked, and walked away.

"She's a bee eye tea see aitch," said Reece.

"She's just cranky, but she *does not* like us being here."

"I don't like being here."

"We're not moving, so don't even think about it."

"I don't know."

"Well, I do. That trooper's out there cruising around. Plus, we're both exhausted."

Reece couldn't stand the idea of letting the dawn catch up with them inside Paul's Flying K. He felt his life force draining into the vinyl booth.

"There's the overpass just a quarter mile up. It wouldn't take us two minutes to get there. We could lie down and sleep." A cloud in the distance radiated lightning like an old light bulb, a soft incandescence in the sky.

"Plus, it might rain," said Kristin.

Lisa waddled out with the food and drinks. The food looked like a truck-stop breakfast should. The plates were off-white and heavy, the silverware scratched and blurry.

Kristin drained the glass of water and called out to Lisa for a refill as she hurried back to the kitchen. A couple of other customers had blown in the front door, a breeze following them that startled a magazine on the floor. A little blow-in subscription card cartwheeled across the carpet. Reece took a bite of toast, and it took Lisa another five minutes to get the juice to the table. He made up his mind that they had to leave.

"Tastes okay," said Kristin.

"The service is what tastes bad." He felt cornered and dreaded trying to get the check. "I thought she would have left a check."

"See, she wants us to stay." Kristin looked like she had caught her second wind, like she was angling to bond with Lisa. He wondered if Lisa felt sorry for Kristin. She had seen her naked in the bathroom, bathing at the sink. Lisa probably thought that Reece was the cause of whatever misery Kristin might be enduring. She probably thought they were homeless, that Reece couldn't keep a job, and that this crazy girl was being dragged around on a bicycle for no good reason. The scenario depressed him.

"Let's get the check and get out of here."

Kristin was silent, but he could tell she was thinking.

"It'll be fun. I've never slept under a bridge. We'll lay the bikes down, and we'll be out of the rain, plus it's cooled down. It's too cold in here, and I'm worried about our bikes."

Lisa bustled over with the bill and handed it to Kristin. Reece reached for his wallet in the zip pocket of his silvery riding pants. Lisa's scrawl looked like either eleven or seventeen, and they both looked at the ticket, trying to discern what they should pay.

"It can't possibly be seventeen."

"Maybe the juice?"

"That's crazy."

"We still have to tip her."

Reece knew she was right. "Let's leave fourteen. I have fourteen here."

Kristin hesitated and managed to catch Lisa's eye and waved her over.

"Eleven twenty-five," said Lisa, handing the little thin receipt on the table back to Kristin and waddling away. Her legs rubbed together.

"How about sixteen?" asked Kristin.

"Sixteen?"

"We're leaving sixteen." She pulled two dollars from her pack.

"Okay, sixteen."

A light rain slapped the windows.

"We better hurry."

"Let me go to the bathroom first. Watch my pack."

Mounting the bikes was painful, and they wobbled down the road to the overpass. The two-lane ducked under briefly. There were no exit or entrance ramps. A stiff wind with fits of blowing rain narrowed their shelter to a dry strip just a few feet wide. Feeling a burden of responsibility to make sure everything went as well as possible, Reece pulled out a tarp and the small tent. The wind made it hard to keep things from flying away. Cars and trucks and big rigs swooshed overhead, a loud *clank clank* each time. Reece sized up the situation. Kristin was squatting, saying she was cold. There was no ledge near the top of the bridge where he had imagined they could sleep. He turned the bikes onto their sides in the tall weeds and grass, laid the tarp on the sloped cement, and he and Kristin pulled the limp tent over them as a blanket and shield from the mist that rode on the gusting wind.

An old woman clutching a grain sack rose as Reece followed Afewerki into the cramped clinic. A teenage boy with balloon eyes and a straw hat with a red silk band, something you might win at a carnival, listened as Emma explained to Afewerki how the boy should take his tapeworm medicine, a big beige tablet. "You must chew it and swallow." She explained the worms would die and he should watch for them, that he might feel sick when that happened, that he should wash his hands after he defecates. Do you have a shintabet at your home? No, he did not. The boy carefully chewed the tablet, making an awful face. Emma spoke to Afewerki, and he handed an orange cup of water to the boy. "Bataam taruno," Emma told the boy, who staggered out of the clinic like he had been cut open.

Light filtered in through the cracks, the door, and the "skylight." Patients sat on one of two crude benches made of planks and biscuit tins. A crazy tilted system of shelves held the medicines used most often—pills and ointments for worms, eye and ear infections, stomach pains, headaches, burns, and a variety of skin diseases, including scabies. There were still thirty or forty people in line. After examining the contents of a small storage room containing large cans of diazepam and codeine and bottles of IV fluids, which he discovered were indeed from Iceland, Reece asked Afewerki if he should help Emma. Emma initially objected, but then agreed. She looked exhausted.

Afewerki had shaved his head since Reece first saw him

and wore a baseballcap advertising Exxon. Outside, the woman doling out the milk powder was laughing. Afewerki stepped onto the top step, holding onto the door frame. He motioned to an old woman who stood. She had some trouble stepping up and held her hand to her back. She limped as if her left hip were very stiff.

"Mendeno?" asked Afewerki. What's wrong? What brings you here today? He had a curious manner of talking softly and with a hint of humor, or maybe it was irony in his voice.

Reece stood back, giving everyone plenty of room, visually inspecting this old woman in rags. She was skinny.

"Rasmatat, hodiun." The lady touched her head and then her stomach, and then cried, mumbling. Reece surmised that her primary problem was that her life was pure hell.

Afewerki turned to Reece and in that low voice, his clinic voice, said that the woman was suffering from headache and stomachache. Emma was listening and said something to her. Reece watched as Emma pulled the old woman's lower eyelid down and then murmured to herself. The lining of the lid was very pale. She asked her if she ate eggs or meat, and did she have worms in her stool? No, no, and maybe. She just didn't know, and tears returned to her eyes. Reece kept a trickle of sadness in check. She looked so helpless sitting there.

"How old is she?" asked Reece. But the woman said she did not know. That her mother knew, that her mother had been dead for many years.

"She's maybe fifty," said Emma.

She looked ninety.

"So, what do you do in this case?" Reece had plenty of experience doing CPR and cleaning tracheotomy tubes, but this was a different ballgame.

"Headache and stomachache, and she's anemic. We'll treat her for that and tell her to buy some eggs if she can, and give her some extra milk powder and some biscuits. Her stomach is not distended, so I don't think she has worms."

Afewerki doled out thirty vitamin tablets with iron into a small yellow envelope. One per day, he told her. He made the motion of putting the pill into his mouth and swallowing. "And, baqan baqan." The old lady stood slowly with Emma's help, murmuring her thanks over and over, and secreted away the packet of vitamins into the folds of her dirty dress. She was barefoot. Afewerki yelled out the door and then motioned for the old lady to go to the middle of the compound for extra rations.

Emma then called in an old man, a shimogele, a term that seemed to have a slight derogatory connotation. The next patient called in by Afewerki sat as if she had come to visit for a while. She looked young, perhaps twenty-five, and had a somber but pretty, round face like a cartoon caterpillar. If it were possible, Reece thought, she seemed slightly plump. "This woman is my neighbor," said Afewerki, and he inquired what the problem might be, even though he already knew.

The woman sat, wringing her hands, talking to her knees in long sentences. She stopped and looked up at Reece as if expecting a solution.

"This one is interesting," said Afewerki.

Reece had no idea what the problem could be and was

also watching Emma with the old man, who, touching his forehead and stomach, indicated another possible case of worms.

"What does she say?"

"She says she is pregnant."

"Is she having problems?" asked Reece.

"She says she is bleeding, but that is not the problem. She has been pregnant for eight years, and the baby will not come outside, she says."

"Eight years?"

"Yes, she is crazy. She has no husband and has no child. She comes once or twice per month. Maybe she is to hear you are coming."

Emma finished with the old man, giving him pills for roundworms.

"What do you think is best?" Reece stood closer to the woman and said hello, "Tenesteling." The woman smiled and said something. Reece felt as if he had been standing there all his life. "Let's look at her eyelids and her teeth." The woman opened her mouth. Reece pulled her lower eyelid down. He looked in her mouth. She had very white teeth up front, but her molars seemed to be rotten. Her gums looked blue and were blue, having been tattooed, making her front teeth seem ultra-white.

"We just tell her to pray for God to cause the baby to come out," said Afewerki.

Reece thought that was probably better than nothing. "She's anemic, so let's give her some of the vitamins. Maybe she'll feel better." His throat tickled. Flies buzzed. He'd forgotten to lock the door to his room, or did it matter?

Afewerki dealt the woman the information offhandedly. She nodded in agreement and began to cry, and she took her packet of pills as he made notes in a dog-eared spiral notebook.

"Do you think she's okay?" asked Reece.

"She will be okay. God will help her. She will sell the pills, and she will be happy."

Afewerki called for the next patient as Emma was calling another as well. A mother and her five-year-old son stepped inside, she being stooped over with his weight. Another woman gripped the door frame, waiting for the woman to move forward. Those smells of milk and wood smoke. The mother with the boy slid him off her back. He was wild-eyed and began to whimper a primal tune. She unwrapped a length of cloth from her waist and held it in her lap as the little boy tried to disappear into her. She coaxed and soothed him, looking back and forth between Afewerki and Reece with a look of incredulity. She laughed, and the little boy uttered a cry, and she shifted back to murmuring to him, rocking back and forth as if constant motion were needed to placate him.

The other woman took a seat against the wall, and Reece tried to visualize her need as well as that of the agitated mother and her woeful son. A sourness in the air. The little boy did not have pants, and his small, uncircumcised penis pointed straight out like a divining rod. It looked like something was wrong with his hand, and he kept pulling it away from his mother, whining and hiding his face. As a mother with a child in the feeding program, they had already been measured and weighed.

Afewerki showed Reece the big yellow card that she carried. "He is gaining weight, see," and pointed to the dots and the hand-drawn curve now reaching into the shaded area, indicating normal. "He is getting fat," he said in Amharic and pinched the little boy's cheek. "Mendeno, mamoosh?"

The little boy cringed. His mother took his wrist and forced his hand out, speaking to Afewerki, who summarized her statements for Reece every fifteen seconds or so. Emma was feeling the lymph nodes in the neck of the other woman who wore a black string around her neck. Her rough and filthy quilted dress swept the floor, and her feet were bare.

The woman in front of Reece was Coptic and had tattooed dots around her neck that connected into a virtual necklace. A small cross was tattooed just above the breastbone. The little boy's left hand was swollen, especially his index finger, which was twice its normal size. The flesh looked angry and red despite his deep brown skin. The boy cried in fits, anxious that no one should touch his finger. His mother soothed him with great energy, holding him still as Reece moved in for a better look. He touched the finger, and the skin was very tight like a drumhead, and the boy began to shout as if he were being killed. The mother gathered him to her and rocked him, speaking to no one in particular.

Reece had never lanced a wound before, but this one needed lancing, and he inquired if there were any scalpels. Afewerki produced a sterile blade within seconds. "We need to wash the hand first with some iodine," said Reece, focusing closer and closer on the finger. Afewerki explained to the mother what must be done, and she explained it to her son, then pulled his unwilling hand back out for all to see. Afewerki moved an empty biscuit tin beneath the hand as Reece opened a prepackaged sponge soaked with an iodine solution. He moved carefully, and the cool, thick, blood-like iodine dripped from the boy's hand into the tin. With a pair of sterile gloves, Reece wiped carefully with a gauze pad the spot where he would nick the swollen finger.

The woman with Emma had shown her a row of festering sores lining her groin, and she had prescribed her medication for miliary tuberculosis: rifampin and isoniazid. She would need to come back once a month for six months, but she doubted the woman would comply.

Reece moved the scalpel in quickly and sliced a quarter-inch slit, which burst with a stream of hot, yellow pus. The boy screwed up his face in horror but did not flinch or scream, but his mother looked as if she might faint. "Ishi, ishi," said Afewerki. "Ishi, mamoosh, bataam taruno." Emma stopped to watch as Reece touched and then cradled the boy's finger with his own. More pus ran out and dripped into the biscuit tin, and then everyone except for Reece gasped. In his gloved hand, he held the outer casing of the boy's finger, including the intact fingernail. It had slid off like a glove. The boy slowly worked himself into a scream, and his mother worked very hard to calm him and hold his wrist.

Emma, Afewerki, Reece, and the mother all craned their heads in the patchwork of light. The denuded finger was red, but not bleeding. It looked raw but had the appearance of a piece of meat that was just beginning to cure. A hole in the hollow of the bone nearest the knuckle looked like it might have harbored some nasty pocket of infection. The flesh was smooth and looked very strange. Reece decided it reminded him most of a burn and asked if there was any Silvadene, the thick antibacterial ointment used for burns. Emma nodded and, to Reece's amazement, returned with a large jar of silver sulfadiazine. The little boy's eyes grew wider and wider as Reece carefully covered his finger with the white ointment, which was cool and soothing. The boy grew calm, and the mother, as well as Afewerki, helped Reece apply a sterile dressing that cocooned the finger.

"You must keep this very clean," Afewerki told the mother. "You must come back tomorrow." He sounded very stern and pointed his finger at her for emphasis.

Emma handed her a packet of famine biscuits, which she incorporated into her dress and, without much ado, alighted into the blue day, the head of the little boy peeking from beneath her dingy shamma.

Without pause or commentary, Emma helped a teenage girl up the stairs. She looked the color of a pale green tomato. She had thin, delicate features and thick hair combed back. She looked miserable and was barefoot. An old, old man teetered in behind her, leaning on a staff of polished, crooked wood. A thick, filigreed silver cross hung around his neck. In his free hand, he gripped the local flyswatter, an ox's tail fashioned to the end of a piece of carved wood, which he flipped with a flourish. He had brought with him a few flies that clung to his reddened eyes, which were oozing yellow discharge. "He is priest," said Afewerki.

Reece thought he heard the helicopter, something in the air. Reece looked at the girl, and she was either trying to cry or not to pass out, and Emma was fortifying her with encouraging words and asking Afewerki for something. Afewerki spoke to the priest and told Reece the girl needed ORS, oral rehydration solution, the no-frills, flavorless Gatorade from plain silver packets mixed into cups of water. She held the cup, shaking and trembling, taking little sips and making a sour face as if she were drinking her urine.

"Mendeno, baba?" asked Afewerki to the old man. His short hair was peppered with gray, as was his scraggly, six-inch-long beard. He smelled of smoke and incense, dampness, and fried potatoes. He wore the crude sandals made from old tires and a puffy brown hat that fit his head. His eyes were tired and deep and almost hidden. Afewerki quizzed him about his eyes, and Reece took a closer look. The bottom lids of both eyes had begun to turn inward, entropion caused by *Chlamydia*, which, if untreated, would lead to completely inverted eyelids, the eyelashes slowly gouging and scarring the infected eyes into blindness. Hunks of yellowish discharge floated like hot frothy butter between blinks. The eyelashes clung together in wet clumps. Despite the nastiness, he looked very stoic sitting there, as if he would still be sitting there a hundred years from now, no matter what happened.

Afewerki showed Reece a box of tetracycline eye ointment, which was used to treat most of the eye infections that they saw, including this case of trachoma, which was common. "We have seen him before," he said. Reece heard the distant chopping of the helicopter and glanced through the door. Afewerki tilted the old man's head back and, with a latex glove, pulled his eyelids down and placed a small line of the ointment across the lid's mucky interior. The old man blinked and listened as Afewerki explained how he must use the medicine three times a day and come back when the ointment was finished.

"Maybe we can give him some soap to wash his hands," said Reece.

"He will sell it," Afewerki said, but handed the old man an unmarked box of square yellow soap and pantomimed handwashing as he spoke to the old priest.

Reece noticed Emma with the can of generic Valium. The girl still held the orange cup of ORS, and Emma was giving her a handful of ORS packets, vitamins, and diazepam as well. She looked a little better.

The priest had words for Reece and directed a solemn discourse at him. He kissed his cross and stood shakily to leave, secreting his ointment in a pocket along with a packet of famine biscuits. "He says for God to bless you," said Afewerki.

Emma helped the young girl to stand as Afewerki called in the next patient. After she disappeared around the corner, Reece asked Emma about the girl. "She's a newlywed, married a week to some old geezer. I think he's wearing her out," said Emma.

"How old is she?" asked Reece.

"I think maybe thirteen or fourteen. Her husband is an old man, older than me. She says that he is bothering her, which could mean anything unpleasant."

In stepped an older mother with a baby on her back, sheathed in a leather carrier decorated with small bells that jingled. The little girl emerged with a blank look and a cloud of sour odors. Her braided and buttered hair shone with small, colorful beads. The mom pulled up the little girl's dress to show her stomach, which was covered with a fine scattering of sharp, raised bumps. Afewerki asked her a few questions, and Reece heard the word for soap, *samona*. The woman turned her daughter this way and that, pointing, stroking the sand-like bumps, making itching motions. "This mother and daughter have scabies," said Afewerki.

Emma tended to a large, powerful-looking man. He was very tall, had a loud voice, and the look of someone who could plow rocks all day and build a barn at night. Outside, the laborers were gathering, the helicopter louder and louder. Reece felt like he was watching *M.A.S.H.* on TV. Afewerki spoke louder and pulled a box from the bottom shelf filled with smooth metal bottles, permethrin, a foul-smelling oily topical medication for scabies. Reece was unaware that mites caused scabies and followed Afewerki's script. Emma nodded her approval. Afewerki had been working with Emma all along. He was trained as a dresser, which Reece understood to be like an LPN or perhaps a medic.

The helicopter roared overhead, pounding the tiny clinic with a fist of wind. Terry circled and set his bulging cargo net on the ground. Barra ran up, crouched, and unhooked the load. Within seconds, Terry spun up and then dove away to the river valley below. Reece followed the addictive sound until it faded.

The little girl had buried her head into her mother's breast, prompting her to nurse the child, although she seemed too old and the mother's breast too flat and flaccid. The little girl, maybe two, stood barefoot on the floor, wedged between her mother's thighs, sucking and looking backward as best she could without losing her mother's breast. Afewerki toyed with her, trying to make her smile. She stared back at him. Outside the clinic, children would flock to Reece, run circles around him, reach for his hand, yell Ferenj!, and ask for caramella, but inside the clinic, they just watched, petrified.

Afewerki pulled on a latex glove and, with a gauze four-by-four, lathered the permethrin on the inside of the little girl's arm. She jerked it away and crawled up her mother's dress like a cat up a curtain. Reece watched, amused, beginning to realize that his drop-in visit would be his first day of clinic work. He wondered if he was helping or in Emma's way.

"Let me know if I'm in the way."

"What?"

Afewerki explained to the woman that she must wash the affected areas with soap and apply the lotion. To do it again in a few days if needed. He explained to her the need to wash the girl's clothes, but that was impossible with water being so scarce, and it was useless to elaborate on all the things that needed washing. Emma's patient left before the little girl and her mother. He seemed worried and turned back to say something to Emma, pleading, and Emma sent him on his way.

"What did he need?" asked Reece.

"He has gonorrhea," said Afewerki.

"And he must bring his wife," said Emma.

Afewerki explained that they did not treat just the male and that he had to bring in the female he was sleeping with as well, or vice versa, and that sometimes it was the wife and sometimes not.

"Oh," said Reece.

An old woman with the saddest face Reece had ever seen struggled up the two steps. Afewerki helped her to the bench where she sat panting. Her head was small, shrunken, and the corners of her wrinkled mouth drooped into a fantastic quarter moon. Her tiny eyes looked through him. She whispered as if from an old rocking chair on a front porch far away, pulling her dress off her left shoulder, exposing what used to be a breast, and above it, hanging down beneath the flesh, her clavicle snapped nearly in half. She couldn't move her left arm, and her voice quavered. Reece imagined she felt she would die, that she knew she had acquired a fatal flaw.

Afewerki and Emma stood back and shook their heads. Emma bit her lip and asked Reece for his opinion. Reece leaned down and lightly fingered the bone. She explained that she had fallen, and her eyes welled with tears.

"There is nothing we can do," said Emma.

"Can she go to Addis?" asked Reece. He felt helpless.

The bone would heal, Emma explained, of its own accord.

"Let's send her on the helicopter," said Reece. He had no idea what would happen, but it sounded like something a mission should do.

"She says her husband will not let her go."

"Where is he?" asked Reece.

"He is plowing."

"What can we do?"

"We can do nothing." Plus, she had just sent a patient to Addis, the man with his intestine herniated into his scrotum. Emma explained to her that she must not use the affected arm. And the woman asked how she could make enjera? Reece suggested they put her arm in a sling, and Afewerki held a stack of famine biscuits for her. Emma found a prepackaged sling, olive green, and after some false starts, she and Afewerki had her arm supported, the best that could be done. "Tell her to let the arm rest, to keep it in the sling and close to her body." Afewerki told her, and she looked comforted as she rose unsteadily to leave.

Afewerki went out to check on the line, and another twenty-eight were waiting. Reece felt his jeans were loose. Dirt covered his tennis shoes, and as the sun began to slant through the poles in the wall, he could see a cloud of swirling dust, almost like a fire. His back hurt, and he realized how tense he was. He was thirsty as well, but did not want to drink water straight from the water can, knowing it hadn't been boiled.

The next patients, two young teenagers, complained of worms. Wosfat. Tapeworms in their feces. Headaches. Stomach pain. One wanted to take his first dose of niclosamide at home, and Afewerki shook his head and said, "No, no, no," because he suspected he would sell it instead. The boy ruefully chewed the large tablet, youthful but already painted with the chiseled look of the older men who moved stones and plowed and sat around drinking talla while the crops grew in the brutal sun. And then more cases of scabies, stomachs and the bends of arms littered with itching bumps, the biting mites invisible to the naked eye, feasting.

An old woman carried a tiny baby into the clinic, the

infant crying weakly and struggling in slow motion. To look at the line of people, one couldn't see these infants and small children hidden on the backs of women. She was his grandmother, and his mother had died in childbirth, and now what could she do? The baby had diarrhea and was growing weaker, she said matter-of-factly, and then she turned him across her knee, clothed in a loose shirt but no pants. Reece winced and moved closer. Emma and Afewerki made sounds of disapproval, *Ai, ai, ai,* and *Tsk, tsk, tsk.*

The boy's rectum protruded three inches from his anus, the incessant diarrhea everting the red and glistening lining. Reece could see the residue of yellow discharge on his scrawny legs. The woman wiped it away with her left hand onto the side of her dress. Reece knew what to do and shared his plan with Emma to see if she agreed, and she did. The old woman held the little boy's buttocks as best she could while Reece poured cool water onto the projecting bulge of tissue to which the boy screamed and kicked, causing some of the water to splatter on the floor instead of flowing into the biscuit tin. The sensitive tissue withdrew an inch or so, and he would need to push it back carefully, and he did, wearing a latex glove, his finger coated with a glop of petroleum jelly. Gently, he poked, and the angry mess pulled itself back into place. Afewerki helped to wash the boy's legs, and then Emma taped the buttocks together. She asked the woman some questions about the diarrhea. Red like blood? Yes, red like blood. How many times per day? I don't know, many, she said. Is he breastfeeding? No. How is he drinking? Okay. Is he vomiting? No.

Afewerki had mixed some ORS in an orange cup, which the old woman first tried to drink herself until Emma told her to give it to the baby with a syringe. How old is the baby? I don't know, and the woman began to try to count days, and it was determined that the boy was six months old. Reece pinched the infant's thigh lightly, and the skin wanted to tent but slowly spread back out. He wondered about IV fluids. The grandmother managed to squirt some ORS into his mouth. He smacked it, and most of it ran down his face onto her dress. Reece found himself staring and swallowing, as if he were the baby, and a pressure built in his chest. The tape came off the boys butt, but the rectum was inside where it should be and then a little squirt of hot yellowish fluid. After cleaning his bottom again and re-taping, this time over a spray of benzoin to make the skin tacky, Afewerki explained the importance of hydration. He placed a small box of ORS beside her. Use clean water, he told her, and she nodded. Use the syringe, and she nodded. There were only a few cans of infant formula in the clinic, and he gave her one of those as well, telling her to give as much as he would take with a spoon until it was gone. Reece thought she said, "Murphy."

Emma laughed. *Murphy,* Afewerki explained, was an injection. He said that the injection was the most highly valued form of treatment. Sometimes they will leave and talk to others and say that they have been cheated if they do not get an injection, he said. Reece said to tell her to come back if the diarrhea did not get better. He had very little knowledge of using antibiotics with infants, but felt that they were doing the right thing. The old woman smiled and bundled up her dead daughter's son, off to the next mishap, her wrinkled brow seemed to say. "If the tape gets soiled or comes off, just leave it off," and Afewerki called this out to her as she walked away.

"Is there ever cholera?" asked Reece.

"Oh yeah," said Emma.

"Yes, there are many graves just down this hill," said Afewerki.

Reece looked out the door. An old man was standing there, looking in. He wore a dingy white skullcap, indicating his Muslim faith.

"Just beyond the fence, you will see later."

"Mendeno, baba?" asked Emma.

The old man, it was hard to say how old, had a spark in his eye. His eyebrows seemed to be animated. Reece looked closer, and the lice there responded to his inspection by freezing.

"He has lice," said Reece. "In his eyebrows."

"Yep," said Emma, "but he is complaining of headache." The lice didn't seem to bother him. The old man's stomach didn't hurt, just rasmatat, a headache, and trouble seeing long distances.

A teen, maybe fourteen, entered with her little sister, five or so. The older sister looked every bit like an adult except for her size and the freshness of her skin. She had a lovely smile and seemed to have some carefree days left in her. She was efficient and professional in the presentation of her younger sister, whom she announced had had an accident. The little girl wore a leather strip and an amulet around her neck. The older sister wore a clean brown dress, and the little one's was dark green. Both were barefoot.

"What is the accident?" asked Afewerki. The little girl was not smiling, but did not seem to be in any pain.

"Oh," said Afewerki. "She says she has lost a rock inside her nose."

"Really?"

"Yes." Reece put his hand out to the little girl, and she looked at it. Afewerki asked which side.

"This one," she said. And he tilted the girl's head back and looked.

The old man seemed to be telling Emma a story and enjoying his visit, talking loudly and tapping his staff on the floor.

Reece looked in the nostril and did not see anything. The little girl spoke shyly. "She does not want to die," said Afewerki. Reece asked Afewerki to block her left nostril and have the little girl blow. He explained, and she blew, but not very hard, and out popped a small stone. She turned and embraced her sister, who comforted her. There was no blood or swelling, and she had no breathing problems. Reece noticed a small mark on her leg and asked about it. Her brother threw a stick, the older sister said. And he put the stone in her nose, she added. Reece cleaned the small puncture with iodine and gave the older sister a tube of antibiotic ointment. Afewerki handed the little girl a packet of famine biscuits, and she tried to stifle a smile.

The old man, with his packet of paracetamol tablets for his headaches, loitered in the doorway, exhorting Allah and asking blessings for everyone.

The laborers had finished carting the grain and other

supplies left by Terry, and the women doling out soybean oil, milk powder, grain, and biscuits began to close up shop in the middle of the compound, pulling tarps over piles and boxes, laughing and talking. Reece had lost all sense of time. The air was still and warm, but promised to cool. The light outside was bright, but the haze of the distance beyond the fig tree and over the rise seemed dimmer. He had slight indigestion from lunch and was very thirsty. There was no shintabet inside the warehouse compound, and he wondered where everyone went to pee or otherwise.

"What do we have here?" asked Emma.

A woman cradled a small boy, perhaps two or three. He pressed his head against his mother's chest, his eyes cutting toward Emma and Reece. The people out front had let her pass. She had traveled on foot from a nearby village, Aferbiny, two or three miles. Away. The accident had just happened, she said.

"What is it?" asked Emma, and the woman lay the little boy on her lap. He did not resist and had a distinct mark on his little dress. She pulled up his dress, a long coarse shirt, and without telling them what had happened, Afewerki guessed first. He was playing, she said, and his sister was not watching, and the little boy walked behind an ox, and the ox kicked the little boy in the chest. The woman used her hands to show the force and shook her head, and said that she thought he was dead, that he did not move, and tears came to her eyes as the little boy lay there on her lap, very still. The hoof had caught him just over his heart, and the flesh was cut almost like a cloven cookie cutter would, red and swollen but with minor bleeding. He breathed slowly but not labored, and did not seem to be in pain while breathing. He did not want Emma to touch him there and made a burst of protests, drawing closer to his mother.

The next three people in line peeped in, watching, sensing a miracle. And it was Emma who used *miracle* first, and then Afewerki and then Reece. With much soothing and a biscuit, Reece listened to his chest and heard nothing unusual. His pulse seemed fine. He would be very sore and should rest, said Emma, and Reece nodded. Afewerki cleaned the area gently with peroxide and dabbed antibiotic ointment around the swelling edges. She was to keep him clean, wash the wound daily, and apply the ointment, and she said, ishi, ishi, okay, okay, and it was a miracle, she said, and everyone thanked God in one way or another and marveled at the little boy. He had flown through the air like a chicken, she said.

Reece wondered if everyone in Godo had worms and scabies. He wondered how many helicopter loads of niclosamide and permethrin had flown through the thin air. The diet was so spicy, he thought, and must be tough on worms. Kosa and wosfat, the worms, could block an intestine, starve a body, rupture a bowel. The cumulative weakness wreaked by the worms alone staggered him. He remembered having hookworms as a kid in Germany and swallowing soft capsules the size of footballs. He wondered if a pound of misery weighed a pound of worms.

A short, thin, very black man staggered in. He wore farmer's clothes, had no hat, and wore tire sandals. His face looked like a shriveled raisin. He had traveled for many miles from an area north into Wollo. His family had malaria, he said, his wife and three sons and two daughters. They will die, he said, unless God helps us. He spoke as if he were twenty, but he looked sixty. His doolah looked heavy. He had no particular smell, and the flies seemed uninterested in him. Emma queried him, and Afewerki whispered to Reece a summarized account. There was fever, vomiting, his wife's eyes had turned to suqwar, sugar, he said. Only the little girl was crying now, and they will die, he said.

"Are they shaking?" asked Emma, and he gritted his teeth and looked a fierce demon. Yes, they have malaria, the man said, they are dying.

Afewerki shook his head. "Mmm, mmm, mmm. Tsk, tsk, tsk."

"Can they come here?" asked Reece.

No, no, no.

Emma explained to the man what he must do, that he must take the chloroquine pills she was giving him, and that his family must take them as she says. They must drink plenty of water, and they should chew on lemons or limes, if possible. The man said he had no money to buy lemons and held out both hands for the packets of chloroquine. Afewerki silently gave him two coins, and the old man bowed his head as if being knighted.

"Let's give him ORS as well," said Reece, and everyone agreed it was a good idea, and the young man who was old walked out bent over with a long journey before him. Reece wondered if they should go with the man. No, that would do no good, said Afewerki, and there are so many people coming here. Reece wondered about how long the man had sat in the hot sun, waiting patiently, perhaps hours. He felt sick for the man, and the day began to weigh on him, a sack of rocks around his neck.

It was cooler, and there was a quiet like the hush of a school that is closed for the day, the few remaining people silent and drifting. Emma told Reece that he should go and rest, but Reece was no longer tired. There was a hum in his forehead, the autopilot, and a vague headache, the altitude he thought, and that persistent tickle in his throat. He was thankful he didn't have to pee and remembered the liter of water he'd had with lunch. He worried that he was becoming dehydrated in a chronic sense. Afewerki counted nine patients left. The guard had let them all into the compound and closed the gate. The horizon was golden now, and the air heavier. The guard was a rough-looking man with a patchy beard, as if someone had grabbed his face and pulled out a fistful of hair. He didn't have any visible scars on his legs or arms, but he looked scarred anyway. The guards in the living compound were always laughing or joking.

Seven of the nine had either diarrhea, scabies, or worms. The other two complained of eye problems. They sat inside the clinic, each on a bench, one facing east, the other facing north. Two old ladies, and Reece had no idea how old they were. They seemed to be sisters or neighbors, but he did not ask. They both had black marks on their palms from carrying hot coals and wore no shoes. One had extensive tattoos on her chest and neck, the other just a cross on her forehead. Reece and Afewerki faced south, and Emma faced west.

The woman facing north toward Wollo, the area where most people had died in the famine, sat and whispered that her husband was blind and that she feared going blind, what would happen if she went blind, and they would die because they had no family other than his two worthless sisters and then she began to list a long line of useless relatives and friends who would abandon them once there was no enjera to eat or talla to drink. Afewerki laughed.

She had taken to brewing the clear, smoky, powerful liquor, katikala, to make money. She had tried to put some in her eyes to cure the infection and had gone blind in one eye for one week, she said. But everyone wanted to drink the katikala today and pay tomorrow, and her husband, because he was blind, liked to drink the katikala and then sleep instead of begging, as God would have him do. And now I'm going blind, she said, and began to weep, her tears flushing little clots of yellow from her matted eyelashes. Reece did not hear the other woman's story, but from the tone and Emma's replies, he imagined her story was the same. Afewerki took a sterile gauze four-by-four and wiped her lashes with saline, working loose the debris. Her eyes looked red and bleary, the lashes already turning toward the eyes. She lay back on the bench and Reece poured a small stream of saline into each eye as Afewerki caught the runoff with more gauze. Tetracycline ointment, and she was ready to go with a packet of biscuits and a single tube of the ointment to take with her. Reece wondered if it would make a difference.

Emma locked the clinic door, closing the padlock. Reece suddenly felt strange and free, like he might leave the ground and float away. Three weeks ago, he could have been hesitating at a four-way stop in Alabama, picking up pinecones, or chewing gum in an elevator. He tried to tie it all together, and nothing happened. The weight of nightfall is the same everywhere, he thought.

"Such a busy day," said Afewerki. He put on his coat.

Children swirled like dust before the rain as they walked to the home compound. Reece did not like the sound or feel of "compound." It felt too heavy, like a fortress, like he would wake in the morning, and the people would have laid siege to the compound. The wide path was very steep. It amazed him, the steepness and rockiness of Godo. He breathed hard and found it harder to talk as he walked. Emma sauntered and did not seem bothered, but Afewerki acted as if they were very slow and pulled ahead. Emma and Reece walked in silence.

A thin trickle of smoke came from the cookhouse hidden behind the gate and fence. Dinner was waiting, and Reece went to his room to clean up and have a long drink of water from the bottle there. The letters from Kristin and his grandparents lay on the table beside the bed. He noticed for the first time that the blanket on his cot was red plaid. He started to open a letter and put it back down. The other guys had been loitering on the narrow, covered stoop that ran the length of their four-room motel. Mariam was listening to a small tape recorder, and when Reece heard country music, he asked him who it was. "Jeem Reefs," Reece thought he said, and looked at the cassette cover, Jim Reeves. Reece wondered how Jim Reeves had made his way to Godo.

"He is famous singer," said Mariam.

Reece thought it sounded like a question and felt that he should affirm the popularity of Jim Reeves. "Yes, he is very popular." He had no real idea who Jim Reeves was, just that he existed. Mariam smiled shyly, nodding his head to the country beat.

In his room, the poles making the roof were crooked.

The white plastic lining the walls sagged. The room was quiet, and the bed creaked when he sat on it. Outside, the team was talking, bantering. He wanted to refer to them as the guys, but that didn't seem right, but neither did "the team." In his first letter from Godo, he wrote "the team of guys I work with," and that seemed sufficient for outsiders.

"I am from a beautiful place in Ethiopia," said Barra. The team, the guys, sat snugly in folding chairs in the dining hut, a kerosene lantern ready to go when darkness fell. The dirt floor held remnants of the grass that grew there not so long ago. Before he could ask where Barra was from, Barra continued. "It is near Shashamane. There are many beautiful lakes." He smiled widely as he spoke, evangelically. "You will come and visit my family?"

Reece looked at Barra, not quite understanding everything he was saying. He was understanding the words, but Barra's manner of speaking indicated he didn't quite mean what he said. "Are they big lakes?" he said.

Barra laughed, leaning his head back as if to sneeze at the sun. "Oh yes, bigger than Zhorzia," and he clapped his hands and laughed and gazed around, and the others laughed a little as well. "Oh, you are not from Zhorzia?"

"He is Ah-la-ba-ma," said Isaac. "You have not been listening, my brother." He chuckled to himself.

"Ah yes, the Ah-la-ba-ma," said Barra, shaking his finger at everyone.

Stooping, Emma pushed the flap aside and stood there. There were not enough chairs.

"I'll get the chair from my room." Reece stood.

"No, no," said Isaac. He poked his head outside and yelled to Ketow for another chair.

Reece remained standing. "Birmingham," he said. "We're talking about Alabama." He had brought a single bottle of water and wasn't sure if he should have brought one for everyone.

Barra looked puzzled. "You say Leningrad?"

Emma laughed and took the chair that Ketow brought, a rickety stool.

"No, no," said Reece. Sitting in the dining hut, the world seemed very real and very strange. Already, the United States was slipping away as an entity, becoming more of an idea or concept.

"We are following these men with beards," said Isaac. He spoke deliberately and sounded drugged to Reece, but he wasn't. "You have seen in Addis Ababa? The men with bushy beards, the Russians?"

"The big billboard in Revolution Square. Marx, Lenin, and Engels," said Emma.

Reece pondered his response. Thus far, the only meaning he could attach to the so-called Marxist regime was petty bureaucracy, in the form of purple stamps. Everyone had a rubber stamp and a pad of purple ink. No one wore red, or flew the Soviet flag, or spoke Russian. He hadn't seen peasants reading *The Communist Manifesto*. "It sounds crazy," he said.

"We pay them no mind," said Emma. "Just go with the flow."

Ketow pushed through the plastic with a big platter of enjera, the pungent smell preceding it, piled with meat still on the bone. A bowl of tibs floated in a red, oily liquid.

"This is kiyawot," explained Afewerki. Kiya, meaning very spicy, meaning nuclear hot.

Reece's mouth watered, and he wondered if they ever ate vegetables. Suddenly, he decided that he would share his box of peanut brittle. He noticed a familiar sound of crickets outside and one lone cricket inside. He wondered what Emma did besides work in the clinic, what sorts of rituals she went through each night. Was Hattie fitting in at Gundo Meskel? "What happens after dinner?" asked Reece.

"I go to bed. I'm not sure what these guys do," said Emma.

"Read?"

"Read and write, and sleep." She laughed, pulled her face into that lopsided smile.

Barra mentioned that he would be going later to have tea in the local tea house. Isaac and Mariam had no plans, although they went out occasionally at night to have tea or coffee as well.

The goat meat was delicious and spicy, and Reece was tempted to drink the water from the pitcher after he polished off his bottle, but it was unfiltered. Except for chit-chat with Emma, most of the conversation was in Amharic. Mariam spoke the least, Barra the most. Everyone ate and ate until only the bottom layer was left, soaked with juices. Reece suspected Ketow would eat this, and he did. Once again, Reece's hand was a mess, and there were no napkins. He couldn't figure out how they could eat such messy food so neatly and without sucking their fingers. No one sucked their fingers, and he wanted to suck his badly, like scratching an intense itch, or sneezing, or laughing in church, and he felt that his inability to clean his sticky fingers was distracting him, altering his breathing, which he monitored closely for twenty seconds.

"It takes practice," said Emma, reading his mind.

Reece told them about Alabama, his grandparents, Kristin, and answered a couple of odd questions about his appearance.

"Your hands are very small," said Isaac

"You are very young," said Barra. "We thought you were teen...teenager." Both remarks caught him off guard. He was twenty-one and had never thought of his hands as small.

Reece had many questions, but his brain bogged down, and he wished to be alone in his room. The red kerosene lantern hissed and burned a deep orange, and at first, nearly blinded him. He felt exhausted and flat and uninteresting. Kristin seemed like a ghost. He looked at his hands and wondered if he should grow a beard.

Barra suggested they sing some songs for Reece. The first one Reece recognized, but they sang in Amharic. It was almost impossible to reconcile the tune with the voices, and he had to strain to listen to the song. In the second stanza, he forgot what the song was and couldn't remember until the refrain. *This is the day, This is the day, That the Lord hath made, That the Lord hath made.* Together they sang like birds, especially Barra, who had produced two cassette tapes of spiritual songs. The singing added a layer of complexity to the team. They sang with purpose and sang as if the songs were their own. Emma hummed and clapped but did not sing.

Mariam had to leave for a moment and came back, and

then there was some noise, some disturbance, and Ketow was talking loudly to someone. That prompted the group to disband, and whatever was happening at the fence must have been resolved, although a few shouts had been exchanged. Reece wondered if he should inquire. Emma stuck her head through the door flap.

"Can't see. Too dark. They'll take care of it, whatever it is," she said. "Could be a beggar."

"Is it safe to walk around at night?" He felt the distance between himself and Emma expand now that they were alone in the hut. That first afternoon in the clinic with her had gone so smoothly, as if they were a team that had worked together for many years. Afewerki was the missing ingredient now, or maybe it was the patients.

"Safe as any place, although I'll only go out with one of the guys. Once it's dark, folks shut themselves in, lock the gates, especially women. Hyenas and wild dogs, don't forget about them."

A silence formed a light frost in the room.

"You're engaged?" asked Emma.

"Yeah. Kristin." A tug deep in his throat snuck up on him. "I have pictures."

"What does she think about you being here?"

"We didn't get engaged until after I had plans to come here. She understands, but wants me to come back as soon as possible."

"Sounds tricky. She's not angry about it, is she?"

Reece thought she was. "I'm not sure."

"Write her lots of letters. That's what I do at night, read and write letters."

"Anybody special back home, or here?"

"Not really."

A longer silence ensued, long enough to read the praise quotes on the back cover of a book.

"Ready for some sleep?" Emma stood. "Ketow will get the dishes."

Reece was tired but wondered how easily sleep would come on his first night in Godo. He longed to call Kristin, but the closest phone was hours away.

The night sky crowded itself with bright stars. Reece had no idea they could be so bright. The stars seemed to pull him upward, and he almost fell looking at them. He said goodnight to Emma and closed his door with a sharp scrape, saying goodnight to Isaac, who had walked him to the door with the lantern. He latched the door and pointed the beam of his keychain flashlight toward his bed. It was like looking through taut, greasy cellophane. The bed seemed to be miles away, and he tripped over his hiking boots. Something clattered against the roof. He could hear dogs fighting in the distance. As he moved, the room moved with him like a man wearing a barrel.

*Dear Reece, I miss you so, so, so much...*and a fog of emotion enveloped him. The big candle on the table by the bed provided enough light to read. After each of the three letters, he laid them on his chest and stared at the roof poles. Something scratched in the wall, something between the plastic and the wall, but he was too tired to imagine what it might be. These letters were real. Kristin was real. He was real. He deliberated whether to write her next or read the two letters from his grandparents, written by his grandmother.

Dear grandson, We received your letters and have been

*reading them over and over. You just be safe, you hear me…*and he smiled, and then almost cried.

The letter from Reece's friend Keith made him feel good and normal, and he prepared himself mentally to write a long letter to Kristin, to let her know how the first day had gone, to reassure her that he wouldn't stay longer than necessary, to try and give her some sense of his purpose there. He fell onto the bed and dropped his pen, almost in a panic. The suddenness of something moving, that something had been diving back and forth across the room for perhaps thirty seconds. It was beyond the reach of the candle, but it was there nonetheless, a bat, flying in an arc from wall to wall, front to back, back and forth. He grabbed his flashlight, the one with a rubber button on top, and he could see it cutting through the beam, as if on a hidden drooping wire. He needed to pee badly. The bat had no intention of giving up its route. He wondered if he should call out and almost did, but thought better of it.

He sat up and leaned against the wall. The bat's speed and angle of turn did not vary. He lit a candle and tried to write, but then closed his eyes. The bat swooped for no more than five minutes, but it seemed an eternity to Reece, and when it suddenly stopped, he shined his light around the room, up into the rafters, and could see nothing.

As he feared, Irigit ran over when he opened the door. Reece waved his hands *No Worries* and pointed to the far-left corner of the compound. Emma had told him to use her toilet, that it would be expected. Irigit understood and walked away. Barra's door was still open, and he stepped into the doorway, silhouetted by several candles. "You are okay?" he said. Reece didn't want to say it, but he said,

"Shintabet." There were sounds of voices from the others, and Barra spoke rapidly from within his room. Reece picked his way through the ankle-high grass with the universe trying to suck him into the sky.

He hadn't brought any toilet paper, paused, and then remembered he didn't need any. The door faced the fence, which in the dark and the light of the flashlight looked like something a demon might weave from roots and bones. He opened the door and flooded the narrow space with starlight. The floor was rough cement, and there was a hole in it, which was surrounded by a toilet seat. A smell of urine. Afterward, he found it difficult to finish his letter to Kristin, which stretched across two mailers. He slept like a dead animal and had no dreams.

After brushing her teeth in the dark, Emma warmed water to bathe. Reece seemed a bit stiff, perhaps shy, but was very capable, not afraid to jump in and get his hands dirty. Having him around would take a load off her shoulders. She thought about how neat his hair was, kind of dorky but cute, and smiled. His legs weren't bad either.

She hung the washcloth on the back of her wooden dining chair and moved the candle to her bedside. She had worked her way through Second Kings, having had her fill of the rulers of Judah. Chapter One of First Chronicles showed little promise, listing the descendants of Adam to Abraham and beyond. She put her Bible aside and wrote a short letter to her mother, mentioning the new guy, Reece, that he was from Birmingham, less than an hour's drive from where they lived, and that he seemed to be serious and knowledgeable. She didn't know why, but she asked about her old boyfriend. Had her mother seen him around? Had he asked about her? Oh, and the new guy was engaged. *Bummer.*

A copy of *My Utmost for His Highest,* her daily devotional, she opened to June 11: "Come to me...Have you ever come to Jesus?" She laughed and then sighed. She flipped to June 16: "Will You Lay Down Your Life?" *Greater love has no one than this, than to lay down one's life for his friends...* Emma agreed with the sentiment and prayed that she, too, would be willing to do such a thing, to sacrifice her life for a friend, to give her life for Christ, literally, if it came to that. Coming to Jesus was one thing, but her bouts with amoebiasis and what could have been a lethal case of dengue fever had brought her to the edge of mortality.

There had been moments when she felt that death was within reach, but God had spared her. Like those around her, she felt illness was a test of faith as well as of flesh. She tried not to second-guess the mysteries of the will of God, but did consider, after her recovery from the undiagnosed fever—after she had felt that her bones were breaking—that God may have ventured into the realm of perfidy. It made her uncomfortable to think such thoughts, but she had been terrified for her life, and that didn't seem right under the circumstances.

She cupped her hand behind the candle's flame and blew. A dog growled in the pathways, a low, vicious growl that went on for several minutes. Eyes closed, she lay there mulling over the day, the next day, a full clinic day. She heard a scratching noise from above, something rubbing the tin roof. She listened. The cordite smell of the extinguished candle lingered. She couldn't tell if the sound was from inside or outside. Something was either trying to get in or get out. She reached for her flashlight, but it was not there. A gasping sound. A pulling sound, scraping. She fumbled for the Bic lighter. A scratching sound on plastic. A chill gelled her spine. A thud. She froze, sensing movement. Something was on her bed. She yelled, "Hey!" and swung her arm, kicking her feet. The lighter lit, and the orange flame trembled in her hand.

"Abet!" came the call of Irigit. He trotted toward Emma's house, rifle at the ready.

Barra, Isaac, and Mariam all came to their doors, peering into the courtyard. Reece snored, oblivious to the excitement.

It was the monkey. Marvin had returned from his adventure, scooting around Godo, avoiding the kicks of farmers and the rocks of little boys. He was lucky not to have been killed by dogs.

Emma laughed, then frowned. She had kind of hoped that Marvin would magically disappear. But there he was sitting on his haunches on the floor, darting his head from side to side. Irigit knocking on the door, Isaac joined him.

"You are okay?" asked Isaac.

"Yes, fine." Marvin scampered under the table. "The monkey has returned. He's inside with me."

"Are you frighting?" asked Isaac.

"No, it's okay. No problem." She heard them murmuring outside, and then all was quiet again except for the dogs' endless fighting in the distance.

She found her flashlight on the floor. Marvin leaped from the tiny stove to the top of the propane refrigerator that hissed in the far corner. She walked toward him, and he scampered into the rafters, lying flat and curling his long gray tail over his neck.

Reece awoke early in the morning with a dull headache behind his eyes, one that had lingered ever since his arrival. Dr. Guthrie said it was the altitude. Godo was between 7,000 and 8,000 feet above sea level, the nearest sea being the Red Sea, which separated Ethiopia and Eritrea from the Arabian Peninsula. A large black fly circled crazy around the room.

He unfastened the hasp on his door. The door creaked open. He saw the dining hut, Emma's house, and the cookhouse. Smoke wafted from the cookhouse window and door. Ketow emerged from the shintabet. Reece waved. Ketow waved. Reece tried to imagine powerlines, a squirrel running across a powerline, and couldn't. The clouds looked different from home. The sounds were very different. Instead of the quiet soughing of wind in pines layered beneath the croon of cicadas, he heard hammering, a child calling out, the *pop, pop, pop* of an engine, the belt-driven mill where villagers ground their grain. The air smelled smoky and dry. What time was it? It was Thursday. Thursday, June 12, 1986. There was an eight-hour time difference between Ethiopia and home. It was midnight back in Alabama, and his grandparents were sleeping.

"You are waking?" It was Barra. He grinned at Reece.

Reece came to his door. "Yes, waking."

"You are working to-day? Yes."

"Oh yeah. In the clinic with Emma."

"Yes, Emma. She is very nice. No?"

"No. I mean, yes."

"Yes."

Reece nodded.

"You are Christian?"

"Yes, yes. Christian."

"Jesus is our friend. We must praise him."

"Of course."

A moment of silence passed.

"What do you do here?" asked Reece.

"I am working the Mission, the Baptist Mission. Same as you, no?"

"I mean, what is your job here?"

Isaac appeared from his room, wearing blue mechanic's overalls. "He is singing for the people. All day singing. He is famous singer."

"You are bad brother," said Barra, laughing.

"I'm not such a good singer," said Reece.

"Barra will teach you to be famous singer." Isaac grinned.

"There's Emma," said Reece. He waved.

Emma wore jeans and a green scrub top. "What's the news, guys? Ready to get to work?"

"Sure thing," said Reece. "Looks like rain."

"It will rain today. The rain is coming," said Isaac.

"Good for foods," said Barra.

"Good for catching water, too." There were rain barrels at Emma's house and the cookhouse.

"Do you catch most of the water?"

"What you mean to *ketch* the water?" asked Barra.

Emma explained. "To catch, in the barrel."

"Yes, to catch," said Barra.

Zenebek emerged from the cookhouse, carrying a covered enjera pan to the dining hut.

"Ready to eat?" asked Emma. "We'll eat and then head down to the clinic, maybe get started a little early. You doing okay?"

"Slept okay. And you?" Reece tried not to look down Emma's scrub top, which blowsed in the front and at the sleeves. She was six inches shorter than he was.

"Well, a monkey woke me up last night. Did I forget to mention the monkey? The guy with burned hands gave it to me as a gift. Crawled under the eaves between the wall and roof last night. Scared me to death."

"Where is he? Is it a he?"

"His name is Marvin. He's a he. I'd show him to you, but he deposited a gift on my table this morning and left the same way he came in."

"Gross."

Inside the dining hut, the smells concentrated. Mariam uncovered the pan to reveal a smoking pile of scrambled eggs mixed with green peppers and onion to be eaten with enjera. Reece's mouth watered. Misrak brought in a pot of hot tea spiced with ginger and cloves. All was well.

Clinic started with a sudden downpour. Patients huddled beneath the eaves, some protected by umbrellas, others soaking up the storm and weathering their spot in line by the fence as best as possible. The rocky ground transformed into sticky mud, clods accumulating on feet like cement.

A coolness, a mist infiltrated the clinic, an interval between seasons, as if a great invisible crossroads ruled by stars had passed over them. An old woman carried to the clinic by two men, one with her legs and the other with her arms and shoulders, received their first attention. She could barely stand. The one who was her son told Afewerki that she had been taken with a fever, that she had lain in bed for many days, that she had resigned herself to die. On each hip were terrible wounds, he said, and what could be done?

"Let's take a look." Emma braced the woman so that she would not fall. "She's so weak." The old woman lifted her chin with each breath, breathing through her mouth, assuaging the pains of her body, puffing them away with concentration.

Reece looked on as Afewerki lifted the oily, grimy cloth of the woman's rough dress. She teetered to the side, Emma losing her stance.

"Whoa."

Reece stepped in and cradled the woman's head and shoulder. "Lay her down? Maybe pull the bench away from the wall and lay her back with her legs propped."

"Okay. Afewerki, can you fold two or three grain bags into a pillow?" asked Emma.

"Ishi," he said, and stepped carefully down to the rocky, muddy ground. He picked his way to the warehouse, where there were stacks of empty grain bags.

"Easy does it," said Emma. The woman looked up, as would a small child, and smiled. She smelled of smoke and sweat, like the hide of a freshly killed goat. The bench was narrow. "Let's wait till he gets back." Emma's head brushed Reece's as she steadied the woman's knees, and Reece held the old woman. Emma realized that she had a strong desire to kiss him. A tiny thrill in her chest worked itself out as a quick exhalation.

Reece knelt to decrease the strain on his lower back. His line of sight was directly into Emma's scrub top. Bent over, her breasts strained against her bra. She stood, keeping her grip on the woman's knees.

"Nice day," said Reece. "Now that it's stopped raining."

"Line's not too bad, maybe forty to start with. I'd expect at least sixty, though."

Afewerki stepped up with bags folded. "Oh, she is happy."

Emma took the bags and arranged them beneath her head. "Okay. Now let's see what the problem is." Reece squatted behind the woman to catch her in case she swayed.

The right side of the dress came up and revealed a deep ulcer over the hip, deep enough to hold a can of soup. A ring of black char lined the wound that glistened meat-like inside. The bone was just there, just visible.

"Yikes."

"Wow."

"Oh my."

The other hip proved less deep but also open and nasty. Her buttocks were red, the flesh above the tailbone chafed and broken.

"How long has she been in bed?"

Afewerki inquired of the son who held his hat in both hands, restless and looking away. "For many days."

"Okay."

Reece had experience with bedsores, but nothing of this magnitude. "Looks like we'll need to pack it. She'll need to stay out of bed for those to heal."

"Could take weeks," said Emma. "But we'll get her on the road."

Reece scanned the medicines on the rough wooden shelves. Ferrous sulfate. Iodine. Magnesium sulfate. Niclosamide. Paracetamol. Baralgin. Benzathine penicillin.

"She definitely needs to move around and eat well, to make this heal," said Reece.

Afewerki translated to the son, who nodded gravely.

"How about we coat the inside of the wound with antibiotic powder? We have some Banalin," said Emma.

"That might help the skin granulate and fill in," said Reece. "Do you think we should coat it with some of the Silvadene first, and then pack with gauze soaked in saline? Have her come back once a day for a dressing change?"

"I guess if we pack it only with the Banalin, the gauze would stick. It needs to dry, though. I'm surprised it doesn't look infected."

"Me too. Looks like fresh cut steak, except that thick black around the edges."

"I say we try the powder, though, to dry it out. It's not oozing or weeping. If the packing sticks, we can pour in saline to loosen it."

"Sounds good. Just have never seen something that deep."

"Shall we clean the wounds?" Afewerki shooed away a couple of curious onlookers peering through the door. "Go, go!"

Reece glanced at Emma. She exuded a tired confidence that was disarming. "Sure, let's clean her up with saline, dress the edges with antibiotic ointment, and then do the packing." She locked eyes with Reece and gave him a lopsided smile.

Reece looked away. He wanted to take a photo of the woman's hip and send it to Kristin. He didn't have the heart to suggest it, though. There was so much to show and tell her.

Wounds dressed, and loaded with vitamins and famine biscuits, the old woman murmured her thanks. When her son and his friend tried to pick her up, she balked, stood under her own power, and told them to get on either side. She was going to walk as far as she could. Pain registered in her eyes like a lizard being squeezed, but she was determined.

"Bataam taruno," said Emma. "Look at her go." She was to return the next day and the next.

"Lying in bed will kill you quicker than anything," said Emma.

"The bullet is quickest," said Afewerki.

"I'd rather be shot than rot away in bed," said Reece.

"I'll remember that," said Emma. "Just in case."

"She will shoot you." Afewerki laughed, peered out the door, and called in the next two patients, a priest with his cane, cross, and flyswatter, and a young woman with a child on her back.

With sixty-two patients behind them, Emma and Reece tidied up the clinic shelves, putting supplies away. Afewerki swept the floor with the homemade broom, shooting the dirt and debris out the door onto the dried mud. Reece fumbled through the box with IV kits. He had started an IV on a young boy who was severely dehydrated and given him a liter of saline over four hours. The kits, like the IV bottles, had been made in Iceland.

"Did you ever meet the Icelandic team who was here?" Reece read the fine print on the kits. The plastic catheter that inserted into the vein over the steel insertion needle was stiffer than he was used to.

"There was a doctor and two nurses," said Emma. "I never met them. They left about a month before I got here, lived in tents. I've heard some stories, though, strange stuff, some of it hard to believe."

"Yes, Svana, she makes me to laugh," said Afewerki. "She is big woman, strong, can drink many things. She has the black hair. Eydis is hard worker, too, with white hair, like white paper."

"Who was the doctor?" Emma pushed her hair behind her ears.

"He was Dr. Gudmunder," said Afewerki. "He is tall man with long fingers. His hair is like arancia, like the orange."

"Black, white, and orange. Sounds like a colorful group," said Reece.

"Yes, many colors." Afewerki rested the broom in the corner.

The guard locked the door behind them. Reece peered through the cracks at the empty room.

"Watch your step," said Emma.

"Why did they leave? Seems the Mission was upset at them for carousing?" asked Reece.

"From what I know, they were hard drinkers, liked to hang out in the tejj bets and drink. Usually it's just men, so the women being there was something of a scandal, I think."

They walked shoulder to shoulder up the steep, wide path, the pink sun settling to their right. "Ferenj!" came the familiar cry.

"Yes, much alcohol for them." Afewerki gave a mean look to two little boys, snot running from their noses, frightening them away. "The Icelanders are looking for some things, which is forbidden."

"Really?" asked Reece. "Like what?"

Up the steep incline, Afewerki paused and spoke with his hands. He told them about the tabot in the nearby church, the sacred replica of the Ten Commandments held in the Ark of the Covenant that Ethiopians believed was kept in a Coptic church in Axum. No one but the priests were allowed to see the tabot or Ark, being hidden within the inner sanctum of the church, the maq'das. Only on feast days was the tabot removed from the church's interior, being covered with ornate fringed fabrics of gold and red.

"When they are here, someone has stolen the tabot from the church," said Afewerki.

"The rumor was they thought it was the real deal, the Ark of the Covenant, that it was being passed secretly from church to church to keep its location secret," said Emma. "When it came up missing, the priests accused them openly."

"The people were angry and rising against them, so they must leave," said Afewerki. He looked sad. "Dr. Gudmunder was speaking to me to study in his country."

"They left in a hurry, is all I know," said Emma.

"Did anyone ever find the tabot?" asked Reece.

"No, but it is rumored to have been hidden in a cave."

"There are many caves," said Afewerki.

"So this tabot was heisted by the Icelanders and hidden in a cave somewhere nearby?" asked Reece.

"Yep, that's the story," said Emma.

They stopped in front of the gate as it swung inward.

The air was cool, heavy white clouds framing the setting sun.

"You are going to the shelter?" asked Afewerki.

"I forgot. Want to go with us?"

Reece said, "Sure," and they turned back up the path, bypassing a large puddle where two little boys were playing, covered in mud. They ran up to hold hands with Emma.

"Yellum!" said Afewerki. He put on his stern face and told them to wash. They ran away a few feet and yelled, "Ferenj!"

They curved left and upward along the path, passing family compounds on both sides. Cooking smoke infiltrated the air, a sense of the day winding down. The shelter sat on an exposed slope above the round Orthodox church. The church was made of poles daubed with mud for walls, a roof of thick straw with a decorative cupola made of tin sheeting. Around the church's perimeter was a graveled walkway. A wooden slotted box with a steel padlock invited visitors to donate money. At the church's center was the curtain-shielded inner sanctum, the Holy of Holies, where the tabot rested. Except for Sundays, the church seemed to be deserted.

The old, sleepy shelter guard snapped to attention when he saw them, his rifle strapped to his shoulder. There were valuable items kept there, including a quintal of teff flour, oil, and pots and pans. A smell of human waste filled the air, an undercurrent beneath the cook smoke and stale body odors.

"Oh my God," said Emma. "Look."

A young boy of five tugged on Marvin, a rope around his

neck, choking the poor little beast. Around him gathered other little boys and girls, some naked, fingers in mouths, gaping at the monkey. Marvin screeched and yanked at the rope around his neck. Overhead, two hooded vultures sluiced through the sky, disappearing in a cloud.

"Bucka, bucka." Afewerki walked over to the pantsless boy with the rope, rather an amalgam of knotted string, and scolded him in Amharic.

The little boy put his hands behind his back and told Afewerki, "Yellum."

Reece walked up, focused on Marvin. The boy's eyes grew wide as he approached. He dropped the rope and ran to his mother, grinning from the doorway of the shelter where she breastfed his baby sister. He buried his head in the folds of her dress.

Marvin kept working on the rope around his neck as Reece stepped on the loose end. "Come here, buddy," he said. Marvin pulled on the rope, trying to free himself. He grimaced, pulling his lips back into a pitiful look.

"Aw," said Emma. "He's so scared. Can you pick him up?"

"I can try," said Reece.

"He will bite," said Afewerki.

"I don't think so." Reece sat on a stone and gathered the rope into his hand. He extended the other hand to Marvin in a peace gesture. Kristin flashed through his mind. What would she think of this? She volunteered at an animal rescue shelter. Marvin would fascinate her.

Emma sat beside him on the same stone. "Can you get the rope off of his neck?"

The guard sat, watching with a bewildered smile. Afewerki paced, glancing into the shelter, into the dimness at bodies sleeping on mats made from grain bags and corn shucks. He had hoped that Marvin was gone for good. Monkeys were unclean. Another young mother, two children gripping her long patched dress, approached him, speaking in hushed tones. She wanted Emma to look at her breast, which was swollen, she said.

Reece edged closer to Marvin, who sat on his hindquarters. Reece picked him up and placed him on his lap. Marvin's little head rotated on his tiny neck. Reece whispered to Marvin that it was okay and loosened the rope around his neck, pulling it free. Marvin simpered a seeming thanks and scampered toward the guard, who barked a warning. Marvin retreated and scratched his head.

"He's so soft," said Reece.

"Like a little baby," said Emma.

"There is a woman," said Afewerki. "She is here," and he pointed.

"Okay," said Emma. "Reece, see if you can pick him up again and get him back to the house."

Two dozen children converged into a loose circle around Reece and Marvin, laughing and pointing. With them came flies. The children squealed, running backward as a group. Reece batted at flies mobbing his face. Grimacing, little Marvin peered with concern at the moving mass of humanity expanding and contracting around him. He scratched his neck. The vultures circled higher.

Reece came within arm's length and reached for Marvin, who scooted away, chattering, anxious, glancing at the children. He darted toward the guard's shack and storage building. The children moved in and took both of Reece's hands. "Caramella?" they said. He sought out Emma and saw her near the shelter door, speaking with the mother, examining her exposed breast. A breeze quickened and sighed through the shelter compound, flapping clothes and scattering flies. He thought about his grandparents, his parents, Kristin. He recalled running through a church graveyard with his cousins when he was a kid. Decoration Day they called it, the first Sunday in May.

Marvin let Reece scoop him up and hold him at arm's length. Reece drew him close, cradling him like a baby. He looked into Marvin's beady black eyes. He saw that Emma was watching. She gave him a thumbs-up.

With the sun setting, the cool breeze washed away the heat of the day, bringing a light chill to the air. To Reece, daytime felt like bright summer and nights like crisp fall.

Dinner was a milder wot, an alicha made from peas, ginger, onion, and garlic. The juices soaked into the enjera, making for delicious, tangy morsels. There were also fried potatoes, which Reece thought tasty and reminiscent of home.

"Where's Barra?" asked Emma.

Afewerki shrugged. Isaac spoke. "He is registering new family for rations. He will come soon. He has big appetite." Mariam laughed. "You must to meet the administrator," said Isaac. "Perhaps tomorrow. He is expecting."

"Yeah," said Emma. "Need to pay your respects, whether he deserves them or not. He's the guy everyone calls the Hyena. Mean as a snake."

Reece had briefly heard the story of Afewerki's arrest. "Sounds like something to look forward to." He cleared his throat. The Hyena sounded like a cruel and devious man. There were certain moments, pauses, since his arrival, when he felt that anything was possible in Ethiopia. The thought of meeting this Hyena made Reece's stomach titter.

"I guess he's like the mayor, except he's appointed, not elected. He's the chief administrator. There's also an agricultural administrator and a minister of finance. "What's the agriculture guy's name?" asked Emma.

"He is Tewodros," said Afewerki.

"He's not a bad guy," said Emma. "Wears a baby blue polyester suit every day. You can't miss him."

Reece nodded, imagining these people, their possible power over him. "Meet him after dinner?"

Isaac said, "He is drinking this time. You must go tomorrow morning to greet him. He will fright you." He laughed.

Emma looked disgusted, but grinned. She could tell that Reece was hesitant. "He won't bite. At least not while you're looking. He sees himself as pretty important, so it's best to meet him before he comes looking for you. Isaac, will you go with him? I have no desire to see him unless I have to."

"Ishi," said Isaac. "You must bring your papers."

"Okay." Reece ate another fried potato, sliced like thick chips. He imagined it would be like meeting with the cranky nursing supervisor that no one liked back at the hospital.

"He is soldier," said Isaac. "He has killed many people."

"Likes to brag about it," said Emma.

Afewerki made a sour face and grumbled, thinking of his father's head wound.

"Jeez," said Reece. Tomorrow was ration day, his first full day during what would be an onslaught of patients, and now this meeting with the administrator, this Hyena. "Should I take him a gift or something?"

Mariam's eyes brightened at the thought, and he nodded. Isaac agreed. "You may bring him some soybean oils."

"What about one of those Mennonite blankets?" asked Reece.

Afewerki scowled at the thought of giving gifts to the Hyena. "No. Oil is good. He will sell it."

"Okay, whatever you think is best." Reece finished his bottle of filtered water and replaced the red stopper.

The gate groaned open, and Isaac peered through the flap of the dining hut. "It is Barra."

Barra entered, wearing his ear-to-ear grin. He was short and dark like the Hyena, but did not have the bloodshot eyes or gold teeth.

"Welcome, my brother," said Isaac.

"Praise God, we are eating foods." Barra settled into his place and ladled alicha from the yellow bowl. He looked tired. He spoke in Amharic, telling Isaac, Afewerki, and Mariam that a new tabot was arriving soon to replace the stolen one. The new one had been procured from the area Bishop and taken for consecration to the Church of Our Lady Mary of Zion, where the original Ark of the Covenant was said to be located. This had taken nearly four months, the famine and fighting in the north contributing to the delay.

Isaac summarized the discussion for Emma and Reece. "There will be a feast soon when the tabot arrives." Without the tabot, the church had no authority to intercede and exercise spiritual authority, such as the casting out of demons from the unlucky who had been afflicted with the evil eye.

"They are lucky to escape, the Icelanders," said Isaac. "The peoples know that it is hidden nearby into a cave." He explained that the priests claimed to feel its power nearby. Had it been removed from Godo entirely, even greater calamity than the famine would have descended upon the town.

"What does the tabot look like?" asked Reece.

"We are not to speak of such things," said Isaac.

Barra looked indifferent. "We are following Jesus Christ. We can talk of such things." He showed with his hands the size of the tabot, said that it was a wooden tablet carved with the Ten Commandments in the ancient tongue Ge'ez, perhaps, Reece gathered, the width and length of a book from an encyclopedia set.

"So, it's not like a chest or an ark?" asked Emma.

Isaac explained that the tabot rested inside the Ark, that only the original tabot given to Moses by God was kept inside the revered Ark of the Covenant.

Talk of the sacred object, mention of evil eye, the aroma of ginger, and the flashing white of Barra's teeth lent the inside of the dining hut a mysterious air. Reece glanced at Emma and could tell she also felt as if she were being made privy to something larger than life, something beyond their ken.

Roosters, dust, and donkeys started the busy ration day. Terry had already dropped one net of grain and was returning with another. He would distribute and take mail then. Reece felt like it had been a lifetime since he'd had news from Kristin, even though it had only been a few days. He had much to share. His letters, composed at night, could hardly keep up with the events.

The line for rations ran to the middle of the compound, heads of households holding their yellow ration cards. Outside the gate, donkeys and the occasional mule waited for their owners to return. The bustle was palpable, filling the air with talk and braying. The clinic line was growing as well, filtering through the gate and backing up the hill.

Reece brushed shoulders with Emma. She wore a blue scrub top with white scrub bottoms and a pair of light hiking boots. He wore jeans and a white scrub top, his standard outfit, with his hiking boots that were too small. Emma pushed back her full-bodied hair, exposing her ears. She put her hands on her hips, ready to start with the first patient, the man who'd had the back of his head split open when the hand grenade went off in the jeep. The wound was clean and ready to stitch properly, versus the loose stitches she had originally placed.

"Afewerki, I saw that old lady in line, the one with the sores on her hips," said Emma. "Let's get her in next. She's too frail to sit and wait."

"Ishi, Emma." Afewerki tilted his Exxon ballcap.

Reece wanted to watch Emma sew, but called in the next patient. He knew already that it would be a long day.

A young mother with a lemon-sized goiter grabbed the door's edge and pulled herself up the steps. On her back, bells tied to her leather child carrier jingled.

Afewerki spoke with the woman. He looked at Reece. "She wants for you to circumcise her son."

"What?"

"That's a new one," said Emma.

Reece considered the request and thought about his options. He'd seen how it was done during one of his nursing clinicals, but had never done one himself. "I'd better pass. Who usually does it?"

"The priest does these things," said Afewerki. He looked amused and bored.

The mother pulled her reluctant son from her back. He clung to her neck, eyes wide as small planets. He wore no pants, and a protective leather amulet hung around his neck. Tears came to his eyes.

"How old is he?"

"The mother says three."

"What do you think, Emma?" She was prepping the suture site with a povidone-iodine solution.

"I wouldn't try it unless you know what you're doing."

"I hate to turn her away."

"She is begging," said Afewerki. The woman whispered to him with urgency. She reached out and took his hand.

Reece thought about how he would circumcise this little boy. There was a kit that doctors used. A bell-shaped plastic device with a hollow straw-like tube at the end was placed over the head of the penis, the foreskin then drawn across the top of the bell. A sterile string was tied around the excess foreskin and then drawn tight, crushing the nerves and blood vessels. A scalpel then traced the outside of the circumcision, cutting the foreskin loose. There was little bleeding, and urine could pass out through the tube while the incision healed. "I could try."

"Better not," said Emma. She popped on her sterile gloves and waited for Afewerki to peel back the suture kit, a silk 5-0 with a curved needle.

"Maybe so," said Reece. He felt bad. Bad that he couldn't do it, and bad that he was considering trying. "Tell her I'm sorry. I can't do it."

Afewerki explained, and the woman looked hurt. "She is asking you are Christian?"

"Well, yes." Reece didn't know what to say. "Caramella?" he asked the little boy who had buried his head in his mother's dress. The little one turned and took the plastic-wrapped peppermint candy from Reece. He held it in both hands and looked at his mother. "Let's give her a pack of biscuits, too, for her trouble," said Reece.

Two hours and twenty-four patients into clinic, Emma reminded Reece that he needed to call on the village administrator, the Hyena, and introduce himself. "He has the skin of a hyena nailed up on the wall over his desk. Creepy."

A slight wave of nausea passed through Reece. Why couldn't the village administrator be a nice guy who appreciated what the Mission was doing? He washed his hands.

"Isaac can go with you," said Emma.

Reece stepped outside into the hot sunshine. He heard sounds of shouting, fighting, it sounded like, coming from inside the warehouse. Isaac was yelling. The women doling out milk powder and oil stopped work. Omar, one of the daily laborers, stumbled out of the building. He was tall, dark, thin, and muscular, normally with a curious smile, but now with downcast eyes. Isaac emerged into the light, followed by Getachew, the shortest of the dozen daily laborers. His eyes were wet, his face exasperated. He was speaking in quick bursts, tearful.

Afewerki came to see what the problem was. The two had been fighting, Omar punching Getachew in the mouth. A line of blood trickled from his frown.

"Omar has been drinking," said Afewerki. "He is always bothering Getachew." Emma glanced out and went back to her stitching.

Isaac reprimanded Omar, berating him for fighting. Little Getachew, still overcome, spoke out to Isaac with sorrow and anguish in his voice. Reece thought he might burst into tears and stood by, thinking it would be rude to walk off amid the drama.

Isaac spoke in turn to Omar and Getachew, chastising them for fighting, especially Omar. Playing peacemaker, Isaac ordered the matter to be settled. Reece watched as Omar kneeled before Getachew. Isaac placed a rock on Omar's shoulder. Getachew exchanged heartfelt words with Omar and then toppled the stone onto the ground. Laughing now, Omar stood and extended his hand, which Getachew shook. He was still hurt, Reece could tell, but seemed relieved by the ritual. Reece motioned for Isaac, sensing that justice had been done, and asked him to introduce him to the administrator.

Isaac's eyes regained the seriousness of moments before. "Okay, we go now. You will meet him this hour, the administrator. It is good." His English was slow and deliberate, with a slight slurring of his s. "He is hyena," he said and grinned.

Reece and Isaac ascended the path, each carrying a tin of soybean oil toward the administrative compound, passing between family dwellings, yells of Ferenj!, and cookfire smoke. Isaac greeted everyone, and Reece tried his best to imitate the greetings. When addressed, most of the women turned their eyes to the ground with embarrassed smiles, which seemed to amuse Isaac.

They passed around Afewerki's parents' compound and into the open market "square." A brown hen with three little chicks on its tail scuttled across their path, quite alarmed. There was a mild commotion in front of the administrative/jail complex.

"Psst," said Isaac. "He is there, on the mule."

Tied to a rail was a fine-looking, saddled, black and mahogany mule with bit and harness. On the mule sat the Hyena, shouting down to a woman.

"Is bad," said Isaac. They walked closer. One of the Hyena's minions tried to position himself between the mule and the irate woman who had tightly braided and coiled hair. "He is taking mule from that woman. She is angry," he said. They passed beneath the outer shade of the fig tree in the center. "Her husband is prisoner."

Reece felt in his bones that they should make the Hyena's acquaintance on another day. "Should we go and come back?"

"No, no. He is here now." Isaac's face registered amusement at Reece's apprehension. "He will not to eat you," and he laughed.

Isaac led the way. The Hyena saw them coming and tried to heel the mule around. It didn't budge. He yanked on the bridle and cursed. He wobbled in the saddle, drunk before noon. Isaac and Reece walked around the mule to face him. He wore olive-drab military fatigues and had his black Makarov semi-automatic strapped to his waist. The mule hung its head, patient. Its hind-flank quivered, and its tail swished at flies.

The woman continued to shout, turning now to Isaac for support. She wanted her mule back. It belonged to her father. It was many hours back to her home. She had to travel to the jail every day to bring food for her husband, accused of stealing another man's plow point. The Hyena had a notion to travel to nearby Aferbiny and pay a visit to one of his many lady friends.

"He is too much drinking to walk," said Isaac.

The Hyena spoke, his voice rough and growling.

"He is saying welcome," said Isaac.

The Hyena reached down his hand for Reece to shake. Reece shielded his eyes from the sun and put forward his hand. Isaac spoke Reece's name, said he was working with the Mission.

The Hyena withdrew his hand as suddenly as it had been presented. "I know who you are," he said in Amharic. He took a deep breath. "You are spy, pretending to help these people." He made a sweeping motion with his arm and lost his balance, falling from the mule. Reece dropped his can of oil and tried to catch him. The Hyena tumbled, knocking Reece aside, his foot caught in the stirrup. Upside-down, he cursed, spitting his words.

"Jesus Christ," said Reece.

Even Isaac looked perplexed, unable to respond. The Hyena's guards came to his aid, grappling with his arms and freeing his foot. The Hyena was livid and unsteady as he stood. He shirked his top and reached for his head as if he had lost a hat. He stared at Reece and turned toward the offended woman, who had grabbed the reins, and raised his hand as if to hit her. Reece flinched. Isaac stepped between the Hyena and the woman.

"Salaam," said the Hyena, a fly resting on his nose, and he turned away. He spat in the dirt.

"Let us go," said Isaac.

"What did he say?"

"He is drunk," said Isaac. "Let us leave."

The woman hit the mule with a stick to make it move toward a mounting stone, muttering to herself.

Emma worked with two patients at once, both suffering from roundworms, doling out mebendazole, Afewerki explaining how to take the pills, how to wash their hands after defecating, a rote lesson that he spoke in a drone. Reece had only been gone thirty minutes, but she felt his absence, as if she had lost a Band-Aid over a fresh cut. Things moved more quickly with him there. The sunshine looked nice on the ground outside.

"I didn't hear gunfire," said Emma. "How'd it go?"

Reece stepped into the clinic. "Not so well." There was an ant on his shoe.

"Was he friendly?"

"No, not exactly. More like drunk. He was trying to ride off with this woman's mule and fell." A young man with a packet of pills slipped past him, making room for the next patient.

Afewerki made his *tsk, tsk, tsk* and shook his head. "He is bad man."

"I gather," said Reece. "How did he get to be in charge?"

"He is being punished," said Afewerki. "They send him to the country to bother us."

"Ahh," said Reece. "Like first place is a week in Godo, and second place is a month."

Emma nodded, and Afewerki looked puzzled.

A man in a loose-fitting robe of rough cloth and wearing a golden-yellow monk's hat entered. He was missing many teeth, highlighted by a wide smile. On his neck amid a thin beard was a terrible weeping rash that appeared to be a nasty staph infection.

"Looks like emphatigo," said Reece.

"You mean impetigo?" asked Emma.

"Well, I'm not sure, but looks like he could use some erythromycin." He'd had a mild case of emphatigo himself, razor burn from shaving.

"He says it is itching. He scratches," said Afewerki. "He is the Abba Paulos."

"Tell him no scratching. That will spread the infection," said Emma.

Reece realized that both he and Emma were stooped over, peering at this monk's face and neck. He could feel her body heat. Her elbow brushed his side.

"Oops, sorry."

Reece felt an electric charge and stepped back. "Want me to work on the next patient?" he said.

"Yeah, I guess so," she said. "I'll take care of this one." She brushed her hair back and looked Reece in the eyes, searching for something larger than the moment.

Reece thought of Kristin, what she would think of Emma. There were hints of jealousy in her letters, asking what Emma looked like, asking was she cute. The old woman with the deep sores on her hips was helped to the door by Isaac and another woman. She stepped up on her own and, with a dignified grunt, entered the tiny clinic.

"Tenesteling," said Reece. The woman nodded and smiled in reply. She waved flies from her face. "Okay if I borrow Afewerki?" The tin roof popped with the heat. He would drink some water after finishing with this woman.

Afewerki had her pull up her dress and reveal her left hip. The bandage looked good, with minimal drainage, and the tape had held. He made small talk with the woman, asking about her health, and did her heart feel strong? Yes, it did, thanks to God.

Emma cleaned the monk's neck with povidone-iodine, brushing away crumbly scabs from pustules with a gauze pad. She spoke to him as if he could understand English. "No scratching." She made the motion of scratching and shook her head no. The monk nodded. His eyes were deep and watery, yellowed around the edges. He lived in the nearby cliffs, a monastic outpost, building a church into the rock by hand. He spoke aloud as Emma opened the large plastic bottle of erythromycin.

"He is inviting to come to the church," said Afewerki, listening as Reece unpacked the old woman's wounds and prepared new dressings.

"Sure. What's the occasion?" Emma had attended the church near the shelter twice on previous invitations and found the outdoor services tedious and bewildering.

Afewerki explained that it was a celebration to honor the Angel Gabriel, the church's namesake, to remember the deliverance of Meshack, Shadrach, and Abednego from the fiery furnace into which they had been cast by the king of Babylon, Nebuchadnezzar.

"That makes me think of Vacation Bible School," said Emma. "Remember the song, Reece?" It felt good to say his name, to be able to talk in English without scruple or worry. The team was great, but she did have to speak with care.

Reece put on a clean pair of gloves to pack the hip. "I do. There was the line about *around the bend we go.* We always had orangeade and cheap cookies."

"Same here." She lingered on a memory and sang out, surprising the monk, "Stop! And let me tell you..."

"What the Lord has done for me..." Reece finished the refrain, but in a reserved monotone.

Emma laughed, and Afewerki looked amused. He tilted his Exxon cap.

"Maybe we're having too much fun here," said Reece. The old woman was taking in the banter with curious crinkly eyes. She pulled up the other side of her dress.

"I think we're allowed to have a little bit of fun." She peered down his scrub top. He had a line of chest hair that ran to his belly button. Emma had a thing for belly buttons and an ache for intimacy.

Eighty-nine patients passed through the clinic that day. Reece lit the candle in his room. He could hear the shuffling of Barra and Mariam on either side of him. Mariam hummed a tune that sounded vaguely familiar. Terry had not dropped mail, so Reece settled onto his cot to re-read the last letter Kristin had written, dated two weeks prior. The new puppy was doing okay, peeing inside her parents' house, though. She had upbraided the puppy, telling him that "Daddy" would be mad. She ended the letter asking him when he might return, saying that she loved him very much. A tightness crept into his throat. He reached for his Bible, the motion of his hand causing the candle flame to waver, and unzipped its nylon travel case. Inside was a photo of Kristin, taken in her parents' kitchen. Her face filled the photo, her curly brown hair full and bouncy. She had that penetrating smile, one that he felt was reserved only for him. He felt a bit sick in his stomach, gazed around the shadowed room, and listened to Irigit talking to himself outside. It was early afternoon back in Alabama. He tried to imagine the heat, the stillness of two o'clock there, the pine trees swaying with slow, steady pulses of wind. It all seemed so very distant, unreal. How could two places so different exist on the same planet, the same ball of dirt, the same sun in the sky? He wondered again how Emma spent her time after dinner each night. She was trying to keep the monkey inside with her, but it came and went as it pleased, easing itself through the gap between the roof and walls. Tomorrow was market day, only a half day of clinic, and he felt relieved.

Emma's kerosene lantern hissed, giving off orange light. Marvin liked to sit in a wooden bowl on top of the short propane refrigerator. Emma had given up trying to keep him off the table, stove, and fridge. He did what he wanted, like a spoiled child. She warmed a pot of water to bathe with. Marvin sat with his tail curled to his face in the wooden bowl, watching her every move, his little black eyes roving over every detail.

"Marvin," she said. She liked to say his name and watch

his reaction. He seemed to know it was his name, or perhaps he liked the tone of her voice. "Now, you can't watch me take a bath. You'll have to close your eyes."

Marvin stared at her and bared his teeth in a monkey grin.

"Marvin, you're a pistol. A real hot mess. Aren't you, Marvin?"

Marvin scratched his eyebrow with his little hand.

"We're gonna have to cut your nails, boy."

She washed her arms with a cloth. A vein on her left forearm was still hard from the IV chloroquine she'd had during her bout of most likely dengue fever. They'd at first thought it was malaria, but the fever patterns and extreme pain in her bones had altered the diagnosis.

Clinics on ration days were a beast. She was dead tired, but thought how much more tired she would be if Reece were not there. She decided to pass on her devotional and just do a chapter in her Bible instead. Tomorrow was market day, and she looked forward to showing Reece the sights and sounds on their afternoon off. Marvin made a sucking sound with his teeth and yawned.

Emma fumbled through a box of ergometrine vials. The woman huddled on the bench beneath the gaze of her husband had given birth the day before but had not delivered the placenta. She was cramping and still bleeding.

"We need a private room for stuff like this," said Emma. "Maybe an addition on the side here."

"That is good idea," said Afewerki. He slapped a fly.

Reece looked up from examining the cruddy eyes of a teenage boy. "She looks pretty spry to have just delivered.

Another room, maybe with a bed, would be nice."

Emma prepped the woman's arm for the IV and heparin lock. She would dilute 200 micrograms of ergometrine in 60 ccs of normal saline and push it over one minute. "Let's get your guy out as soon as he's ready, and then close the door."

"Will do," said Reece. Having rinsed the eyes, he pulled down the lower lids and laid down a line of tetracycline ointment in each. He capped the tube and handed it to the young man who wore a Bob Marley t-shirt and farmer's shorts with wide leg openings. The man blinked his eyes several times and mumbled something to Afewerki.

"He is asking the murphy," said Afewerki.

"What?" asked Reece. "Tell him no shot is needed. He just needs to use this two to three times a day until it runs out. He can come back if the infection does not go away."

Afewerki delivered the news in a tone that reminded Reece of someone being told that their child had died.

Emma laughed. "Never fails." She capped the IV with the heparin lock, flushed it with a few ccs of saline, then taped it down.

"He is jealous of this woman's injection," said Afewerki.

The young man understood that he was finished and thanked them in a hushed tone. He dawdled in the doorway. Reece handed him a packet of famine biscuits, and all was well. "Amenseganolo," and the man stepped outside.

Afewerki stopped an old man trying to come in the door and motioned him back so that he could close it.

"Afewerki, tell her I'm giving her medicine to make the placenta come out. Tell her she may have some cramping pains. Maybe we should get a grain bag in case it comes out."

Reece volunteered to go and get one. Babies and placentas were virgin territory for him.

The woman wore a dirty dress of rough fabric, patched in many places. Emma removed the swath of cloth around the woman's waist and handed it to her husband, still standing in the same spot with his hands folded.

With grain bag in hand, Reece closed the door behind him and prepared to see what a placenta looked like. The woman pulled up her dress around her waist unabashed, seeming to be eager to get it over with. She tried to squat, but Emma motioned her to sit on the bench.

"Was it a boy or a girl?"

"A girl," said Emma. "Ready?" She inserted the 18-gauge needle into the IV port. "Afewerki, she'll need to push like she pushed out the baby, tell her."

Reece held the dusty grain bag, a gift from Canada. He shifted from foot to foot, not sure what he should do. He supposed he would catch the placenta and put it in the bag. Afewerki cracked his knuckles.

A minute passed. Two minutes passed. Emma wore tan shorts and a blue cotton t-shirt with the name of her home church on the front and the number 47 on the back. She had played softball on the church team. She was silent, watching the woman's eyes. Reece couldn't help but notice Emma's smooth ankles, staring at them as she crouched beside the woman, waiting for something to happen.

The woman frowned and panted, pushing her fists into her thighs. Blood trickled from her vagina into a biscuit tin placed between her legs.

"Push," said Emma. She went to her knees, gloves on.

The woman rolled her head back, groaned, and strained

once, twice, and the placenta slid into Emma's waiting hand, trailing a foot of ivory umbilical cord. "Good Lord." She let the bloody mess drip into the tin. "Reece, the bag."

Reece stepped forward. The placenta looked like a thick, bloody steak that had been pounded. He let the organ drop into the woven nylon bag. Afewerki had turned his back, arranging boxes and bottles on the shelf. He was not fond of blood.

"Well, that's that," said Emma. "She did great. Let's have her lie back a bit and let me massage her fundus, try and stop this bleeding."

Reece watched Afewerki unbusy himself from the shelves and speak to the woman. Reece held the placenta like a sixteen-pound bowling ball.

Emma pushed her fingers deep into the woman's abdomen, finding the hardening uterus to massage and induce contractions to stem the flow of blood. "Bataam taruno," she said. The husband continued to stand in one place, hands folded.

On the roof, doves alighted, scratching and flapping on the hot metal. Above them, a cloud shaped like a giant hand seemed to cup itself over the village of Godo. A breeze swooshed through the many cracks of the closed door into the clinic. A drop of blood fell from the bag onto Reece's hiking boot.

"She will bury this beneath a tree," said Afewerki. "So that she will have more children."

"So, no one's going to eat it?" asked Reece.

"Are you kidding?" asked Emma.

"Such a horrible thing," said Afewerki. "It is forbidden. Only the animals do such things."

Emma continued her deep tissue massage.

"I didn't mean it that way. I mean, back in the States, some women eat it, kind of a New Age thing."

Afewerki looked utterly horrified.

Emma chuckled. Reece looked uncomfortable holding the placenta, and now he was being defensive. His face registered an apologetic wonderment of the moment that seemed innocent to her. "People are very picky about what they will eat around here. They follow all the Old Testament rules."

"We cannot to eat the meat slaughtered by the Muslim," Afewerki was quick to add.

Reece said, "Hmm, that's interesting." He felt like a blank slate being written on too quickly to comprehend the impression of the stylus.

Emma kneaded the fundus a few minutes more and, satisfied that the flow of blood was stopped, cleaned the blood away and asked her to remain until she felt steady on her feet. She could have used a liter of IV fluid, but seemed to be strong despite the birth and loss of blood. Her husband finally found the nerve to sit beside her and held the orange cup of rehydration solution for her as she sipped, a look of relief on her face.

After clinic, Afewerki accompanied Emma and Reece to market. He wore long, Western-style pants and a light blue, short-sleeved, button-up shirt. He was somewhat aghast that Reece was wearing shorts. He had become used to seeing Emma in her khaki hiking shorts, but was still uncomfortable with the idea.

"Some are asking, who is the new farmer?" he said to Reece.

"Why is that?" Reece looked alarmed.

"Because you are wearing short pants like the farmer."

The people of the market stood shoulder to shoulder, those arriving earliest taking places in the shade of the giant fig tree, but most tolerating their places in the hot sun blocked by hazy clouds. High above, a pair of jets, MiG-23s, shrieked thinly through the stratosphere, visibly ahead of their noise plume. To the pilots, Godo looked like an octopus with a circle of short, stumpy arms.

Reece wavered and wobbled.

"You're fine," said Emma. "Just watch to make sure you don't step on anybody."

Reece took tiny steps, moving forward between Emma and Afewerki. He planned to buy a few things but wasn't sure what he needed or even what he was looking at. He stared hard at a cloth piled with tiny black pins, then realized they were cloves. He saw lined woven baskets filled with yellow, umber, orange, and red powdered spices, women squatting on their haunches, looking up with hard and wrinkled squints. Bags of green coffee beans. A woman gripped a hen's legs between her toes. Foot-long sections of maroon sugar cane. The banter and chatter of trading melded with the musty aromas of charcoal, sweat, milk, smoke, and leather to make the market a living animal.

"Sentino, *and* kilo mooze?" Emma asked the price of bananas from a young woman sitting beside her pile of thumb-sized fruit.

"Sidist, *and* birr," said the young woman, indicating that six of the tiny bananas would cost one birr, the equivalent of fifty cents. She sat on a large stone, knees nearly to her chest. Even though it was warm with the sun hot, the woman wore a long, faded, full dress of light green and yellow that hid her feet with a thick cloth over her shoulders. A shiny black cloth tied around her head bundled her coiled braids onto the back of her neck.

"She says six for a birr," said Emma.

"I'll take six," said Reece.

"I'd better get a dozen, some for Marvin," said Emma. The monkey was learning to stay in the compound, or at least he came back to eat. She couldn't bear the thought of putting him on a leash like Barra suggested. She peeled off a worn and dirty 1-birr bill from the roll in her pocket.

"Yellum," said the woman, shaking her head no.

"You must give her a new one," said Afewerki. "She does not want the old one."

Emma grumbled and gave the woman a fresher-looking bill, then dropped her bananas into a grain bag.

They moved deeper into the fray, walking a tightrope between squatting vendors. Reece saw potatoes, tomatoes, and onions. Little scales weighed out portions of ginger, incense, and niter-kibbeh using D-cell batteries as a counterweight.

Emma bought limes to make limeade, some potatoes to fry, and showed Reece two men making custom sandals from old tire treads. A thin, slack-jawed man with a white shamma coiled on his head tapped little nails with a ball-peen hammer, attaching straps cut with a large, curved knife to the tire soles.

Reece lost his balance and stepped backward, knocking his heel against a scale used to weigh chickpeas, six hundred grams for one birr. The woman chastised him, and Reece staggered, trying to right himself without causing further harm. Emma steadied him, catching his elbow. He grabbed her forearm, and for a moment it seemed as if they might have to dance to keep from knocking each other over.

"Whoa, this is making me dizzy," said Reece.

"Let's head back to the compound," said Emma. "Or do you want to see more?"

Reece felt overwhelmed, and a great weariness descended on him. "Sounds good. Head back for now. This is a madhouse."

"There is a man who is seeking medicines," said Afewerki. "He is here."

A man wearing a woman's cable-knit sweater and farmer's shorts stood apart from a row of rough, hand-forged axe heads to show them a deep cut on the back of his leg across his hamstring.

"The ox has stepped on him," said Afewerki.

"Ouch," said Reece.

Emma considered having the man come to the clinic on Monday, but there was definite infection there, redness and tenderness. She feared going to the clinic and having a line form from thin air. It had happened before. She looked at Reece. "What do you think?"

"Probably some peroxide and ointment, leave it open to heal?"

"That means we need to go to the clinic." Emma felt her day slipping away. She wanted to invite Reece into her house for some limeade and maybe even have dinner with him, cook him some fried potatoes, which he said he liked. She longed to just have a decent conversation without having to rely on Afewerki or going through the tedium of pre-thinking every word so that it made sense.

"I can go if you want to head back," said Reece.

"No, I can go. No problem," said Emma. She could have just sent Afewerki to do it. It was a simple procedure, but it was also his afternoon off.

"Heck, we can both go. Let's just take our stuff with us. Afewerki, you don't have to go. I appreciate you coming to market with us."

"No, no, I will come with you. You may have some problem," said Afewerki.

"It's okay, we'll be fine," said Emma.

"Either way is fine by me," said Reece.

Emma rolled her eyes. "Heck, I can just go by myself."

"Let us all go." Afewerki asked the man if he could leave his wares and come to the clinic. He said he could and called for his son to take his place among the axe heads.

A Saturday afternoon nap sounded like heaven to Reece, and he quickly followed Emma's lead by stretching out on his cot and letting the stillness take him into slumber. As he dozed, his head swarmed with the images of Godo, the bright faces, the tattered clothing, children on women's backs, huts made of sticks and mud, the rough cement floor of the clinic, the clay water pots carried by little girls from the stream so far away, a good half-hour walk downhill. With his door ajar to allow some air to circulate in the hot room, flies found him quickly. He covered his face with a blue bandanna, but the heat was too much, making it feel like he was pulling air through thick foam. There was a racket outside, the gate closing, a goat bleating. He remembered they were having goat for dinner. Isaac had mentioned it. The goat, a fat one, had cost thirty birr.

He swiped at the flies, catching one in his hand without trying. He opened his hand to look, and it was gone, flying madly in circles, angry or defiant. It occurred to Reece that they were about to slaughter the goat. He rose to close his door, but it was too hot. He peeked out and saw the goat tied and held by a young man he did not recognize. He was shouting and held a long knife in his hand.

Reece winced and sat on his bed. He had never seen an animal slaughtered and felt sad. He put his fingers in his ears, but then relented. He could hear Isaac talking to the young man. He heard a woman's voice, Misrak, perhaps anxious to get cooking. The goat had a black head and a white body. He wondered how old it must be, whether or not it knew what was about to happen. He heard a steady bleating, a call almost, a child calling for its mother. He closed his eyes and listened, hoping for the cries to stop. There was shouting, the goat seeming to scream now. He heard a thump and opened his eyes. The goat, with its throat slit, ran into his room. Reece jumped onto his bed, but the goat came to him, crying, spurting bright red blood as it stumbled. Reece jumped off the bed and, against the wall, reached the door. The goat followed, then a crash of Reece, the goat, and the butcher in the doorway. Reece smelled alcohol on the man's breath, smelled the hotness and iron of the blood.

Isaac grabbed the rope around the goat's neck and pulled it away as its legs collapsed and its cry bled to a wet gurgle. He spoke hot words to the man who had botched the job and yelled for him to finish.

In a daze, Reece reentered his room, blood on his shoes, and surveyed the mess.

Emma thought the goat story was sad but funny. She'd slept right through the horror, the scenario's genre according to Reece. Misrak had wiped blood from the floor, but most of it had soaked into the grainy, unfinished cement. He was able to get a new blanket from the stash in the warehouse, but his only sheets would be stained for life. Before dinner, there was a hot hoosh of the goat's liver and green peppers as a prelude to the big meal, which Reece declined, and Emma as well, stating her dislike of organ meats.

For dinner, there were tibs, sautéed hunks of goat meat, and a spicy wot of goat and berbere. The taste of the gray teff enjera was growing on Reece. He liked the pungent malt-vinegar taste and how it soaked up the juices. The wots were so spicy, though. One bite and his head began to sweat.

"How do you like? How do you say, gebeya, this market?" Barra looked to Afewerki. "You show him this, no?" He ate with precision, making neat bundles of meat and enjera. He was an efficient chewer as well.

Reece took a long drink of water. "Very nice. It was very crowded."

"Yes, many peoples," said Mariam.

"He did good, bought some bananas." Emma dangled her fingers juiced with meat drippings.

Marvin peeped in the room, his little black face embedded in a swash of gray whiskers. He started to come in, and Barra yelled, "Nyet! Yellum!" Marvin recoiled but did not retreat, remaining near the entrance flap.

"Poor Marvin." Emma wore a long-sleeve t-shirt, anticipating the coolness of evening. Her cheeks looked red.

"He is poor?" asked Isaac. "He is rich monkey."

Emma laughed.

"Go, go!" Barra stood, clapped his hands, and Marvin scampered away from the hut.

Reece wiped sweat from his brow, being vigilant not to use his left hand while eating. He remembered the monk's invitation to the church. "Tell me about the church celebration," he said to Afewerki.

"To the St. Gabriel Church. The people are believing that the angel saved the men from the fire of the king. They are into the furnace and are not killed."

Reece and Emma both knew the story from the Book of Daniel. "Meshack, Shadrach, and Abednego. Was it Gabriel or another angel that saved them?"

"The people are believing this to be Gabriel."

"He is saint for church, just here." Barra pointed over his shoulder and sucked his teeth. "The people are believing in him, no? But we are believing in Jesus Christ." He laughed a small laugh.

"Can we go into the church?" asked Reece.

"I don't think so," said Emma.

Afewerki gestured. "It is best not to go inside unless you are invited. The ceremony is outside. Not so many people can go inside. The priest will come outside. There will be many people." He explained again that the tabot inside was the representation of the tablets written by God, the Ten Commandments presented to Moses on Mt. Sinai.

"How is that different from the Ark of the Covenant?" asked Emma. She thought about the Icelanders and the rumor that they had stolen the church's tabot.

Isaac spoke. "The Ark is in Axum, near Eritrea." It

was the original Ark kept by Solomon in his temple, he explained, and brought to Ethiopia by his son with the Queen of Sheba, an Ethiopian woman according to tradition. The son's name was Menelik, the first ruler of Ethiopia to descend from Solomon.

"It sounds like the tabot is the covenant without the actual ark, which had magical powers," said Reece. "Something to simulate the original Ten Commandments."

"Yes, the tabot is resting inside the church, the maq'das. Only the priest can to see it. No one can to see but the priest." Barra gesticulated a vast, wondrous space with his hands. "We believe this thing."

Reece wanted to know if every church had a sacred tabot. Yes, this was exactly true, said Afewerki. Every church had its tabot that the Patriarch of the Ethiopian Orthodox Church had blessed. Without its tabot, the church had no power to guide the people.

With the enjera platter cleaned of its wot and tibs and a few bones in a bowl, the only thing left was some of the soggy bottom layer soaked in juices. Irigit helped Zenebek clear the table of the serving pan and cups. He had feasted on stewed kidneys and the goat's tongue, a delicacy, and would finish the wot and what enjera was left. A few drops of heavy rain fell, causing all to hurry back to their rooms before the deluge. The air was crisp and wet, the sky purpling to the bruise of dusk.

Reece stood with his hand over his head as if that would help. "Can I heat some water on your stove?" He walked with Emma to her tiny house.

"Sure."

Afewerki lingered, stooped beneath the dining hut's

overhang, watching Reece with Emma. When the door closed behind them, he remained, waiting. When he saw light flare from the window, the kerosene lantern, he dashed home through the rain, coming harder now.

Inside, the rain pattered like fingernails on the tin roof. Marvin sat huddled in the bowl on top of the refrigerator. Reece twiddled his thumbs as Emma removed the lid from a jerry container of water.

"You tip this over and I'll hold the pot." Her hair fell across her eyes, and she brushed it back. The kerosene lantern whooshed like a jet plane.

Reece tipped the dark blue container, and water sloshed into the pot, splashing onto the floor.

"Careful," said Emma. "A little girl had to carry that water up a steep hill."

"I've seen them with those heavy clay pots. That's ridiculous. Do the men not carry water?"

"Nope, never. Men plow and take care of the animals, and drink tejj and talla." She loosed a lopsided smile that knocked Reece off balance. The bobbing shadows made the scene seem like TV.

The stove's magneto clicked, and an orange flame settled to blue. Marvin peered down from his perch, watchful. Water on the bottom of the pot growled and hissed when put to the flame.

"Have a seat." She looked toward her bed to make sure she didn't have any dirty underwear or bras lying about. "Seems like it takes twice as long to heat water at this altitude."

"I still have a mild headache. I'm guessing it's the altitude." He sat and leaned back, thought better of it, and put the chair back on its legs. "I like the way you hang your clothes up with those bamboo rods." He could see little wrinkles in the folds of her arms below her bicep. She looked strong but pale in the wash of the kerosene's reddish glow.

"Thanks. Afewerki helped me make it. I'd like to make a little bookshelf and maybe put in a shower. I've talked to Thomas about it. He's supposed to be getting me a spigot to screw into a barrel." She reached and rubbed Marvin on his tiny head. His little eyes darted back and forth, up and down. "Got a face like a baby."

"Looks human." Reece was at a loss for words, could feel an attraction growing for Emma. Everyone loved her, and she'd been through hell. She was efficient, Johnny on the spot, and had what he thought of as natural beauty, a rough prettiness without makeup. She looked good with mussed hair. He cleared his throat. He tapped his fingers on the small wooden table. The lantern hissed. The stove hissed. Rain dotted the roof.

"So, how is your fiancée doing? Kristin. Do you miss her?" Emma squatted with her back to the wall. She watched the curtains tremble behind Reece.

The specter of Kristin loomed large in the room. Reece felt her presence, called up by the utterance of her name. "She's doing okay, I guess. She wants me to come back as soon as possible, though."

"You're here for two years, though, right?"

"That seems to be what's expected. How long have you been here so far?"

"Going on fifteen months. Sometimes it feels like fifteen years and sometimes like fifteen minutes." She eased to her rump and stretched out her legs.

"Tomorrow's Father's Day. I nearly forgot."

"Yep," said Emma. "My dad's out of the picture, I'm afraid."

"Sorry to hear that," said Reece.

"Water's boiling. Just take the pan with you."

"Right." He stood and stretched his leg. He watched Emma busy herself by her bed, arranging her things. He wanted to stay and talk, ask her about the Icelanders. "Is there any kind of church service here tomorrow?"

"Sometimes. The guys usually get together for breakfast and sing a few songs, have prayer. I suppose I should care more, but I'm always too tired to think about organizing a service."

"Do you know what time?"

"About the same time as breakfast, eight or so. I need to hit the hay, and your water's getting cold."

"Right, okay, well, I'll see you tomorrow then."

Emma closed the door behind him and latched it. The rain, which had waned, now threw itself at the ground in waves. Marvin cowered inside his bowl.

Reece awoke to the sounds of doves chalkboard-scratching the tin roof. He could hear Barra singing in English, "Love lifted me, Love lifted me..." He opened his door, scraping its bottom on the cement floor. Water dripped from the roof where the sheets of tin overlapped, and the sun was a glorious orange. He smelled wood smoke. Isaac's door was open, and he emerged with a worried face.

"Brother, you are sleeping well?" Isaac wore brown knit pants and a clean, white button-up shirt with a pair of black Sunday shoes. He looked a new man compared to his mechanic's overalls.

"The rain helps. I still have this headache that won't go away." Reece regretted the complaint and said something positive. "It's a nice day, a day to rest?"

"Yes, to rest. You will come to have service wiz us?"

"Sure. There?" He pointed to the dining hut.

"Yes, there."

"We have some bad news during the night," said Isaac.

"Really? What?"

Barra stepped from his room with an eager but grim face. He wore New Orleans Saints sweatpants that were two sizes too big and an old sweater. He was barefoot. "Mendeno?"

"The thief has been coming in the night," said Isaac.

"The Hyena is a greedy man," said Barra.

"How do we know it was him?" asked Reece.

"We are not sure, my brother," said Isaac. "Maybe it is the Hyena's workers. We have seen them before. We catch them with the gun."

"He is greedy man," said Barra. "He is stealing oil from us."

Reece took Barra at his word, but what could he do about this troublesome administrator? "That's what we gave him to let Afewerki out of jail, soybean oil."

"We shall pray for him this day," said Isaac.

"Maybe I should visit him again, ask him about it," said Reece.

"No, no," said Barra. "Do not do this."

"God will punish him," said Isaac.

"But the devil will reward him," said Reece.

Barra and Isaac looked puzzled. Mariam opened his door, stretched, and waved. Reece nodded to the silent Mariam.

"The devil is powerless against God," said Barra.

Reece shuffled his feet. That's not what he meant. He searched for the right words. "Yes, I suppose God will punish him."

Misrak appeared from the cookhouse with a smile on her face, carrying breakfast on a platter to the dining hut. She wore a long, aqua print dress, her hair in a bun.

"We must eat," said Isaac.

Yelling came from Emma's house. A sound of banging. The door flew open, and Marvin hurried into the yard and climbed the small tree near the dining hut.

Emma walked out with an angry air, with tousled hair and wearing a simple, white terry-cloth robe. "He did his business on my table!" She turned back inside to clean up the mess, a small miniature bowel movement that looked human.

Reece laughed and explained to the team, who began laughing, especially Isaac. Barra looked disgusted, and Mariam smiled. "Let me see if I can help her," said Reece. He looked at his t-shirt to make sure it was clean.

"Bad monkey," he said to Marvin in passing. Emma's door was still open. "Knock knock."

She already had the mess scooped into an empty can when Reece stepped in. He lingered in the doorway. "Can I help?"

"Well, not really." She tightened the front of her robe. "You could throw this can in the shintabet. Dingdang monkey. *Worse* than a baby."

"At least a baby uses a diaper," said Reece, reaching for the can.

"Not around here." A rooster crowed from the compound behind the house, the government clinic. She looked irritated, realized she looked irritated, and tried to put on a more cheerful face. "Just hate to wake up to that is all. Maybe give me some good news." She put a pot of water on the stove. "Tea?"

Afewerki arrived and knocked on the door. "Hallo," he said. He saw Emma in her robe and turned away.

"Hey, it's okay," said Emma. "Want some tea?"

Afewerki cleared his throat. "Tea is good for the night."

"Did you hear about the thieves?" asked Reece.

"Lord," said Emma. "Again?"

"Yes, in the night," said Afewerki. "They will accuse me. You will see."

"They better not," said Emma. "I've had enough of that. Let me get dressed, though, and I'll have tea ready for whoever wants it." She ran her hand through her hair and checked out Reece's legs.

Isaac called from the dining hut, announcing that breakfast was ready.

The afternoon was hot and Sunday languid. Emma suggested that Afewerki show her and Reece some of the caves in the area, in an area just west of town, along a deep, sloping chasm. They passed the path down to Sokoro stream, where most men sent their daughters and wives to fetch water, wending down the side of the steep, scrubby escarpment. Next, they forayed to a rising cliff edge, the path swaddled in gesho shrubs, its leaves used to flavor talla, the smoky homemade beer. Twenty feet up, Reece could discern an opening in the rough basalt. Afewerki said it was a crypt, that there were skeletons inside.

"Can I climb up and look?"

"That is bad idea," said Afewerki. "These are bodies of the very poor. They cannot afford another way."

"Is it sacred, or taboo to look?" Emma wore a red bandanna that gave her a hiker-girl look.

"The people will murmur among themselves if they know this."

The climb looked fairly straightforward, and Reece stepped onto a boulder and hoisted himself to the first ledge. "I'll be quick. I just want to see."

Afewerki held his tongue and watched, holding Reece's 35-millimeter Ricoh. "Do you want picture?"

Reece continued up the slanting face, hand over hand, until he reached the lip of the crypt, about eight feet wide and two feet high, which expanded in height toward the back, where it was as black as night. He stepped into an indentation, reached for a handhold above the opening, and pulled. A twisted torso of bones lay tangled with another decayed corpse. The bodies had been tossed in without much care. They must have been fairly old, as the skin on the skulls was eaten away, and the bone was very dry. The floor of the shallow cave was covered in silt, which poofed as his foot slipped and touched a disengaged leg bone. He looked down, and Afewerki snapped his photo.

"Get down before someone sees you." Emma stood with folded arms, with no desire to see the carnage.

Reece descended. "What did they die of?"

"No one knows," said Afewerki. "Let us go to see the

donkeys." He had told them about a large cave where donkeys congregated during the hot hours of the day. If someone needed his donkey, he knew where to look. Afewerki took a lime from his pocket and punched a small hole in it to suck a bit of juice.

Within minutes, they arrived at the donkey cave. Reece felt the cool air emanating from the tall slit in the rock, four feet at its widest. There was no sound coming from within. Emma passed inside first. It was very dark with a patch of light coming through an overhead shaft farther up the cliff face. Reece and Afewerki followed. Now there were sounds of hoofs on soft dirt. Gradually, the scene came into view as their eyes adjusted, a herd of nearly one hundred donkeys milled about in the vaulted chamber, twitching ears, moving as a flock of starlings but without sound. The smell of donkey was quite strong in the coolness.

"Wow," said Reece. The donkeys pulled back, snorting, pressing to the walls.

"Bizarre," said Emma.

"It is cool here. They can rest until it is time to work." Afewerki spoke while holding his nose. Emma had noticed that he was susceptible to unpleasant smells. Often, he put a piece of lemon peel in his nose to mask clinic odors.

They retreated into the sharp light. Reece's feet hurt. He needed a half-size larger boot. "How many caves are in the area? And where do all of these priests and monks live?"

"Some are living in the caves," said Afewerki. "To the north by one hour are more caves." He turned and retraced their path, now going uphill again. The sky was a clear and brilliant blue, a porcelain glaze.

He led them back toward the village among a few outlying huts and then toward the edge of an escarpment that fell away steppe-like for a thousand feet or so. The path down was narrow and rocky between dry grasses and scrub. Afewerki led them down the path and then veered to begin picking his way along the steep slope among boulders and large rocks. Emma kicked a stone and stumbled, grabbing for earth. Reece grabbed the waist of her pants from behind, keeping her from tipping downslope.

"Thanks."

Reece could feel the altitude, his heart beating with the exertion. Afewerki looked as if he were on a cakewalk and paused to keep from leaving them behind. Coming into a clearing, the view south was deep and wide.

They picked their way through the rocks like goats, leaning ever more into the slanting cliff to their right. Finger-length brown lizards flitted from stone to shadow. Reece stepped over a line of large black ants busy with work.

"How much farther?" Emma wiped sweat from her forehead.

"Just here," said Afewerki. "You will see a holy place."

"A cave?" asked Reece.

"It is a church," said Afewerki. "It has been made into the rock."

"Does a priest live there?" asked Emma.

"He is a monk. He has come to the clinic for medicines. He has made the church with his hands, into the rock."

Fifteen minutes more passed as they worked their way around the curving slope. House-sized boulders hung from the cliff above, ready to smash them into pieces. Reece examined his skinned shin and cuts on his hands. Everything was sharp or rough in Godo: thorns, the rocks, everything. He watched Emma's calves working, straining against the uneven ground.

Afewerki turned with a big grin on his face. "You are coming? Just here, coming soon." He adjusted his ballcap. Afewerki had once walked forty kilometers for a stamp.

Emma was thirsty but didn't want to complain. She was eager to see the church carved into the rock. Dr. Guthrie had told her about the rock-hewn churches in Lalibela, monoliths carved from a single block of stone dating from the twelfth century A.D. The Icelanders, too, had visited this church that she hoped would appear soon.

Within another ten minutes, Afewerki stopped and gazed up, scanning the cliff through shoulder-high scrub.

Reece thought there seemed to be a faint path, but couldn't be sure. "Looks like the end of the world." He paused and stared out over the vast gulf below and the flat-topped ambas in the distance. His toes ached in his boots. Above, the clear sky appeared to be within arm's reach.

Afewerki pointed. "Here," and he turned to climb hand over hand.

"We should've brought Marvin," said Emma. She tried to see what Afewerki was seeing. She looked back at Reece and caught his eye. An urge to kiss him, like stepping onto a bus just because it stopped in front of you. If Afewerki hadn't been there, she just might have.

After climbing ten feet or so, a ledge twenty feet wide extended from the forty-foot cliff face to the lip they had just scrambled up and over. To straighten the wall for the entrance, the monk had mined two feet into the face, creating a rough frame for an entry carved with an arch. A wooden door painted green stood open. Piles of dusty rocks and chips lay about. Farther down the ledge stood a tiny square house with a roof of corrugated tin. The brisk wind blew, flapping their clothes in bursts. From within came sounds like chopping wood.

"He is inside," said Afewerki. "Abba!" he called. The monk was called Abba Paulos.

The chopping sound stopped, and the monk came to the door. He looked displeased at being interrupted. Emma recognized him right away, the monk with the staph infection on his neck. He wore a golden-yellow skullcap and a dirty robe of matching color. Afewerki explained the ferenji had come to pay their respects, that they were interested in his work, to see the church he was building.

"Can we go inside?" asked Emma. The hot sun was especially intense in the open.

"The women cannot to go inside," said Afewerki. "It is forbidden."

"Come on, really?" She wasn't too surprised, though, knowing the culture, the pushed-aside lives that women led.

"How long has he been working on this?" asked Reece.

"He has been working many years." Afewerki turned and asked the monk. "He says for eleven years now. This is his second church to build. God has given him the dreams to build. He will show us, he says, but only because there is no tabot inside. The church is not finished. Perhaps by one year or two years."

The old monk disappeared into the gloom before Emma could get a good look at his neck, to see if it was healing. "Is he using his medicine?"

"I will ask," said Afewerki.

Reece and Afewerki stepped up one step and then down two into the roughly square chamber. There was a scaffold of rough poles along the side. The ceiling caught Reece's attention, at least fifteen feet high. As their eyes adjusted, the room, four hundred feet square, came into view. A pickaxe leaned against one of the four basalt columns that stretched from floor to ceiling. A rudimentary wheelbarrow with an iron wheel sat half-filled with sharp slices of rock. The rock's face was a light brown to gray, reflecting the bright sunlight through the door in a soft glow. Only the corners remained dusky.

"Holy cow," said Emma from outside, looking in. The monk turned and shook his finger at her.

"This is something else," said Reece. "How does he survive, food, money?"

"The people bring to him food. He is asking now for ten birr to help him finish this place."

The old monk took his pick and, with stooped shoulders, began hacking away slowly at the uneven floor toward the back. There were no flies inside.

"You have any birr on you?" asked Emma from outside.

"No. We can come back," said Reece. His voice echoed in the cave-like interior. "Afewerki, I have two fifty-cent pieces for now."

Afewerki took the money and placed it into a Merti tomato can sitting near the door. The old monk paused. "Xavier meskin."

"Minem aydelem," said Afewerki. "He says he must continue to work so that he can do his prayers."

"Amenseganolo," said Reece. He bowed his head.

Back outside, the dull crack of the pick on stone continued from within. "Well, that was pretty cool," said Reece. "Amazing how this is his life's work. One man. One task." He remembered his feet hurting.

"Pretty cool for you, I guess. If I bring him ten birr, maybe he'll let me see inside." Emma looked serious. "Let's get back. It took us nearly an hour. Are you guys thirsty?"

"No." Afewerki tumbled down the hand-over-hand segment of the path, falling but landing on his feet. "Oh, damn! I am sorry." He looked up at Emma, who was surveying the tricky descent.

"Need a rope," said Emma.

"I think you can back down it like you came up. I'll hold your arm until you get your footing right." Reece kneeled.

"No, I've got to do it myself. Maybe you go down first and catch me if I fall."

"Really?"

"Yeah."

"Okay. Here I go."

He turned around and dug his fingers into a tiny crack in the rock, lowered a leg, and searched for a hold. Afewerki directed from below. "To za right. To za left."

"Sounds like you're doing the Hokey Pokey." She could see down his shirt, the line of chest hair that led to his navel. "Be careful."

Reece found another foothold and lowered himself full stretch. He took his left hand away, and then his right slipped. Instead of falling backward, he jumped and landed hard, pushing the air from his lungs with an *Oomph!* "Shit on toast," he said to Afewerki who was helping him stand.

Emma was already on her way down. She kept her belly close to the wall and seemed to float. She dropped the last two feet, raising a cloud of dust, and grinned at Reece. "You okay?"

"Fine. Let's go," he said, limping just a bit. "Dang boots are too small."

Back at the compound, it was a lazy afternoon. Reece and Emma took naps. Mariam and Isaac played several games of Uno with Ketow. He had just gotten the hang of the game and howled with laughter at every move, as if he had never before imagined having such a good time. Afewerki puttered around at his parents' compound, helping his two younger brothers with Amharic lessons and helping his dad sharpen the household knives and axe. Barra was out and about socializing with members of the village's kebele, the farmer's cooperative, discussing urgent matters such as the high price of sugar.

Emma awoke. She hadn't brushed her teeth after lunch, and her mouth felt fuzzy. The sun was still bright and orange, heading down in the west. The compound seemed empty. She could hear sounds of talking from the dining hut and walked with a toothbrush and cup of water to the back of her tiny house. The grass was getting high. Through the tangle of the head-high fence, made of poles and living plants, she glimpsed the government clinic. Someone was there. She turned her back, rinsed, and spat into the grass. She looked back through the fence, and it was him, the Hyena with his gold teeth. He was alone and held a Kalashnikov.

The Hyena pulled back the bolt. He pointed the rifle at Emma, not saying a word.

"What do you want?" asked Emma. She took a deep breath.

"Americano," he replied and spat, his lower lip packed with the narcotic leaf qat.

Emma froze. Should she call for help? A fly landed on her cup, trying to get at the liquid there. Marvin came around the corner of the house. She tried to focus on the monkey. "Come here, buddy." Her movements were stiff. Her heart raced.

Marvin sat back on his haunches, staring at her, picking his ear.

"To'ta," said the Hyena, and he laughed. He pulled the trigger and called her a bitch, shamuta.

The blast shocked Emma. Marvin screamed and ran to the tree.

All hands came running—Isaac, Mariam, and Ketow. Reece heard the shot from his bed, the commotion, and sat up. He stood too quickly, had to pause as everything went black for a few seconds, and stumbled to his door.

"Shamuta," the Hyena said again, grinning and turning as everyone gathered around Emma.

Isaac railed at the Hyena through the fence, telling him he should be arrested. Mariam's eyes flashed, and Ketow stood by nervously with his rifle, looking from face to face.

"What's going on?" asked Reece. He zipped his pants.

"That bastard fired a shot at me," said Emma. She was shaking. "At my feet, I think. Dammit." She grabbed the fence, hoisted herself up, and yelled, "Hey!" at the Hyena who was out of sight now and too stoned to care.

Reece could still feel the Sunday malaise. Mixed with this outburst, the day seemed extra sour.

"He will suffer," said Isaac, huffing with excitement.

"Does the mission know what's going on up here with this guy?" asked Reece.

"They know," said Emma. "Just part of the territory. I suppose we should pray for him."

"Yes, to pray," said Mariam, who trembled.

Reece didn't quite know what to do. "Should we go after him? He can't just fire his gun at you and get away with it."

"He probably can," said Emma.

"The peoples fear him," said Isaac.

"I get that," said Reece.

Afewerki ran into the compound. The news had traveled quickly. "You are okay?" he said to Emma. She explained what had happened. "We will cut his throat," he said in a temper.

"Yikes," said Reece. "He deserves it."

"Well, what would Jesus have to say about it? I have to remember that," said Emma.

"He will say this." Afewerki made a cutting motion across his throat.

"Ouch," said Reece.

Dinner was goman, wild greens, and an alicha made with fresh white potatoes. Emma and Reece, both dressed in jeans and a scrub top, passed on the offer of extra berbere spice, but the others sprinkled it liberally over their potatoes, making impressive sounds of satisfaction with each bite. Reece excused himself and brought back his box of peanut brittle from the States.

"Oh, caramella!" said Barra. He rubbed his hands together. "What it is?"

"It's made with peanuts and syrup, very sweet. Peanut brittle."

"I love peanut brittle," said Emma. "You better give me a big piece."

Reece ripped into the foil pouch and pulled out a jagged, flat chunk. "It's very sticky. Sticks to your teeth." He handed the box to Emma, who took a piece and passed it on to Isaac, then Mariam, Barra, and Afewerki.

"Ah." Mariam laughed. He wore his shirt with the huge front pocket. Emma said he could put a bowling ball in there. To her surprise, he'd known what a bowling ball was.

"Very delicious," said Afewerki. He chewed up and down.

Barra licked his like a sucker before putting the whole piece into his mouth. He chewed and chewed with a big smile.

"You are good brother," said Isaac.

The box went around one more time before it was empty.

"That was so good." Emma leaned back in her folding chair. "I miss having sweets."

Reece decided to try a joke. "Here is a joke." The room grew quiet. "Did you know that the Disciples owned a Honda?"

No one spoke for a moment. Barra looked perplexed. "Who is the de-zibles?"

"You know, the Apostles. Matthew, Mark, Luke, John—"

"Ah, yes, yes," said Isaac. "Of Jesus Christ."

Emma nodded, waiting for the punchline.

"What is Honda?" asked Isaac.

Emma laughed. She knew it was next to impossible to tell a joke and get the expected laugh.

"It is a car, a Japanese car," said Reece.

"Yes, Japan," said Mariam.

Reece felt the joke going flat. "Well, it says in the Bible that they all met in one Accord." He immediately knew he would have to explain Accord.

"Yes," said Barra.

"Is joke?" asked Isaac.

"Japan," said Mariam.

Only Emma was laughing, and the team gazed at her in wonderment.

As the chill of evening slipped over Godo like a thin glove, Reece asked Emma questions he'd been saving for when they might be alone. Afewerki, though, had stayed with them as the others said goodnight.

"I'm the youngest of six sisters. The only one not married," said Emma. "Have a younger brother."

"Wow." Reece was an only child. "Would you ever want to have that many kids?"

Emma looked startled. "Heck no. Maybe one or two, but not seven." She laughed at the thought, showing a serious, lopsided smile that made Reece's stomach flutter.

"Your family is big family," said Afewerki. "I have two brothers and one sister, praise God. None has died."

"I've seen your brothers herding the goats," said Emma. "They're adorable."

"Cute? This means pretty?"

"Sort of. Good looking."

"Yes, good looking." Afewerki propped his hands on his knees.

Reece drank the last bit of water in his bottle. "What about a boyfriend?"

Afewerki cleared his throat. "Emma? She is no boyfriend."

"No boyfriends," said Emma. "I was seeing someone a

few months before I came over. Just didn't work out. Different ideas about life." She looked wistful. "What about you, Afewerki? Any girlfriends?"

Afewerki made a sour face. "No, no. Women only want to get married. No, no."

"Aww," said Emma. She gave Reece a curious look. "So, how long have you been engaged?"

Reece scratched behind his ear. "About a month before I came over, almost two months now."

"Wow, that must have been tough, having to leave her. What does she think about it, you leaving and being gone for so long?"

"She's not happy about it. But I told her I had committed to this before I met her, literally a week before we met."

Emma wanted to say it sounded like a disaster waiting to happen, but didn't.

"I really, really miss her." He wanted to say that he was finding it harder and harder to visualize his life with her, but didn't.

Monday started slow, with only ten patients in line, when Emma, Reece, and Afewerki entered the clinic compound. Reece held to the elbow of the old woman with the deep hip ulcers. She was walking on her own, though still weak, and was the first patient of the day.

She pulled up her thick, dusty dress before she sat down. The dressings from Saturday hung limply from the silk tape.

"Let's have her stand, make it easier on everybody," said Emma.

Afewerki motioned her to stand and braced her. Reece held up the dress, exposing the first hip.

"Have her stand sideways so I can sit on the bench and work." Emma peeled off the gauze and let it and the packing drop into the biscuit tin. "Eschar is peeling off." She put on a glove and peeled back a black rind of dead tissue ringing the ulcer.

"Oh, baby," said Reece. "Pink and healthy underneath." The wound seemed less deep as well, closing in on itself.

Emma dropped the six inches of scab into the trash and dabbed at the tiny dots of blood the eschar had drawn around the wound's edge. "Maybe no packing, just the Banalin powder and a dressing over it?"

"Yeah, that works," said Reece. "This is the worst of the two. I'll bet the other one looks even better."

Emma finished the left hip and began work on the right. It also looked much better and shed its substantial rim of eschar, revealing clean, pink skin beneath. The old woman thanked them, holding Emma's hand in her own and bowing toward Reece.

"Minem aydelem," said Afewerki, as heavy splashes of

rain swept the roof. The drops sounded like small stones. It rained in waves as if someone were scattering grain and then stopped. Patients without umbrellas had crowded into the compound beneath the clinic's eaves.

"Ciao," said Emma as the old woman gathered her dress and stepped into the humid air. She grabbed her son's arm for support. The rain had brought the smell of steamed earth, the thin air struggling to hold the moisture.

Reece remembered hearing a child's screams during the night. It seemed to have gone on for hours. "Did you hear that screaming last night?" he said.

"You know, I did," said Emma. A middle-aged man entered the clinic and sat on one side, a mother with child sat on the other.

"Yes, there is a child, a young boy who is very sick," said Afewerki.

"Has he been to the clinic?"

"No, no," said Afewerki.

"Is he close by?"

"Yes, near to here. His family is very poor. He has a ghost in his leg, and he will die."

"What?" asked Reece.

"What's wrong with his leg?"

"It is very large. He has fever," said Afewerki.

"We need to see if we can help."

"You may try," said Afewerki. "He will most likely die."

"Can he come to the clinic?"

"No. He cannot walk. You must go there."

The day yielded seventeen cases of diarrhea, fifteen with tapeworms or roundworms, six instances of scabies, six eye infections, three flesh wounds, and a young bride suffering from anxiety and shock, a slow but productive day overall. Afewerki mentioned in passing that the Hyena was spreading rumors about the clinic, how they were using expired medications, which had been occasionally true. Of the tons of supplies flooding the country, many had been held in storage for more than two years before finding their final destination.

After clinic finished early around four, Emma, Reece, and Afewerki visited the tukul with the sick little boy who was screaming in the night. The ramshackle hut did not have a fence and sat amid a gathering of three others in similar disrepair. A large hole in the thatch roof was visible from the outside. The mother, a short woman stooped with toil, met them in the tiny dirt yard. She had a soiled rag tied around her head. From inside came sounds of plaintive moaning, a cry of continuous deep-seated pain.

They crowded into the rank hut that smelled of urine and frankincense. A lump of amber aromatic sap sizzled and smoked on top of a smoldering lump of charcoal. The thin spiral of smoke melded with the shaft of light coming through the roof's ragged hole. The boy lay on a rough bed made of poles laced with leather straps. A few empty grain bags served as his mattress. He looked their way, seeing through them.

Emma came to his side and touched his head. He was burning with fever. His frightened eyes widened, creased at the corners with pain. His teeth were large, white, and dry. Bits of desiccated foam clung to his cracked lips. He was naked, except for a small cloth across his waist. He was too weak to move, with only the strength to utter his pitiful cries.

Reece moved in to have a closer look at the boy's leg. The right leg, below the knee, was swollen, with the skin ashy and tight, but without any open sores. He watched Emma stroke the boy's head. "Afewerki, can she tell us what happened? When it started? Can he eat?" asked Emma. The boy was very thin, the skin between his ribs sucking with each labored breath.

"It has been two weeks." He paused, listening to the mother tell the story. "She says that he has a ghost in his leg, that he is very hot. He will not eat enjera, she is saying."

"We need to get him on an antibiotic, some paracetamol, and get some food and liquids in him," said Emma. "He's right pitiful."

"He's beneath the opening in the roof. What happens when it rains?" asked Reece. "I'll donate the money to have the roof fixed, tell her."

"Let's buy some soft foods, bananas and oranges, maybe some potatoes she can boil for him."

"She says he will die soon," said Afewerki. "But she is grateful for what you are doing. She says for God to bless you."

Reece felt a lump in his throat. He could see the boy's heart beating through his thin chest.

Reece and Emma walked back to the clinic for supplies, while Afewerki went a few huts over to hire a man to patch the roof. Once back, Emma started a 20-gauge IV with a liter of the Icelandic IV fluid, a dextrose-saline mixture. The boy was severely dehydrated from his fever. Reece held the thermometer under the boy's armpit.

"If he can't swallow the chloramphenicol, we'll have to

do injections," said Reece. The clinic had no IV antibiotics. "Hundred and four temp."

"Jesus," said Emma. "Probably 105 then by mouth." Leaning over the boy, her hair covered her face. "Can you hold my hair back while I tape this?"

"Me?" asked Reece.

"Yeah."

Reece wedged himself between the bed and the fire ring, trying not to fall. He reached from behind and drew Emma's hair back with both hands and balanced over her. He watched her neck and shoulders, the bones of her vertebrae outlined beneath the scrub top.

"Thanks."

Afewerki fidgeted, then squatted, observing the proceedings.

The boy's eyes drifted as the fluid dripped into his vein. He had a distant look, as if he were being transported from one universe to another. His lips moved. His mother sat on his bed, soothing him with her voice.

"Let's see if he can swallow these pills," said Emma.

Afewerki explained to the mother. Together they sat him up, moving his legs. He howled in pain, looking from face to face for relief or explanation.

"Careful of the IV," said Reece. With no IV pole, he held the bag at chest level.

"His leg is so hot," said Emma.

The boy's mother placed a single paracetamol in his mouth, then an orange cup of water to his dry lips.

"How old is he?" asked Reece.

"Asra-hoolet," said Afewerki. "He is twelve."

The paracetamol slipped out of the boy's mouth as he tried to swallow.

"Damn," said Emma. "We've got to get his fever down. Tell her to try again."

The boy moaned.

"May need a feeding tube for the meds," said Reece.

"Could be," said Emma.

The boy's mother tried again. The pill floated on top of his tongue, with the water spilling from the corners of his mouth. His eyes focused as he watched his mother's hand bring the cup to his lips again. He swallowed hard, and the pill was gone.

"Three more to go," said Emma. "What's his name?"

"His name is Fekadu." Afewerki handed the woman another paracetamol tablet and two antibiotic tablets. She placed one to her tongue to see if perhaps it was bitter. It took a few minutes, but finally the boy swallowed them all and lay back exhausted with the effort.

"He needs the IV overnight," said Reece. "Maybe let the rest of this bag go in and do a heparin lock? Give him another liter tomorrow?"

"He already looks better," said Emma. The boy's eyes had relaxed, his moaning subsiding to a mumble. "Afewerki, can you find some bananas, bring some back, and see if he can eat? We'll stay here until the fluid runs in. Reece, can you go back to the clinic for the hep lock?"

"Ishi," said Afewerki as he ducked out of the hut, past a small gathering of children who were peering in with very wide eyes at the proceedings.

"Caramella?" asked one as he passed.

Afewerki barked, and the children ran to the path, alarmed but then laughing. "Ferenj," said one shyly as Reece headed downhill to the clinic.

With the young boy Fekadu stabilized and rounds at the shelter complete, everyone sought the comfort of their rooms for a bit of silence and rest before dinner. Emma washed underwear and bras and hung them on a line strung across the room. Marvin was nowhere to be seen, and that was a bit of a relief to her. She secretly hoped he would escape into the great, vast wilderness around Godo. She thought about the monk in the carved church and made a face at the idea that she could not go inside. She would return with a donation, and perhaps he would change his mind. A knock on the door, *rap, rap, rap*, very light. She knew it was Afewerki.

"Yes?" She slipped back into her scrub bottoms.

"Emma?"

She opened the door. Barra stood behind him a few feet away. She watched Afewerki's eyes survey her laundry. He seemed to be choking, the color draining from his face.

"Oh, oh," he said.

"What's up?"

"I do not mean to bother you." He looked everywhere except into her tiny house, as if he were trying to make eye contact with some unseen person.

"No bother." Emma smiled at his clumsiness.

"Marvin has been kill-ed."

"What? He's dead? How?" She stepped outside, pushing Afewerki aside. He nearly fell. "I'm sorry. Tell me."

Barra came forward and took her hand. He kept his eyes down as he spoke. "The monkey has been kill-ed by some boys. They catch him and kill him."

"Jesus," said Emma.

"They take out his eye," said Afewerki.

"Yes," said Barra. He held Emma's hand. "You must not worry. The monkey was stealing some foods, and they catch-ed him."

"Where is he? The body?"

Barra looked at Afewerki. "No, he is dead. He is gone."

"Did you bury him? You should have told me first."

"He is monkey. He is gone now. You must not worry," said Barra.

Afewerki looked pale, shaken by having to deliver the news.

"Do we know who did it? I mean, you can't just kill a monkey, can you? Boys did it?"

"Is best to forget," said Afewerki.

Emma scowled and dipped her shoulders.

"The monkey was dirty. He is gone now," said Barra. He smiled.

"Okay, thanks," said Emma.

"You want play Uno?" asked Barra. He laughed, trying to cheer her up.

"No, but thanks. I'll see you at dinner."

"Yes, dinner," said Afewerki.

They agreed during dinner that Reece would start a Bible study group to meet on Tuesday evenings. Reece wasn't sure what sort of lesson plan he would follow. He had read the Bible through twice, had all sixty-six books memorized in order, and knew about two dozen passages by heart, but he was not an expert in any particular area. He had thought about the Book of James, but decided to first pursue the Ark of the Covenant, its origins, its history, its significance from a Biblical perspective. He enjoyed history more than evangelism. A quick search of his Bible's concordance had revealed numerous references, most in the Old Testament but some also in the New Testament. He hoped the discussions would shed light on the relationship between Ethiopia and the Ark and maybe even on the activities of the Icelanders, whom he was very curious about. He wished he could have met them. Iceland seemed as mythical, as rugged, and as far-fetched as Ethiopia. The original Ark of the Covenant had been imbued with mysterious powers of destruction. He wondered again if the Ark could be in Ethiopia, as everyone seemed to believe, hidden away in a chapel of the Church of Our Lady Mary of Zion in Axum in the north of Ethiopia. It seemed as strange as reading *The Martian Chronicles.*

Reece fetched a basin of cool water from the cookhouse barrel. He had not brought a washcloth or towel, so he used half of a bandanna to wash with and the other half to dry. Terry would fly in tomorrow, hopefully with mail for him. He fingered the short stack of letters building on his bedside table, picked up one, pulled out the lined paper, and smelled it. He smelled again, searching for a hint of home, a hint of something familiar. Kristin's letters merely smelled of paper. He tried to think of something positive, looked at her photo pinned to the wall with a thorn. Every little move was an act of improvisation. He longed for something sweet, anything. A Little Debbie snack cake hovered in his mind. He thought about Emma earlier that day, squatting in front of him, asking him to hold back her hair. He shook his head, as if to sling stinging droplets of sweat from his brow. The little boy, Fekadu. How was he doing? He could hear a faint moaning in the distance. Perhaps it was him. He couldn't tell. It was too early for the dogs to fight, and he dreaded their noise.

Emma put her underwear and bras away. The thin air made drying clothes quick, even indoors. She washed her hands, digging beneath her nails to get at the orange stains of the berbere. The book of First Chronicles proved to be a chore, with endless genealogical lists and a history of King David's reign, the father of Solomon. She breezed her way through chapter after chapter, skipping the lines of names, seeking narrative. She read of priests, of spices, of the death of the disobedient King Saul at the hands of the Philistines. David was then appointed by God as the ruler of the Israelites and returned them to the city of Jerusalem, conquering the lands around him. She lingered on Chapter 13, reading of David calling the Hebrew people back to Zion and with them the Ark of the Covenant. Reece seemed to be very interested in the Ark. As the Ark, with its holy tablets, was being escorted back to Jerusalem, the oxen pulling the heavy gold-layered box of acacia wood topped with two cherubim tumbled. A man named Uzzah reached out to steady the Ark, but God was displeased and struck him down. *Weird.*

She sat on the edge of her squeaky cot and blew out the candle, plunging the room into darkness. She heard the shrill moan of Fekadu floating through the still night and propped her head on a pillow. They had done what they could, except to evacuate him to Addis, which would get her in trouble with the business manager, Thomas Watson, unless it was a dire emergency. She closed her eyes and could only think of Marvin, how horrible his death must have been.

Fekadu soiled himself during the night, soaking the grain bags that lay between him and the leather webbing of the crude bed frame. That was a good sign, all agreed, showing that his kidneys were working, that he was processing the fluids being given intravenously. Reece went back to his room and took his spare sheet to put over Fekadu. He suggested that Fekadu be taken outside—perhaps they could carry him into the sun for a few minutes. His hips and sacrum were showing signs of wear, redness, and chafing from the constant pressure of lying in bed.

Emma tested the heparin lock and started another 500 ccs of saline to run in over two hours. Reece and Afewerki fashioned an IV pole from a heavy stick lodged in a biscuit tin filled with rocks. Fekadu sat up, supported by his mother. The morning light flooded the open doorway, and a shaft swimming with dust came through the hole in the thatched roof. Fekadu took shallow, rapid breaths, his eyes searching for something to help the pain in his leg. Emma removed the thermometer from his armpit. "Hundred and two. Better."

Reece palmed two paracetamol tablets for the mother to give her son, and then the antibiotic. Fekadu had lost significant weight, down to about fifty pounds, they estimated. "Is he eating?" asked Reece.

Afewerki replied, no, that his mother said he was not eating.

"Tell her to try the bananas again and even enjera, just that she should try," said Emma. "If he doesn't start eating, we'll need to put down a feeding tube. Let's send some famine crackers back up here. Tell her he needs to try and drink too, even though we're giving him this IV fluid." She slowed the drip and counted for a full minute.

As they left, the neighbor Reece had paid to mend the roof walked up with a load of straw and his tools. He had long, slender legs and was missing several teeth. He doffed his hat in passing and looked very grave as he set about his task.

The day was dominated by many cases of diarrhea, young and old alike, requiring cups of ORS for most and IV fluids for one young teenage girl. An hour before noon and lunch, Emma asked Reece if he could handle the clinic with Afewerki. She had an errand. She didn't say that it was to visit the monk and see the effect of a donation on his reluctance to show her the inside of his hand-carved church. It reminded her of her dad always making her sit in the back seat of their giant station wagon.

Sure. Why not? It seemed to be a very routine day, although the woman, whose hip sores they were treating, had not shown as usual. Emma gathered a pack of famine biscuits and took a packet of iodine swabs with her. She had a crisp 20-birr bill as well. On the black market, one US dollar was going for eight birr, so it was a small gift, but considering the average family wage in the countryside was a meager twenty to thirty birr per month, her gift was large.

With the sun out in full force, she fetched an Atlanta Braves ballcap from her tiny house. She washed her hands, drank from one of the cold IV bottles, and set off through the village toward the west, where the magnificent cliff line worked its way down as steppes to the narrow valley below. She thought about the cool of the donkey's cave and imagined they were crowded there, sheltered from the sun's blast. The path at first was the same used by women going to fetch water, then she veered right, following rough ground through thorny shrubs. Half an hour later, the path veered downhill, and she tried to remember how high or low she should proceed, following the cliff rising above her to the right.

Within half an hour, she realized that she had gone too far and turned back, now on a faint path that seemed at times like it was not a path. She was thirsty, and her nose felt burned. Vultures circled high overhead, gliding, searching. She wished now that she had brought someone with her. Getting lost with a friend could be fun, but not alone. She searched the cliff above for clues. There would be a wide ledge. She would have to climb hand over hand about ten feet. The rock face of the church would be there. She stopped and listened to the wind, gusting now, straining to hear the thunk of pick on rock. Gesho shrubs and thorn bushes ran together. The path was lost. She looked down and then up. Her foot slipped in the dry, crumbling dirt, and she fell on her side, gaining a great streak of brown on her white scrub top.

She heard them first. Low sounds of talking and laughing. She crouched. The sounds were coming nearer. Above her and perhaps fifty feet away, she saw a full afro, glimpsed army green, then a bare leg. She felt silly, as if hiding something, and stood. She moved forward, keeping to her goal of finding the path again. It couldn't be far. She had perhaps overshot her mark by ten minutes, she thought. She heard a voice, this one coming from below. She twisted between the shrubs, scratching her arms. He caught her gaze and stopped. He put the butt of his AK-47 on the ground and nodded at her. "Allo," he said, grinning.

Emma raised her eyebrows but said nothing, veering away from him. A dread filled her gut. Someone was approaching from below, the sound of dry twigs breaking. Another afro, this one with a homemade wooden pick embedded into the hair, the Hyena's bodyguards. Her stomach heaved. She turned to check behind her. The one above her was calling to someone and standing his ground. The one below was now cutting her off. He brandished his rifle, complete with an unsheathed Izhevsk bayonet. The blade caught her eye. It looked incredibly sharp.

And then there he was, the Hyena himself, wearing reflective aviator sunglasses. He said nothing as he steadied himself on the uneven ground. He wore full-length fatigues and combat boots. His gold-rimmed teeth glinted between his thin lips.

"Well, if it isn't the American bitch," he said in Amharic. He spat. The others held their eyes on her, waiting. The one who wore short pants with wide leg openings pulled up his pant leg and began urinating on the ground.

Emma pushed forward, head down. She was vaguely aware of the shifting positions of the three men. They were converging on her. A hand grabbed her shirt and pulled, choking her to a stop. They were in a small clearing of rocky ground. The dirt was like talc, a fine powder.

She jerked her shoulder away. The top of her head felt hot. Her mouth was dry, and her heart beating much too fast. Her midriff was showing, her shirt bunched in his hand, the one who had come from below. His friend finished urinating and moved closer. The Hyena kept the higher ground, looking down.

Emma grabbed a wrist and dug in her nails and pulled. She grunted and fell forward, free from the bodyguard. His legs were bony, shiny, with a large tropical ulcer over the shin.

Emma thought about screaming, but not yet. She felt that she could extricate herself, get back to work. She sensed that the Hyena was either drunk or stoned, but she couldn't tell. He stepped down to more level ground. She could see herself reflected in his shades. She felt dizzy, sick.

Now the two guards were pulling her shirt in different directions, and the cloth was tearing. She mumbled *No* and then allowed herself to scream as long and hard as she could. She stood there in her bra, a heat of anguish building in her chest. She reached for a stone but was thrown backward onto the ground, which was very hot, burning her hands. She filled both hands with the fine dirt and tried to stand. A leg kicked her off her feet onto her back, knocking the breath from her. She threw the dirt, but it rained back into her eyes. The bayonet came now to her face, inches from her nose.

"Damn you," she said. And then they moved in, breaking into muffled shouts and grunts as she punched and kicked. The Hyena, his manhood failing him, lingered, watching his young stooges in a stupor, holding his penis in his hand, a glaze of laughter taking him.

"Tew! Tew! Wu tah! Basta, basta!" The monk in his yellow robe and skullcap yelled down at them from the ledge above. He shook his staff, topped with an Orthodox cross.

The two young men let go of Emma, and she broke into a run with only one shoe on. The Hyena looked alarmed and doubly confused, staring up at the monk, who continued to berate them, telling them to leave, that they were desecrating holy ground, that he would call down curses upon them if they did not leave immediately.

Emma, holding back a sob, stopped her retreat. She looked up at the monk and then back at the men standing stupidly. They looked ashamed. She circled back around and picked her torn shirt from the ground and slid it on. She grabbed her shoe and hurried her foot into it, taking off into a run, away from the dumbfounded group. A dirt devil sixty feet in height materialized from nothing, stirring up a cloud of rotating dust and debris. The orange funnel whipped about in jerks, as if deciding which way to go.

The Hyena looked up one last time at the monk who was holding forth his staff, as if parting the Red Sea. He swallowed and motioned for his thugs to come, to go, a look of bewilderment and fear blazed onto his face.

Where the path would allow her to run, Emma ran, pushing through scrub until she regained the open path that led uphill. She struggled for deep breaths, her forehead dripping with sweat. She tasted aluminum foil. She felt fingertips digging into her wrists and shoulders. A young girl of twelve with a clay water pot looked back at Emma. She stopped and put her hand across her mouth, looking down at the ground as if she could guess what had happened. Emma paused at this girl's beautiful face, her head covered with a pretty scarf of turquoise and blue. She wanted to tell her to run as well, but continued on. What should she do? She could only think of home, her mother, then her father, and she shook her head. *Reece.* She wanted to see Reece, to tell him what had happened. She just needed to tell him, to talk as soon as possible before she collapsed into a sobbing heap. She passed a young boy with a dozen goats, and a sense of calm descended upon her. The boy was only six or seven and held a tiny whip. He looked much too young to be in charge of goats, perhaps all his family owned in the world. "Ferenj," he said. Emma smiled and passed him, feeling more confident as she walked between compound fences, hearing the sounds of women calling to one another. A skinny hen with five chicks hurried across the path in front of her.

A peace settled within Emma as she returned to her tiny house. Ketow let her in and looked at her with curious eyes. He could see her torn shirt and spoke rapidly. She only nodded and went inside to change into clean clothes, then she would go to the clinic and talk with Reece. A wave of empty helplessness filled her chest. She could feel those hands grabbing at her body, the sneers, the laughter. She felt chilled, wondering if it had happened. But then there was the monk shouting down at them. He had saved her, no doubt. She sat on her bed and put her head into her hands, losing herself in memories of childhood, her father hitting her mother, her father whipping her with a belt through a thin cotton dress, how it had hurt so deeply. Vacation Bible School, images of old women with white hair serving cookies and orangeade. Time seemed to slow.

There was a knock on her door. She listened. She could hear a vague noise of voices in the distance. A fly landed on her folded hands. The knocking resumed.

"Emma?" She heard her name. "Emma?" It was Reece.

"Hey," she said.

Reece pushed the door open, scraping the rough cement floor. "You okay? Ketow said there was a problem."

She was silent. She saw Reece in his jeans and white scrub top, untucked. Peering over his shoulder was Afewerki.

"Emma?"

She burst into tears, crying into her hands.

Reece pulled the chair to the bed and sat with her until she could speak. Afewerki stood in the doorway, arms folded across his chest.

"What happened?"

Emma took a deep breath. She felt a thread of control returning. "I went to visit the monk, to see if he would let me into his church."

"Alone?"

"Yes, alone."

Afewerki edged into the room, drawing closer. "The monk has done this to you?"

Emma looked up, seeing him for the first time. "No, he helped me. It was the Hyena and his two guards. They... attacked me."

"You've got to be kidding," said Reece.

"They grabbed me. One had a knife on the end of his rifle."

"Are you okay?" asked Reece. He wanted to ask if they had raped her, but couldn't bring himself to say the words.

"Just bruised, I think. I fell. They ripped my shirt. That's all. The monk came and started yelling. They stopped, and I ran."

"Jesus Christ," said Reece.

"Very bad," said Afewerki, his face contorted with anger. "We must kill him."

Emma's expression remained the same. "Right now, I just want to get back to the clinic. You guys go, and I'll be down in a few minutes. Okay? I promise I'm okay."

"No, you should rest or just relax," said Reece.

"Relax? How am I supposed to relax?"

"Well, there *is* a patient who asked to see you specifically," said Reece.

"Good, I need to work, that's all. Just let me have a few minutes, and I'll be down."

"No, we must go for Dr. Guthrie," said Afewerki. "To have the Hyena arrested."

"That would be nice," said Reece.

"Not now," said Emma. "Go. I'll meet you down there. Go!"

"Okay, okay," said Reece. "You're a tough cookie."

Emma smiled and put her hand to her chest, fighting a surge of despair.

The woman who had requested to see Emma had a cloudy blue eye and a clear brown one. Her hair was shaved closely to the scalp. A long, muscular neck flowed beneath a narrow, sculpted jaw. Her skin was that of brown sugar, and she had been raped, by who she did not know, just that a man had entered her hut during the night and forced himself on her. It was dark, and she could not see his face, although she thought it was probably her neighbor's husband, but she couldn't be sure. She talked in hushed tones and wept.

A rush of rage surged within Emma. Her heart thudded in her chest.

"Do you live alone?" asked Emma.

Afewerki replied she did. Her husband had left during the famine and not returned.

Reece busied himself quietly with a severe burn. The young boy, who had epilepsy, had fallen into the cookfire and burned his thigh and hand. His mother had rescued him quickly, but not before the hot coals had seared his flesh. The little boy cringed as Reece wiped dirt and debris from the edges of his wounds with sterile gauze soaked in saline. The afternoon was proving to be pleasant, a cool breeze beneath a breathy, cloudy sky.

The woman took Emma's hand and cried into it, with Emma sitting beside her. She had been born in another village to the east, near Gondar and Lake Tana. Her mother was there, living alone as well. If only they could be together. She wasn't sure if her mother was still alive, but felt in her heart that she was. Emma thought about her mother, living alone since she had left.

"Does she think she might be pregnant?" asked Emma. "I know it's too early to tell, but..."

Afewerki asked and replied that, no, the woman said that God had cursed her and that she could not have children. That was why her husband had not returned, she was sure.

The sounds of the little boy screaming distracted Emma for a moment. The boy was slow for his age, she could tell at a glance, his head overly large for his body, snot running from both nostrils. "Is she afraid to go back to her house? She can stay in the shelter if she needs to. We have a guard there."

"No, she cannot to leave her house," said Afewerki. "Someone will steal."

"Does she want to report this to someone, to the authorities?"

"No, no she cannot. She cannot prove anything she says. It will only bring more trouble. She is complaining to urinate. There is burning and pain just here." Afewerki pointed to his lower back.

"Probably has a urinary tract infection from that bastard. Once we have the little boy out of here, I'll do a quick exam." Reece was finishing up the bandages on the boy's thigh and hand. The woman clung to Emma.

"She wants the murphy, an injection," said Afewerki.

"Lord, and she may need it. Ask her if she's allergic to penicillin."

"She does not know," said Afewerki.

Reece interrupted. "I'm through here. Can you tell the mother to bring him back tomorrow for another dressing change?"

"Ishi," and Afewerki explained this to the grateful mother, who thanked Reece and then thanked God.

"Let's step outside," said Reece, "so that Emma can examine this woman." And they did.

That afternoon, Emma wound up flying back to Alem Ketema with Terry for a couple of days just to gather her senses after the attack by the Hyena and his cohorts. News of the incident filtered back to Addis Ababa, where the Mission's head administrator, Ben Ashberry, and Dr. Guthrie determined to file a formal complaint against the Hyena. No one seemed to know what his real name was, and they had to begin there, then take the issue to the Central Committee in charge of law and order in the administrative zones established by the Marxist government. Emma was neither for nor against having the Hyena punished, but she was determined to find out just how evil he was and to raise a cry against him from within the community. She had a gut feeling that he was responsible for the rape of the woman who had come to the clinic and of many others as well. According to Afewerki and Isaac, the Hyena was very unpopular with the local peasant association, the kebele, whose responsibility it was to operate a low-level social court within their jurisdiction. While Ashberry and Guthrie worked from the top, Emma would hammer away at healing the people of Godo.

When Emma returned to Godo the following Friday, Reece was thrilled to have her back. As Terry landed the Bell 412 just an hour after clinic started, Reece realized just how excited he was, being nearly speechless as Emma walked away from the helipad, crouched, her hair flying wild in the downwash of the blades. She headed straight into the clinic, holding a grain bag of mail.

A lopsided smile crept onto her face.

"Hey." Reece put his hand on her shoulder, and she

came in close for a hug.

"Hey, yourself." She hugged Afewerki, causing his face to flush. She was back in the clinic—the smells of smoke and milk, the orange plastic cups, the crooked shelves of medications, the two benches, and the empty biscuit tin that served as a waste can.

"You need to get settled first?" asked Reece. "We've got it under control here. Missed you, though." A lump formed in his throat.

"How many are in line?"

"Ration day, so plenty, maybe sixty."

"I figured. I could see from the helicopter."

"You must rest for now," said Afewerki.

"Baloney," said Emma. "I'm rested. Eye infection there?" She nodded at the old man leaning on his doolah.

"Yep, eyelashes turning in. Trachoma," said Reece.

She rolled up the sleeves of her Shocco Springs t-shirt, a Baptist retreat in Alabama. "Our lady with the hips been by today?"

"First thing, as usual," said Reece. He had Afewerki explain the procedure of dosing the tetracycline eye ointment to the man. "Three times a day."

"And tell him to keep the flies away from his eyes, to wash his face as well, keep the junk out of his eyes," said Emma.

"What is junk?" asked Afewerki.

"This yellow mess in his eyes, the discharge," said Emma. "Need to be more technical, I guess."

Reece laughed. Afewerki laughed, and then Emma laughed. The old man looked confused.

"Junk," said Reece. "That's what it is."

"Or maybe gunk," said Emma.

"He is crying yellow tears," said Afewerki.

"Exactly," said Reece.

"How's Fekadu? The little boy with the ghost in his leg?" asked Emma.

"His fever is down, but he wasn't eating. I put a feeding tube down, and I'm pushing a mix of Nido powder and water. He seems less weak, but his leg is still hot and painful."

"I have mail for most everybody, especially you." She handed letters to Reece.

Reece instantly felt guilty. He had missed a couple of nights writing his daily letters to Kristin.

Talk that evening around dinner began with speculation on how God would punish the Hyena and his helpers.

"They have a bushy bushy hair," said Isaac, "to catch the fire." He laughed.

Emma asked Reece if he'd had Bible Study yet. He replied no, but said he was preparing for the first meeting next Tuesday, after dinner, and that he would discuss the Ark of the Covenant as a symbol of hope for God's people.

"This Ark is with Ethiopia," said Barra. "It belongs to the people of our country."

"How did it get here again?" asked Reece.

Barra explained that Menelik, the son of King Solomon and Sheba, an Ethiopian woman of great beauty, had brought the Ark back to Ethiopia, that Menelik was the first of the Ethiopian emperors to be descended from Solomon.

"And Haile Selassie, the last emperor, was also descended from Solomon?" asked Emma.

"Yes," said Isaac, "but he is disappeared. Mengistu has kill-ed him, but no one knows where to find his body."

"Is the Ark safe, where it is? Seems like the military government would try and take it or perhaps destroy it," said Reece. "There is fighting in that area, right?"

Mariam, usually quiet, spoke up in Amharic. Axum was in Tigray, and there was fighting there between the Ethiopian government and the Tigrayan People's Liberation Front.

"The Ark is to become mov-ed," said Afewerki. "When there is danger, the priests hide it."

Barra broke in and explained that, many centuries ago, the Ark had been taken from Axum during an invasion by Muslim armies.

"Where was it taken?" Emma sensed Reece's interest in the mysterious Ark and found herself becoming more intrigued as well.

"Gragn, a terrible man, he destroys Axum. The Ark is tak-ed away to Lake Tana, to the sacred island there, Daga Stephanos," said Barra. His white teeth glistened in the fading light. If the conversation continued much longer, they would need to light the lantern.

"But the Ark has returned to the church in Axum?" asked Reece.

"Yes, the Ark has return-ed," said Barra. "But it may be mov-ed from place to place. There is fighting. No one knows these things but the Church."

"It has many powers," said Mariam. Afewerki translated for him.

Reece recalled the story of Joshua and the siege of

Jericho, how Joshua had marched the Ark around the city walls and, at the blast of a trumpet, caused the walls to come tumbling down.

"Yes, this story is true," said Barra. "This Ark has many powers from God. It is made from woods with many golds. Inside is the tabot, written by God."

"And the new tabot for the church here is coming soon? It was stolen and is being replaced?"

"Yes, maybe by one month," said Barra. "There is feast day."

"To remember Santos Gabriel," said Afewerki. "It is a holy day. The tabot will come on that day, it is said."

"I'd like to see that," said Reece. "But there is no Ark coming, right? Just the tabot?"

"Ow, yes, only one Ark, but many tabot." Afewerki inspired deep. "But you must not ask many questions. The people will murmur against you."

Reece grinned. "Because of the Icelanders?" He wanted to speak with them very badly about their interest in the Ark.

"Yes, many are suspicious." Barra put a sour look on his face.

"Maybe the Hyena stole it," said Emma. "If he thought he could sell it for a few bucks..."

Her remark elicited chuckles, especially from Barra. "Ah, why you say these things? God will punish the thief. He will not to live." His eyes narrowed just a bit.

"So, do you think the Icelanders stole the tabot from the church?" asked Reece.

Barra looked from face to face. "Yes. The people believe this thing."

"Did they take it with them?" asked Emma.

Mariam spoke, and Afewerki translated. "He says that the tabot is hidden by the Icelanders in a cave."

Isaac moved to the lantern, pressurizing the kerosene with the plunger.

"I'd like to find it," said Reece. He had come to Ethiopia for many reasons, one being adventure, and thus far, he had not been disappointed.

Afewerki shook his head. "No, no. You cannot say this. The people will become angry."

Emma rolled her eyes, used to hearing what she could and couldn't do. The Icelanders, though, had been run out of town because of the stolen tabot, so she should be careful.

They parted ways, and Reece asked Emma if he could warm a pot of water to bathe with, and she asked him to have a cup of tea with her. She did not invite Afewerki. He walked with them to the door of her tiny house, stood there, dawdled, and then departed, saying good night.

Emma left the door open, shadows from the lantern dancing on the walls. She respected Reece's commitment to Kristin, but his engagement somehow seemed irrelevant under the circumstances. From what Reece had said, the engagement sounded forced, as if he had felt badly about leaving Kristin behind, and that he had proposed out of guilt, and that such a bond was not legitimate.

Reece busied himself, pouring water from a jerry can into a small pot. "Want me to heat this for tea first?" He felt clumsy and awkward, like being the first customer in a store just as it opened.

"Sure. I'm not tired. Got some rest in AK. It was good

to get away and talk to Lisa. She's so cool. Terry's lucky to have her around."

"Do you think anything will happen? You know, with those guys, the Hyena?"

"I don't know and don't care at this point. I've got more important fish to fry. Do you want to know his real name? I found out in AK."

"What? His real name isn't the Hyena?"

"I wish it were. His name is Emanuel Wundafresh." She smiled.

Reece laughed. "That's a mouthful. Sounds like a German loaf bread."

"Something like it." She dropped two tea bags in the pot and four heaping teaspoons of sugar. "You like cloves in your tea? It's nice."

Reece thought about clove-flavored chewing gum. He didn't like cloves or licorice. "No, maybe just the sugar. I love sweet tea."

"You ever eat at Milo's back in Birmingham?"

"Oh yeah, they had the best sweet tea."

"Too sweet, but good with those salty French fries," said Emma.

"Stop it. I'll start drooling in a second." He watched tiny bubbles form at the bottom of the pot.

"How's Kristin? I know you got a bundle of letters from her."

Reece winced. "She's fine. She bought a puppy." He cleared his throat, trying to bring an image of her into his mind.

"So now you're a daddy, huh?" She stirred the pot with a spoon, helping the sugar to dissolve.

Reece blushed. "I wouldn't say that."

"You want to have kids?"

"Well, if the time is right. Eventually. We never really discussed kids."

"I'd like to have two, I think."

"Two is good. Two would be good, I think."

Emma thought about how she had always been drawn to guys who were the oldest or the only child. She supposed it had something to do with her being the youngest child in her family.

"It's not boiling yet, but it's steaming," said Reece.

"Ready enough." She retrieved two orange famine mugs from the rickety shelf and carefully poured the hot tea. "Here." She handed the dripping tea bags to Reece on a spoon.

He looked around for a garbage can, but there wasn't one, and he just held the spoon as if it were a thermometer.

"You're gonna lead a Bible Study on Tuesdays? Talking about this Ark of the Covenant?" She sipped her tea, blowing to cool it. "They already seem to know a lot about it."

"Maybe I'll learn something," said Reece. "I know it sounds crazy to think this three-thousand-year-old relic with supernatural powers still exists, but if it does, it has to be in Ethiopia from what I've gathered. The Old Testament gives its exact dimensions, that it was made from acacia wood layered in gold, that it had two golden cherubim on top, that it was carried with poles."

"How big is it supposed to be?"

"Not as big as you might think. Something like four feet by three feet and two feet high. The measurements are given in cubits, the length from your elbow to the tips of your fingers."

"And it can strike people dead?"

"Apparently. Only those chosen by God can see it or touch it. There is one priest in Axum who has access to it. And only when he dies is the next caretaker appointed."

"Well, it doesn't stop the famine or the locusts or cholera." Emma crossed her legs. She had kicked off her shoes and socks. She looked at her toes and then noticed that Reece was looking as well. "Those are my toes."

"Nice toes." Reece looked out the open door. He could see winks of light from the team's rooms. He assumed that Afewerki had left for his family's compound, that Irigit was in his place near the gate. He had to pee, but didn't want to go.

"I've got a little crick in my neck," said Emma. She pulled her head to one side, stretching.

Reece froze. He searched for words. He wanted to ease up to her and nonchalantly begin to rub her neck and say, "Here?" A great battle in his mind ensued. He was paralyzed and realized the moment was passing, slipping from his reach. "Do you have anything here, like paracetamol or aspirin?"

"Yeah." Emma relaxed. She had thrown Reece, and he was struggling. She did not pursue the matter, even though she did have tension in her neck. Having someone rub her neck would feel absolutely like heaven at the moment. "So, you can take your tea with you if you want."

Reece shifted his feet, scratched his neck, stretched to yawn, but didn't. Suddenly, the room seemed foreign, out of bounds, a distant place he would never see again.

It was Saturday, market day, and only half a day in the clinic. Clouds that dipped to the ground cloaked Godo, a hot sun fighting its way through from above. All seemed still, calm. Opening the door, the clinic echoed scuffing sounds beneath the ring of their voices. Within the patches of silence, Reece could hear his heart beating. He chased a fly from his eyes. He still had bed hair, flattened on one side. Emma's hair was pulled back tight in a neat ponytail. Afewerki read the small print on a shiny tin of antacid tablets, waiting to call in the first patients of the day. He wore his baggy jeans with a brown, collared pullover that was a bit tight in the shoulders. Of the group, his dress looked the most American, the most casual.

The guard came to the door with a serious face and spoke to Afewerki. Something was wrong. He looked back toward the gate with an alarmed look. Afewerki swung down to the ground, followed by Reece. Emma leaned out to look, fearing it was the Hyena and his men.

A man on hands and knees begged for mercy. He crawled past the short line of patients inside the gate, who pulled themselves tighter as he passed. A thin layer of graying hair covered his scalp. He wore tattered shorts and an old military shirt of army green. Dirt clung to his bleeding knees.

"What in tarnation?" asked Emma.

Reece went to the man's side with Afewerki. The man smelled rancid, of smoke and sweat. A host of flies buzzed his body.

"He is in great pain," said Afewerki.

"Where?" asked Reece. He looked to see if the man's legs were broken or wounded. Why was he crawling?

"What's wrong?" asked Emma.

Afewerki spoke to the man, who lay his head on the rocky ground and moaned. "He cannot to urinate," said Afewerki. "It has been three days."

"Ouch." Reece felt the man's pain in his own bladder. The man was truly suffering, in agony.

Afewerki asked the man if he could stand and then motioned for Reece to help him. They each took an arm, and the man yelled as he stood, gripping his knees. The man's arms felt hard, strong. Reece paused, wincing. The man's grip on his arm was intense, long, dirty nails digging into his flesh. The man stood, bending at the waist, and moved forward with Reece and Afewerki. "Amenseganolo," he said, sweating, his skin pale. He grabbed the door frame and stepped into the clinic, doubled over, moaning with the exertion.

"Let's drop his pants and see what we can do," said Emma.

His pants fell to the floor. The man's testicles were grotesquely swollen, filling and stretching his scrotum to that of two angry, brown grapefruit. The skin looked hot and ready to tear. He could not stand straight. But even bent over, the bulge of a bursting bladder showed just below his waistline.

"Sit him down," said Reece. "Needs a catheter asap."

The man kept his legs spread, unashamed, seeking the best posture to relieve the incredible pressure. Emma moved to the small box of catheters on the shelf and chose an adult red-rubber catheter. Reece prepped the man's penis, sterilizing it with an iodine solution. He changed into a pair of sterile gloves and took the catheter from Emma.

"Afewerki, turn his head so he's not breathing on this thing while I put it in."

Reece inserted the tube, and the man cried out but did not move. Reece slid in the catheter until he met the resistance of the prostate. He pushed, and the man howled. "We need to lay him back to make the path in straighter." Emma directed Afewerki to scoot out the bench and sit behind the man, holding him as he leaned back. Reece kept his grip on the catheter. His lower back complained, trying to maintain an awkward position. He kneeled and pushed again. He put a hand beneath the man's testicles and lifted. The man screamed. The catheter would not go in.

"Need a bigger, stiffer catheter," said Emma. "I wish we had a Coudé."

"Or a Foley," said Reece. "One that can stay in without sliding out." Sweat dripped from his eyebrows. "One more time." He pushed again, and the man moaned. No luck. He pulled out the catheter and let it drop to the floor. "Damn."

Afewerki shifted his hips. He looked clumsy holding the man. Doves lit on the roof, scratching their nails, gouging the tin.

Emma peeled back a 16-French red-rubber catheter, larger in diameter and stiffer than the last. Reece cleaned the tip of the man's penis, which seemed to get smaller and smaller, and changed gloves. "Here we go."

"Hold up," said Emma. "Where's the urine going once you get it in?"

"Oh yeah, forgot about that."

Emma scooted the biscuit tin over to the bench. "This'll

have to do."

"Here goes." He pushed the tube in slow and steady until meeting resistance. The man started to sit up, gargled a moan, and arched back. Reece pushed with one hand and squeezed the man's penis with the other. He pushed harder, sweating. The catheter pushed back. He held his ground and kept the pressure steady. The catheter slid in with a pop, and a gush of dark yellow urine leapt from the tube.

"Jesus!" said Emma.

A steady stream poured into the biscuit tin. The man groaned. For a full two minutes, the urine gushed. The flow went to a dribble. Emma palpated the man's bladder. It was still tight. She pressed on it, and he sat up. "Sorry."

"Chicorilla," said the man, his face beginning to register relief.

"Could be a clot in the tube," said Reece. "Need a syringe." He kept his grip on the catheter.

Emma opened a sterile 60-cc catheter-tip syringe. "Might need to flush it."

"Hope not." Reece inserted the catheter and drew back the plunger. A knotty clot of blood sucked into the syringe. "Okay." The flow of urine resumed, still trickling after three full minutes.

"Maybe two thousand ccs of pee," said Emma.

Afewerki helped the man to a sitting position. He looked slightly disgusted at the whole affair, and Reece laughed at his facial expression, one of stepping into a pile of dog feces. The man breathed heavily, as if having run a long race.

"Clamp it and keep it in?" asked Reece.

"I'd say antibiotics. Take it out and recath if needed," said Emma. She had Afewerki count out a ten-day supply of trimethoprim and sulfamethoxazole, large white pills, horse pills, she called them. "Let's get him a loading dose now. He should stay in the shelter unless he lives close by."

Reece withdrew the catheter and patted the man on the shoulder.

"Xavier meskin," the man said with tears in his eyes.

Reece and Emma spent the afternoon at the market together, shopping for spices and fruit. Reece wanted a pair of tire sandals. After measuring his foot, a young skinny man wearing a large wrap around his head went to work, trimming with a curved knife and tacking on straps with tiny nails. Reece felt silly wearing the sandals and holding his pricey hiking boots, which were too small. The sandals felt good, a little rough over his toes. Afewerki was off with his father, facilitating the purchase of two donkeys.

"She's selling packs of famine biscuits." Reece nodded toward a young woman with a dozen packets spread on a cloth in front of her.

"You'll see a lot of that. Nothing we can do."

"Good for the economy, I guess."

"Maybe," said Emma.

They stepped between rows of women squatting, walking with care. An old woman with deeply wrinkled skin held a panting hen's legs between her toes while counting a handful of change on a dirty handkerchief.

"Check that out." Reece pointed to a man at the edge of the great shade of the fig tree. A half dozen tattered books lay in a crude wooden box. "Let's look."

Emma led the way and smiled at the used-book salesman. He looked very professional, wearing nappy knit pants with a dingy, white long-sleeve shirt. Only his floppy, patched hat gave him away as a country dweller. He spoke rapidly to them in a low, confident voice, as if he were behind a counter of precious valuables. He motioned for them to take a look.

"Look. *War of the Worlds,* there," said Reece. The paperback was missing its front cover. The pages were fragile and golden yellow.

"Those two are in Arabic," said Emma. "What about this one? German?" She picked up a thick hardback still with its torn jacket. "*Íslending...asögur,*" she read.

"You like?" asked the man. He spoke some English. "Ice-land, book."

"Huh?" asked Reece. He opened it to the end pages. There was an engraved frontispiece of a Nordic warrior in full regalia. On the inside front cover was a bookplate that read, "Gudmunder Thorsson."

"Hmm," said Emma. "This belonged to that Icelandic doctor."

"Sentino?" asked Reece.

"Amist birr, five birr," he replied.

"Sost birr?" asked Reece, bargaining.

"Ishi, sost birr." He handed the book to Reece, who counted out three bills.

"There's a letter or something here." Reece unfolded a piece of graph paper with handwriting on it. "It's in Icelandic, I suppose."

"What are you going to do with the book?" They stood very close together, letting others pass behind. Reece could smell her breath, something like cool water.

"I don't know. It just makes this place more real. Others have gone before us, that sort of thing."

"Afewerki told me that Dr. Thorsson was worshiping demons," said Emma.

"Do what?" asked Reece. They walked past piles of lentils and peas spread on old tarps. The market bustled around them. "Some kind of Viking cult?" He palmed the hefty book, fanned the pages, and smelled them.

"Beats me," said Emma. "Smell like a book?"

"No. Smells like incense, sweet. Sweet paper." Reece spotted a woman selling okra. "Oh my God, look. I love fried okra."

"Yep, okra," said Emma. "Didn't expect to see that?"

"No, not really."

"Bamia," said the woman. She held up a pod of okra and shaded her eyes. "*And* kilo, *and* birr."

"That's cheap," said Reece, but he waved his hands no.

They wandered through the market, shoulder to shoulder, looking but not buying. Calls of "Ferenj!" followed them.

Reece pointed out a man begging, displaying a large sore over his shin. The wound looked grisly.

"I've seen him before," said Emma. "He makes his money begging and isn't interested in a cure." She dropped a ten-cent piece onto a ragged piece of plastic. The man nodded and spoke in a whisper, thanking her.

That night, after a fiery dinner of spicy dorowot, Emma retired to her room, determined to write home about being attacked on her way to the church carved into stone.

She lingered with her pen and paper, unable to get started, then resorted to her daily devotional instead. The text rang hollow. *We must get to the point of being sick to death of ourselves, until there is no longer any surprise at anything God might tell us about ourselves. We cannot reach and understand the depths of our own meagerness.* She didn't want to feel sick of herself, but wanted to feel better. She had brought the attack on herself by making herself vulnerable. Whether the Hyena had followed her or their meeting had been chance, she didn't know. Regardless, why would God allow such a thing to happen when she was there doing His will?

Instead of writing about the attack, she told her mother more about Reece. He had nice legs, she said, and was shy. She recounted their afternoon at the market and long stroll through the village, winding up at the shelter where the sun had been quite beautiful as it rounded down from the sky, close enough to touch.

In his room, Reece went through his prayer list of forty-seven names. The list grew and shrank as prayers were answered, as new challenges descended upon friends and family. He prayed, especially for Kristin, that God would give her the patience she needed to await his return. He even prayed for the Hyena that either he would see the light and come to know Jesus Christ as his Savior, or that God would punish him mightily in the tradition of the psalmist David's enemies. After his prayers, he picked up his Bible and continued his survey of verses related to the Ark of the Covenant. He reread the twenty-fifth chapter of Exodus, the detail of the Ark's dimensions, and a description of the throne of mercy built on top of pure gold.

God had directed Moses to place two cherubim on top, each with wings raised and facing one another. God communed with Moses and his successors there, between the cherubim.

Observing the tradition of the Ark and keeping replicas of the tablets in their churches, the Coptic Christians of Ethiopia still held much in common with their Hebrew ancestors from whom they had been converted by the Syrian missionary Frumentius in the fourth century AD. One of the key thrusts of the Baptists in Ethiopia was to bring more bearing onto the traditions of the New Testament, which introduced Jesus Christ and his teachings. Coptics accepted the New Testament but were still firmly rooted in the Old Testament, much more so than their Western Christian brothers and sisters.

In the Old Testament, God spoke directly to the people through his appointed mediums such as Moses. The Ark was the ultimate symbol of this direct communication. Centuries later, the coming of Christ had made God accessible to all who believed, bypassing the earthly connections through prophets and the instrument of the Ark, giving one and all free discourse with the Maker through His Son. Reece pondered the cultural implications, let his mind wander, and became confused. He supposed what the Baptists had to offer was a more egalitarian form of salvation, one that came with twenty-four/seven customer service through direct prayer. Moses had given the Ark's blueprint to a craftsman named Bezalel, who built the Ark according to instruction. Reece supposed that the team would know all of this, but he was curious to hear their thoughts and to learn more.

Even though they were eight thousand miles from home, Sunday morning felt like Sunday morning, vaguely stiff and formal, an air of suspended guilt. Today, Barra would look over the weight percentile data of children in the feeding program and prepare his monthly report. The trend had been steadily upward as the famine and drought gave way to the unprecedented influx of international aid and the returning rains. There would come a time when the distribution of wheat, sorghum, soybean oil, milk powder, and other foodstuffs would end. Emma suspected that within a year, feeding operations would cease and that most of the nurses at the feeding stations would either return home or take on new assignments. The Southern Baptists had been active in Ethiopia since the 1960s, expanding from evangelism and rug making into other mission areas. The famine had been a prime opportunity for them to firm up their presence in Shewa Province.

Emma awoke with a headache and pain in her lower back. She had run out of tampons from home and relied on whatever was available in Addis, usually thick pads that she hated. She had lucked onto a stash of Italian Teeve tampons, though the boxes looked to be a decade old. At least she didn't have to resort to strips of absorbent, pounded tree bark as did women in the village. The Sunday malaise, combined with her period, made her wince and think of her bed back home, how her mother would bring a heating pad and take care of her. She took a double dose of paracetamol and warmed a dark, chewy roll in a pot. She opened the door to her tiny house and looked out over the dewy grass. Even the air seemed like Sunday air, as if it were pouring from the basement of an empty, concrete-block Sunday School room.

Reece turned to his open Bible, the book of Exodus, and continued reading the detailed plans of the Ark, of its acacia-wood poles plated with gold, and of a table with golden utensils. "And you shall overlay it with pure gold, and make a molding of gold all around." Then there was a lamp stand of pure gold with golden bowls and ornamental knobs and flowers. Verse 40 of chapter 25 read, "And see to it that you make them according to the pattern which was shown you on the mountain," referring to Moses' forty days and nights on Mt. Sinai during which he received detailed instructions to build the Ark and its accoutrements.

With doves scuffling on the roof, Reece continued through chapter 26, reading of the portable tabernacle made of ten curtains of woven linen. In the center of the tent, behind a veil, was the Holy of Holies where the Ark was to be kept when the tent was erected. "You shall set the table outside the veil, and the lamp stand across from the table on the side of the tabernacle toward the south; and you shall put the table on the north side." Everything in its place. He glanced ahead to chapter 27, where God gave Moses the dimensions for an altar to accompany the Ark, exacting in its detail. There was a knock at the door.

"Hello, brother." Barra pronounced brother as *brazzer*. His flashy, white smile seemed too bright for the Sunday morning gloom.

"Good morning." Reece stepped outside in his bare feet. Barra's black shoes looked freshly polished.

"Yes, we have another thief in the nighttime, stealing

some grains and oil."

"Really?" asked Reece.

Isaac and Mariam came from their rooms to join the conversation.

"Very bad," said Barra.

"We can't just stop the thieves when they come?" asked Reece. "And why don't they steal the medications?"

"You cannot eat the medicines," said Barra.

"We arrest one thief, one time, and tie him," said Isaac. "Dr. Guthrie tells us no, we cannot do that. The Hyena is laughing us, but we can do nothing. And he tells the people that our medicines have poison."

"But the people still come."

"Yes, they know he is liar," said Isaac. Mariam nodded his agreement.

Emma waved as she made her way to the shintabet at the far end of the yard. A thin trickle of smoke emerged from the dimness of the cooking hut.

The short silence was interrupted by Barra. "Ato Wundafresh is not to like you. He makes threat to you." Barra was the only member of the team who referred to the Hyena using the respectful address of Ato or his real name.

Reece fidgeted. "I figured that. I think maybe I need to talk with him." He watched Emma retracing her steps back to her tiny house and waved again.

"It is no problem to talk wiz him," said Isaac. "But he will not listen."

"He kill-ed many men," said Mariam. He looked frightened as he said it.

Suddenly, the sky looked foreign to Reece, the haze in the distance like fog. Why such animosity toward them when they were doing such good things for the people? He was happy to see Emma walking toward them now. She had brushed her hair back into a loose ponytail. She looked soft and vulnerable.

"Hey, guys."

Reece caught her up with the conversation, becoming angry as he spoke, remembering the attack. Something had to be done. Right?

"I guess we have to stay focused," said Emma, "on working the clinic and getting as much of the food out as possible."

"God will punish him," said Isaac.

"Yes," said Mariam.

There was a banging at the gate. Ketow had not arrived, and Irigit had left earlier. Isaac went to check. Reece could see that it was the man with swollen testicles. He was sweating and had a pained look on his face.

"Let's get him to the clinic and cath him again," said Emma. "Dang, I almost forgot about him."

"Let me put my shoes on." Reece could feel the man's bursting bladder.

Following the catheterization and the draining of 700 ccs of blood-tinged urine and the patient's return to the shelter where he was staying until he could urinate on his own, everyone ate a late breakfast of inkolal, scrambled eggs with peppers, accompanied by flat dabo bread and hot, strong coffee. His readings from Exodus fresh on his mind, Reece asked if Coptic Christians still practiced the sacrifice of animals as prescribed in the Old Testament.

"No, no," said Barra. "It is forbidden. Only the Falasha

do such things." He explained to Reece that the Falasha were Ethiopian Jews who lived near Lake Tana. Reece knew that Jewish people no longer sacrificed animals and wondered why the Falasha still did so.

"It is a mystery," said Barra. "They come to Ethiopia long ago. Also, the Habasha Christians still follow the old ways. They do not boil the meat into the milk, like the Falasha."

"What is Habasha?" asked Reece.

Afewerki, who had joined them, laughed. "Habasha means the way of Ethiopia, like the Habasha food is enjera."

"Ah," said Reece.

"Habasha shoes." Emma pointed at Reece's tire sandals, which he had taken to wearing in the compound.

"Yes," said Isaac. He laughed. "But Falasha is Ethiopian Jew."

While Barra worked on weight percentiles of children in the feeding program, a long and lively game of Uno ensued inside the dining hut. The cards were worn, warped, and tattered. A red four was missing, as well as a green seven. Reece made two liters of purple, sugar-free Kool-Aid, which created a festive atmosphere.

After a dinner of leftover dabo and fried goat meat, Reece retreated to his room. He picked up his reading in Exodus at chapter 28. There, Moses was told by God to appoint his brother Aaron and his sons as the chief priests who would intercede with God through the Ark. Beginning with verse 3, the voice of God instructed how to make special garments that the priests must wear. This included a "breastplate, an ephod, a robe, a skillfully woven tunic, a turban, trousers, and a sash." The ephod was made of linen using gold, blue, purple, and scarlet thread. On the ephod, precious stones of onyx engraved with the names of the sons of Israel were to be mounted in gold. Chains of pure gold were to accompany the breastplate, which was to be studded with sardius, topaz, emerald, turquoise, sapphire, diamond, jacinth, agate, amethyst, beryl, onyx, and jasper. The robe was to be entirely blue.

Reece imagined the priestly clothing as bulky and dazzling. Verse 43 indicated that Aaron and his sons had to wear the special Ark costume "when they minister in the holy *place,* that they do not incur iniquity and die." It sounded like the garb was protective in some manner or that the clothes merely set apart its caretakers as special. Perhaps the vestments were a tool that the powers of the Ark used to distinguish its keepers from others. He had never paid much attention to these words before and now found them to be very strange, especially since he was in the country rumored to harbor the original Ark. He estimated the distance between Godo and Axum, where the Ark was kept, at roughly four hundred miles. And a new replica of the Ark's tabot would be in the church below the shelter in less than a month. He wanted to attend the ceremony.

While in college, Reece had taken an undergraduate class in the Old Testament as an elective. Surprisingly, it was there he learned to question the true meaning of the Bible. The professor had been thorough and reasonable, explaining the stories of the Old Testament, such as Noah and the Ark or the parting of the Red Sea by Moses, as tools of understanding versus literal truth. The distancing of the scripture from hard fact had unnerved Reece at first and made him uncomfortable. Two students had even dropped the class, feeling that the professor was profaning the Word of God. One had to learn to read between the lines, said the professor, in order to fathom the Hebrew mind of the period.

He plowed through the next chapter with interest, reading of the daily sacrificial rituals performed on the altar of the tabernacle. The details were so concrete, even specifying that the fat covering the kidneys was to be burnt on the altar. Bulls and rams slaughtered. Verse 20: "Then you shall kill the ram, and take some of its blood and put *it* on the tip of the right ear of Aaron and on the tip of the right ear of his sons, on the thumb of their right hand and on the big toe of their right foot, and sprinkle the blood all around on the altar." What a bloody mess there must have been each day. There were to be offerings of bread as well, and oil and wine of which Aaron and his sons were commanded to eat. Amid the bloodletting, the protectors of the Ark would be well fed.

Both Reece and Emma awoke early, opening their doors at the same time and waving like neighbors. One of the water bearers was emptying her clay pot into the cookhouse barrel. The Mission paid her three birr for each pot that she brought.

"Hey," said Emma.

"Hey, yourself," said Reece. "Up early?'

"I couldn't stop thinking about that little boy Fekadu. Can you still hear him moaning at night?"

"Not as loud as he was, though."

"I just wanted to get by there before clinic started, see if he's eating on his own. Should probably leave the feeding tube in for now." She smoothed wrinkles in her scrub pants.

"We should take the IV out, since he's getting fluids through the tube."

"I'll do it. Want to go with me?" She mused, thinking their little conversation was kind of like a shift change at the hospital, when the outgoing nurses filled in the oncoming shift about each patient's status.

"Sure. I'd like to see the new roof, too. I was thinking about the man at the shelter, the guy with swollen testicles." He winced. "I've got to pee now, and that's what made me think of him first thing. He must be miserable."

"Yeah. Well, you go ahead. We'll make an early round together. Sounds like fun."

Barra poked his head out of his door. "Good morning! How is it?" His hair looked a bit nappy, normally impeccable. He wore a long-sleeve sweater somewhere between pink and red. It made him look a bit wild.

"Good morning," said Reece. "We're just shooting the bull."

Emma laughed, anticipating Barra's reaction.

Reece caught on. "I mean, we're just talking about the patients."

"Yes. You are not to shoot the bull?" Barra laughed and broke into a bit of song, and then laughed again.

Reece laughed, realizing his newness to Ethiopia. A brief flash of a grocery store, aisles filled with boxes of 'Nilla Wafers and fresh apples, frozen lasagna.

"We're going to see a couple of people before clinic," said Emma.

"You are hard workers." Barra took Reece's hand in his own and let it fall.

Reece wanted to say "hardly working" but caught himself. Mariam's door opened. He looked out, waved, and then disappeared.

After five minutes to freshen up, Reece and Emma departed for Fekadu's humble hut. Villagers passed them, whispering their greetings. Fekadu's mother was outside sweeping the patch of dirt in front of the entrance with a handful of stiff straw left over from the roof. The new section stood out dull yellow from the dark gray of the old roof.

"The only thing now is that he's inside that dark hut all day," said Reece. "At least he had sunshine when it wasn't raining."

"Dehna," said Emma to the mother.

"Dehna," the mother whispered. She bowed her head and covered her smile with her hand. Inside, her son Fekadu lay on his back, whimpering, his mouth open, dried saliva webbing his lips.

Emma felt the boy's leg. It was still swollen and hot

and felt chalky and dry. She motioned to the mother. The mother understood and helped her bring Fekadu to a sitting position. He groaned and winced, bobbing his head as if in the grips of vertigo. Afewerki appeared, having learned of their plans from Barra. He stood back, surveying the scene.

"Hey," said Reece.

Afewerki spoke to the mother. "The ghost is still in his leg, she is saying."

"I guess we need to fight the ghost harder," said Emma.

"I guess we need to feed the ghost," said Reece. "Let's mix some more Nido powder with water and push it down the tube."

"Maybe do another liter of fluid before we take out the IV?"

Fekadu reached up and pulled the tube from his nose.

"Damn," said Reece.

"He wants to ride the horse," said Afewerki.

"What?"

"He says this."

"Let's check his fever. I hope it's not a white horse," said Emma.

"Tsk, tsk, tsk," said Afewerki.

Reece pinched the skin on the boy's dry hand. There was minor tenting. He pressed his fingertips over the boy's shin on the swollen leg and left small indentions. "He's dry, but this leg is pretty edematous. Is he still urinating?"

Afewerki inquired, and the mother said, Yes, a little, "Tenish, tenish."

"He needs another clean cloth or sheet to cover himself with," said Emma. "Afewerki, can you go to my room and bring back the sheet on my bed, the one that's on top of the mattress?"

"I will," he said and left, ducking out of the hut.

The mother stood by, helping her son to sit up. He was going limp and trying to lie back down, a delirious look on his face.

"Temp is still 102," said Emma. "Let's put the feeding tube back in and push his meds with the Nido. I want to listen to his lungs before we give him more IV fluid." She helped the mother lay Fekadu back on the rough bed. He coughed, a slight rattle in his chest, and moaned.

They finished with Fekadu and moved on to the shelter, having to go quickly to make breakfast and open the clinic.

The man's disfigured scrotum looked better, the swelling of his testicles down, but he still could not pee. He welcomed them with open arms, pulling his pants down as they approached, much to the chagrin of the young mothers milling about, who turned their heads and groaned.

"Terry has to bring us more catheters," said Emma. "We only have two more that'll work on this guy."

Afewerki asked the man if he had taken the antibiotic yet, and the reply was No, that he had lost the pills. Afewerki shook his head, suspecting that he had sold them. "He must come with us to the clinic." He yawned.

"Yep," said Emma.

"Who would buy a sulfa drug from this guy?" asked Reece.

"Who knows?" Emma helped the man pull his pants up. "Anyway..."

That evening, Reece retired to his room and wrote a quick letter to Kristin, telling her of Fekadu, the man with the swollen testicles, and a little boy with polydactyly who had ripped off his extra toe playing soccer. It had been hanging by a thread of flesh, and he had sliced it free with a scalpel. The mother had taken the toe to bury it. He did his best not to mention Emma, but found it hard not to. He worked so closely with her and found her increasingly attractive. Trying to rid himself of images of Emma's breasts, he shook his head. She had what he would call a very healthy chest, not too big, but present. He fought an urge to knock on Emma's door to see about heating a pan of water for bathing.

Instead, he plunged back into Exodus, amid the minutiae of instruction passing from God to Moses atop Mount Sinai. God commanded Moses to build an altar to burn incense, once again covered in gold, including rings with which to carry the altar, much as the Ark. Reece knew that gold was an excellent conductor of electricity, and where did the Israelites get so much gold? Considering the costs, God was wise in making sure that each person traveling with Moses through the wilderness would contribute a monetary offering of half a shekel toward the upkeep of the tabernacle, the Ark, the altars, and all the sundry accessories such as lamps and lavers. There was to be a census to make sure that all were numbered. Those not contributing the half-shekel "ransom" would be visited by plague, God said.

There was a departure from the use of gold in the construction of a bath made from bronze, in which Aaron and his sons were to bathe before entering the tabernacle. Reece knew a little about bronze, that it did not generate sparks when struck by another metal or other hard surfaces. Much emphasis was placed on cleanliness, as if there ran some risk of contamination within the portable tabernacle. Also, expensive oil was to be used daily to anoint the altar, the Ark, and all the utensils. The oil was holy and not to be reproduced for use by any but the appointed priests. The washing, the sweet-smelling incense, the holy oil—Reece fathomed a portrait of extreme ritual, one that would be difficult to maintain daily unless there was good reason. He remembered the sweet smell of the incense sizzling on the coal in Fekadu's house. He gazed around his rectangular room, candle shadows bobbing, feeling the ancientness of the place he was in, the closeness to the soil of the Old Testament, to words that he had glossed over so many times before. What did it all mean?

Tuesday flew by in a whirl of clinic and shelter duty. The little boy who had fallen into the fire returned to have his dressings changed after missing a day. The gauze was filthy and stuck to his arm, requiring much soaking to release. The old man with swollen testicles was doing better. They had shrunk to nearly half their grotesque size, and he was beginning to dribble urine on his own. Young Fekadu was stable, but not much better in terms of fever. He still had a wild look in his eyes, which is what frightened Emma and Reece the most.

At dinner, Reece hesitated to eat for the first time when presented with dulet, a mixture of chopped tripe, liver, and tibs mixed with shredded enjera. Emma shared his dislike of organ meats but did not balk, eating as much as Barra, who especially loved dulet. Following dinner, they had their first Bible study together.

Reece opened by introducing the topic of the Ark of the Covenant and asked Isaac if he would lead them in prayer, which Isaac did, using his slow, intoxicated English voice. Reece asked them again if they believed that the original Ark was kept in Ethiopia.

"Yes," said Barra. "Eh-ti-o-pia is special to God. We are only country of Africa to remain free. No?" He was referring to the colonial domination of Africa, the carving of Africa by European powers such as France, Germany, and Belgium. The Italians had occupied parts of Ethiopia but had never been able to formalize their rule, a source of pride among Ethiopians.

The others agreed as well. The Ark was real and was located in Axum, unless it was being hidden due to the fighting there. Only the priest of the Church of St. Mary of

Zion and his helpers knew its location at all times.

Reece skimmed through the blueprints of the Ark and its accoutrements, bringing the talk around to Moses, a very mystical figure, someone imbued with extraordinary powers who spoke directly with God on top of Mt. Sinai.

"He has learn-ed from the Egyptians. No?" asked Isaac. "They teach-ed him many things. You know this story of the snake?"

Reece knew the story, how God told Moses to instruct his brother Aaron to throw down his rod in front of Pharaoh, the Egyptian leader, whom they were petitioning for the release of the enslaved Israelites. Aaron did so, and the rod became a snake. But Pharaoh's magicians reproduced the act. It was then that the snake of Moses consumed the snakes produced by Pharaoh's conjurers.

"Was it a miracle or magic?" asked Reece.

"It was a miracle, of course," said Emma.

"Moses was always in these mysterious situations." Reece recalled the burning bush, using his *Cruden's Concordance* to find the scripture in Exodus chapter three. God spoke to Moses from the burning bush, and Moses was very afraid and doubtful of what he was seeing. God told him to throw down his rod, and it became a snake, just as it would later when he was convincing Pharaoh to free the Israelites.

"So many snakes," said Isaac. Mariam laughed.

Reece knew that Moses had been raised among the Egyptians by Pharaoh's daughter, being schooled in Egyptian science, magic, and rites. When he was forty, Moses witnessed an Egyptian beating one of his fellow Hebrews and killed the Egyptian, hiding his body in the sand. Moses then fled to the land of Midian, where he lived for forty years until God called him to lead the Hebrew exodus from Egypt.

"Moses was a smart man," said Reece. "But when he was trying to free the Hebrew people through the use of plagues such as turning the water into blood, Pharaoh's magicians were able to perform the same miracles, just as they reproduced his feat with the rod and snake." He paused, watching the interior of the dining hut dim a bit. The days were long, the darkness of night cinching down, the light lasting two hours or more after sunset.

"It seems strange," said Emma, "that the Egyptians produced the same results as Moses, although eventually Moses came out on top."

"God is winner," said Isaac.

"Yes," said Reece, "but the Egyptians used magic to perform their miracles, whereas Moses channeled God, although he had probably been taught the secrets of Pharaoh's magicians."

"Moses is Jesus Christ of Old Testament," said Barra. "He is saving the peoples of God. Praise to God."

"Yes, exactly," said Reece. "And after the Hebrew people are freed and following Moses in the wilderness for forty years, God speaks to the people through Moses and the high priest Aaron and Aaron's sons, actually coming to Earth, appearing through the Ark. To worship God, the people had to sacrifice animals, burn incense, and consult with the priests."

"With Jesus," said Emma, "the children of God, we, anyone who believes, can communicate directly with God through prayer. He sacrificed himself so that we would no longer have to sacrifice animals or rely on priests."

"Yes," said Barra. "We pray to God. He answers our prayers. No?"

"That's right," said Reece. "No more need for magic tricks, it would seem."

Emma pulled at the neck of her pullover and reached over and touched Reece's hand. "Magic tricks?"

"Well, you know, turning a rod into a snake is a kind of magic trick."

"What about when God killed all of the firstborn in Egypt, was that magic?" asked Emma.

"Some of the plagues called down by Moses, the Egyptians could not reproduce. You might say their magic was not strong enough."

Mariam spoke. "We praise to God, to Jesus." He then spoke in Amharic.

Isaac interpreted. "God's power is greater than the magicians. Praise to God."

"Not at first, it wasn't," said Reece.

"Okay, we get it," said Emma.

"Moses was a high priest trained under the Egyptians. He knew their tricks. That's all I'm saying. The Egyptians, without God, could do some pretty cool things, like build pyramids and turn rods into snakes. I just think we have to look at that. It's in the Bible."

Isaac, Barra, Mariam, and Isaac looked at one another, then back at Reece, and then at Emma.

"God is good," said Mariam.

"Yes, He is," said Emma.

"Of course, He is," said Reece. "Who would like to end in prayer?" He closed his Bible. He opened and closed his concordance. He felt his heart beating faster than it should. Barra volunteered and launched into a lengthy prayer.

As Emma walked away, Reece called after her. He took long strides to catch up with her. "Cup of tea?" He just wanted to be near her.

"Sure, come on in." She turned and waved goodnight to Afewerki. He hesitated, then turned away. Above, a large gray cloud sat on top of Godo, hanging there within a stone's throw. Crickets chirruped in the tall grasses around the base of the house.

"Want me to light the lantern?" He left the door open behind him.

"Yeah." She pulled on a long-sleeved t-shirt. "Chilly."

"Yep, gets that way after sundown." He sat and leaned the chair back on two legs. He laid his Bible and concordance on the table beside an empty orange cup and a shallow dish holding limes.

"Nice Bible study." She filled a pot with water from the gravity-feed filter and lit the stove.

"Thanks. I get carried away sometimes. I've got some chamomile tea, if you want it, in my room." Reece gripped a lime in his hand and smelled it. He scuffed his boots on the cement floor. "Do you think Moses crossed the Red Sea or the Reed Sea?"

Emma paused by the stove. "What do you mean, Reed Sea?"

"Some scholars believe that Moses and the Israelites crossed through a lake area filled with reeds, that the Egyptian chariots following them sank in the mud, that the story of Moses parting the waters is just an elaboration to demonstrate how God saved them from Pharaoh's army." He held up the lime as if he could see through it.

"You going to light the lantern?" asked Emma.

"Oh, forgot." He pumped the primer on the red lantern and looked around for matches.

"Here." Emma handed him a large box of strike-any-where matches. "I've never heard this Reed Sea story."

The match flamed. The lantern hissed and whooshed. He dialed down the flame, which flooded the room with light.

"It's from a class I had in the Old Testament. The Hebrew people were skilled storytellers, not always interested in relating the facts but rather some larger truth that made for a good story."

Emma opened the fridge and pulled out the sugar, which she kept there because of ants. "The Red Sea is the better story. Any good news from home?"

"About the same. My grandfather's garden is coming in strong, lots of tomatoes."

Emma laughed. "What else?"

"Kristin moved to day shift from night shift, which is good, she says. Night shift always messed with my head." He put the lime back in the bowl.

"I hated night shift."

"Me too."

Outside, Irigit was whistling, tapping a biscuit tin with a stick.

"What about you? Anything new?"

Emma stood to check on the water and find the tea bags. "No, just that note from Dr. Guthrie about filing an official complaint against what's-his-name, the Hyena."

Reece watched her graceful but tired movements from shelf to stove. "Haven't seen him around. I wonder if it's true that he's sick."

"I know he went to the government clinic for some kind of infection." A chill swept her arms, and her nipples hardened. A flash of heat swept down her spine. "I can't stand the sight of him."

Reece wanted to hold her. "He can pretty much do as he pleases, it seems." He looked away from her breasts resting beneath her t-shirt.

"I'm praying that God will take him away," said Emma. She handed Reece a cup of steaming sweet tea.

"Maybe he'll drink himself to death."

"Maybe a bolt of lightning..." Her hand trembled.

The next day, after tending to Fekadu and visiting the shelter where the man who couldn't pee was now peeing like a racehorse, and who seemed not in a hurry to leave, Reece, Emma, and Afewerki opened the clinic, the door swinging out to a crystal clear view south over the hills toward the unseen Wenchit River.

Reece had a dream that the Hyena came to the clinic, and he was more surprised than Emma when the Hyena showed up that morning, his hand pressed to his swollen jaw. Emma stared at him, standing there in the dirt. The Hyena spoke to Afewerki and stepped up into the clinic. He sat beside a woman in her late thirties who had twelve children. He leaned back to rest against the wall. He was dressed not in his military garb, but in shabby knit pants with a dirty white short-sleeve shirt and cheap flip-flops. His big toenails were thick and hard.

"He is suffering from the cuts in his mouth," said Afewerki.

Emma looked at Reece, asking him with her eyes to address the Hyena. She stepped outside to catch her breath.

"Tell me about these cuts." Reece prepared himself to treat the Hyena as he would any other patient. He was hoping that an injection of penicillin would be called for.

Afewerki made a face. "He is chewing much qat, making his gums to bleed. Now there is infection."

"What is qat?" Reece moved in front of the Hyena, who put his hand out for Reece to shake. Reece hesitated.

"You must shake his hand," said Afewerki.

Reece took the moist, bony hand, surprisingly soft, and listened to Afewerki explain that qat was a plant of which the narcotic leaves were chewed. Many people were addicted to qat, he said, especially the taxi drivers in Addis Ababa. Reece opened his mouth and motioned for the Hyena to do the same. He looked at the Hyena's bared, greenish teeth, stained from the qat. The skin beneath his lower front teeth was eroded and bright red, exposing the top portion of the roots. There was a vestige of purple from the gentian violet applied at the Government Clinic. The lymph nodes under his jaw were swollen, giving him a puffy, sad look.

Emma came back in and moved the mother to the other bench. She took long, slow breaths to keep her composure. The woman had missed her period, and what could she do? She did not want another child. She spoke in whispers. Emma had no means to test for pregnancy. She kneeled beside the woman and watched Reece tending to the Hyena. He caught her eye, and she looked away. "Afewerki, tell her there is nothing I can do. Does she have any other complaints? We can give her a thirty-day supply of vitamins, in case she's pregnant. That's about it."

Afewerki raised his hand, waiting for Reece to say something about the Hyena's mouth.

"Go ahead and finish with Emma," said Reece. "We'll have him rinse with peroxide and start him on an antibiotic."

"He wants murphy," said Afewerki, smiling.

"Gladly," said Emma.

"My pleasure," said Reece.

Afewerki explained to the mother that there was nothing to be done. Did she want the vitamins to improve her health in case she was pregnant? The woman said, No, that she did not want to give birth, that perhaps the vitamins were a bad idea.

"Yeqirta," said Emma. She held the woman's hand for a moment.

"Chicorilla," said the woman in resignation, but with a smile. On her way out, she gave the Hyena a cold look.

The Hyena's mouth foamed from the peroxide, and he spat into the biscuit tin, making a foul face. He cursed and stuck out his tongue. He stood and spoke.

"He is thinking you are to trick him," said Afewerki.

"No, I'm trying to help him. He should rinse again."

"He will not," said Afewerki.

"Does he still want the injection? Tell him it will be penicillin in his hip. Is he allergic to penicillin? Ask him."

"He does not know. He wants to see the medicine, to make sure it is not expired."

"Okay."

The Hyena took the vial of penicillin procaine and scrutinized the small print. Afewerki showed him the date of March 1988, translating the date into the Ethiopian calendar.

"He's okay?"

"Yes, but he wants to see the needle first, to see that it is new."

"No problem." Reece fished out a sterile 10-cc syringe and an 18-gauge needle.

Wide grew the Hyena's eyes.

"The needle is like a spear," said Afewerki, translating.

"The penicillin is thick and must go deep into the muscle, tell him."

"How many men has he killed?" asked Emma.

"No, no, no," said Afewerki. He shook his finger at Emma.

"Let's do this or not," said Reece.

The Hyena stood and unbuttoned his pants. He cursed under his breath and put both hands to the wall of metal sheeting. Afewerki exposed the upper portion of the buttocks as Reece mixed the powder with 10 ccs of sterile saline. He expelled air from the syringe. Afewerki cleaned with alcohol swabs the spot Reece pointed to. In went the needle. The Hyena jerked and thrust his hips. Out came the needle.

"Dammit," said Reece.

Afewerki scolded the Hyena, trying to suppress a grin. Emma was on the verge of laughing and excused herself. She walked to the warehouse to kill time, inspecting the twenty-foot-high stacks of grain.

The Hyena moaned, realizing that Reece would have to start over again. He raised his hands in defeat and sat with his pants undone.

"He wants tablet," said Afewerki.

"Really? And waste this penicillin. I can put a new needle on."

"No, no," said Afewerki, translating. "He wants tablet."

Reece obliged and counted out a ten-day supply into a small manila envelope with a button-tie closure. "Three times per day, tell him. If he needs to come back, tell him he should."

Afewerki explained, and the Hyena nodded, fastening his pants. He looked down and left the clinic, mumbling to himself.

After clinic, they decided Fekadu needed to start penicillin injections and discontinue the chloramphenicol. He seemed stable but not improving, plus they were risking aplastic anemia using the chloramphenicol. The paracetamol helped, keeping his fevers within reason. He wore a red-and-blue-striped polo shirt that swallowed his thin body.

"He needs sunlight every day," said Reece. The hut smelled like sour beer and smoke. "Tell his mother to pull his bed outside for an hour in the morning, but not in direct sunlight. We can help if needed."

"Ishi," and Afewerki explained to the mother, who nodded, wringing her hands. She wore the same old brown dress, falling apart at the seams.

Fekadu moaned and smacked his lips as Emma pushed the Nido solution down his feeding tube. "He's much better in terms of hydration, although his lips are still cracked," said Emma. She brushed tenacious black flies from his face. The swollen leg, with pitting edema, had taken on a light, earthy tone.

Afewerki explained the injection and rolled Fekadu toward him, taking care with his leg, positioning it on top of his other leg. Fekadu shouted when Reece began to push the penicillin into his shriveled buttock and tried to sit up. His leg trembled. Emma reached in and helped Afewerki hold him. Following the injection, they stayed for another ten minutes in case of an allergic reaction.

"Onward," said Emma as she led Afewerki and Reece from the hut.

"Ferenj!" came the familiar cries of children ready to hold their hands as they walked down the steep hill to the clinic.

Afewerki bluffed, barking at the kids to go away, but

the kids weren't buying it, taking Reece and Emma by the hand anyway.

Clinic that day was a barn burner, with ninety-five patients. There had been a record number of snotty noses and what appeared to be an outbreak of bronchitis. Reece, Emma, and Afewerki were late to dinner and ate the dorowot cold.

"Dang, that's spicy," said Emma. Both she and Reece broke into sweats from the berbere.

"What about that guy wearing the suit made out of grain bags?" asked Reece.

"He looked cute," said Emma. "Shirt, short pants, jacket."

Afewerki laughed.

"What about that poor woman who fell and bit the end of her tongue off?" asked Emma.

"Ugh, don't mention it," said Reece.

Afewerki shivered, laughing again.

They ate slowly, the food roaring with spice, and Afewerki lit the lantern as the chill and dark of night descended on Godo.

Two weeks passed with many days of heavy rain. A tinge of green was returning to the long-distance views, dominated by the earthy bronzes of the distant ambas. Dr. Guthrie had arrived by helicopter to meet with the Hyena about the attack on Emma. He wanted to go alone, but Emma insisted that she come, leaving Reece to run the clinic.

Terry cut the helicopter engines, hopped out, and handed Reece the mailbag and a paper sack of oatmeal cookies from Lisa. It was late morning with forty-two patients in line.

"How's it going?" Terry wrinkled his unibrow, jutted his sharp chin, ran his hand back through his strong brown hair. Veins popped on his hands.

"Busy enough," said Reece.

"Hey, Afewerki."

"Hello to you, Terry." Afewerki wiped his wet hands on his pants and shook Terry's.

Reece looked in the mailbag and fished out his letters, two from Kristin, one from his grandparents, and one from the pastor of his home church. "Thanks for the cookies, man."

"No problem, dude."

Terry walked uphill. He wasn't keen on watching Reece peroxide wounds. There was a teahouse off the main square near the administrative compound. He sat on a stone in the shade and ordered a gingered and cloved, hot, sweet tea that came in a heavy beer mug. He could see the entrance to the Hyena's headquarters.

Inside the dim building that smelled of dirt and sweat, Emma and Dr. Guthrie faced the Hyena, who sat behind his rough wooden desk. The Hyena wanted to see Dr.

Guthrie's travel permit to visit Godo. Just beyond a doorway to a back room milled his two sidekicks, who had taken part in the attack on Emma.

"Look, I can't get a permit for every little move I make. I have clearance from the RRC to travel upcountry. You've seen that before." Dr. Guthrie's sun squint was in full bloom. Emma could sense the bile in his voice. He spoke in loud, abrupt Amharic, but without need for an interpreter.

"I could arrest you." The Hyena smiled and tapped a black ballpoint pen on his desk.

"And if you lay one more finger on any of our workers, it's you who will be dealt with. I've filed a formal complaint. God knows what good it will do, but do not threaten me."

The Hyena grinned, his gold teeth flashing in the poor light.

Emma folded her arms across her chest, goosebumps washing across her back and shoulders. "Tell him I'll travel with an armed guard from now on, with orders to shoot."

Dr. Guthrie did not interpret, and the Hyena held forth his hands in inquiry.

"Suffice it to say, we will pull out of Godo if harm comes to our workers, and you will be to blame. Our work here is not done, and you are endangering the lives of many who would suffer if we left." He knew the best way to get the Hyena to cooperate was by giving him regular payments in cash. Bluffing was second best.

"Why she is visiting the holy man in the caves?" asked the Hyena. "The people now are talking. She is like the

Icelanders, trying to steal."

Dr. Guthrie rolled his eyes and explained to Emma. She muttered *Shit* under her breath. "The issue is not what's in a cave, but how you and your men attacked and injured Ms. Smith here." His voice was rising in volume and slowing in tempo. "Not to mention arresting Afewerki and knocking his father in the head." His fingers were flexing. Dr. Guthrie was a solid piece of beef in his too-tight, short-sleeve button-up shirt.

The Hyena opened a drawer, pulled out his Makarov pistol, and laid it on the table. "We will work together. But you must tell this woman that she cannot steal from the people. She will be greatly punished if she continues to seek things that do not belong to her."

Dr. Guthrie held back. "I won't tolerate any more acts of violence against our volunteers." He leaned on the Hyena's desk. "I need you to know that."

The two young men with globe-sized afros entered the room, smirking, smiling at Emma.

Emma's mouth tasted of brass, and her heart raced.

The Hyena laughed, a forced laugh. His guards laughed as well.

"Here's a copy of the complaint." Dr. Guthrie placed an envelope on the Hyena's desk and motioned for Emma. "Ciao," and he turned to leave.

Terry joined them for the silent walk back to the clinic. A little girl took Emma's hand. "Ferenj," she whispered. Emma smiled at her.

Dr. Guthrie paused as they passed the line of patients sitting on rocks against the fence. "Mendeno, baba?" he said to a wilted man with no hat. The man shaded his eyes and gazed up. He looked frightened. His nose was disfigured, twisted, as if it had been torn away and replaced. Dr. Guthrie squatted and looked at the man's hand. A tremendous deep sore ate the flesh between his thumb and index finger. Old sores scarred his legs. Terry looked away, noticing how calm the breeze was, perfect for taking off.

"Yaws," said Dr. Guthrie. "Very contagious. You might want to go ahead and see him. Wear gloves, though." He told the man to follow them into the clinic.

"Hey," said Reece. "Who's this?"

The man with yaws hesitated, then stepped into the clinic. His eyes were watery and wide. Neither Reece nor Emma had seen a case of yaws before. The disease was caused by a spirochete, related to syphilis, which also disfigured its victims in later stages.

"He is from Wollo," said Afewerki.

"Ah," said Dr. Guthrie. "Poor guy. He'll need a big wallop of IM penicillin." He asked the man how long he'd had the sores, and the man replied, perhaps two years. "Do you have any Pen-G? He'll need 1.5 million units."

"Yes, we have." Afewerki retrieved a vial from the shelf and handed it to Emma. The man spoke, just above a whisper. "He is thanking God."

"A good place to start," said Dr. Guthrie.

"Are we here much longer?" Terry said from the doorway.

"Hold your horses." Dr. Guthrie frowned. "So, Emma, you okay?"

"I suppose so, I think." She winked at Reece.

"So, how did it go?" asked Reece.

"Like talking to a brick wall," said Guthrie. "I think he

knows he's walking on thin ice. I'll let you know if anything happens on our end. In the meantime, be safe and
avoid him like the plague."

"What if he continues to steal?" asked Reece.

"It's a small price to pay, considering. We can tolerate
that, but we can't tolerate him roughing up anyone, especially Emma. I wanted to put my fist down his throat to be
honest."

Emma smiled. "I had similar ideas about my foot."

"And be careful about getting close to any artifacts or
showing interest in what the church here is up to. He may
be right when he said that people are talking. We have to
avoid any appearances of repeating the mistakes of the
Icelanders."

Emma stood ready with the penicillin.

"Are there any other Icelanders still in Ethiopia doing
volunteer work?" asked Reece.

"Not that I know of," said Guthrie. "Why?"

"I found a book that belonged to the doctor who was
here, and it had a note inside. I was just curious about
what the note said."

"There's an Irish Jesuit in Addis who speaks Icelandic
and used to live over there. He might be your best bet."

"Maybe on a trip back to Addis."

"You and Emma both have R and R coming up soon.
Well, got to be moving on. Terry's in a hurry, and I've got a
cattle clinic this afternoon near AK."

Dr. Guthrie headed to the helicopter, and Emma had
the wispy man with the disfigured nose stand to receive an
injection that would wipe out his disease in a single dose.
Following dinner, Afewerki returned to his family's com-

pound. Emma had hugged him again, patted his back, and said good night. He could still smell her, an earthy, feminine smell. The lotion she used reminded him of the sweet, cream-filled sandwich biscuits from Saudi Arabia that he bought at market. He had felt paralyzed when she hugged him. *What could it mean?* She was unlike any female ferenj he had ever met. She had once mentioned that she would love for him to see her home back in Alabama. His little brother came into his small room and took the enjera dish away to be washed.

On his wall were pages torn from a magazine left by the Icelanders. There was a photo of a red-haired woman wearing a white sweater with black decorative trim around the neck. The other page was an ad for a watch made in Iceland. He grabbed a chewing stick from his small table and rubbed his teeth, thinking what it would be like to be alone with Emma, perhaps on a walk, perhaps at one of the Italian restaurants in Addis Ababa. He knocked over a cup of water and disturbed the fat hen roosting above his bed in the rafters.

Before locking up, Emma called out to Irigit and passed him a cup of hot, sweet tea. He took the cup with two hands, a shamma wrapped around his neck and shoulders. He thanked her and went back to his post by the gate, humming a tune. She closed the door and felt the need to visit the shintabet. She sighed and gathered the necessities, opening the door again.

"Abet?" asked Irigit.

"Chicorilla. No problem," said Emma. "Shintabet."

"Ishi." He chuckled.

She ambled past the dining hut to the far corner of the compound. The sky was violet, already filled with the brightest stars. The chill of evening brushed her arms. She used her flashlight to check for spiders and other critters. She wished that someone would raise the toilet seat off the cement floor. Squatting was hard work and awkward, so she wound up sitting on the seat with her legs bent in front of her. The cold smell of her waste was unpleasant as usual.

What was Reece doing? *Probably reading his Bible, thinking about the Ark of the Covenant.* The Bible study the night before continued with Moses and the Ark. God had commanded Moses to make the seventh day of the week a holy day, given him the tablets of stone, and sent him back down Mount Sinai. But the Israelites had strayed in his absence, had built a golden calf to worship. An angry Moses threw the tablets to the ground, breaking them. He burned the golden calf, crushed it to powder, scattered it upon the water, and made his people drink from it. Moses then had the men take sides. Those who chose the side of God stood apart, and Moses went throughout the camp and killed the others, three thousand in number. God then saw fit to have Moses carve two new tablets upon which He once again wrote His ten commandments, replacing those that were broken. The way Reece was telling the story made God seem like a magical madman and Moses his earthly wizard. There was verse 4 from Genesis, chapter 6.

"There were giants on the earth in those days, and also afterward, when the sons of God came in to the daughters of men and they bore children to them. Those were the mighty men who were of old, men of renown."

Reece insinuated God had been a visitor from another planet, that these sons of God had had relations with humans, creating a superhuman species that was part God or part alien. This had been early, prior to the great flood and Noah and his ark. Why had there been a flood? Why had God destroyed everyone but Noah and his family? According to the Bible, God had found the people wicked. But this occurred just a single verse after the "sons of God" created children with human women. Emma had never really thought much about it before, or had her attention drawn to these sons of God. Reece was very convincing. The others had only nodded and given questioning looks, as if themselves pondering some new but perhaps dangerous idea. Reece was excited about the church service celebrating the new tabot in two weeks, which was worrisome to Emma, given the warning from the Hyena and advice from Dr. Guthrie.

Reece changed underwear before going to bed. He'd not had a proper bath since arriving in Godo. To Kristin, he had sent more rolls of film. He worried about the photos of Emma, what Kristin would say. He'd purposely only taken pictures of her working in the clinic, usually stooped over a patient, cleaning ears or listening to a phlegm-rattled chest. There was also the photo of the old woman whose bedsores they were treating. She still came most every day and was making substantial progress. There were lots of long-view scenic shots, pictures of black and orange roosters, and a photo of poor Marvin sitting in Emma's doorway. He wanted Kristin to feel Godo, to be able to touch and smell it. He had a small box with a stone and a feather in it that he was planning to mail back soon, perhaps with a handful of kollo for her to eat, the hard nuggets of roasted sorghum flour that farmers kept in their pockets as a snack while plowing.

He wrote Kristin a quick letter, a summary of his day, moved through his prayer list, and settled in with his preparation for the next week's Bible study. He continued to read through Exodus, following Moses back down from Mt. Sinai after forty days and forty nights of instruction from God. When he descended with the new tablets, the Bible said that his face shone, frightening the people, so that he wore a veil. Whenever Moses entered his tent, a "pillar of cloud" would descend to guard the entrance. To Reece, he couldn't help but imagine God as some sort of space astronaut imbued with radioactive powers that manifested in Moses's glowing face, the pillar of cloud, and the mysterious powers within the Ark itself. The thought made his stomach feel empty. Never before had he had such clarity and insight. Being dropped into the middle of nowhere, where the land and sky and everything in between was strange, was frightening, yet liberating. There were so many questions.

Once back among the people, Moses had called for offerings of gold, cloth, wood, and precious stones with which to make the Ark, the tabernacle, and its accompanying utensils. The artisan Bezalel was trusted with the making of the Ark. The details were astounding. Gold was beaten into thin sheets and cut into threads to be woven into the garments of the priests.

"Then Moses looked over all the work, and indeed they had done it; as the Lord had commanded, just so they had done it. And Moses blessed them." (Exodus 39:43)

In his letter to Kristin, he noted how the tabernacle had been erected in the last chapter of Exodus, how the Ark had been placed and partitioned, surrounded by a veil. Once erected, "the Glory of the Lord" filled the tabernacle. By day, a cloud covered the tabernacle, and by night it was ruled over by fire. Was it fire, or was it an electrical phenomenon playing off the gold-infused tabernacle walls? He noted that the next mention of the Ark was not until the sixteenth chapter of Leviticus, the chapters prior to that being concerned with animal sacrifice and the dilemmas of sores, scabs, and discharges from the body. The priests were required to bathe and put on special garments before entering the Ark's presence. Much emphasis was on cleanliness, as if the temple were subject to contamination. Reece thought of the space-like suits worn by workers who assembled sensitive electronics. He finished his letter, and his thoughts turned to Emma. He wondered what she would look like in a bathing suit. Her curves came through the scrubs she wore. Dr. Guthrie had mentioned swimming at the Addis Ababa Hilton during an upcoming R-and-R break. He hoped that he and Emma could go together, but who would look after the clinic?

After a month of treatments, the old woman with hip sores was deemed cured. Granulated pink skin had closed over the gaping hip holes. She was walking on her own and gaining weight as well. Fekadu's fevers had abated after the first injection of penicillin. He had broken into a tremendous sweat, soaking his bedclothes. He was still puny, and his leg was weak, but he was sitting up now under his own power. Emma worried that he would fall into the cooking fire, but every child faced that danger each day.

It was Saturday, a market and ration day. Godo burst with activity. Goats bleated in the hot sun, waiting to be sold. Vendors crowded the market, doing brisk business in the waning shadows of famine. The clinic line stretched up the hill. Inside the clinic compound, a line of mothers with children stood, waiting to be weighed. Another line waited for grain, and another for milk powder and soybean oil. The nuclear oven of the sun bore down on Godo as if all were well.

A middle-aged man had been hit in the eye with a doolah. Vitreous humor leaked from the swollen eye, oozing from the iris. The pupil was no longer round, but shaped like a keyhole. His vision was intact, but all was blurry in that eye.

"Let's wash the eye and get some tetracycline ointment in there. God, it looks awful," said Emma. The lids were puffed and purple. The wound extended to a cut above the eye.

Afewerki grimaced, murmuring, "Tsk, tsk, tsk."

"Need to put a patch across it, I would think." Reece thought about the verse in Leviticus that said all discharge from a man was unclean. Anyone who touched a man with discharge was to bathe and change clothes. Probably not a bad idea, but it seemed far-fetched in the case of fluid from inside the eye.

The man seemed resigned to his fate, although he was worried that he could not plow with only one eye.

"Tell him to drink plenty," said Emma. "He needs to stay hydrated and build up new fluid inside his eye."

The man left with his eye patched, a dose of penicillin in his hip, and with instructions to return the next day, even though it was Sunday. His shoulder hit the door frame on his way out, and he cursed, then apologized.

A woman with a large piece of lime peel in her nose entered, followed by a younger woman with a massive goiter that seemed to be a fetus growing in her neck. Emma turned to the woman, and Reece to the girl. Afewerki positioned himself in the middle of the action, translating for both.

The goiter transfixed Reece. He had seen several smaller goiters around Godo but none this large. The goiter was made of three lobes that formed a rough protruding hemisphere, reaching from just under her chin to her breastbone.

"Massive," said Reece.

"Yes," said Afewerki.

Emma glanced over. "Not much we can do."

"Mendeno?" Afewerki asked her. "Does the goiter cause you problems?"

The woman replied that it made it hard to swallow and breathe, but that she had not come because of the goiter.

"I suspected that," said Emma. Her patient was suffering from nausea; bad smells were making her vomit.

"This woman complains that her hands have become dry," said Afewerki of the woman with the goiter.

Reece caught Emma's look, and she rolled her eyes. He checked the woman's hands, and they were very dry and chapped as if she had been mixing cement with them, the skin wrinkled and pink. "Do they hurt? They look like they hurt."

"Yes, much pain," said Afewerki.

"What happened?"

"She has found some powders to wash with, and she thinks that it is Omo, the washing powder for clothes, but it burns her hands."

"It's a chemical burn, almost like a lye burn. Where did she get the powder?"

"She bought in market. She trades it for some eggs."

"Doesn't look infected," said Reece.

Afewerki moved over to help Emma.

"Does she think she might be pregnant?" asked Emma.

Afewerki translated, and the young woman put her face into her hands and laughed, but then began to cry.

"How many days since she has had her period?"

"By two months," said Afewerki.

"It's okay," said Emma. She sat beside the unmarried woman, twenty years of age. She had large feet and smelled of something bitter. "We'll do what we can to help. Is she on rations?"

"Yes," said Afewerki.

Reece donned a glove and dipped into a large can of petrolatum jelly. He had the woman hold out her hands and applied a dollop to each. "Ask her to rub it into the skin. Should make it feel better."

The woman's goiter bobbed up and down as she breathed. She smeared the petrolatum onto her palms, oohing at the slickness.

"I'll put some inside one of these gloves, and she can apply it as needed. She can come back if she needs more." He took a tongue blade and filled a glove with a generous helping of the salve.

Emma was bagging up a month's supply of vitamins with iron for her possible mother-to-be. "Yours could probably use the vitamins as well. It has iodine, in case that's the reason for her goiter."

"Right," said Reece.

Emma asked the young woman if she knew who the father was, if there was anything else she could do, and the woman said, Yes and No, and that God would see to her needs. She thanked Emma, dried her eyes, and left with her vitamins and a pack of biscuits. Reece's patient left, stroking her lubricated fingers one against the other. He stood there close to Emma for a moment, noticing the fine hair on her neck, feeling the heat from her body radiate. He stepped outside for a breath of fresh air and gazed back through the door of the tiny clinic, feeling that he was still inside.

Reece awoke to a rapping on his door. He stood from his squeaky cot, and it was Afewerki.

"Today is to celebrate the new tabot. It has arriv-ed."

Reece paused, thinking, still half asleep. The new tabot, to replace the one stolen, had arrived in Godo. "When? At the church?"

"Yes, the church," said Afewerki. "Shall we go? Perhaps by one hour."

"Sure, I'd like to see what I can. Will it be okay for me to go?"

"I think will be okay. If the priest asks you to leave, you must leave."

"Okay," said Reece. "I'll be ready."

Afewerki told Emma as well, but she declined and warned Reece that he should not go, that the Hyena was spreading rumors about them. Reece insisted, saying that he wanted to see the tabot, to get as close to the replica as he could, to see if he could "feel its power." She nodded her grudging but bewildered approval. Reece had a huge cowlick, and it made him seem like a kid, innocent and harmless. A volley of gunshots cracked the Sunday morning idyll. It was a call to service at the church.

Afewerki and Reece climbed the path. A stiff breeze riffled the gathering crowd, billowing their shoulder-draped shammas. Reece wore a clean pullover with jeans and the hiking boots that hurt his feet. Afewerki wore jeans as well, along with a plaid shirt that was too big for his frame. The shake of a tambourine and boom of a large two-sided drum played like warm-up music at a rock concert. Around the church, farmers gathered in their best patched shorts, shirts, and tire sandals.

Afewerki and Reece made their way to the edge of the crowd. There were only men, no women or children. Reece could see the shelter behind and up the hill. At the entrance to the church stood two deacons dressed in ceremonial robes of white linen edged in saffron yellow. One steadied a large bronze Orthodox cross mounted on a staff, and the other wielded a roomy purple umbrella fringed in orange. The white smoke of incense from within leaked through the doorway, curling at the edge of the tin roof. The farmers, many with their rifles, milled about, chatting with one another. It was a special day, the Feast of St. Gabriel, as well as a welcome for the new tabot that the Patriarch of the Ethiopian Orthodox Church, the Abuna Takla Haymanot, had blessed. Reece's stomach trembled, and he belched an essence of rotten eggs.

"Are you feeling well?" asked Afewerki.

"I feel queasy, a little nauseous."

The two young musicians, wearing white shirts embroidered with the Orthodox cross, marched around the church. The drum was huge.

"Shall we go?" asked Afewerki.

"No, not yet. Can we sit?" Others had begun to sit on the hard, rocky ground.

"I will stand."

Reece squatted. His stomach swam into his chest, and he belched again. He looked through his knees at the scene before him. He saw rifles and staffs, scruffy hats. The only colors to break the monotony of greens and browns were the brightly trimmed white vestments of the deacons and the purple umbrella. He imagined describing the ceremony to Kristin. He thought about her peanut-butter fudge.

He belched again, the hot and eggy gas burning his throat.

The crowd of men continued to grow. Some women from the shelter had eased downhill to sit on stones and watch from a distance, covering their smiles with their hands. After half an hour of waiting, the drum and tambourine picking up pace, the priest appeared in a yellow robe of linen with golden sashes, emerald trim, and a matching headdress, a poofy skull cap.

Reece's stomach had settled somewhat, but he still felt nauseous. His butt hurt from sitting on the ground, and his back ached. The hot sun appeared, then disappeared behind large, white clouds moving from east to west. His eyes were growing tired from squinting. Each minor discomfort seemed to be adding up to something insufferable. He stood, relieved to see that the service was getting underway, but stood too quickly, causing his vision to blur, then blank into darkness. He reached for a wall that was not there and nearly fell.

"Abet?" Afewerki caught him by the arm.

"I'm okay." Reece regained his balance and felt the nausea sink lower into his abdomen. He felt "puny," as his grandfather would say.

The young man who had been playing the drum took the purple umbrella from the deacon and held it over his head. The priest withdrew to the eaves of the church. He carried a large book, the Coptic Bible.

The crowd, gathered in a horseshoe around the church, fell silent as the priest invoked the Holy Day and began a call-and-response that Reece could not understand. The men answered the priest in one voice, a strong, understated chorus that made Reece shiver. "Where is the tabot?"

he whispered to Afewerki.

Afewerki put his finger to his lips.

The priest was then reading aloud the story of Shadrach, Meshach, and Abednego from the Book of Daniel, chapters 1 through 3. Reece shifted from foot to foot. Afewerki had said that it would be brought from within the maq'das, the Holy of Holies at the center of the church. The priest read slowly and deliberately, often losing his place on the oversized pages. Reece was thirsty, his throat dry. He belched and tasted acid, smelled the rotten eggs. His head swam.

Before delving into the account of the three Hebrews being bound and tossed into the fiery furnace for their refusal to recognize the God of Nebuchadnezzar, the priest handed the Bible to the deacon beneath the umbrella and first told the story in his own words, gesticulating toward the heavens. The men around Reece nodded, shifting their rifles. One man spat on the ground and was reprimanded by his neighbors. He looked truly hurt and hung his head as the priest regained the Bible and began reading once more. Reece felt that a beam of light was about to find him and transport him back to Alabama to the hammock between two pine trees at his grandparents' house. He felt sick and elated.

The priest ended the reading, and after another round of call and response, he lifted his arms. Reece looked toward heaven with him. Gunshots! The sound of thirty or so rifles firing shook Reece from his reverie. Afewerki was doubled over, trying to catch his breath, laughing at him. Reece looked to see if his feet were touching the ground. His heart was slowly disengaging from his throat and settling back in his chest. As the service had begun with a volley of rifle fire, so it had ended. He let a smile come to his face and tried to comprehend all that was occurring. "Jeez," he said.

"Oh, your eyes are very big...when the guns..." Afewerki laughed, and others smiled at the startled ferenj.

"Is it over?"

The crowd of men stirred but did not break up.

"No, no. The priest is coming again, soon."

Reece watched the two deacons enter the church and emerge with censers dangling from chains, streaming white smoke. The crowd made a path for them as they walked around the church, leaving a fragrant contrail of incense. Reece belched and grimaced. At least half an hour passed as attendees trotted uphill and into the bushes to use the restroom. The tambourine and drum had reappeared, counting down the priest's reappearance with a steady beat. There was a commotion coming from up the hill, a woman shouting.

Afewerki met the guard from the shelter, who was complaining that the farmers were using the pit toilets reserved for the women. Women merely squatted, covered by their long dresses. Men tended to urinate through the wide leg holes of their shorts, but had to remove them otherwise. Afewerki told Reece that he was going to the shelter. Reece stayed behind, feeling unwell, hoping that the next part of the service would start soon.

Afewerki followed the old guard to the ridge, and a group of women had gathered, hurling insults at a young man squatting over one of the open shintabet holes. "Shoot him in the butt," he told the guard. The guard raised his rifle. Afewerki said, "Yellum!" He was only joking, and the old guard frowned at his missed opportunity. The young man said nothing, being in the throes of an intestinal fury. The women continued to yell at him and taunt him, but from a distance. "Ai yi yi," said Afewerki. "What a hell." He told the guard to hold on and let the man finish, but to threaten any others who tried the same thing. "Ishi," said the guard. The stench of pit toilets drifted into Afewerki, and he pinched his nose and hurried back to the church.

Reece looked pale. "You are sick," said Afewerki. "You must to rest. Shall we go?"

"No, no. I want to see the tabot." A gripe wrenched his gut.

"Do you want to vomit?"

"Not yet. I think I can make it." The drumbeat reverberated through his abdomen.

The deacon emerged from the church and raised his hands to quiet the murmuring crowd. In a deep voice, he announced the appearance of the new tabot of the Church of St. Gabriel, freshly blessed. A few turned to see if Reece would react. He had only an interest now in keeping his stomach under control and glimpsing this sacred relic from the Old Testament.

The drum and tambourine ceased as the priest appeared. He bent to pass through the door, carrying on his head the tabot made of wood. The tabot was wrapped in a rich red and pink cloth with gold edging that draped across the priest's shoulders. The fabric was patterned with red diamonds, containing a gold center. On top of the priest's yellow robe, the effect was blinding, causing Reece to look away and belch once again. Rotten eggs. He wished for some secret power of the tabot to reach out and touch him. He refocused, trying to latch onto any energy that might be emanating from the covered tabot. The people began to clap, and the tambourine and drum fell into place in front of the priest, who walked through the crowd to the path.

The farmers with their rifles and doolahs enclosed behind him, forming an entourage. They were going somewhere. Women began to follow, and small children. A young girl took Reece's hand. "Ferenj," she said. He repeated the word back to her.

Reece became a part of the flow, passing down the narrow lane that led to the village center. They passed Afewerki's house, then entered the empty marketplace. Splashes of color began to appear in the growing crowd, brightly colored scarves, and Western t-shirts advertising plumbing and IBM. The music and movement mesmerized Reece, making him forget his queasiness. His feet seemed light, and there was no air resistance against his skin. The tabot remained fixed in his field of vision, just a dozen feet ahead. Afewerki was by his side, but Reece had forgotten him. The crowd circled through the square and headed out toward the western side of the village, taking the path to the village's main source of water, the spring located downhill, a thirty-minute walk.

The sun bore down on the moving swath of people. They passed an enormous fig tree, the rocky path cutting through ground otherwise denuded of trees and shrubs. Reece's nausea returned, and he slowed, trying to keep his balance. A tremendous urgency penetrated his bowels, and he lagged to the side of the column into stiff yellow grass. Afewerki followed.

"I have to go back. Now." Reece looked around for a place that he could run to, but there was none. He veered off the path to avoid the pressing crowd. Their faces blurred, then seemed ultra clear. They were dancing. Women were ululating.

"Let us go," said Afewerki. "You are sick. Come."

Reece stopped and bent over to relieve the cramping. The pressure was unbearable. He moved on, breathing slow and deep. He belched. Rotten eggs. They reached the end of the trailing crowd and moved back onto the path. Each footfall raised a slight whir of dust. Within five minutes, they neared the village market area and met the Hyena with three sidekicks, the two with the large afros, and all three with rifles. The Hyena wore his Makarov at his waist.

Reece said, "Oh, Jesus," and did not stop or greet them.

The Hyena spoke in a concerned voice. He was going to follow the priest and make sure there was no trouble, guard the tabot, and so on. Why were they not going? Was the walk too difficult for the ferenj? He laughed.

Afewerki stopped. He took the hand extended to him. He told the Hyena that Reece was sick.

"Well, he can cure himself," said the Hyena.

"I must go," said Afewerki, wondering when the Hyena would release his hand.

Reece banged on the gate. He didn't think he could make it. Where was Ketow? Afewerki ran up behind and called over the fence. Mariam came from his room and opened the gate. "Abet?" He looked puzzled as Reece pushed by him, running with his buttocks clenched. He made it past the dining hut, unbuttoning his jeans, pulling on the zipper. The fence joined the sky to the ground. He pushed on the door. He pushed, then pulled. "Jesus Christ, Mary, Mother of God…"

Soon after, Emma checked Reece's temperature, which was 99.2, a low-grade fever. Reece's diarrhea continued, involving frequent trips to the shintabet every ten minutes or so. Emma suspected giardiasis or amoebiasis, probably the latter, considering the rotten-egg belching. He hadn't vomited yet but could barely take a sip of water without gagging.

The first 200 milligrams of chloroquine were going into his gluteus maximus. Emma gripped the amber ampule and snapped off the top. She withdrew 5 ccs of the clear liquid and tapped out the bubbles in the syringe. She motioned for Reece to turn on his side. "You'll have to unbutton your pants," she said.

Reece felt an icy wind blow through his chest. His hands shook as he pulled down his pants just enough for Emma to palpate his hip for the sweet spot. Her hand was soft and warm. He tried not to look at the needle but couldn't help himself. "Skin and bones," she said. The needle slid in, and he felt the liquid knotting in his muscle.

"Thanks," he said, and staggered up to stumble out to the shintabet. It was raining. He slid his too-small boots on, not bothering to lace them. He felt dirty and longed for a hot shower. Chills shook him. Mud splashed onto his boots, and then he kicked a stone, sprawling to his knees in the grassy muck. He was stunned, and a voice seemed to tell him to crawl, and so he did on hands and knees.

Afewerki rushed to his aid. "You are falling," he said. "Give to me your hand."

"I'm a bad person," Reece said to the ground. He remembered images of the tabot brightly wrapped and balanced on top of the priest's head, like a casserole dish wrapped in a blanket. He had felt an energy emanating from beneath the cloth. This same energy was ordering him to crawl through the mud in the rain to the toilet. How could that be? He put his hand in Afewerki's and stood. The rain came down harder, and he moved forward.

Later in the day, Reece broke into an intense sweat with shaking chills. The team was anxious, especially Afewerki, who suggested that Reece could die of such a thing, and of course, it was true. Emma checked on him every fifteen minutes until dark, when she sat by his bed for an hour, not talking, just thinking, musing on what it meant that Reece was there, that he was so sick. Already, a rumor was spreading that the tabot had made Reece ill because he was secretly planning to steal it, like the Icelanders. When Barra told her this, she groaned, knowing that it was the Hyena who was spreading the lie. But she had warned Reece.

The next morning, he was very weak. His intestinal trouble continued, although with improvement. He hadn't eaten in over twenty-four hours and was amazed that he had anything left to give the shintabet. He stayed in bed that morning. For lunch, Zenebek made him a plate-sized kita, plain flatbread cooked over the fire. He managed a few mouthfuls of the crispy-chewy bread, drank a liter of water, and for the first time ceased to belch, which was a great relief.

"Well, if you do come, make sure and wash your ding-dang hands." Emma was irritated that Reece was insisting on coming to the clinic after his meager lunch. "I think you should rest more, but..."

"No worries," said Reece. "I need to get out of bed. Was hurting my back lying there."

"Ahh, you must rest," said Afewerki. "We are fine today with the clinic." He looked to Emma for support.

"No, really, I'm okay," said Reece. "Just let me wash my hands again like Emma suggested."

Emma and Afewerki went ahead. "He's stubborn," said Emma.

"Yes, like the mule," said Afewerki.

Emma laughed.

Scabies, scabies, yellow diarrhea, headaches, wosfat (roundworms), kosa (tapeworms), and then a nasty case of warts. The young woman, a teen with a beautiful smile, her face framed with a red and purple scarf, a thick wart-like growth covering the soles of her feet. Walking was painful. The warts were hard and discolored, a watery brown, and had calluses on them.

"Can't cut them off," said Reece. "You'd have to cut the bottom of her foot off."

"There's nothing we can do," said Emma. Each day,

there was at least one person who fell beyond their abilities.

The woman laughed when Emma offered to buy her some shoes.

"She will keep the money," said Afewerki.

"Let's do it anyway," said Reece.

Only Afewerki had money with him, and he handed the five-birr bill to the woman with a stern set of instructions to buy shoes. The woman blushed, covering her mouth, and said, "Thank you." The highlight of the day was an old woman with maggots between her toes.

That night, Emma turned to her devotional. The entry for July 29 ended: "Is there anyone except Jesus in your cloud? If so, it will only get darker until you get to the place where there is 'no one anymore, but only Jesus...'" Clouds taught faith. She wondered if her increasing interest in Reece could become a hindrance to her relationship with God. Pretty much every guy she had dated had done everything but bring her closer to God. Celibacy had crossed her mind in the past, but she did want children, and sex was an appetite that she appreciated.

She wrote her mother that she was glad Reece was better, but that she was feeling a bit queasy herself. She lay down, watching the shadows from the candle milk across the inside slant of the roof. Jesus in her cloud. She laughed, remembering Reece sprawled on his hands and knees in the mud, in the rain. She got up to make sure her door was latched and lay back on her squeaking cot. The sheets needed washing. The candle flame leaned this way and that, strong and blue at its base beneath a teardrop of sun orange. She pushed her hand beyond the elastic of her pajama bottoms. She imagined Reece's profile in the shadows as if he were watching. Her hand trembled into a rhythm, and she closed her eyes. The sound of Irigit whistling inched closer to her house. She'd forgotten to make him a cup of tea. The rap on the door startled her, and she lay still for a few seconds before responding.

"Yes!" Her voice came out too high-pitched.

"You still up?" It was Reece.

She reached over and blew out the candle, and then cursed. "Hold up!" She fumbled for a match to relight the candle.

"Sorry to bother." His voice came through the door, through the cracks, through the curtained window.

Emma ran her fingers through her hair. She opened the door, and it made a mighty creak, enough to wake the village. She was eye level with him, being up a step. There was dampness between her legs. She had just imagined him, and there he was.

"Hey." She blew out a deep breath like cigarette smoke.

"Hey, yourself." Reece was upbeat, unable to sleep. He felt that he had been raised from the dead following his acute abdominal crisis. "Saw you had a light on and wondered what you were up to."

Emma could see Irigit hovering in the darkness. "Come in. I'm about to make some tea. Want some?"

"I'm having trouble sleeping, so maybe not."

"How about some of that chamomile tea you brought from Addis?"

"Sure," he said, "I'll be right back."

She filled the pot with water and then began sweeping.

Reece was wearing shorts and his tire sandals. "Here." He handed the blue box to her.

"Have a seat." She moved the candle to the small table near the stove.

"Thanks for giving me that injection. I'm a believer in the murphy now."

"Still take the pills, though, just in case."

The candle's light toasted her face golden. Reece thought of a browned pancake. He thought of warm syrup. "Does Zenebek or Misrak wash your clothes?"

"Need your clothes washed?"

"Yeah." He tapped his fingers on the table.

"Just give them to Misrak. She washes the clothes."

"Do you pay her?"

"She gets paid by the Mission to wash and cook for us."

"Oh." Reece felt the words backing up in his mind. There was something he wanted to say. How could he say it?

Emma sat and put her elbows on the table. Reece's hair was just long enough in back to curl. She wondered what his hair felt like. "We should put in a garden, you and me. Grow stuff. I have seeds from home."

"What kind?" He tried to make eye contact but wound up looking over her shoulder. He could feel the weight of the starry sky through the roof.

"Tomatoes, lettuce, green beans, cucumbers." She stood and poured the steaming water into three orange plastic mugs, each with a tea bag, chamomile for them, and Lipton for Irigit.

"How can we plow up the dirt? It's mostly rocks."

"Maybe Afewerki's dad can help us. He's always out

plowing."

"Sounds good," said Reece.

She handed the mug to Reece and went to the door, still ajar. She peered into the darkness. Steam wafted from the cup. "Irigit?"

"Abet?" Irigit jogged over from the gate. He wore his floppy hat, and a shamma wrapped around his shoulders and face like a scarf. The evening had cooled, dropping into the low sixties. He took the cup with both hands, grinned his big grin, and rattled off a full page of lively Amharic that neither Reece nor Emma understood. He sighed and bid them goodnight.

"I should go," said Reece.

"You just got here. Finish your tea, for goodness' sake." She imagined a deserted café at closing time.

Reece felt a stirring in his pants and tried to think of something other than Emma's breasts. He imagined the dog named Stones that Kristen had adopted and then re-named Walter. He thought about Pastor Scoggins at his home church, who had severe acne scars on his face and webbed toes. "Tell me about your church."

"Okay." Emma raised her eyebrows. "It's a small Baptist church in Hueytown, about two hundred members. Not too big, not too small. How big is yours?"

"It's, uh, small, about a hundred. Half the church is in the choir on Sundays."

Emma laughed. "Do your choir robes match the pew cushions?"

"Green and red, so maybe not."

Dogs growled and snapped from outside the walled compound, an evil sound.

"I feel bad for the dogs around here, especially the mamas." Emma supped her tea.

"Afewerki's old mutt is covered with scars and can barely walk. Just how it is, I suppose."

"How's Kristin?" She scolded herself for asking, but she couldn't help it.

Reece relaxed. "Okay. Sad, though. Tells me how sad she is."

"That's too bad."

"Unfortunate, I guess."

"That she's sad?"

"Yeah, that she's sad." He shifted in his chair.

"So, how's the Bible study going? Are you ready for tomorrow night?"

"A little behind since I've been sick. I'm in Leviticus. Do you know the discharge chapter? I think it's chapter 15."

"About a woman being unclean when she has her period?"

"That and it goes on and on about male discharge as well. If a man has a discharge—he made air quotes—then he has to bathe and will be unclean until evening."

"Weird. The women here are considered unclean for seven days after their period."

"Do you think that would make for a good Bible study?"

"Well, maybe not."

"I'm just reading through the Old Testament now, filling in the gaps between references to the Ark."

"So, did you get to see it?" She wanted him to leave or jump her bones so that she could finish what she had started.

"It was covered. The priest balanced it on top of his

head. The people were going nuts. I hated to leave, but had to."

"That's as close as you'll ever get. Probably for the best."

"I felt something. Call me crazy," said Reece.

"What do you mean?"

"Like I think the tabot did make me sick. Kind of like the rumor, although I have no plans to steal it."

"Oh, come on." She looked at Reece, his jaw set, a shadow darting from ear to chin.

"It's like it was calling out to me. Like I could feel it, the danger or maybe something powerful, something electric."

He looked serious with his hands folded across his lap. Crickets chirruped beneath the dogs' gnashing of teeth, growls, and yelps.

"Hmm."

"How's Fekadu?" Reece had missed their morning visit.

"Doing good." Emma canvassed the inside of the tiny square house, the dark corners, the bright white stove. Shadows flowed like seawater across the surfaces. "He's eating enjera."

"That's great."

"He doesn't look so desperate now. He looked like he wanted to die, to be rid of the pain in his leg."

"I guess we don't know what the problem is or why the medicine is working, but it is," said Reece.

"God's giving us the green light, I guess. His mother believes he has a ghost in his leg, though."

"I think Afewerki believed her. He seemed convinced there was nothing to be done."

Emma crossed her legs. "Kind of like the evil eye, the

buda. I'm not sure that he believes it, but it frightens him."

"What has he told you?"

"The weavers, potters, and metal workers are the ones who have the evil eye. They come into the village on market days, but otherwise they're outcasts. No one dares look them in the eye. If you do, you're cursed."

"Like this?" He made bug eyes at Emma.

Emma laughed. "Something like that. At night, they visit graveyards and turn into werewolves, maybe more like a hyena."

"Afewerki is a little jumpy about ghosts and such," said Reece.

"He was Coptic before the Mission came. He became a 'Christian' before he took the job with us."

"Hmm." Reece finished his tea. He looked over at Emma's bed. A small pile of laundry lay at the foot of the cot. His back felt sticky against the chair, and his feet were cold. "I should be going."

"Well, glad you're better." She watched him leave and then closed her door for the night. She smelled burning candle, and Reece.

With the flowery taste of chamomile in his mouth, Reece said his prayers and delved into the Old Testament. He wondered at the endless sacrifices of animals, the anointing of the altar with blood, yet no one was to partake of that blood, "the life of all flesh" (Leviticus 17:14). Chapter 18 dealt with the general abomination of uncovering the nakedness of one's relatives. The verse prohibiting the lying of a man with a man, though, carried no corollary banning a woman from lying with a woman. Why was that?

"When you reap the harvest of your land, you shall not wholly reap the corners of your field, nor shall you gather the gleanings of your harvest." Leviticus 19:9

He considered that by volunteering as a nurse, he was, in essence, leaving the gleanings of his own prosperity to those who could not afford to sow their own fields. That seemed useful. Chapter 21 was a virtual repeat of chapter 20, with an addition at the end noting that a man or woman who was a medium would be stoned to death. Wasn't Moses, though, a medium between God and the Israelites? And Moses's feats of turning rods to snakes? Would that not make him a magician? And what was the big deal about those with defects being forbidden to approach the altar, to make sacrifices? Half the people in Godo had some sort of defect, a withered hand, a missing finger, tropical ulcers. What was the point of all the sacrificing? Why would God care about slaughtered animals or sheaves of wheat? A man among the Israelites "blasphemed the name of the Lord" (24:11) and was stoned to death. In the same chapter, God told Moses, "Whoever kills any man shall surely be put to death" (24:17). That seemed fickle. Reece's heart rate rose, and he felt it bobble, skipping a few beats, thump thumping in his throat. The condoning of slavery. He reached the end of Leviticus and closed the book, but could not sleep, and placed a pair of brown socks across his eyes.

Isaac was first up and out into the early morning chill, followed by Barra washing his face, and Mariam brushing his teeth with baking soda.

"How are you, my brothers?" asked Isaac. He combed his hair with a pick.

"Yes, it is good day, praise to God," said Barra. He splashed water on his face and made a satisfied sound.

Mariam asked about the ten thousand birr that the Mission was planning to give to the people of Godo to buy oxen. The famine had consumed most of the cattle, which were crucial for plowing. The Mission had donated similar funds at its other feeding stations, but the Hyena had caused them pause in Godo.

"Is good idea," said Barra. "I have spoken with Ato Wundafresh of this thing. He is happy for the people to have this money."

Isaac laughed. "Hyena will buy new house." He chuckled more.

"No, no," said Barra. "It is good thing for people. We must to trust him. Yes?" He inspired, creating a wheeze of agreement.

Ketow opened the gate, and Misrak entered, ready to get the fire going for breakfast. Isaac whistled at her, and she gave him a sour face. Mariam blushed and waved a short wave.

From his cot, Reece listened to the banter, not understanding their words. A rooster crowed nearby, and then another. The crowing set his teeth on edge. It was such an insistent sound. He kicked the covers from his feet and wiggled his toes. A faint sour of rotten eggs crept past his lips as he sat up. He seemed to have gotten through the crisis, but something was lingering. He reached for his chloroquine and swallowed a bitter 500-milligram tablet with water from an Icelandic IV bottle. He wondered what the Hyena was doing at that moment. Did he yawn and stretch before he got out of bed? Reece imagined the Ark of the Covenant, shooting bolts of electricity. He wasn't quite sure how the Bible study would go that night.

Emma awoke early and took a sponge bath. She squeezed the juice from a lime, mixed it with a little sugar to wake herself, and smacked her lips. She combed her hair and put on a red bandanna. She would have to tell Reece that she had dreamed of the Ark of the Covenant. She dreamed that it had been in her tiny fridge. She listened to the team talking and laughing outside.

Breakfast was fit-fit with a bowl of berbere powder to sprinkle on top. Barra had bought a large clay jar of milk curds and sprinkled some of the hot pepper on top, slurping and expressing deep satisfaction. Reece and Emma declined his offer to have some. After eating and brushing his teeth, Reece put his dirty clothes in a pile on his bed to be washed. Afewerki hooked up with them on the walk down to the clinic with a stop at Fekadu's along the way.

"He's outside," said Emma. "Bataam taruno!"

Fekadu was sitting up in bed, pulled from within the dark hut. He sat with his legs folded, coughing into his hand. His leg looked less swollen, but still dry and ashy, as if it had been held over a fire to smoke.

"He is much better!" said Afewerki.

"How's his appetite?" asked Reece.

Afewerki interpreted for the mother who was busy cleaning feces from the floor. Fekadu's little sister, bottom exposed, gazed at them. The mother used her hand like a squeegee and slung the waste behind the tukul. She wiped her hand on her dress and scolded the little girl.

"He is eating very well," said Afewerki.

"Is he drinking the Nido?" asked Emma.

"Yes, she mixes with water."

Fekadu lay back, running his eyes from one to the other.

"He fears you are bringing the murphy," said Afewerki.

"Murphy, yellum," said Emma. "But he needs to finish the pills."

Afewerki explained, pointing his finger at the mother. She nodded. "Ishi." Fekadu murmured and took a deep breath.

"Does she have soap to wash her hands?" asked Reece.

"Samona?" Afewerki said. "No, she has no soap."

"Let's get her a bar, okay? To wash her hands with."

"She is saying to praise God," said Afewerki.

They moved on in the morning sun, a mild pink hanging beyond a bank of baby blue clouds. They walked in silence, their shoes scuffing the hard dirt and rocks. A man was cursing a cow, hitting its flank with a heavy stick.

"What the..." said Emma.

The cow limped, protecting its back leg. The man raved and shouted as the cow hopped, stopped, hopped.

Reece walked toward the man. Afewerki called for him to stay.

"Hey," said Reece. "What's going on?"

The man stared at Reece and then at Afewerki. He let fly a slew of language.

"He is catch-ed the cow eating the teff," said Afewerki.

"He became angry and broke the leg. See." He pointed to the broken leg, the bone snapped in half. The cow huffed, frothing at the mouth.

"So, why is he out on the path beating it?" asked Emma.

"He is taking to be slaughtered. He must go quickly."

The cow lowed a pitiful moan and staggered, a vacant stare in its eyes.

Reece put his hands on his hips, ran his hand through his hair. "Damn."

"Okay, we must go now," said Afewerki. "The animal must be slaughtered before it is to die."

The man resumed his cursing and beating of the cow, as the three continued in silence down the hill.

"Maybe there's some good news at the clinic," said Reece.

"That was awful," said Emma.

"It is the way of the people," said Afewerki.

"I guess it is." Reece eyed the back of the line that crept up the hill along the fence. "Looks to be thirty or so."

"More will come," said Emma.

A large cloud loomed, two bunnies side by side in the sky. A hawk circled below, soaring the currents.

Afewerki greeted the grizzled clinic guard. Inside the compound were Isaac, Mariam, and half a dozen day laborers. Two were fashioning a doorway in the clinic's side that faced the warehouse. Cement was being mixed in a crude box made from the food pallets dropped months ago by the Polish military.

"What's going on?" asked Emma.

Isaac walked up. "You like? We build for you new room, like hospital room."

Afewerki explained they were adding a new room onto the clinic. Emma had suggested it one day, to have a place to put the patients who needed to lie down.

"Nice," said Emma. "Great. Go for it."

The first patient of the day turned everyone's stomach. How the man's leg came to be in such a horrid condition was not apparent. They first had to unwrap a dirty length of thick, opaque plastic from the leg and foot. In his twenties and very thin, he looked the definition of starved. A lolling, piercing gaze. Sharp bones beneath stretched skin. A restless tongue that seemed to look for water.

"Oh my God," said Emma.

Afewerki retched and stepped outside into the cloudless morning to catch his breath.

"Holy cow," said Reece.

"Are you in pain? Does it hurt?" Emma forgot she needed Afewerki to interpret.

Reece motioned for Afewerki to come back inside.

Afewerki put his Exxon ballcap back on and held his hands up as if surrendering. He spoke rapidly in Amharic and laughed a pained laugh.

Emma looked at Reece and then back at the leg. There was no meat from just below the knee to just above the ankle. A goo of rotted blue flesh bundled over the ankle like a roll of fat going over a collar. The foot was a gel hanging from the bones. The toes were indistinguishable. Below the knee, the edges of flesh seemed fresh, as if just cut, but there was no bleeding. The exposed bones shone white and plastic.

"He was walking on that foot," said Reece.

"We have a wire saw," said Emma. "Jesus, I just want to

cut that foot off."

"Why doesn't it smell?"

"Smells like formaldehyde?"

"Maybe."

Afewerki recovered, his lips twisted. "Oh, it is terrible." In a low voice, he asked the man what had happened.

The man spoke in whispers, telling of being shot through his calf while fighting against the Eritreans near Massawa. He had been captured but escaped and was making his way home to Addis Ababa. An infection had lodged in the wound, causing the flesh to die and fall away. There was no pain, he said.

A woman with a child on her back peeped in the clinic, covered her mouth, and turned away. The workers mixing cement peered inside, their bare hands covered in slurry.

"He wants to cut away," said Afewerki.

"We can't do that, though," said Reece.

"Maybe we could. It wouldn't hurt," said Emma.

"But he'll need an artificial limb, and the end will need to be sewn up. I wouldn't try it," said Reece.

"Look at how pretty the bone is."

"Looks fake almost."

"I say he's earned a helicopter ride to Addis Ababa," said Reece.

"I tell you, Thomas will give us heck, but maybe you're right. Jesus, I want to cut that thing off so bad. It's awful."

"He must go quickly," said Afewerki.

"Terry will come tomorrow, I hope," said Emma. "If not, we'll need to put him in a jeep if there's one around."

"Hell, let's wrap it up. I can't stand to look at it anymore," said Reece. "What's your name?"

"His name is Assenake," said Afewerki.

With Afewerki's help, Reece cleaned the exposed and wounded flesh below Assenake's knee with iodine solution. They wrapped the dead, gooey, gelid foot in a grain bag. Just for visual relief, he wrapped the exposed bones with a roll of sterile gauze.

Without a proper place to let him stay in the shelter, Reece volunteered his bed until the man could be evacuated to AK and then Addis. The question then became, where would Reece sleep? Emma had the most room, but he would have to sleep in a sleeping bag on the cement floor. Afewerki was against allowing Assenake to sleep in Reece's bed, saying that he was a soldier and used to sleeping on the ground.

After dealing with the rotten foot and leg, the rest of the day seemed a breeze, a mishmash of tapeworms, trachoma, and scabies. With Assenake in Reece's bed, the mattress fortified with plastic and grain bags to protect it from the oozy foot, the team milled around inside the compound as if confused, as if the order of things was out of kilter. Barra had gone in and said a long prayer with him. Everyone who came into the compound had to take a peek and see this man whose leg had died. Emma had pumped him full of antibiotics, which would take care of any lingering infection. Assenake had fleas and lice, so they gave him a new set of clothes, a pair of blue work pants and a pink t-shirt with "Panama City!" airbrushed on it. Afewerki's mother shaved Assenake's head and eyebrows with a razor blade, taking out dozens of crispy lice in the process.

At dinner, a fiery feast of the ubiquitous dorowot, conversation meandered.

"We have Bible study, no? This night?" Barra folded a piece of oily boiled egg with enjera and put it to Mariam's mouth. "Take it, my brother."

"Yes. We'll check on Assenake and then get started," said Reece.

"You may wind up with fleas in your bed," said Emma.

Barra made a sour face. "It is unclean. You are very brave man."

"He deserves a break." Reece gauged the puzzled looks. "I mean, he has had much suffering. He needs a break. He needs to rest, I guess."

"Ah, yes," said Barra. "To rest."

"Where you will stay the night?" asked Afewerki. He was sitting on his hands.

Reece looked at Emma and cleared his throat. "I think Emma has plenty of room."

Silence.

"Yeah, I think that's fine. It should only be one night," said Emma.

"The floor will be hard," said Afewerki.

"Did Misrak take Assenake some food?" asked Reece.

"I go," said Mariam, "to see."

The spongy gray of the enjera soaked in pepper sauce made Reece think of the man's rotten foot.

Following dinner and a brushing of teeth, everyone gathered back in the dining hut for Bible study, during which Reece revisited the idea that aliens had communed with earthlings, basing his thoughts on the reference to the "sons of God" in Genesis chapter six.

"I think you need to give that one a rest." Emma sighed,

not quite sure of what to make of Reece's take on the scriptures. Sure, it was interesting, but...

"Yes, my brother. There is only one Son of God," said Barra.

"Jesus the Christ," said Barra.

Mariam inspired an agreeing "Ow."

Reece nodded, thinking perhaps he had said enough for one night. His mind raced with ideas.

Afewerki looked at the faces around the table. "You are sleeping with Emma this night?" he said. He cleared his throat.

Reece looked at Emma. "Well—"

"He's sleeping on the floor, just until he gets his bed back."

"Ah, yes, yes." Afewerki looked troubled. "I must be saying goodnight." He stood and folded his hands, waiting for Barra to let him pass.

"Yes, it is long day," said Isaac.

Reece forgot to end the study with prayer and stood. He wondered what Kristin would think of him sleeping in Emma's house. He could see down Emma's scrub top and stifled a rush of airiness in his chest. Against his wishes, his mind wandered. He wondered how soft her breasts would feel in his hands. He shook his head.

"Why are you shaking your head?" asked Emma.

"No reason, I suppose. Do you need a few minutes before I come in?"

"Yeah, give me five minutes." She followed Reece into the night. The stars were within reach and so thick. Two, or perhaps ten, dogs gnashed their teeth and roared in the distance, screaming and yelping.

On his way home, Afewerki passed the teahouse, light escaping through cracks in the walls and from beneath the straw roof overhang. A heavy scent of incense filled the air. Inside, he could see eyes and teeth glowing in the light of candles.

"Afewerki!" someone called from within.

Afewerki paused, forgetting what he was doing. "Abet."

Outside came the Hyena with a bright smile. He was drinking katikala. Afewerki smelled the alcohol.

"Look, it's the thief," he called back inside. He laughed and grabbed Afewerki's hand.

Afewerki froze. The Hyena was squeezing his hand. Without thinking, he blurted, "The ferenj is sleeping this night with Emma, the nurse. I must go." He tried to pull away from the Hyena, but could not. Two men with AK-47s stepped out of the teahouse. They were drinking the clear and smoky katikala as well.

"My goodness!" The Hyena laughed and relayed the information back to his bodyguards, who laughed as well. They had seen Emma in her bra when they had assaulted her on the path to the rock-hewn church. "He is a lucky man. No?" The Hyena bent over, laughing so hard he began to choke. He needed to urinate badly and knew just where he would go. He patted his pistol on his hip and, without a sound, walked shakily toward the Mission's compound, bodyguards in tow.

Afewerki regretted his words, but continued on his way home. Just that morning, had Emma not hugged him when they met at the clinic?

On his back, Reece watched the shadows of Emma's candle swirling on the ceiling. He tried to imagine Kristin. The earthy smell of the cement floor beneath his back cloyed his senses. Emma had been very quiet, sitting on her bed, stretching her arms, and yawning. Reece wondered if she was going to read. He closed his eyes.

"My neck is stiff," said Emma.

"What?" asked Reece. He felt a rush of blood to his face.

"My neck is really stiff." Emma ached, and Reece was right there on the floor.

Reece felt a rush of adrenaline as he emerged from his unzipped red sleeping bag. "Maybe I can help?"

"Yeah, maybe just give my neck a good rub. Would sleep a lot better, I think." Her heart raced as Reece approached through the dancing light. She could see his erection.

Reece felt the ground slipping away beneath his feet. "Maybe if you sit in the chair, I can..."

"Yeah, right." Emma stood, wearing a pair of silk pajama bottoms and a scrub shirt. She wasn't wearing a bra. Reece's hands were cold. "Oh!"

Outside, behind Emma's little square house, the Hyena stood in the adjacent Government Clinic compound. His stream of urine just made it through the fence to the whitewashed walls. Behind him, one of his minions suggested that the two ferenjis were at that moment fucking like donkeys. This made the Hyena laugh, lose his focus, urinate on his shoe, and curse.

Reece could barely breathe. He heard a laugh. Emma seemed to melt in his hands. She leaned forward, letting Reece's hands go lower. Nine months of famine, months of tapeworms, months of black flies, months of being lonely—

The first shot from the Makarov 9 mm seemed like a loud noise that had nothing to do with reality. With his heart in his throat, he could only think of the engagement to Kristin. Had he made a mistake? Her parents didn't even like him.

The first shot passed through the wall.

The second shot hit Reece's skull, entering above his cheekbone. Although his body fell sideways to the floor, Reece continued to caress Emma, sliding his hands beneath her top and cupping her perfect breasts. They felt so warm. Why was she screaming?

Famine
Struggle Me This
Half Smile
Finding Her
The Icelanders
Anywhere and Everywhere
Mother Time
Emma